More books by S.M. LaViolette & Minerva Spencer

Minerva's OUTCASTS SERIES

DANGEROUS

BARBAROUS

SCANDALOUS

THE REBELS OF THE *TON:*

NOTORIOUS

OUTRAGEOUS

INFAMOUS

THE SEDUCERS:

MELISSA AND THE VICAR

JOSS AND THE COUNTESS

HUGO AND THE MAIDEN

THE ACADEMY OF LOVE:

THE MUSIC OF LOVE

A FIGURE OF LOVE

A PORTRAIT OF LOVE

THE LANGUAGE OF LOVE

DANCING WITH LOVE

A STORY OF LOVE*

THE MASQUERADERS:

THE FOOTMAN

THE POSTILION

THE BASTARD

THE BELLAMY SISTERS

PHOEBE

HYACINTH

SELINA*

THE BACHELORS OF BOND STREET:

A SECOND CHANCE FOR LOVE (A NOVELLA)

ANTHOLOGIES:

THE ARRANGEMENT

THE WILD WOMEN OF WHITECHAPEL

THE BOXING BARONESS

THE DUELING DUCHESS

THE CUTTHROAT COUNTESS

VICTORIAN DECADENCE: (HISTORICAL EROTIC ROMANCE—
SUPER STEAMY!)

HIS HARLOT

Praise for Minerva Spencer & S.M. LaViolette's

THE ACADEMY OF LOVE series:

"[A] pitch perfect Regency .... Readers will be hooked." (THE MUSIC OF LOVE)

★*Publishers Weekly STARRED REVIEW*

"An offbeat story that offers unexpected twists on a familiar setup."

(A FIGURE OF LOVE)

Kirkus

"[A] consistently entertaining read."

(A FIGURE OF LOVE)

Kirkus

Praise for THE MASQUERADERS series:

"Lovers of historical romance will be hooked on this twisty story of revenge, redemption, and reversal of fortunes."

Publishers Weekly, STARRED review of THE FOOTMAN.

"Fans will be delighted."

Publishers Weekly on THE POSTILION

Praise for Minerva Spencer's REBELS OF THE TON series:

NOTORIOUS

★A *PopSugar* Best New Romance of November

★A *She Reads* Fall Historical Romance Pick

★*A Bookclubz* Recommended Read

"Brilliantly crafted...an irresistible cocktail of smart characterization, sophisticated sensuality, and sharp wit."
★*Booklist* **STARRED REVIEW**

"Sparkling...impossible not to love."—*Popsugar*

"Both characters are strong, complex, and believable, and the cliffhanger offers a nice setup for the sequel. Readers who like thrills mixed in with their romance should check this out."

—*Publishers Weekly*

"Packed full of fiery exchanges and passionate embraces, this is for those who prefer their Regencies on the scandalous side."—
Library Journal

INFAMOUS

"Realistically transforming the Regency equivalent of a mean girl into a relatable, all-too-human heroine is no easy feat, but Spencer (Outrageous, 2021) succeeds on every level. Lightly dusted with wintery holiday charm, graced with an absolutely endearing, beetle-obsessed hero and a fully rendered cast of supporting characters and spiked with smoldering sensuality and wry wit, the latest in Spencer's Rebels of the Ton series is sublimely satisfying."

—**Booklist STARRED review**

"Perfect for fans of Bridgerton, Infamous is also a charming story for Christmas. In fact, I enjoyed Infamous so much that when I was halfway through it, I ordered the author's first novel, Dangerous. I look forward to reading much more of Minerva Spencer's work."

—**THE HISTORICAL NOVEL SOCIETY**

Praise for S.M. LaViolette's erotic historical romance series
VICTORIAN DECADENCE:

"LaViolette keeps the tension high, delivering dark eroticism and emotional depth in equal measure. Readers will be hooked."

-PUBLISHERS WEEKLY on HIS HARLOT

"LaViolette's clever, inventive plot makes room for some kinky erotic scenes as her well-shaded characters explore their sexualities. Fans of erotic romance will find much to love."

-PUBLISHERS WEEKLY on HIS VALET

Praise for Minerva Spencer's *Outcasts* series:

"Minerva Spencer's writing is sophisticated and wickedly witty. Dangerous is a delight from start to finish with swashbuckling action, scorching love scenes, and a coolly arrogant hero to die for. Spencer is my new auto-buy!"

-*NYT Bestselling Author* Elizabeth Hoyt

"[SCANDALOUS is] A standout...Spencer's brilliant and original tale of the high seas bursts with wonderfully real protagonists, plenty of action, and passionate romance."

★*Publishers Weekly STARRED REVIEW*

"Fans of Amanda Quick's early historicals will find much to savor." ★*Booklist STARRED REVIEW*

"Sexy, witty, and fiercely entertaining." ★*Kirkus STARRED REVIEW*

Praise for S.M. LaViolette's Books:

"Lovers of historical romance will be hooked on this twisty story of revenge, redemption, and reversal of fortunes."

★*Publishers Weekly* **STARRED REVIEW**

"A remarkably resourceful heroine who can more than hold her own against any character invented by best-selling Bertrice Small, a suavely sophisticated hero with sex appeal to spare, and a cascade of lushly detailed love scenes give Spencer's dazzling debut its deliciously fun retro flavor."

★*Booklist* **STARRED REVIEW**

"Readers will love this lusty and unusual marriage of convenience story."

NYT Bestselling Author MADELINE HUNTER

"Smart, witty, graceful, sensual, elegant and gritty all at once. It has all of the meticulous attention to detail I love in Georgette Heyer, BUT WITH SEX!"

RITA-Award Winning Author JEFFE KENNEDY

<u>HIS VALET</u>

<u>HIS COUNTESS</u>

<u>HER BEAST</u>

<u>THEIR MASTER</u>

<u>THE HALE SAGA SERIES: AMERICANS IN LONDON</u>

<u>BALTHAZAR: THE SPARE*</u>

*upcoming book

Hyacinth

The Bellamy Sisters
Book 2

Minerva Spencer
writing as
S.M. LAVIOLETTE

CROOKED SIXPENCE BOOKS are published by
CROOKED SIXPENCE PRESS
2 State Road 230
El Prado, NM 87529

Copyright © 2023 Shantal M. LaViolette

All rights reserved. No part of this publication may be reproduced, distributed, or transmitted in any form or by any means, including photocopying, recording, or other electronic or mechanical methods, without the prior written permission of the publisher, except in the case of brief quotations embodied in critical reviews and certain other noncommercial uses permitted by copyright law. For permission requests, write to the publisher, addressed "Attention: Permissions Coordinator," at the address above.

To the extent that the image or images on the cover of this book depict a person or persons, such person or persons are merely models, and are not intended to portray any character or characters featured in the book.
If you purchased this book without a cover you should be aware that this book is stolen property. It was reported as "unsold and destroyed" to the Publisher and neither the Author nor the Publisher has received any payment for this "stripped book."

First printing February 28, 2023

ISBN: 978-1-951662-60-8

10 9 8 7 6 5 4 3 2 1

Any references to historical events, real people, or real places are used fictitiously. Names, characters, and places are products of the author's imagination.
Photo stock by Period Images
Printed in the United States of America

Chapter 1

London

Even with a half-naked woman on his lap Sylvester Derrick, eighth Duke of Chatham, was bored.

But that wasn't unusual—neither the boredom nor the half-naked woman.

No, what was unusual was that Sylvester hadn't simply got up and left hours ago—when he'd first begun to *get* bored. He blamed his inertia on the weather rather than laziness, but he knew that was a lie. While it was true that it was wretched outside, it was truer still that his arse had been in his chair so damned long the two seemed to have become fused.

He shifted the girl's plump bottom from one leg to the other and she made a soft grunting sound, like a sleeper disturbed, her arm tightening around his shoulder.

"I'll stick," Sylvester muttered over her shoulder when the dealer gave him a questioning look.

The young buck next to Sylvester took a hit on a four showing and received a ten. The boy stared at the two cards and savagely chewed his lip before—amazingly—asking for another card. It was a knave, which meant twenty-four showing.

Sylvester snorted.

The idiot gave a gurgle of surprise and dropped his head into his hands. "Bloody hell!"

"No hysterics," Lord Angus Fowler—who sat on the boy's other side—growled. The cantankerous Bristol shipbuilder shook his leonine head at the dealer. "I'll stick."

The version of *vingt-et-un* at Number Nine Leeland Street—known more commonly, but less flatteringly, as the *Pigeonhole*—was different than most played in other London hells, not that every gambling den didn't have its own variations of the popular game.

This variant was played with two packs, the dealer was allowed to double, the second card was dealt face-up, and—most interestingly—the dealer was required to take a card on anything less than fifteen. Sylvester found the game more entertaining than any other he'd played and, therefore, compelling enough to come to such a godforsaken part of the city.

The dealer flipped his card, revealing a queen to go with his four, and then dealt himself another card. A second queen hit the table.

"Bloody hell!" the young fool beside Sylvester groaned again, louder this time. "I could have won if—"

"You shut your gob or leave," Fowler snapped, scraping his winnings across the green baize with a scowl.

The younger man shoved back from the table and lurched unsteadily to his feet, glaring belligerently down at the gargantuan industrialist. "I'll—I'll—"

"You'll go and eat some supper before you shoot the cat and embarrass yourself worse than you already have," Sylvester advised, before Fowler lost his patience with the lad and did something all of them would regret.

The younger man turned and blinked blearily down at him, his gaze flickering to the right side of Sylvester's face. He grimaced and then coughed. "Ah, yes. Supper."

He staggered away and Fowler chuckled.

"It must be bloody nice to be a *dooook* and scare little boys away with a glance," Fowler taunted. "Us mere mortals usually have to give them a boot in the arse to be rid of them."

Sylvester smiled, even though his facial muscles were out of practice and he knew it was not a pretty sight. As harsh and uncivil as Fowler was, he liked the other man a great deal. Not only was sea captain-turned-shipbuilder clever and amusing, but he elevated plain speaking to an art form.

The whore who was sitting on his lap—Delia, Sylvester thought her name was—shifted restlessly, her hand going to Sylvester's face. The unscarred side.

She stroked him and whispered into his neck, her bottom rubbing suggestively over his groin. "What about you, Your Grace? Have you worked up an appetite? Are you... hungry?"

Hyacinth

Sylvester knew that Delia wasn't talking about the surprisingly excellent supper the Pigeonhole laid out for its victims as an incentive to stay.

But her carnal words did nothing to stir him, so he ignored her offer.

The deal passed to the lugubrious Lord Framling, a man who'd been losing as steadily as Sylvester and Fowler had been winning. Sylvester had at least two thousand in his pile and Fowler even more.

"You going to supper or staying?" Fowler asked, as they waited for fresh packs of cards—which was Framling's prerogative.

Sylvester opened his mouth to say *neither* when the door to the card room swung open and a newcomer hovered in the doorway.

"Ah, fresh meat," Fowler said, pausing in the process of stuffing some of the notes on the table into his pocket. The big Scot sized up the young man and snorted disparagingly. "Although he doesn't look like he'll have much to contribute to my purse."

Sylvester had to agree. The newcomer was a stripling who couldn't have been more than eighteen. He was a spindly lad and his well-made clothing hung on his tall, thin frame. Thick spectacles perched on a long, bony nose that looked out of place above a full but tight-lipped mouth. As he came closer to the table Sylvester readjusted his estimate—the boy looked closer to fifteen than eighteen. He was nothing but sharp angles and fine-boned fragility.

He looked far too young to be out and about by himself at such an advanced hour.

"Here then," Fowler said, eyeing the youngster with a look harsh enough to strip the barnacles off a ship's hull. "I think you took the wrong door, lad. The nursery's one house down."

The others chuckled and even Sylvester snorted.

The boy's skin—pale, soft, and not yet sprouting hair—flushed darkly. He took off his hat, exposing hair that was the shocking orangish-red of an actual orange, and dropped his skinny carcass into the chair where the last stripling had sat. He placed his hand on the table and when it came away, there was a tightly rolled wad of banknotes in its place.

Fowler chuckled. "I guess that shuts me up."

Sylvester studied the boy's flushed profile. Strawberry blonde eyelashes grew thick and without any curve from lids that rode heavy over pale sea-colored eyes. His fine hair was overlong and brushed his collar. Even a heavy dollop of pomade could not stop the frizzy curls, except around the boy's temples, where the corkscrews had been brutally scraped back to expose fair skin with blue veins pulsing beneath.

The lad turned toward Sylvester, obviously aware of his scrutiny. Not by a blink or even a change in breathing did he show any surprise at Sylvester's hideously scarred face. That alone was unusual in Sylvester's experience. In fact, it might be unique. Even Fowler had gawked at his mutilated cheek the first time they'd met. But the boy just fixed him with a pale, fishy stare.

Well.

But then the lad's eyes drifted to Delia and his flush—which had just started to recede—returned with a vengeance, flooding his peaked face. The boy swallowed so hard it looked painful.

Sylvester chuckled at his obvious discomfort and gave the woman on his lap a nudge. "Up you get, darling." She was putting his leg to sleep and wasting her time on him; it was better for them both—not to mention the nervous boy—if she found a lap that paid better.

Delia unfolded herself from Sylvester's lap with the languid stretch of a cat, making sure to thrust her not insubstantial breasts up against Sylvester's chin in the process. He tucked some money between the twin moons and her sleepy eyes widened at the amount.

"Coo, much obliged, Your Grace." She licked her full, rouged lips. "Are you sure you don't—"

"Not tonight," Sylvester said, his gaze still on the boy's wide-eyed stare—which had become even wider when Delia had turned the full extent of her charms in his direction. Really, the lad was looking at the woman as if he'd never seen one before.

A waiter came to deliver fresh packs of cards and take orders for drinks.

"Brandy," the boy said in the warbly uneven tone of a young male in the process of becoming a man.

Sylvester nodded at the waiter to indicate he would have the same.

Viscount Framling gave the waiter card money, split open two fresh packs, and commenced to shuffle.

Outside the wind blew hard enough to rattle the shutters on the building.

***

Hyacinth

Hyacinth Mary Bellamy, the second oldest daughter of the Earl of Addiscombe, carefully turned up the corner of the face-down card: an ace.

She flipped it over and pushed more money toward the dealer. "Split and double down."

Hy ignored the low murmuring that came from the other players. She couldn't blame their irritation; she had enjoyed an unusual number of splits in the course of the evening.

The dealer dealt her two cards: a nine and an eight.

"You lucky little bastard," the big gruff player—a man called Fowler—grumbled as he stayed with his hand, a five showing. This was a better group of card players than Hy usually encountered, but then again this wasn't a collection of grooms, postilions, and footmen in a country posting inn; this was one of the highest dollar hells in London. Complete with prostitutes.

The dealer flipped his cards to grumbles all around the table: seventeen. His hand beat all but Hy's and the scarred man next to her.

Hy glanced at her winnings, several towers of neatly stacked coins and a small collection of notes. She'd increased her stake money by one hundred and twenty pounds. It was the most profitable evening of cards she'd ever had. She could have earned a lot more if she'd wagered more aggressively, but her naturally cautious nature was difficult to suppress.

Besides, this was only her fifth night out and she still had ample time to accumulate the funds she needed without becoming reckless.

Hy would have liked to continue playing, but it was late and she had to be careful about returning home.

"I'm out," she said. She took the small leather purse from her pocket and began to put away her winnings.

"Leavin' already?" Fowler growled, leaning back, one huge arm slung over his chair, his dark green eyes as hard as agates. He was a ginger, too, although nowhere near as red as Hy.

Nobody was as redheaded as Hy.

Hy nodded at the man and then remembered what her best friend Charles was always telling her: "You've got to *speak* to people, Hy. Even if it's only to say *hello* and *goodbye*."

"Yes," she said. That answer seemed far too bald so she added, "Thank you, sir, it was most enjoyable." Hy stood and tucked the purse inside her coat, the fat roll of money making a bulge over her left breast. She stopped her body from dropping a curtsy at the last minute, turning the action into a rather awkward bow.

Fowler laughed. "D'ja hear that Chatham? The lad *enjoyed* takin' our money."

The Duke of Chatham looked up at her, his light brown eyes glinting with humor. The wound in his cheek—an odd, circular scar—pulled the right corner of his mouth up, exposing his canine tooth and the ones on either side of it, giving him a perpetual sneer.

The longer he looked at her, the more Hy relaxed: he did not recognize her.

Hy should have been ecstatic about that, but she couldn't help feeling a bit insulted: this was at least the third or fourth time they'd been introduced—or *re*-introduced, rather—this Season.

Of course, all the other times Hy had been wearing a dress and her hair had been a dull brown.

Besides, why *should* he recognize her? Hy was... well, *Hy* and the duke was one of the *ton's* preeminent connoisseurs of women, and a matrimonial catch who'd been pursued relentlessly by every marriage-mad mama in the *ton*, not that Chatham seemed inclined to marry any time soon, if the gossips were to be believed.

And those were only the proper rumors she'd heard.

The *im*proper rumors—those she'd overheard while gambling in the various London hells—described Chatham as a libertine with the sexual appetite of an ancient Roman senator. She knew what that meant: the duke enjoyed the sorts of *unusual* activities that wealthy, powerful men went to exclusive brothels to engage in.

Hy knew that proper, decent, moral women did not think of such places, except with disgust. She also knew she was none of those things because she had an almost burning desire to visit a brothel—especially one of the wicked ones called birching houses.

Not that she would ever dare to do such a thing. It was one thing to masquerade as a man at a card table and quite another to do it in a house of prostitution, no matter how much she might like to try.

It suddenly occurred to Hy that she could now reflect on what her mother called her *unnatural and perverted* urges without feeling guilt and shame.

Charles would call that progress.

As Hy studied the duke's face she recalled all the tittering she'd overheard at the *ton* functions she had attended. Many, many women had whispered to each other how hideous the duke's mutilated face was—even while they were setting their caps at him.

Hyacinth

Personally, Hy didn't think his scar was so horrifying, unless a person thought about how badly it must have hurt when it happened; *that* was horrifying.

Hy thought it gave him an air of rugged danger and improved upon an otherwise average face. But then she was odd that way, liking ugly or damaged things. At almost six feet tall with shocking orange hair, freckles, *and* spectacles Hy was hardly a diamond of the first water, herself, so it didn't seem fair to expect perfection and beauty from others.

"What is your name?" The duke's accent—unlike his friend Fowler's—was of Hy's own class, crisp and diamond hard.

Hy and Selina had already discussed this eventuality—her encountering people she knew—although she'd never imagined she'd have to put her lies to the test with somebody like the Duke of Chatham.

They had decided that a name as close to her own was the wisest choice. "Hiram Bellamy, Your Grace." She cleared the froggy sound from her throat and added. "But I answer to Hy."

The duke's shrewd gaze made Hy's skin prickle beneath the men's clothing she wore.

"Any relation to the Earl of Addiscombe?"

Again, Hy had anticipated this question. "None that I know of, sir."

Fowler laughed. "He sure doesn't play like Addiscombe."

The men at the table, all except the duke, laughed with him.

The duke's speculative gaze made Hy feel more than a little uneasy. But it seemed she was worrying for nothing because, after a long moment, he nodded and said, "No, he most certainly does not."

Hy experienced a pang at hearing her father's skills—or lack of them—spoken of so derisively, but she wasn't surprised. The earl was a dreadful card player, no matter how much he loved gambling. Or perhaps *because* he loved it so much.

The duke kept her fixed with his piercing stare, so Hy held his gaze, unwilling to back down. After all, it wasn't too often that she had an excuse to openly gawk at such a man.

The Duke of Chatham was that rare beast: a wealthy, bachelor duke of marriageable age—not that he appeared to be looking too hard for a wife, much to the chagrin of her Aunt Fitzroy and every other matrimonial minded mama in England.

In addition to being a well-known libertine, he was also accounted top of the trees when it came to riding, shooting, fencing, and was a pugilist of some renown—a Corinthian, in other words.

Hy wasn't certain what, exactly, a Corinthian was—although her brother Doddy was wild to belong to the group. She could only assume a Corinthian was the embodiment of masculine ideals.

Strangely, the duke did not *look* like a debauched pugilistic rake. Well, other than the prostitute he'd had on his lap. He was above average height and of normal build, although his shoulders and chest appeared well-developed. The unscarred side of his face was neither handsome nor ugly. He looked, with the exception of the scar, shockingly normal.

Especially when compared to his friend Baron Fowler, who only lacked longer hair with plaits, a kilt, and a six-foot broadsword to complete his resemblance to a barbaric highlander on the warpath, although the man's Scottish accent was oddly blunted, as if he'd lived more of his life outside of the region.

"Have you been playing long?" the duke asked her.

Hy just shrugged. She hated vague questions.

Fowler gave one of his loud, good-natured guffaws. "There, see what you've done, Chatham? You frightened the lad and cut off his garrulous babbling."

Again, the others laughed, all except the duke.

"Do you play here often, Bellamy?" Chatham asked, apparently not dissuaded by her reticence.

"This is my third time," Hy said.

"You must join us again sometime and give poor Mr. Fowler an opportunity to win back some of his money." When the duke smiled the undamaged side of his mouth pulled up higher, exposing a second pointy canine. "If you do come back, you will need to arrive earlier—we usually begin our play at midnight. I know it is an unfashionable hour, but we are elderly and must start our entertainments early in the evening."

Fowler gave another bellow of laughter.

Hy exhaled the breath she'd been holding. "Thank you, Your Grace, I shall bear that in mind. You honor me with your invitation."

Which I shan't be accepting any time soon.

Hy had been lucky to escape recognition once, she might not be so lucky again. "I bid you goodnight." She turned away, forcing herself to move slowly, rather than sprint from the room—and the duke's disconcerting stare.

***

Hyacinth

Sylvester watched the tall, skinny boy leave, his gait the awkward, self-conscious walk of a very young man who was newly on the town.

"Quite the cool-headed little bastard, wasn't he?" Fowler asked, holding up two fingers for the hovering waiter.

"Too cool for you," Sylvester said, his gaze flickering to his friend's much diminished pile of money.

Fowler thought that was hilarious. "Aye, but I think I wasn't the only one taken in."

Fowler was right, the stripling had worked the table more skillfully than men who'd been playing for thirty years. While Sylvester had no way to prove it, he knew the boy was aware at all times of what had been played and what remained in the deck—an impressive skill when a person was counting into not one, but two packs of cards.

Not only that, but he'd employed a playing strategy that was logical, consistent, and without emotionalism. It had been a pleasure to watch him decimate the others even though Sylvester had also lost money to him when it had been his turn at bank.

To be honest, it had been a while since Sylvester had enjoyed much pleasure at the card tables—or anywhere else—which must have been why he'd issued the unusual invitation to the lad.

"An odd humor to invite him back here to play, wasn't it?" Fowler asked, as if reading his mind.

"I enjoyed watching him take your money."

Fowler gave Sylvester's diminished pile a pointed look. "Aye, I know what you mean."

Sylvester snorted and gathered up his winnings.

"What? You leavin'?"

"I have an early appointment tomorrow."

Fowler looked at his watch. "You might as well stay awake and go to your meeting from here."

Sylvester ignored Fowler's bossy suggestion. "Do you want a ride?"

Fowler scowled. "I'm staying."

"As you wish." Sylvester headed for the door.

"Don't forget that I'll be wantin' you to go with me to Tat's to look at that pair of chestnuts," Fowler called out behind him.

Sylvester didn't bother answering; Fowler would show up at his house and drag him off whether he agreed to go or not.

His carriage was ready and waiting for him when he stepped out into the horizontal wind and rain. He'd told John Coachman to be ready at three and the man knew Sylvester valued both his servants and cattle too much to keep them standing in the rain.

A burly footman opened the carriage door and Sylvester stepped into the plush interior, which was warm thanks to a cast-iron brazier set in a special slot in the floor. Sylvester put his booted feet on the brass lid of the warmer and relaxed against the soft leather seat, his mind sorting through the evening.

The Pigeonhole allowed its punters to play some interesting games and the stakes were among the highest in London, but it was in a part of town Sylvester wouldn't want to ride through without armed men.

Fowler had convinced him to go the dangerous gambling hell because of the play, but normally Sylvester would not have bothered.

Still, there was not much he could be bothered to do these days. Even bedding his mistress seemed like a chore—which is why he'd not paid a visit to her in over two weeks. He knew matters had become grim when he'd rather use his own fist than go to a beautiful, skilled lover whom he paid hundreds of pounds to cater to his every whim.

Sylvester was disgusted by his moodiness, but no longer surprised by it. His father—as Sylvester knew all too well—had suffered from a similar melancholic disposition. Unlike his father, however, Sylvester did not have the luxury of eating a bullet. At least not yet.

Sylvester's lips twisted at the overly dramatic and self-pitying thought.

Poor, hideous, rich you, his inner critic mocked.

Sylvester yawned, wincing as he stretched out his sore body. He'd gone to Jackson's for the fifth day straight. It was excessive behavior and he'd known as much even without looking at the famous pugilist's frown. Not that *The Gentleman* would dare to say anything other than, "Welcome, Your Grace."

He massaged his shoulder and smiled; one of the few benefits of being a duke was never having to hear the word *no* or argue with anyone.

Except with Your Grace's mother, his mental companion whispered gleefully.

Yes, except her, Sylvester conceded.

A grown man afraid of his own mother!

Sylvester refused to be drawn into another tedious mental argument with his own conscience.

Instead, he rested his head back against the soft leather and thought back to tonight, and the odd young man at the gaming hell.

Hyacinth

Chapter 2

Hy waited until her Aunt Fitzroy and Selina had been gone for an hour before changing into her *Hiram* outfit and sneaking out through the conservatory, leaving one of the big windows unlatched for later.

She walked several streets from her aunt's address before hailing a hackney cab. The light mist from earlier was turning into a persistent drizzle, but it was better to be damp than to be seen by any of her aunt's servants.

The first hackney that stopped was so old and rickety Hy could hardly believe it would make it all the way to Leeland Street without the wheels falling off. The driver looked as ancient as his coach.

"Where to?" he demanded. When Hy hesitated, he snarled, "Well? Do ye, or don't ye?"

"Number Nine Leeland Street."

The driver snorted, as though Hy had said something funny. "Get in, lad."

The coach wasn't as filthy as she'd feared and she settled in for the rather long ride.

As usual, her mind wandered to the reason for these late-night jaunts. Hy had painstakingly accumulated almost eighteen hundred pounds, but she needed at least another thirty-five hundred. She'd not won all the money in London. Indeed, she'd been saving up her winnings for nearly eight, long years, counting her pennies and planning for the day she could set off on her own life.

At first, she had hoped that her friend Charles would join her, but last November he had become so ill that Hy knew he would never be able to share the future they'd plotted and planned together.

Charles's illness had cast a shadow over her plans—over her entire life—but he had urged her to seize the future she wanted, and so she had planned to make her move this spring.

Hyacinth

And then, a month ago, she and her sisters had discovered that their father, the Earl of Addiscombe, owed five thousand pounds to keep moneylenders from tossing her entire family out of Queen's Bower, their home.

Hy knew that most people—even her beloved siblings—thought of her as emotionally remote, or even emotionless. While that was true, to a degree, even she could not conscience running off and leaving her family in such dire straits.

No, it was her duty to at least cover the interest for a year. Although she wasn't stupid enough to think that things would change for the better even after she'd done so.

Her father would not stop gambling. And he would not stop losing.

Hy, whose brain was a logical machine most of the time, experienced an uncharacteristic throb of futility when she thought about her father.

But that was not something she could concern herself with right now; she needed to keep her thoughts focused and sharp.

Not only did she need the money for her family, but Hy was also determined to earn enough so that Charles could go to the seaside, which his physician had told him would ease his health problems.

Hy grimaced at the thought of Charles's probable reaction when she tried to give him money. Her best friend was a proud man, but he wasn't foolish. Hopefully he would take the money. Or perhaps she could give it to his grandfather and swear him to secrecy as to where it came from? One way or another, she would make sure he could afford to leave London. She not only adored Charles, she *owed* him. If she were the sort of person given to dramatic declarations, she would say that he had saved her life. Or at least made it worth living.

Once she'd taken care of those two obligations, she could set off on her own. And if she felt a twinge of something that felt shockingly like remorse or homesickness at the thought of leaving her siblings and Queen's Bower behind, well… She would get past that feeling once she'd seized the reins of her own future.

Hy was sure she would.

She suddenly noticed the rain had begun to fall harder and blocked what little light shone from the increasingly infrequent streetlamps. Yet again it was a miserable night to be out and Hy probably should have stayed home.

But, for some reason, she'd been too restless to simply catch up on her sleep.

A face pushed around the edge of her thoughts like a willful child peeking around a door: the Duke of Chatham's face.

Hy was startled that the man had sprung to mind.

No, you are not, a voice whispered in her head. *He is the reason for your earlier than usual departure from your aunt's house.*

Hy pondered the accusation for a moment and was forced to admit there was some truth in it.

She *did* hope the duke would be there tonight, even though he was a distraction she could ill afford. She also, wickedly, hoped he had a woman on his lap, she hoped his hand—his elegant hand with its intriguing ring on the thumb—drifted languidly over the woman's body and settled on her thigh, as it had the last time.

In the privacy of her room, Hy had recalled Chatham's idle yet sensual stroking of the woman's scantily clad body. But in her mind's eye it had been *her* own body—far less lush and feminine than the whore's—that he'd caressed with an air of confident masculine possession that had sent arrows of arousal to her sex.

Rather than indulge in a private orgy of self-castigation at enjoying such a fantasy—as her mother would have demanded she do—Hy had instead embraced the vivid images.

And then she had—with very little guilt—sated her body's relentless demands, just the way Charles had encouraged her to do.

Which brought her thoughts in a circle around to Charles.

But thinking about her friend was pointless. He was gone, gone, gone. At least as far as Hy was concerned.

And nobody would ever understand her like Charles.

***

Sylvester glanced at his watch and then at Fowler, who was chatting up a group of young chits straight from the schoolroom under the gimlet eye of at least four chaperones. The girls' faces were angled up at the towering man like flowers tilted toward the sun. The Scotsman did burn brightly, his dark red hair the color of a live coal under the blazing light of several hundred candles.

Hyacinth

Sylvester wished he had the other man's optimism—the belief that one of the women in this room was his perfect mate and would provide him with what his life was missing: children, family, and love.

He knew that Fowler would deny it, but the man was a hopeless romantic. He had the rough, unpolished exterior of a blacksmith but the heart of a poet. He also had more money than the king; hence the reason his big peasant feet were allowed over the thresholds of so many grand aristocratic houses.

Well, money and his elevation to a barony. Yes, Lord Angus Fowler, owner of the nation's largest shipbuilding enterprise, was welcome anywhere in Britain, especially in this time of war.

Sylvester envied his friend his optimism. His own heart had shriveled up and blown away a long time ago. If he remarried—*when* he remarried—it would be an emotionless business arrangement just like any other he engaged in for the future of the dukedom. Romance and love were two concepts that he'd lost interest—or belief—in a decade ago.

Sylvester's eyes settled on one of the girls in Fowler's bouquet—by far the loveliest young woman he'd seen this Season—even in several. He'd not noticed her before, which was not surprising as he normally avoided making eye-contact with debutantes or their handlers, but he looked his fill now. She was an intoxicating blend of full pink lips; enormous, heavy-lidded blue-violet eyes; and thick, glossy, golden hair that would hang down past her arse when it was unbound.

She had his dead wife Mariah's coloring and yet the two women could not have looked more different. This girl was all sweet innocence and smiling joy and the way she was staring up at Fowler—not with apprehension as the other blooms were doing, but with her lips parted in an expression of genuine interest—said she had intelligence and a curious nature to go along with her beauty. An unusual combination in Sylvester's experience.

But as unusual as she might be, Sylvester had no interest in staying at the insipid ball just to look at her. He was ready to leave. Now. He put down his empty glass and made his way through the hot press of bodies over to Fowler and his garden of beauties.

The chaperones noticed him first, their eyes widening slightly, but for such dignified matrons a slight widening was tantamount to yelling. They would be wondering what the Duke of Chatham—a man who'd eluded parson's mousetrap for almost a decade—was doing approaching a group of girls barely out of the schoolroom.

They would be hoping.

Some of them would already be scheming...

Sylvester picked one of the chaperones at random—Viscountess Fitzroy—and bowed over her hand.

"What an unexpected pleasure, Your Grace," she cooed, forgetting all about the rich man she had on the hook—a mere baron—in contemplation of a much bigger fish. She gestured to the girl in the white dress, the beauty. "I believe you've met my niece, Lady Selina Bellamy, before."

Bellamy? Sylvester stared at the girl. How odd to hear the same name in less than a week.

But other than a similar pale coloring, this curvaceous, feminine angel bore no resemblance to the gangly and awkward young ginger he'd met at the Pigeonhole.

The surname was just a coincidence.

"Of course, I recall Lady Selina," Sylvester lied smoothly, bowing over her hand. When he straightened, he found her eyes on *his* eyes, rather than the right side of his face. She was even more exquisite up close. Her skin was like blushing crème silk and her coral pink lips looked sinfully soft. That fact that he had no recollection of meeting such a glorious specimen of femininity really was a sign that he was getting far too old and jaded for all this.

Fowler jostled his arm and Sylvester realized he was still holding Miss Bellamy's hand and staring down at her. He relinquished it and looked up to find the Scotsman glaring at him.

Sylvester bit back a smile at the other man's territorial behavior and moved on to meet the rest of the entirely forgettable bouquet of young ladies, most of whom cringed, winced, or avoided looking at his face entirely.

When he'd finished, he turned to Lady Fitzroy to take his leave, but she was ready for him and pounced.

"Lady Selina's partner for the waltz turned his ankle and had to beg off," she murmured to Sylvester.

He glanced at Fowler, but the viscountess set a hand on his arm. "Perhaps you might partner her, Chatham—you know a single dance with you will make her Season."

The wily viscountess had snared him with very little effort—thanks to bloody Fowler. What else could Sylvester say but, "Of course, my lady." It was a struggle to hide his irritation. He doubted very much that a diamond such as Selina Bellamy needed any help from him, but he had no choice.

"Would you do me the honor of dancing this set, Lady Selina?" he asked, aware that Fowler's eyes were burning a hole through his head.

The beauty looked startled, but not unpleasantly so. "I would be honored."

It was immediately clear that Lady Selina was an able practitioner of the rather scandalous dance, but Sylvester could see she'd not been dancing it for long.

He smiled down at her and asked, "When did you receive permission to waltz, my lady?"

"It has been several weeks now." She cut him a shy, but not terrified or repulsed, look. "I have not seen you at Almack's, Your Grace."

"No, I have not returned since being denied entry." He tried his best to avoid the tedious—and yet exclusive—Wednesday night affair, despite the fact one of his cousins, Lady Sefton, was a patroness and repeatedly offered him vouchers.

"They turned a duke away?"

"They did, indeed."

"What heinous infraction did you commit?"

He laughed, charmed by her teasing. "I was three minutes late."

"Ah. So you've not returned because you've been nursing wounded sensibilities."

"Just so, my lady." He smiled down at her. "But now I might have a reason to brave the dragons and return."

She flushed prettily at his compliment—which he had no intention of turning into deed—and the rest of the dance passed in comfortable chatter about what she'd done in London since her arrival.

While the dance wasn't unpleasant, Sylvester was grateful to be able to hand her safely back to her chaperone when it was over. He carefully avoided making eye-contact with any of the other matrons and turned to Fowler.

"I'm off and wanted to know if you wished for a ride?"

Fowler was staring at the Bellamy girl with the intensity of a parched man gazing at a glass of water. "I'm going to stay a while," he muttered, not taking his eyes off the girl.

"As you wish." Sylvester made his escape and was hatted, gloved, and coated a quarter of an hour later, comfortably ensconced in his coach, and headed to the Pigeonhole.

Once inside his carriage, Sylvester couldn't help wondering about his friend. He'd not seen such a rapt expression on Fowler's freckled face before. Sylvester had known him for almost seven years, but never had he seen the big man show his heart so nakedly.

He thought about the girl Fowler had been gazing at. Sylvester knew a little about the Earl of Addiscombe, he could recall playing cards against the man years ago. He'd not seen the earl since Addiscombe had been forced to retrench and had tucked himself and his family away in the country.

The girl was obviously looking for a wealthy husband and with her beauty and charm there would be plenty of men on offer. Sylvester had a difficult time imagining her choosing Fowler. For all that he was an excellent friend and entertaining associate, the man could hardly be called handsome or charming.

Not that Sylvester was one to talk.

He stared out the window into the night. It was a week for summer storms, and here he was again, heading out into one. And why? Boredom, yes. But also curiosity, although he hated to admit it., he had enjoyed watching the Bellamy boy play cards and wouldn't mind playing against him again.

How pitiful was that? Headed into a tempest to play cards with a mere stripling. Ha!

The carriage rolled to a smooth stop and Sylvester saw he was already at the tall brown brick building. Outside it was raining horizontally and he opened the door without waiting for his footman to lower the steps.

"Evenin', Yer Graze," the Pigeonhole's familiar mountainous doorman Alfred greeted as he ushered Sylvester into the gambling den, the wind trying to tug the heavy wooden door from his huge paw.

The Pigeonhole—which was really called Jensen's—was a pared down operation, the men who came to play not interested in gilt furniture or luxurious décor. Walls had been knocked out on the ground floor to make a supper room, which was also utilized for games like E.O., Hazard, and Faro. The second-floor rooms, where Sylvester was bound, accommodated two tables each, except for the Green Room, which was only large enough to hold one table. It was also the room which usually hosted the highest stakes games. Jensen allowed the players to call their own games and serve as bank in exchange for a percentage of the money that changed hands, which made it an appealing alternative to hosting games at one's house.

Hyacinth

Sylvester's mouth curved into a smile when he saw the back of a familiar ginger head. Perhaps the evening might hold some entertainment, after all.

There were three other men—all of them young—in addition to Bellamy, but Sylvester knew none of them. They must have known him—at least by description—because all three gawked at his scar and then flushed when they realized they were staring.

Hiram Bellamy was carefully stacking his most recent winnings in precise towers on his right side. He must have noticed some subtle change in the room, although nobody had spoken and the door closed without making a sound, as Jensen had felted it.

Bellamy looked up, his blue green eyes opaque behind the thick spectacles. His mouth, which had been tightly pursed, curved into a tentative smile when he saw Sylvester.

Something about the younger man's obvious pleasure at seeing him caused an odd tightening in Sylvester's belly. He could not recall the last time anyone—other than Fowler—had appeared genuinely glad of his company.

"Good evening, Your Grace," the boy said in his low, froggy voice.

"Good evening, Hiram." He glanced at the others. "Gentlemen." He took the empty seat beside the boy. "You appear to have done well this evening. How long have you been here?"

"I ar—" his voice broke and he cleared his throat and tried again, "I arrived early, just after eleven, sir."

"Hoping to find Lord Fowler, were you?"

The boy merely smiled.

Sylvester nodded to the servant who appeared with a tray of five rouleaux and deposited them on the table beside him.

Sylvester extracted five five-pound counters and pushed them forward as his opening bet.

The boy's eyes flickered to the money and back to Sylvester. He hesitated and then gave a slight nod, as if he'd come to some sort of internal agreement. And then he put forward the same amount.

The other three men stared pensively and then made their own far smaller bets.

And then the first cards were dealt and the time for small talk was over.

***

Sylvester should have left when the boy did. Not only did he begin to lose after Hiram cashed in his counters and departed, but the play became strangely flat with the lad was no longer there.

He had greatly enjoyed watching the systematic way Bellamy played. Although he was just a young scrub, he was already a master of the game.

Sylvester stayed perhaps another half hour before deciding it was time to leave—foul weather, or not.

He briefly considered visiting Juliet but decided he couldn't be bothered making the small talk that was necessary even with one's mistress. It was probably time to cut their association as he no longer had the desire to use her services. He didn't know why he couldn't be bothered to go to her—especially after he'd gone to such trouble to hire her away from a birch house he frequented. Not only did Juliet not balk at rough play, but she seemed to genuinely enjoy the sort of bed sport he did. But for the past six months their exchanges had felt… flat, for lack of a better word. Indeed, he'd paid more visits to her former place of employment than to her. It was foolish to prolong the relationship and Juliet—who was a mature woman his age—would accept the severance with equanimity.

Sylvester sighed. He should go and see her tonight and raise the matter—why put off the inevitable—but he was too bloody tired.

He yawned hugely as the carriage rumbled through the worsening weather, his thoughts yet again returning to Hiram Bellamy and the boy's ability to remember the cards.

Sylvester wondered just how many packs Bellamy could keep track of in his methodical mind. He had no mean skill in that department, himself, which was part of the reason he enjoyed playing double pack games so much.

He yawned again, his eyelids suddenly heavy. Lord, he *was* getting old; it wasn't even three o'clock and he was ready for his bed.

Sylvester was just starting to drift off when the carriage passed one of the few streetlamps that existed in this poor section of town. Slumped against the pole, hatless, and leaning into the wind was Hiram Bellamy—as if Sylvester had conjured the other man just by thinking about him.

"What the devil," Sylvester muttered. He sat up and pulled on the cord.

The vent opened. "Yes, Your Grace," his coachman yelled over the storm.

"There was a boy back there—against that light post."

Hyacinth

"Aye, Your Grace, I saw him."

"Stop and send one of the footmen to go fetch him. Tell him Chatham is offering him a ride."

"Yes, Your Grace." The vent snapped shut, the carriage rolled to a smooth stop and Sylvester felt the vehicle shudder as one of the footmen hopped off. Outside the rain had begun to fall in sheets, the wind driving hard enough against the carriage that it swayed and shook on its springs, reminding Sylvester not a little of the opening scene in *The Tempest*.

Chapter 3

It wasn't Hy's way to regret outcomes which had already occurred and which could not be altered, but she had to admit to feeling something very close to regret about losing her evening's winnings.

Although it wasn't really accurate to call it *losing* it if one was robbed.

Regardless of what one called it, Hy was the fool who'd climbed into the hackney without considering the consequences.

She'd been lulled into a false sense of security by the hack's meticulously maintained exterior. As if criminal behavior and good housekeeping somehow could not coexist. As a result, she'd been too busy mentally plotting her gambling schedule for the coming week to notice when the carriage slowed and then stopped altogether. Not that she could have done much about it if she'd noticed sooner.

The hackney had stopped in the darkest spot between the streetlamps. Granted, lamps were few and far between in this part of the city but still, it made no sense to stop in such a place unless evil deeds had been planned.

The door flew open and the force of the wind banged it against the hack's side. Two men stood in the battering wind and rain.

"'Why, ee's jest a scrawny squib, 'Arold," the smaller of the two men observed, needing to shout to be heard over the weather.

The bigger man, Harold, Hy assumed, flicked his comrade a look of irritation before speaking to Hy. "Yer specs, lad." He didn't wait for Hy to understand, instead reaching out and taking her glasses. Why would he want her spectacles? What possible use could they have for *her* glasses?

Hy squinted at the now blurry pair.

"'And over yer dosh and they'll be no throble."

Her brain struggled to decipher the words; he wanted her to do *what*?

But Harold was not a patient man and he reached into the carriage with a swiftness at odds with his bulky size and grabbed Hy's shoulder, yanking her from the coach and knocking her hat from her head in the process.

"Nice cover!" the smaller man said, taking off his own hat and replacing it with Hy's, which even without her glasses she could see was far too small for his head.

"The money," Harold growled, his rain-slicked ruddy face only inches from hers, his big hand going to the buttons on Hy's coat.

She comprehended his intention and batted away his hand. "I'll get it," she said, shoving her hand into her overcoat and extracting the roll of notes from her breast pocket before he tried again.

Harold snatched the bills and squinted at her, his expression difficult to read in the rain and wind, he opened his mouth, as if to say something, but his associate, the smaller thief, had plans of his own.

"Yer gloves and coats, too." His hands landed on her shoulders and he grabbed her woolen overcoat and yanked. "Unbutton it," he shouted when he couldn't simply tear it off her body.

Hy pulled off her gloves and he snatched them away from her, trying—and failing—to shove his own hands into them. Hy fumbled with the big silver buttons on her overcoat. She barely got the last one open before the coat was ripped from her back.

Not to be outdone, Harold grabbed her fob and watch, pulling hard enough to tear her breeches and send her stumbling backward.

"Coat, too," the smaller man said, although he'd never fit into it.

Yet again Harold impatiently yanked the garment from her body.

Hy had just regained her balance when Harold shoved her away from the carriage.

"G'won," he said, "Before ol' Jemmy 'ere decides to take yer breeches and boots, too." His foot landed on Hy's bottom and he kicked her hard enough to send her sprawling to her hands and knees.

Hy bit her tongue as she fell, her mouth flooding with blood, her forehead knocking against the street. Bits of gravel bit into her palms and stung badly enough to make her eyes water. By the time she pushed up onto her knees, the carriage had rumbled off, quickly obscured by the weather.

Hy grunted as she lurched to her feet, swaying against the battering wind and rain as she looked up and down the street, unable to see more than a few feet in either direction. The only streetlamps in this part of town were on corners. Hy hadn't been paying attention, so she had no idea of which direction was which. She picked the dull glow that was brightest and began to walk toward it.

The only good thing she could say about the wretched weather was that she appeared to be the only idiot out in it. Well, her and the robbers, who'd probably found themselves a nice cozy inn by now and were in front of a fire enjoying her money.

Hy swallowed down her fury and kept walking. By the time she reached the corner she was soaked through to her bones. She slumped down at the base of the streetlamp. Perhaps she should just sleep there? A lamplighter would find her at dawn, either drowned or frozen to death by the unseasonably cold rain.

Yes, she was feeling sorry for herself.

A minute, she would rest for a minute and then get up and continue walking.

Hy was leaning heavily against the pitted lamppost when she heard the distant sound of carriage wheels on the rough street. It could be more robbers—or the same ones coming back for the rest of her clothes. Hy decided she didn't care and slumped against the post, too tired to run and hide from whoever was coming.

Luckily, the carriage rolled by without stopping.

She turned her hands palm-up and sucked her lower lip between her teeth with a hiss as the rain washed away the dirt and blood with a surprising sting.

"Sir?"

Hy shrieked and whirled around.

A young man stood a few feet away in costly-looking livery, complete with a heavy wool overcoat. The footman or groom was regarding her with such a puzzled look Hy could only assume her screech had sounded less than masculine.

"What do you want?" she demanded in a much lower tone.

"His Grace of Chatham is pleased to offer you a ride."

Hy squinted, but the rain made it impossible to see beyond the footman's expensively clad shoulder.

"Chatham?" she repeated stupidly.

"Aye, sir. His Grace's carriage is not far away."

Hy shook her head, almost amused by her choices: she could stagger home in the rain—if she could even *find* home—or she could accept a carriage ride from one of the most notorious libertines in England. Not that her virtue—such as it was—would be in any danger as she was garbed as a man.

Actually, a man accustomed to the most beautiful and accomplished women wouldn't be interested in Hy even if she were dressed only in her chemise and stockings.

Hy realized the servant was being buffeted by rain while she dithered.

"Lead the way," she said. A carriage ride was better than wandering the streets.

Hy followed him through the rain, wincing as her tattered breeches rubbed against her torn and bleeding knees.

The carriage was a monstrous black lacquer thing with Chatham's escutcheon on the door. Lanterns blazed on hangers beside the coachman and light shone from between the louvers covering the windows.

The footman opened the door and a wall of heat smacked Hy in the face.

The man who leaned forward was indeed the duke. He looked far different showing only his unscarred profile and Hy realized that perhaps he wasn't as average looking as she'd thought. Indeed, without his roguish scar he was handsome in a dignified, proper sort of way.

She climbed in without waiting for the servant to lower the steps and took the seat opposite the duke. The footman quickly shut the door against the howling wind and rain.

Hy cleared her throat. "Thank you, Your Grace."

"You are welcome."

Hy pushed back her wet hair and was about to wipe her face on her shirtsleeve—a pointless gesture since her sleeve was soaked, too—when a folded handkerchief appeared in front of her.

"Thank you," she said again.

He nodded.

Hy dried her eyes and cheeks and then used the handkerchief to mop up the dripping hair around her face.

"I take it you have been relieved of your winnings?"

"Yes. The hackney driver stopped the carriage and two men took my money, watch, hat, and coats."

"And your spectacles."

"And my spectacles," Hy agreed. "I believe they may have been associates of the porter who summoned a hack for me outside Jensen's. In fact, I now question whether the man who fetched the carriage really was a porter there."

"I daresay you are correct." The duke's tone was dryly amused and he stretched out his long legs, brushing Hy's almost equally long legs in the process. She jolted at the slight touch, but he appeared not to notice.

"It is unusual for young men to come gaming in such neighborhoods by themselves, Mr. Bellamy. In the future you would be well advised to accompany friends."

Hy nodded, as if she were genuinely considering the man's suggestion, as if she *had* friends to accompany her. She imagined bringing Selina along—and trying to pass off her gorgeous sister as a man—and almost smiled.

Hy glanced down at the duke's erstwhile snowy handkerchief and saw it was now liberally smeared with blood and filth. She held it up. "I'm sorry, but I have ruined your handkerchief."

The duke shrugged. "Where shall I have my driver drop you?"

Hy had been thinking about that, too. She could hardly have him leave her outside her aunt's house. "I shouldn't like to inconvenience you. I can walk from Your Grace's house."

Even Hy knew where Chatham House was. After all, it was one of the biggest private residences in London, sprawled across three lots on Berkeley Square.

"It is no inconvenience and you are hardly in any condition to walk." His Grace's eyes dropped to Hy's knees. She followed his gaze and sucked in a breath. The breeches—one of the three pairs she'd had made by a tailor she'd paid well to ignore her gender—were shredded and blood was oozing through the rips and soaking the surrounding fabric. Hy used the ruined handkerchief to brush away an embedded piece of gravel and then flushed when the stone made a soft *ping* on the brass brazier warming her sodden boots. She'd never seen such an ingenious invention before and briefly wondered how it managed to heat the coach without setting it on fire.

The duke cleared his throat, reminding her that he'd asked a question.

"I am staying with elderly relatives," she said, not entirely lying. "They do not know where I've gone, or even that I'm out so late. I should not like to show up in this state. It will be better if I arrive quietly and enter through the servants' entrance without attracting any attention." She gave him a wry smile and met his gaze, both actions she had to perform consciously but which Charles had always claimed put people at ease. "My aunt would need smelling salts if she saw me in such a condition." That much was the truth.

The duke nodded. "Very well. I'll take you home and my man will fix you up. Once you are presentable, I'll have a hackney summoned to take you home."

Hy opened her mouth, but then shut it when he tilted his head, his expression curious. Indeed, it *would* be abnormal to refuse such gracious assistance.

"Thank you, Your Grace."

"You are new to London?"

"Yes, this is my first visit."

"Down from school?"

Hy wished. She had tried to persuade her parents to let her to sit in with her younger brother, Doddy, during his lessons with the vicar, but her mother had been adamant.

"Absolutely not," Lady Addiscombe had snapped. "You are already odder than necessary, Hyacinth. The last thing you need is"—the countess had flapped her hands in an unusual display of frustration as she'd searched for the words she wanted—"even more oddities."

Fortunately, Hy had met Charles, and the vicar's knowledge became irrelevant. Charles had taught her enough mathematics that she could probably tutor it herself, not that women were allowed to do such a thing.

The duke was watching her with an interested look, making her realize that he was waiting for an answer while her mind was wandering, something it had a tendency to do.

"I did not go away to school," she admitted truthfully. "I was raised by my uncle and aunt and taught by the local vicar. They have no children and are training me to manage their small estate in Hampshire." Small estates in Hampshire were something Hy was extremely familiar with, considering she'd grown up on one.

"And did you learn to play cards from your uncle?"

Hy hesitated.

"Or did you learn by sneaking off to your local inn?"

She looked up at his change in tone to find the duke smiling, the unmutilated side of his mouth curled up, the skin at the corners of his eyes crinkling in genuine amusement. Hy felt an odd kick in her chest at the attractive expression.

"Er, mostly I taught myself."

His eyebrows rose in two elegant arches. "You learned to play cards by playing with yourself?"

"Yes."

His head tilted at her abrupt answer. Even Hy, with her abysmal social skills, could see more information was needed.

"It is not difficult. You deal out hand after hand and then play them all. Naturally you know more about all the hands than you would in a true game, but repeated playing demonstrates the various scenarios and helps to develop a methodology." She shrugged. "As to rules or strategies, I've read Hoyle, of course, along with a few others." Her father had numerous volumes devoted to card playing, all of which had appeared untouched by human hands before Hy had consulted them. If only her father had consulted the books, perhaps her family might not be in such an unpleasant bind at present.

"Once I learned the basic approach I played extensively." As extensively as one could play around the tiny village of Little Sissingdon. She certainly couldn't play at home. It would have been worth her life if her mother had ever caught Hy—or any of her siblings—with a pack of cards.

Chatham nodded and Hy enjoyed a moment of satisfaction at having navigated one of the dozens of social hurdles that faced her daily; hurdles which had increased one hundred-fold since leaving her quiet, predictable home in Little Sissingdon and arriving in London.

"You don't find the added dynamic of other people changes the experience—your approach to placing wagers, for example."

"No."

The duke kept looking at her, so Hy responded with a question of her own—yet another helpful diversionary tactic that Charles had taught her to employ. *People love to talk about themselves, Hy. If all else fails, ask questions.*

"Why would other people change how I play?" she asked.

"Many people watch other players' expressions, posture, and so forth to gain a sense of the play."

Hy could have told him that she judged people's expressions as well as a fish fired a pistol. Instead, she said, "I watch the cards, not the people."

He gave her another of his slight smiles. "I know you do."

"Is that wrong?"

28

"It would not seem so. After all, you won a great deal tonight. But—" he stopped and then gave a slight shake of his head, as if he'd changed his mind.

"But what?"

"I was going to suggest that perhaps a bit of people-watching might have spared you the loss of your winnings and the rough treatment you received in the hackney earlier."

Hy pondered his observation a moment and then shook her head. "No. I doubt I would have noticed anything amiss if I'd watched the driver more closely. I am not a competent student of human nature."

The duke let out a bark of laughter, even though Hy had not been jesting.

His laughter momentarily transformed the hard lines of his face and made him appear more youthful. Hy had noticed laughter often had that effect on people. She'd also noticed that people frequently laughed for reasons beyond her comprehension. It wasn't that she didn't possess a sense of humor—although her family would probably have something to say on that subject—but she rarely found things humorous enough to laugh about.

Charles had advised her to look for signs that something should be taken as amusing—generally the smiles and chuckling of others—and react accordingly. Of course, it was difficult in a conversation with only two people to know what might be amusing, and this situation seemed even less humorous than usual.

Very well, a direct approach seemed best.

"Why did you laugh?" she asked.

"It was less a laugh and more a snort of surprise."

There was something Hy appreciated: exactitude. "My words surprised you? Why?"

"In my experience people rarely admit to their deficiencies so openly."

"Oh." She pondered his observation and then shrugged. "Well, it is never wise to make generalizations based on anecdotal evidence."

His eyes widened and Hy wondered if she'd said something rude or inappropriate. They stared at each other in silence. Hy was just about to open her mouth and apologize—something she was accustomed to doing several times a day, even when she wasn't quite sure *why* she was doing it—when he spoke.

"Generally," he said.

"I beg your pardon?"

"You said it wasn't wise to make generalizations. Isn't *that* a generalization? There must be times that it *is* wise. For example, stepping in front of a moving carriage is *always* a bad idea. If one wishes to keep living, that is."

Hy stared at him. Was he teasing her—something her siblings took great pleasure in doing—or was he serious?

He must be teasing.

She turned to look out the window, preferring the less complicated view of the city streets to the man across from her.

***

Sylvester smiled when the boy turned away without answering his question. He was not accustomed to being dismissed, but he suspected it wasn't intended as an insult. Even on short acquaintance he could see Hiram Bellamy was one of the stranger birds he'd ever met.

He was a person of seeming contradictions. His slim, delicate build and the prim, precise way he spoke would have got him thrashed on a daily basis had he gone away to school. Especially if he had fleeced his mates at cards as efficiently as he'd done earlier tonight.

Yet as fragile as he appeared, he was taking tonight's injuries in a stoic fashion. He might look like a weakling, but he did not behave like one. His knees were badly torn, as were his hands, and there were even some scratches on his forehead. And the loss of hundreds of pounds must cause a severe, if different, sort of pain. But rather than indulging in a display of self-pity, young Hiram was staring out the window with an expression of calm.

Yes, he was a strange bird.

"Is the Pigeonhole the only place you've played in London?"

The boy turned to him, his smooth brow wrinkling. "Pigeonhole?"

"Yes, the hell we were playing in is often referred to as the Pigeonhole."

"Oh. I thought it was called Jensen's."

"The Pigeonhole is a nickname."

"Why is it called that?"

Sylvester almost groaned. Good Lord, but the lad was green. "Because pigeons go there to get plucked."

Hyacinth

Hiram Bellamy chewed that information over for a moment. "Oh. Well, I've played at another establishment but I have to say I prefer the, er, Pigeonhole."

"Where else have you played?"

"Cox's."

Sylvester stared. Robert Cox's hell—which had no amusing nickname—was one of *the* most dangerous places to play cards in the city. Perhaps all of England. Sylvester could scarcely believe the boy had left Cox's establishment alive.

"How did you fare?"

An expression of disgust settled on Bellamy's pale, narrow face. "Poorly." Sylvester chuckled and the boy scowled at him. "I am pleased to amuse you."

"You should be pleased that you are still alive. The fact that you fared poorly is probably the only reason you are walking and talking. If you'd departed Cox's at two o'clock with your pockets bulging like they were tonight, you wouldn't have been left with your boots and clothing."

The boy hesitated and then gave a grudging nod. "I daresay you are correct. I don't think it is possible to win a large sum of money at Cox's."

Sylvester could believe it; at least not if you arrived alone and looked like the boy across from him.

"You believe you were sharped?"

"I'm almost certain of it, although I could not quite discern how."

"Were I you, I should not noise that about without proof."

Bellamy fixed him with a glare no other man would ever consider turning in Sylvester's direction. For some reason, the insolent young pup's fierce expression just made him feel like laughing.

"I would hardly spread tales of such a thing," he said stiffly, his expression so rigid Sylvester didn't have the heart to point out that he just *had*.

Instead, he changed the subject. "So, have you come to town only to tour the city's most dangerous hells or are you availing yourself of the other entertainments of the Season?"

The boy snorted and muttered something Sylvester could not hear.

"I beg your pardon, Mr. Bellamy?"

He looked up from his scratched and bleeding hands, which he'd laid palms-up on his thighs, like two pale fish belly up.

"My aunt would like to trot me out, but I have managed to avoid it. Thus far."

Sylvester chuckled at his unvarnished response. "Don't care for dancing?"

"God no!"

It was the first sign of genuine emotion the boy had displayed. Well, except for his obvious discomfort regarding the prostitute the last time. "If you don't care to dance at a ball there is always the card room."

"Chicken stakes," Bellamy said scornfully.

"Ah, and you like to play deep."

Bellamy eyed him as if he suspected Sylvester might be mocking him. And then he clamped his mouth shut and turned back to the window, dismissing Sylvester yet again.

Sylvester accepted his dismissal in good humor. He closed his eyes, relaxed against the soft squabs, and turned his thoughts to his own activities this Season.

He would be thirty-six this year and Mariah had died more than ten years ago. Over a decade without her and he'd done very little about the tedious process of acquiring another bride and impregnating her, even though he knew it was his duty. To say that his heart had not been in the hunt these past years was an understatement.

And this year had been even worse. He'd scarcely managed to drag himself to more than a handful of functions. Tonight—when he'd gone to speak to Fowler and had been forced to dance—was the closest he'd come to any marriageable young ladies in ages. It horrified him that while his marital candidates had got younger and more innocent, Sylvester felt jaded and a thousand years old.

It wasn't so much being stared at in revulsion that bothered him as the depressing reality of conversations with eighteen-year-olds. It was hard to believe his wife, Mariah, had been only a few years older than that when they'd married.

Sylvester could now think of his dead wife and brief marriage without pain, but that did not mean he'd forgotten the humiliation of his wedding night. He could not forget it, nor did he ever wish to repeat it.

Not that he was even capable of such innocence and infatuation anymore. Not only was he much older now, but he'd shed his romantic inclinations long ago, just like a crab shucked its old shell. Sylvester now knew something he should have known at twenty-three but hadn't: the only reason any woman would agree to have anything to do with him was because of his position and wealth. He was Chatham, one of the largest landowners in Britain. He was a man who could trace his family history back centuries before The Conquest. He controlled six estates, hundreds of people depended on him for their livelihood, and he was on several powerful committees in Lords.

On the other side of the equation were some not so positive facts. The scar did not look any more appealing than it had when he'd married Mariah. Also, thanks in large part to Mariah, he was cynical and no longer susceptible to—or interested in—being charmed or seduced by a pretty face and desirable body.

And lastly, he'd stopped worrying about how the rest of the world viewed him. He did not care if people thought him a deviant sybarite ruled by his baser passions because he *was* one. He refused to be ashamed of what he liked.

If Sylvester were to meet his twenty- year-old self on the street—the age he'd been when he'd fallen in love, or at least infatuation, with Mariah—he doubted he would recognize himself. And even if he did know that younger man, he would certainly have nothing to *say* to him.

Thirty-six-year-old Sylvester was intolerant of stupidity and was curt to the point of rudeness when faced with it. He took care of his estate, his people, and his Parliamentary duties, but he no longer looked upon his ducal responsibility as if it were a sacred duty, which is what his father had relentlessly drummed into him. It was just his job. A job that brought him little joy, but then what right did he have to expect a luxurious existence *and* joy.

Sylvester told himself that he was alone, but not lonely. Some days he believed that.

Some days he did not.

If he had learned one thing from his wife, it was that there was no better way to be lonely *and* miserable than to be married to a woman who despised you.

Unfortunately, the only alternative to remarriage was accepting his cousin and heir, Andrew Derrick, the Marquess of Shelton.

Sylvester despised Shelton and the feeling was mutual.

Which meant that Sylvester couldn't avoid the arduous process of finding a wife, marrying her, getting her with child, and hoping that child was a male who survived the vicissitudes of infancy.

No doubt Mr. Hiram Bellamy—with his penchant for mathematics and analysis—could assess Sylvester's conundrum and offer him odds. Sylvester smiled at the thought and then shoved the subject from the forefront of his mind. If there was one topic that made him feel more exhausted than wife hunting, it was thinking about his heir.

The carriage shuddered to a halt and Sylvester opened his eyes to find Hiram Bellamy looking at him, his bright blue-green gaze as clear as a tropical sea, his face utterly expressionless.

What an odd, odd boy.

Sylvester nodded toward the door. "We are here."

Chapter 4

Chatham House was an enormous Portland stone monster, the biggest house on a square packed with big houses.

A bone-thin man dressed in the clothing of a butler waited within, attended by two footmen.

"Bevins," the duke said, pausing in the act of removing his hat and shaking off the rain to stare at his servant. "What the devil are you doing up at this time of the morning?"

Before he could answer a voice from above startled them.

"Ah, there you are, coz!"

All eyes turned toward the top of one of the two sets of stairs, this one curving up the right side of the room. The most beautiful man Hy had ever seen stood with one hip propped against the stair railing, a glass in his hand. Beside him were two women dressed—or undressed, rather—in chemises and stockings.

But even the shocking sight of the scantily clad women could not pull Hy's attention away from the man, who was a vision of male perfection.

Beside her, the duke sighed audibly. "Shelton, what an unexpected... pleasure." His voice was as dry as a heavy layer of dust.

The other man—Shelton—chuckled. "Such a warm welcome, old man." He grinned, exposing teeth as perfect as the rest of him. "I hope you don't mind that I've brought a few friends?" He turned to one of the women and whispered something in her ear. She giggled and turned and he swatted the second one on the bottom with a sharp *smack*. She shrieked and then collapsed into a fit of giggles with her friend before the two of them scampered unsteadily out of sight.

Shelton descended the stairs, his movements as graceful and beautiful as his person. He wore only buckskins that rode low on his narrow hips. His abdomen and chest were sculpted alabaster, his perfection only enhanced by three rather savage scars on his torso.

Even Hy, with her dismal social skills, could recognize the expression on his face—mocking—but she wasn't astute enough to determine whether his mockery was directed inward or outward.

When the vision of masculine perfection reached the bottom step, he turned his gaze on Hy, cutting her the swiftest of dismissive glances from his cold blue eyes.

"What's this, Syl? A new playmate?"

There was an insinuation in his voice that Hy did not understand. If she did not know better—and if she were not dressed as a man—she would have thought the insinuation was sexual in nature.

She turned to the duke when there was no answer. Chatham was removing his coat, his expression bland, as if he'd heard nothing untoward. Perhaps this was yet another of those times when Hy simply did not understand subtext?

The duke turned to his butler. "Take Mr. Bellamy to the blue room and inform Tackle he will need dry clothing."

Hy opened her mouth to demur that she did not need dry clothing, just an overcoat. But the duke had already turned away and was headed up the stairs.

The angel, Shelton, lifted his eyebrows and smiled slyly at Hy before pivoting on one bare foot and following Chatham, who was rapidly disappearing up the same staircase the other man had just descended.

"If you will follow me, sir." Bevins was looking at Hy in an assessing, shrewd way that made her feel as if he could see right through her waistcoat and shirt to the strips of torn sheeting she used to bind her breasts.

Hy ignored the ridiculous suspicion, chalking her fear up to the fact she did not have much experience with butlers since her own parents had not been able to afford one for many years. She found her aunt and uncle's butler, Deacon—who was an unholy terror when it came to ferreting out irregularities—equally intimidating.

But nobody knew that she wasn't what she appeared to be—a young man—it was only her nerves teasing her; she was safe.

Bevins led Hy up to the third floor, where he opened a door and ushered Hy inside. She glanced around at her surroundings and deduced they were, indeed, blue. Blue carpet, blue bed covering, blue drapes—

"I will fetch Mr. Tackle, sir."

"You needn't go to all this bother. All I really need is a coat and then I can—"

Hyacinth

The butler's eyebrows shot up, his expression making Hy's face heat all over again for some inexplicable reason.

"His Grace said I might borrow a coat," she explained. "I live not far from here. I—"

"His Grace instructed me to inform Mr. Tackle, *sir*."

Hy realized that an order from the duke was… well, an order from the duke. Bevins had no intention of doing anything but following his master's instructions to the letter. He turned on his heel and the door shut with a soft but emphatic click.

Hy went to the nearest mirror and surveyed the damage. It was about as bad as she'd expected. Still, with her hair plastered to her skull and splotchy red cheeks and blue lips she looked even less like a woman than usual. So that was good.

She found the washstand and took a fresh towel from the rack beside it, using it to dry her hair. Her neckcloth was soaked as were her shirt and waistcoat. Really, every part of her was wet from standing out in the street for so long.

Well, she could do without a dripping cravat strangling her. She pulled it off and was in the process of squeezing it dry when the door opened behind her. She startled and spun around.

Hy had to blink a few times to make sure she was seeing what she was seeing. The man was dressed in the raiment of a gentleman's gentleman, but he was as big as an ox. His head was huge and perfectly round and his hair was shaved to a stubble, exposing ears that resembled lumps of cauliflower. His nose looked like a tomato that had been stepped on. His small, dark eyes fastened on her hands and her sodden neckcloth before flickering over her person and finally settling on her face.

"Good evening, sir. I understand you need a bit of assistance." His voice was an improbably high fluting sound at odds with his monstrous size.

"Just a coat," Hy said, snatching up the towel she'd just set down and draping it around her neck, intensely aware of her bare throat. "I'm afraid mine was taken."

Tackle's gaze moved to Hy's knees. "Perhaps I might help you clean up a little, sir."

It didn't sound like a question, but Hy opened her mouth to tell him not to bother.

"We wouldn't want to bloody one of His Grace's coats."

Even Hy understood the hint.

37

The door opened behind the big man and a maid entered with an ewer billowing steam.

The valet nodded at the maid. "Thank you, Dotty." Tackle turned to Hy. "If you'll have a seat, sir."

Hy sighed and took a seat, giving herself over to the big man's care. The sooner she did what the duke had ordered, the sooner she could be gone.

***

Sylvester needed a drink. Maybe even several. "Brandy?" he tossed the word over his shoulder.

"I already have one. I hope you don't mind, but I took my old suite of rooms," Shelton said.

Sylvester could hear the smile in his cousin's voice.

Shelton raised his glass. "I also had Bevins send up a bottle of this lovely specimen to my rooms."

Naturally, his cousin had helped himself. Andrew Derrick, Marquess of Shelton, and Sylvester's heir, had always helped himself to whatever belonged to Sylvester, including, for a time, Sylvester's wife.

"So," he said, turning back to his cousin, who was standing in front of the blazing fire, utterly at ease in his half-naked state, leaning elegantly against the mantle. "I take it you've outrun your quarterly allowance, Shelton."

His cousin wagged a finger at him. "That's not very friendly, Chatham. The first time we've seen each other in—why how long has it been—" he tilted his head back and stared up at the coffered ceiling as Sylvester lowered himself into a seat beside the fire.

"Two years come the end of June," Sylvester said.

That brought Sheldon's head back down, his eyebrows arched with amusement. "I'm pleased to know you recall the last time you saw me with such exactitude."

"I certainly recall your last departure with exactitude."

Shelton's handsome face shifted into an insincere pout. "Oh, now, don't be that way. I do hope you are not still angry with me?"

Sylvester didn't bother answering.

"It was a mistake old, chap—surely even *you* have made one of those?"

Hyacinth

"Oddly enough I have not yet *mistakenly* ruined a girl's reputation and future, impregnated her, and then left her hanging in the wind."

Shelton threw back his head and laughed. "No, all of London knows your proclivities, Syl, and they certainly do not run to virginal young girls."

Sylvester found his cousin's digs and insults as boring as the rest of him.

He did not, however, find the subject boring. In fact, his cousin's behavior to the young girl two years earlier had infuriated him and was the reason he had not completely ruled out remarriage. It irked him to think that his death would benefit the arrogant man slouched against his mantle. However now was not the time to brood on such matters.

He propped his ankle on his opposite knee, sat back, and prepared for even more boredom. "So, tell me how are matters in Yorkshire?"

This time when Shelton laughed, the sound was pure bitterness. "You'd like that, wouldn't you Syl, thinking of me spending the last two years at Rose-bloody-wood."

"If I have to think about you at all, Shelton, I supposed I'd prefer to imagine you at Rosewood," Sylvester agreed, not bothering to hide his smile. Rosewood was his cousin's only property. It was modestly sized, ramshackle, and situated in a part of Yorkshire that was even colder and more backward than the rest of that godforsaken county.

Shelton clucked his tongue. "Two years, but you are still the same old petty, hateful, jealous Chatham."

Sylvester did not bother to dispute his cousin—mainly because the same thing could be said about Shelton. He had not changed. He was still angry, and he was still bent on making Sylvester suffer.

"I haven't been in Yorkshire, Syl."

"I know." Sylvester swirled the amber liquid. "Your steward sent me a letter last month and told me about the condition of Rosewood and the surrounding farms. He asked me to advance enough money to make basic repairs and pay your servants."

Shelton slammed his empty glass onto the mantelpiece. "I *fired* that bloody steward months ago! What the hell is he doing still meddling in my affairs?"

This was a discussion Sylvester did not wish to have now. Or, indeed, ever. It was a discussion which had taken place at least a dozen times over the years since Sylvester's father had died and the management of his feckless cousin's affairs had become *his* responsibility until Shelton turned thirty-five.

"The man is trying to save your estate," Sylvester pointed out.

"Rosewood can go to hell for all I care." Shelton's handsome face was distorted with some of the worst emotions a human being was capable of feeling—jealousy, envy, hatred, loathing, fury—and it was all for Sylvester.

Matters hadn't always been so poisonous between them. Indeed, Shelton had, once upon a time, adored Sylvester and had clung to him like a burr when he'd first come to live at Chatham House, a skinny little orphan of four who'd been three years younger than Sylvester.

Shelton made a rude snorting noise when Sylvester remained silent. "What? No clever retort, Syl?" He snatched up his glass and strode to the decanter. When he returned, the liquor was almost at the top. He took a noisy slurp and shot Sylvester a look that made his hands twitch to thrash the younger man.

Andrew was a destructive, hate-filled, careless toddler in a man's body and yet women fell like wheat beneath a scythe at his cousin's golden beauty and a good many men seemed to find his ridiculous, costly, and dangerous notions of fun as compelling as the Pied Piper.

As far as Sylvester could tell, he was the only person who seemed immune to his cousin's considerable charm. Well, his friend Fowler didn't care for him much, either, but mainly because of the way Shelton had treated Sylvester over the years.

"Why are you here, Shelton?"

His cousin's irritation was gone in the blink of an eye, replaced by his signature sly smile. "I paid a visit to Chatham Park and was surprised to find your dear mama there."

"Yes, she did not come to town this year." A fact for which Sylvester was profoundly grateful.

"She suggested I come to see you in London."

The dowager duchess was so transparent. She would hope a visit from his loathsome heir would badger Sylvester into remarrying. Well, she wasn't entirely wrong. Sylvester had to admit the idea was not without merit: not only would robbing his cousin of his expectations be pleasant, but, if he married and produced an heir, he could then put Andrew from his mind for the rest of his life. Except for periodically bailing him out of scrapes, of course.

"I'm sure you two enjoyed your tête-à-tête."

Shelton laughed. "The visit was as brief and acrimonious as always. I'm pleased to report that she hates me more than ever. I was afraid to drink or eat anything while I was there, so I didn't linger above a few hours."

Sylvester was grateful his mother hated somebody else more than she hated him.

"So, here you are, Shelton," he said. "How much money do you need this time?"

"How kind of you to offer, Syl."

"I only ask so that I might avoid a horde of angry tradesman encamped on my doorstep."

His cousin shrugged, as if running himself into debt was nothing that deserved comment. Sylvester supposed that was true since Shelton had been doing the same thing for years—dating back to Sylvester's marriage to Mariah, in point of fact.

"I am not here for money, coz."

Sylvester raised his eyebrows.

"I am above the hatches."

That would certainly be a first—if it were true.

Shelton thrust his hand into his breeches pocket and pulled out a crumpled piece of parchment. "Read this, if you do not believe me."

Sylvester took the paper and stood, going to his desk to get his reading glasses. Shelton laughed when he put them on, but he ignored him. He glanced at the paper: it was a statement of deposit from a reputable bank in Leeds and it showed a balance of almost £1,000. He looked up.

"How in the world did you manage that?"

"Ingenuity, old boy. Good old-fashioned ingenuity."

It was Sylvester's turn to snort. "Counterfeiting? Smuggling?"

"Very droll. As it happens, I have invested in a stud operation."

"Ah, breeding horses," Sylvester said, unable to keep the weary amusement from his voice. If there was a feckless younger son or heir in England who didn't fancy themselves a horse breeder Sylvester had yet to meet them.

"Go ahead and sneer, soon our hunters will be known all over Britain."

"For lack of wind? Exaggerated gait?"

"Mock all you like. All you need to know is there will be no dunning agents looking for money."

"What about constables?"

Shelton gave a short laugh and sipped his drink, refusing—for once—to be drawn.

"So, you have money. Then why have you come here to stay?"

"You've got nothing but room in this great, draughty old pile. So, why not?" He flicked a lazy gaze over Sylvester's face, his mouth tightening as he took in the scar, an unreadable expression flickering across his perfect face. Sylvester smiled, amused by Shelton's reaction to his disfigurement. It pleased him that looking at his face pained his perfect cousin.

"You never considered taking your newfound wealth up to Yorkshire—perhaps investing it in your property? You might even breed horses there if you ever repaired your stables."

"I considered it. And then I dismissed it."

"I take it you wish to stay here for the duration of your visit?"

Shelton pouted. "Am I not welcome here, Syl? Do you wish me to find other lodgings?"

Sylvester *did* want him to find other lodgings, preferably in the Outer Hebrides. But he refused to give the other man the satisfaction of knowing just how much his presence irked him. "You are welcome to stay as long as you wish."

Shelton smiled; clearly aware Sylvester had not so subtly side-stepped his question. "It is time I considered parson's mousetrap, myself. I can marry a suitable young miss, take her up to Yorkshire, breed her, and embrace the wholesome existence of a gentleman farmer." His eyelids drooped and his smile turned sly. "Or do you think my reputation is so tarnished that I won't be welcome within a hundred yards of a *ton* function?"

Unfortunately, Sylvester knew his cousin would be welcomed with open arms—not only because of his position as a duke's heir, but his appearance was irresistible to many women. He looked like an angel, so people tended to forget he was *not* one.

He also possessed a respectable estate, even if Rosewood was in wretched condition, and of course his war record was excellent. Indeed, Shelton had been hailed as a hero for his daring deeds.

That should not have been enough to erase the fact that his cousin was a bitter, immoral man who used other people without any thought to the consequences, but it would be. The *ton* adored pretty people, be they male or female.

Sylvester met his cousin's cold gaze. "I really could not care less about you, your reputation, or your reception in *ton* circles, Sheldon."

The other man hooted with glee. "By God, I've *missed* you, Syl."

Sylvester somehow doubted that.

Shelton studied his nearly empty glass. "It will be eleven years at the end of July."

He wasn't surprised Shelton knew how long it had been since Mariah's death, but he had no interest in discussing the matter. Especially not with his wife's last lover.

Instead, he tossed back the remainder of his brandy. "I take it you have already settled in?"

"I'm quite cozy, thank you."

Sylvester set down his glass and stood. "I am thrilled to hear it. If you will excuse me, I've some business to attend to." He turned and headed for the door.

"The boy?" Shelton asked, falling into step beside him. "What's that all about? It's not like you to hang about with callow striplings."

"He was robbed by his hack driver on the way from the Pigeonhole."

Shelton snorted. "*That* boy was playing at Jensen's? I didn't get a good look at him, but he doesn't appear to be much older than twelve."

Sylvester smiled. "No, he doesn't, does he?"

"Who is he?"

"Just a young buck on his first trip to London." Sylvester stopped, his hand on the door handle. "I will bid you a good evening, Shelton. Please see that your two, er, *friends* are gone before first light and don't invite them back again."

Shelton chuckled. "Very well."

"And one more thing."

"Yes, Syl?"

"The next time you call me *Syl*, I will kick you down the front steps into the street."

Sylvester savored his cousin's expression of surprise as he made his way to his chambers.

He needed to get out of his clothes, which felt unpleasantly damp from only a few minutes out in the weather. He shuddered to think how cold Bellamy must be.

Tackle was not in his chambers and Sylvester assumed he must be helping the boy. He stripped, shivering as he peeled off his clothing even though the fireplace in his bedchamber was raging.

Naked and covered in gooseflesh, he opted for the heaviest of his dressing gowns—a plush green velvet lined with black silk.

The door opened just as he was tying the sash.

Tackle's dark eyes went to Sylvester's discarded garments, which he'd draped over the clotheshorse. "I'm sorry I was not here to attend you, Your Grace."

Sylvester waved his words away. "How is the boy?"

A rare smile took control of Tackle's harsh slash of a mouth. In all the years the man had worked for him—through the war and the decade after—Sylvester had never seen such a gleeful expression on the ex-prizefighter's face.

"What is it? You look like the cat that got the cream."

Tackle rocked back on his heels and met Sylvester's gaze. "Yes, as to the boy, Your Grace…"

Chapter 5

Hy paced, because that was what she did when she was anxious. Well, that was *one* of the things she did—certainly the least odd thing. She also did long division, challenging herself with larger and larger numbers.

At the moment, however, Hy was a bit too frazzled to enjoy any division.

The big valet had helped clean up her knees and hands and had put some sort of sticky poultice on the worst of the gouges. He'd also brought a fresh shirt, waistcoat, coat, and then had looked perplexed when Hy had refused his help to strip and change into the new clothing.

His stare had been uncomfortably penetrating before he'd left and Hy wondered if the man had guessed the truth.

She'd speedily changed into the fresh clothing once he'd gone and was now garbed in a clean shirt, waistcoat, coat, and cravat.

Hy was five-feet-eleven-and-a-half in her stocking feet, which meant the duke's shirt and coat weren't terribly long on her, but he was far more muscular and the clothing hung from her narrow shoulders like a coat on a hanger. Hy still wore her own breeches, but only because she'd insisted strenuously.

She was especially grateful the valet had brought a fresh cravat as it was critical to hide her lack of an Adam's apple.

The valet had promised to return with an overcoat, but Hy was severely tempted to slip out of the house before then. In fact, that was probably a wise idea.

Hy was just reaching for the handle when the door opened. She was expecting to see Tackle, but it was the duke who stood on the threshold, and he was wearing a dressing gown and slippers.

And apparently nothing else.

Hy's gaze dropped to the v of chest exposed by his robe and she was fascinated to see that he had freckles on his chest. So did she. But then Hy had freckles everywhere, while the duke's face—other than the scar—was unblemished by the unsightly marks that Hy's mother had tried so hard to eradicate.

His hair was messy, as if he'd just raked his fingers through it. Or just risen from bed.

Hy swallowed, and then did it twice more as her mouth inexplicably flooded with moisture. Some long-buried part of her—an awareness that she kept suppressed because it was too raw and unpredictable to fit into her logical, well-planned life—began to wake up, to shake itself, and look around.

And it *liked* what it saw. It liked it a great deal.

The duke cleared his throat, making Hy realize she'd been staring—probably gaping at him like her little brother stared at a sack of sweeties—and standing far too close.

She stepped back but couldn't make herself look away from his body.

Even rumpled and half naked he still managed to exude authority.

He also looked astonishingly enticing.

And all that stood between her, the duke, and his complete nudity was a single tug on his dressing gown sash...

The thought struck her hard, like a punch to the abdomen, robbing her of breath.

Where had *that* come from?

"Hiram?"

Hy noticed handsome men, of course, but she could not recollect feeling *moved* by looking at one. She had felt nothing other than a vague sort of admiration for the duke's cousin, Shelton, a man who was far more classically handsome than Chatham.

And yet her fingers twitched to pull that sash and—

"*Hiram?*"

Hy's head jerked up. Judging by his tone, it wasn't the first time he'd said her name.

"Er, yes, Your Grace?"

He lifted his hands and she saw he was holding a coat—a luxurious black wool overcoat that was much nicer than the one that had been stolen.

"Come here," he said when she just stared.

Hy swallowed and shuffled toward him, her feet strangely leaden. She kept her eyes fastened on the coat rather than his distracting body or his face, which was far too interesting with its sharp clean edges on one side and the odd, puckered swirl of a scar on the other.

Hyacinth

"Thank you," she said, reaching out to take the coat.

But instead of handing it to her, he held it up for her to slip into. "Allow me," he said, his low, deep voice vibrated through her.

A duke holding up a coat like a valet? Offering to dress her like a servant?

Hy gave a slight shake of her head; it was the perfect conclusion to an already dream-like night.

She looked up from the coat, this time because she wanted to, not just because she knew it was polite to look people in the eyes when speaking to them.

Hy had to squint to bring him into sharper focus. They were almost the same height, although he was perhaps half-an-inch taller. In the brightly lighted chamber, she saw there was a good deal of gray at his temples and lines fanning out from the corners of his eyes. On the unscarred side of his face there was a deep groove etched from his nose to the corner of his mouth. As she'd noticed earlier, his eyes were a coffee brown shot through with lighter shards the color of sherry and rimmed with yellowish gold. They were a beautiful and unusual color, the lids heavy and sensual.

Hy caught a tantalizing whiff of him—the scent of clean, salty skin and some expensive cologne—but she wanted more. She was seized by an insane urge to shove her nose into the hollow at the base of his throat and fill her lungs with him.

"How old are you?" she blurted. The question surprised her so much she didn't have any room left to be appalled at her rudeness.

The duke, also, looked surprised—but more amused. His mouth pulled up to exhibit a mouthful of white but somewhat crooked teeth, the front two slightly overlapping, the overlong canines adding to the impression of a feral sneer.

"One hundred and four."

Hy flushed. "That was a rude question. I apologize."

The duke held the coat up higher. "I will be six-and-thirty on my next birthday. How old are *you*?"

"I will be three-and-twenty. What?" she demanded when his eyebrows lifted skeptically. "You think I am lying? That I am younger?"

"You don't look three-and-twenty," he murmured, his burnt caramel eyes dropping to her cheeks.

Before Hy could come up with an explanation for why she had not even a hint of facial hair, the duke held up the coat. "Turn around and put this on, Hiram. Your lips are blue."

Hy knew he was right; she was shivering. She turned and slid her arms into the silk-lined garment, her limbs awkwardly angled to avoid any chance of contact. For some odd reason her skin felt raw and the hairs on the back of her neck stood up.

He might be only half-an-inch taller, but his shoulders were far broader, and she felt like a child dressed in her father's clothing, the cuffs of the coat covering her fingers.

Hy sensed rather than felt the hard heat of him and had yet another insane urge—this time to press her body back against his.

What in the world was wrong with her?

His chest lightly bumped against Hy's back as he adjusted the collar and she jolted and spun around, taking a step back.

The duke's mocking smile was gone, replaced by a pensive stare. "Tackle has called a hackney and it is downstairs waiting, Hiram."

Hy pulled the coat closed around her body, hugging it to herself. "Thank you, Your Grace. But I have no—"

"You can repay me the next time you see me."

Which Hy hoped was never. But she nodded. "Thank you, Your Grace."

"You are welcome."

Hy turned to leave, but the duke stopped her. "I am playing at Weller's on Friday—why don't you join me?"

Hy gaped. The club was famous—and infamous for the fortunes won and lost there; it was rumored that Charles James Fox had once thrown away £36,000 in a single night.

"Er, I'm not a member, sir."

"Come as my guest."

Hy's mind raced; what did she have to do four nights hence? Could she get away?

"You don't have to make up your mind right now, Hiram. I will leave your name with the host if you decide to come. I'll be there around midnight. I hope to see you." The duke opened the door and the huge valet stood waiting in the hall. "I will leave you in Tackle's capable hands."

"Good night, Your Grace."

The duke watched her leave without speaking.

"Right this way, sir," the valet said.

Hyacinth

Hy held her breath until she was sure the duke could no longer see her and then exhaled shakily as she followed the servant down the stairs.

Her reaction to Chatham's state of undress had been extreme, but understandable. After all, she was a woman and he was an attractive man who'd been all but naked. But it had been her other impulse that had startled her—her desire to stay near him.

While it wasn't true to say she *disliked* the touch of others, she did not seek out physical contact. And yet something about Chatham had been extremely appealing. The last time she'd wanted to touch a man had been with Charles.

Hy was both intrigued and concerned by her body's reaction to the duke. The last thing she needed right now was to behave like a fool in front of such an influential and powerful man. She would have to make sure their paths did not cross again.

"Where do you wish to go?" Tackle asked, breaking into her thoughts.

Hy named an address in a far less grand area of the city, a place where somebody like modest Hiram Bellamy might live. The valet opened an umbrella and guided her down to the waiting hack. He gave the driver the address, handed him money, and within moments she was on her way.

Hy waited until they'd turned the corner and then opened the vent. "I've changed my mind. Drop me at the corner of Jermyn and Bennett Street," she said, naming a corner that wasn't far from her aunt and uncle's house. "You can keep the extra fare money."

"Oh, aye, I plan to," he retorted, and snapped the vent shut.

Hy collapsed against the worn leather seat as the carriage rumbled through the rainy night. What an unusual evening. Not to mention an unprofitable one. Luckily she had taken only part of her stake money with her tonight.

Even so, every loss was a setback she could ill afford; a loss her family could ill afford. There were less than two months before her father's loans would be called in and Queen's Bower—her family's home—and everything else the earl had used as security for his gambling debt would pass to some stranger and her brother and sisters would lose their home.

Because neither of her parents appeared to believe their six children deserved know about their imminent ejection from their home, Hy had needed to sneak around and find her father's loan documents and read them herself.

The amount had been staggering. She'd known immediately that she could not possibly pay down the principle. However, the annual interest payment—all that was necessary to prevent the calling in of the loan—was within the realm of possibility. Almost five thousand pounds. That is what she needed. With five thousand pounds they could purchase a year's reprieve. Time to think and plan now that Hy and her sisters knew the truth. They'd not told their brother. Poor Doddy was only fourteen and hardly deserved to have such a burden dumped on his young shoulders.

She'd been doing well saving money, but she could not afford another night like tonight.

By the time the hackney dropped Hy off the rain had lightened. She cut through a mews and used a broken garden gate to work her way back to her aunt and uncle's. She looked both ways but saw nobody moving about on the well-lighted street. Wrapping the rich wool coat tightly around her, she jogged down the narrow rubbish alley that led to the back of the house, glorying in the freedom of men's clothing, even though her knees were throbbing and stinging. Dressing as a man was almost as wonderful as getting to play cards.

Hy was about to crawl in through the window she'd left unlocked when a loud *sssst* made her jump. She turned to find the door to the servant's entrance open.

Hy pulled the window shut. "What are *you* doing?" she whispered at her sister as she brushed past her into the dimly lighted hall.

"Waiting for *you*!" Selina hissed. She raised a finger to her lips, grabbed Hy's hand, and dragged her up the stairs. It was a miracle they made it up to Selina's chambers without detection as the charwoman would be moving around shortly.

Selina shut the door and then whipped around, her astounding blue-violet eyes accusatory. "I was just about to wake Deacon to send somebody to go looking for you. It is after four o'clock in the morning!"

Her sister's threat sent a bolt of fear through her. "You must promise me that you will never alert anyone like that, Linny. It would be disastrous if everyone found out what I've been doing."

Selina ignored her. "Where were you?" Her gaze dropped to the oversized coat Hy was unbuttoning. "And that is *not* the coat you went out in. And where are your glasses and hat?"

Hy went to her nightstand and took out her spare pair of spectacles, putting them on before she shrugged out of the coat and handed it to her sister. "I'll need to return all this," she said, gesturing to the garments on her torso. "You can store it with my other toggery after it dries. Er, perhaps you might give it a brushing. Or ironing. Or whatever it is that such garments require."

Selina scowled. "I don't need your advice about how to clean and tend to clothing, Hyacinth." She snatched the coat. "Where did you get these things?" she demanded, her eyes brimming with questions.

"I got them from a—from a kind Samaritan who gave me a ride in his carriage after I was robbed."

"Robbed!"

Hy flinched. "Good God, Selina, you'll bring the whole house down on us shrieking like that. Don't fuss, I am fine." Hy held out her arms to her sides to demonstrate, but her sister's gaze was already on her legs.

"Oh, Hy, your poor *knees*."

"They will be fine; they are just scratched. But the robbers took all my money." She had to swallow before she could spit out the hateful confession. "Almost £300, Linny."

Selina looked up, her mouth agape. "Three. Hundred. Pounds."

It wasn't a question, but Hy nodded.

"But that is—"

"Gone," Hy finished.

"I was going to say that is a fortune. However did you win so much? The most you ever brought home to Queen's Bower was thirty pounds. Which is still a great deal of money."

Hy found her sister's naiveté amusing. "This is London, Linny, not a rural posting inn." She shrugged out of the duke's tailcoat, wincing at the soreness in her shoulders and back, which she hadn't even realized had been hurt. "The men playing tonight had no limit. And they were rich. Very rich. I could have wagered far more, but now I am glad I didn't."

And one of them was the Duke of Chatham, she could have added, but did not. She could only imagine how her sister would squawk if she learned Hy had been playing cards with the wealthy, infamous duke.

"Three hundred pounds," Selina repeated in a wonderous tone.

Hy pulled off her cravat and tossed it over a chair and began to remove her waistcoat.

Linny took the neckcloth off the arm of the chair. "This is not your cravat, either. It is the nicest linen I've ever felt," she muttered more to herself.

"No, it isn't. I told you—I was robbed. They left me out in the rain without a coat, Linny. I had to walk for a good quarter hour before somebody stopped."

"Oh, Hy—what if somebody *hadn't* stopped? What if you were still out there? Alone."

Hy would never understand such bizarre behavior: why think about things that *hadn't* happened?

"Somebody did stop, Linny." She held out her waistcoat and shirt and Selina took both and examined them with a critical eye.

"These are far nicer than yours, too."

Hy didn't bother answering that. What difference did the quality of the clothing make? But she didn't want to annoy her sister, who saw to the secret mending and washing of Hy's garments, so she kept her mouth shut.

Beneath the shirt Hy wore only strips of an old sheet wrapped around her chest. She barely had any breasts to disguise, but Linny had argued it would be immodest to go without anything.

"Who was it, Hy?"

"What?" she asked.

"Whose clothes are these?"

"Just one of the players—nobody you would have heard of."

"Hy?"

"Hmmm?" She looked up from her thoughts to find her sister pointing at her boots. Hy sat and stuck out a muddy boot.

"Eww," Linny said, but grabbed the boot all the same, tugging off one and then the other. Selina might look like a delicate English rose, but her pretty sister was as tough as an old shoe, not to mention opinionated, and fierce when it came to protecting her family. She reminded Hy of one of the fluffy hens that always pecked her hand when she had to collect eggs: soft looking but feisty.

Selina rinsed her dirty hands in the bowl of cold water on the dressing table. "You cannot continue to risk yourself in this manner, I will not allow it."

Hy bit her tongue to keep from saying what she wanted to say, which was that her sister was not her master. She'd never told any of her siblings about her plans for the future because she suspected they would—except perhaps her eldest sister Aurelia—start squawking about how dangerous her idea was. Aurelia, Hy suspected, had plans for her own future that would set everyone's backs up, as well. Her older sister was an illustrator who could easily earn a living off her drawings, although she probably couldn't earn enough to pay their father's annual debt.

"Are you listening to me, Hy? *Hy*?"

"What?"

"Did you hear what I said?"

"Yes," she lied. "But don't worry," she said, assuming Selina had still been harping on how unsafe her evening jaunts were. "I will engage a hack for the entire evening in the future, that way I will not be dependent on porters."

Selina's brow wrinkled, her expression skeptical. "Do you think that will be enough?"

"I could borrow one of uncle's pistols."

"A pistol!"

Hy winced. "Shhhh."

"Don't you *shush* me, Hyacinth Mary Bellamy."

"Sorry," Hy muttered, and then yawned. "Do we need to discuss this right now, Linny?"

Selina's fierce expression faded into one of concern. "Of course not. You must be exhausted."

"When did you get home?" she asked, handing her the strips from around her chest and then pulling on a nightgown.

"Ages ago. The ball was horribly flat and Aunt Ellen said we might come home early. I've already had a few hours rest. Is there anything I can do for you? Are your hands and knees paining you?"

Hy shook her head, relieved she'd been able to distract her rather dogged sister from the subject of gambling. Selina wouldn't forget the argument, but there was little she could do about it given the fact she was out with their aunt most evenings.

"No, Linny, I think sleep is all I need right now."

"You're not going out tonight, are you?"

"No, Linny. Not tonight."

Selina gave a sigh of relief. "Good. I'm glad to hear you've got *some* sense."

Hy wondered what her sister would say if she knew that the Duke of Chatham—widely viewed as the most eligible bachelor in England—had invited her to meet him at the most exclusive gaming club in London.

She decided that was information better kept to herself.

Chapter 6

By two o'clock that afternoon Hy felt like a sleepwalker.

"Hyacinth!" The Dowager Lady Fitzroy's piercing voice startled Hy from her doze and she jolted upright and blinked.

She'd been sitting at her ladyship's desk, where she'd been pulling out the requisite parts of the newspaper, when she must have dropped off into a doze.

Lady Fitzroy liked nothing but the society section and became irritated if any news of the War invaded her bubble of ignorance.

Hy knuckled her eyes and rubbed away the sleep before going to the doorway that separated the old lady's bedchamber from her sitting room. "Yes, my lady?"

"Aren't you finished yet? What are you doing out there? Are you sleeping?" Her watery but still sharp blue eyes traveled over Hy's person with the ruthless scrutiny of a military commander. "You look dreadful today. Have you not been sleeping?"

"I stayed up late reading last night." It was only partly a lie.

"Hmph. You shall ruin your looks if you continue on that way."

"Yes my lady."

The old lady's eyes narrowed, as if she might argue, but then she seemed to change her mind. "Bring me Lily before you finish with the paper."

"Yes, my lady." Hy took a deep breath, held it, and then went to fetch Lady Fitzroy's ancient pug, Lily, from the dressing room, where she liked to hide away and sleep.

The poor old pug was plagued by terrible gas, which meant everyone else—especially Hy—was plagued by it, too.

The dog was a constant source of conflict between the dowager and her daughter-in-law—Hy's Aunt Ellen—neither of whom liked the other very much.

The dowager was especially fond of bringing the pug into the sitting room when Aunt Ellen was receiving visitors, just to embarrass her.

Hyacinth

Hy had to admit the dog was a pretty effective weapon in the war between the two women, which evidently had been going on almost as long as the one against Napoleon.

Lily gave a disgruntled snort and emitted a quiet but eye-watering *pfft* when Hy picked her up. The poor thing was all skin and bones, just like her mistress, and—but for the stench—it was no hard work to carry her to the bedchamber.

"Ah, thank you, Hyacinth." Lady Fitzroy held out her arms, her smile radiant and her deeply lined face scrunching up until her lips were puckered. *"Mwah! Mwah!"* She kissed the foul-smelling, unresisting dog on the snout, her old face lighting up like a sunrise. "And here is mama's little darling." The dog—so old it could hardly wag its little corkscrew of a tail—appeared to be the only creature which elicited any affection from the old lady. Her grandchildren, daughter-in-law, and grown son most certainly did not.

Hy found it fascinating that the old woman didn't seem at all bothered by the dog's smell. She had hoped that she, too, might become inured to it, but that hadn't happened yet.

"How can you bear it, Hy?" Selina had asked her more than once.

"I'd take a dozen farting dogs over attending a single ball," had been Hy's truthful, if not exactly polite, response.

The dowager looked up from her pet, her features gradually settling into their habitual scowl.

"That is a very ugly dress, Hyacinth. Is my daughter-in-law stinting on your wardrobe now that your pretty sister has come to stay with us?" Her steel gray eyebrows arched high, until they resembled curved saber blades preparing for battle. "Because if she *is*—"

"Aunt Ellen bought me several very nice dresses, my lady," Hy assured her. Indeed, the younger Lady Fitzroy kept buying her gowns even though Hy hadn't even worn most of the outfits her flighty, but kind aunt had inflicted on her when Hy had first arrived.

Aunt Ellen continued to purchase clothing six weeks later, even though she'd long since given up hope of convincing Hy to voluntarily accompany her and Selina on their morning visits, to balls, routes, Venetian breakfasts, romps in the park, and a dozen other frivolous activities which comprised each day.

Hy was grateful beyond belief that Selina had joined her in London. Not only had she alleviated the pressure to attend *ton* functions, but Hy hadn't realized how much she had missed her family until her sister arrived. She hadn't expected to be so homesick and did not look forward to a recurrence of such wistfulness when she left home for good at the end of the Season.

"My younger sister Laura was far prettier than I was," Lady Fitzroy barked, loudly enough to make Hy startle.

She blinked at the old woman's sudden segue but had no response.

Luckily Lady Fitzroy needed none to continue. "She was the favorite of us three girls. *An angel* was how people always, always described her." Lady Fitzroy's mouth twisted, an expression of youthful envy and bitterness forming beneath a lifetime's worth of wrinkles and liver spots.

Hy could only stare, amazed. Decades had passed, the other woman was long dead, and yet the dowager still resented her prettier sister? Truly, Hy would never understand some people.

Lady Fitzroy's gaze settled on Hy and it was like she could hear her thoughts. "Oh, you may scoff, my dear, but keep in mind that Viscount Fitzroy married *me* even though Laura was such an *angel*." Her mouth curved into a slow, sly smile and triumph, glee, and smugness rolled off her in waves. "He married *me*."

Hy nodded; not because she understood the woman, but because so much emotion required a response.

"I was tall and gawky and plain." She gave Hy a pointed look. "Not as tall and gawky and plain as *you*, of course. Nor did I have your rather unfortunate hair." Her eyes lingered on Hy's hair, or what little showed of it beneath the cap she always wore to hide its offensive hue. "Tis a pity for you that people do not properly cover their heads with wigs and powder anymore."

Hy smiled at that, unoffended. She *was* tall, gawky, and plain. And her hair *was* gaudy. Why be upset about the truth? Personally, she was beyond grateful that wigs and powder were no longer in fashion, no matter how it might have made her hair easier to hide.

"I tricked him."

Hy cocked her head. "I beg your pardon, my lady?"

Lady Fitzroy's eyes widened slightly at her own admission, her face twisting into a complicated expression Hy could not discern.

"I *said* that I tricked my husband. I knew he was going to offer for Laura—just like every other besotted male in London that year—and so I instigated a situation that left him no choice." Her eyelids drooped even more than usual. "Poor Geoffrey." She clucked her tongue and chuckled. "He thought he was so clever, but I was cleverer still." She smoothed the piebald old dog's fur with a hand that trembled. "I knew Laura was in love with him, and he with her, but I fixed it so none of that mattered."

"How did you do that?" Hy asked, curious despite herself.

"Oh, that doesn't matter. What matters is that I *got* him." A slow smile spread across her face. "He was *so* handsome—the catch of the Season—and he married me. Poor Laura never did marry, and when our parents died, she came to live in *my* house. With my husband and my children. She never said so, but I knew she always believed all of it should have been hers."

Hy could only stare. Empathy was not one of her strengths, but it almost suffocated her at that moment. Empathy for this woman, for her long dead sister, and for her husband. And pity—for the things people did to each other to get what they wanted, no matter the cost.

The old woman seemed to come back from somewhere far away.

"Bring me my writing desk, Hyacinth." Her voice was brisk, the long-ago episode forgotten, if not forever, then at least for the moment.

Hy brought the small bed-desk to her, settling it carefully to avoid the dozing pug.

Lady Fitzroy took out a square of lavender parchment. "This is for Lady Harwood. Don't forget to tell Deacon it must be delivered immediately. I would hate for Lady Harwood not to find a fourth."

"You're not going out tonight, my lady?"

"No, I'm feeling liverish."

Whatever that meant.

"Er, shall I summon your physician?"

The dowager waved a hand as if she were shooing away a bothersome insect. "No, no, I don't need him quacking me. I just want to make sure this letter is delivered."

"I will deliver it myself, my lady."

"Good girl—but not alone! You take a maid with you this time instead of striding off across the city in that mannish way of yours. In my day young girls had more couth."

"Yes, my lady. I'll take a maid," she lied. The old woman looked tired today and Hy knew she must feel ill to beg off a night of cards. "Shall I summon Miss Lawrence for you?" Lawrence was Lady Fitzroy's dresser, a woman almost as old and crusty as her mistress.

"Yes, please do. I shan't need you again, you may take this evening for yourself."

"Yes, my lady."

A free night meant more cards and suddenly Hy—who'd been dead on her feet only a short time ago—didn't feel nearly so tired.

She would do what she'd promised Selina and arrange for a hackney tonight, not that Selina needed to know she'd be free. But if her sister *did* find out, then Hy would be able to tell her that she'd taken precautions.

Hy knew that her aunt's youngest footman, Will, was probably her best chance of finding a decent hackney driver. Will had seen her slipping out of the house one night—dressed in her Hiram outfit—and had looked amused rather than shocked. He'd also promised not to tell, and that had been *before* Hy had given him a monetary incentive to keep her secret.

Once Lady Fitzroy had finished drafting her message, Hy went to her chambers to fetch a bonnet and cloak, yet again grateful that it was Lady Fitzroy whom she had to please now, rather than her Aunt Ellen.

Oh, it wasn't as if her aunt was cruel or exacting, but she'd been adamant that Hy *must* engage in all the pleasures the Season had to offer and that she *must* find a husband.

Luckily, it had not taken her aunt long to realize that Hy was a nightmare when it came to socializing.

Hy knew the only reason her aunt had invited her, rather than Selina, is because Hy was older than her beautiful sister. The convention of *launching* girls in order of birth—as if they were newly constructed ships—was as asinine as everything else that had to do with a London Season. By rights her sister Aurelia should have come before Hy, but—for once—Aurelia had disobeyed their mother and refused. Instead, she'd taken a job in Scotland, using her superlative illustration skills in the service of one of Britain's most respected and reclusive naturalists.

It had long been Aurelia's dream to support herself with her art, and now she had achieved her goal.

Oh, how Hy envied her!

In any event, her aunt had been almost laughably relieved when Hy had—after two weeks of hell—suggested that she become companion to the dowager Lady Fitzroy and begged Aunt Ellen to allow Selina to come up from the country and take Hy's place.

Aunt Ellen had been seeking a companion for her mother-in-law for years and none of the women she'd hired had stayed more than a few weeks. Needless to say, she'd been thrilled by Hy's suggestion.

Hy found the dowager easy to deal with when compared to most people. The old woman made her likes and dislikes very clear, so Hy never had to guess. Guessing—and getting it wrong—was where Hy usually got into trouble because she was terrible at reading people.

While the dowager was given to hurling the occasional object and hurling insults even more often, she was old and couldn't throw very hard and her insults were the type that had no power to wound. Hy was notorious among her siblings for having a hide so thick that nothing could pierce it. Mostly that was because she usually wasn't even aware that she was being insulted.

The only part of being the old lady's companion she did *not* like—apart from her gaseous hound—was the dowager's requirement that Hy accompany her to the occasional social event.

For instance, sometimes Her Ladyship wished to go to such-and-such a ball if her card playing cronies were attending. Usually, the old woman allowed Hy to accompany her into the card room, but there had been a few occasions when she'd foisted Hy off on one of her friends' grandsons.

Those times were the absolute worst: for both Hy and the unfortunate male.

It was a little tedious to accompany Lady Fitzroy to the houses of other elderly ladies and sit and watch them play Whist—which many of them played horribly—but at least Hy had been wise enough to deny knowledge of the game, or card games in general, when the old woman had asked if she played. She'd learned long ago that her rapacious playing style usually ended up angering other people as she tended to win a great deal.

Not only that, but she despised playing partnership games as most players weren't up to her skill level. That wasn't hubris, it was a plain statement of fact. She did one thing in life very well, and that one thing was playing cards.

Indeed, Hy's current arrangement made for a fairly pleasant life, unless one counted the persistent fear about her family's financial problems.

But that was something she was working toward resolving.

Ignoring her employer's order to bring a maid with her, Hy donned her lighter cloak and absently tucked an escaped curl beneath her cap before she mashed her oldest bonnet over it.

Thus far she'd managed never to be seen without a head covering, which disguised how short she kept her hair. Thanks to her mother's insistence that she use a dark brown rinse to dampen the bright color, few people in the *ton* knew just how vivid her hair was. Only when she went out on her gaming evenings did she completely wash the dye from her hair. Surely nobody would ever put together the drab, brown-haired female with the red-haired, bespectacled lad across the card table from them.

While it might be unusual for a girl of not quite three-and-twenty to always wear such matronly headgear, nobody had protested. Why should they? Only her Aunt Ellen had—very briefly—believed it was possible to find Hy a husband. But she'd given up on that plan as soon as Selina had arrived.

Hy could never attract a wealthy man and save her family by marrying, but if everything went according to plan—and she did not suffer another hackney robbery—she would soon have the necessary funds to purchase a year's respite for her siblings.

Perhaps a year might be enough time for her sisters to meet and marry men they actually loved, rather than sacrificing their futures for a rich husband.

Hy had won almost two hundred pounds last night. If she could manage such a win every time she played cards—without the subsequent robbery—she would have the necessary funds well before the two months were up.

Or you could accept the Duke of Chatham's invitation to Weller's this coming Friday night and perhaps win all the money in one night...

Hy's pulse sped up at the thought.

It was the highest stakes club in London. She would never be allowed in without a member to vouch for her.

It was the opportunity of a lifetime.

Not to mention you will be playing with the duke again.

Hy frowned at that thought. *I enjoy playing cards with Chatham because he's an excellent player and doesn't wager like an idiot. That is all there is to it.*

Playing at Weller's wasn't just an opportunity to recoup her losses of last night, it was also a rare opportunity to pit her wits against the best players.

Those are the only reasons I'd accept the Duke of Chatham's invitation, Hy told herself.

Yes, the only reasons.

Chapter 7

Hy was up almost two hundred pounds and she'd only been at the table an hour. She was playing deeper than she'd ever done before. Mainly because she was eager to make up for her loss. She knew desperation was a terrible reason to change her bidding habits, but it seemed to be working well tonight.

She was also feeling more at ease than she'd ever done before, thanks to Will's help. The young footman hadn't needed to go out and find a trustworthy driver. In a stroke of luck, Will's own brother Jerry drove a hackney.

Of course, she'd had to pay out a considerable amount for such security. First, she'd had to liberally grease Will's palm to not squeak beef on her, and then she'd needed to engage Jerry's services for several hours. Still, the sense of relief she felt knowing that he was waiting and that his brother was aware of her whereabouts, was well worth the money.

Hy had paid Jerry until two o'clock, which is when he should come and collect her. That would allow her to get back to her aunt's house and into bed before Selina came home from—

"Well, look who is here."

Hy started and looked up to see Baron Fowler and the Duke of Chatham.

"He doesn't look happy to see us, does he, Chatham?"

The duke's mouth twitched, but he said nothing. Hy's face was hot under his cool, amused stare. A stare she'd thought about more than she had liked during the prior twenty or so hours.

"You're just in time to sit in," Lord Delbourne said. He turned to Hy, whose deal it was. "Bellamy is almost finished at bank."

Hy fanned out the remains of the double pack—fewer than a dozen cards. "I believe that hand was it for me."

"Excellent." Fowler dropped into the chair across from Hy, and His Grace took the empty seat beside her.

"Mind if I take the deal?" the big Scot asked the table at large. When nobody demurred, he gestured for the waiter to bring two new packs and then turned back to Hy, his bright green eyes glittering with amusement as he looked at Hy's money.

"You've done alright for yourself, eh, lad?"

Hy suddenly wished she'd put some of her winnings away.

She nodded.

Fowler smirked, his sharp gaze drifting over the other players at the table. "Has Mr. Bellamy been talking your ears off and distracting you from your play tonight, Delbourne?"

The bone-thin aristocrat laughed, the sound a bit too hearty. Hy supposed the effete earl didn't feel quite comfortable with a man as rough as Fowler.

For her part, she wished Fowler's eyes and sense of humor were not quite so keen.

"The boy has had his share of luck," Delbourne admitted, cutting Hy a rather sour look.

"Is that right, Hiram?" Fowler asked. "Have you been lucky?"

She opened her mouth to say she didn't believe in luck, but then—based on the hostile look she was getting from the other players—decided to just nod.

Fowler thought that was hilarious for some reason. Thankfully, the waiter brought the cards before the baron could tease Hy any further.

Fowler opened the packs and commenced to shuffle, his fingers nimble for all that they were as thick as the spokes of a coach wheel.

"Now," he said, finishing his last shuffle with a snap. "Let's play some cards."

***

"Move aside, darling, you're crushing my jewels."

The Marquess of Shelton, His Grace's obnoxious cousin, had shown up an hour earlier. Ever since his arrival, Hy's *luck*, as Fowler liked to call it, had steadily gone downhill. Or perhaps that had just been her concentration and mood.

The prostitute did or said something to Shelton and the golden god chuckled before murmuring—just loud enough for Hy to hear—"Yes, of course that's for you, love, but you mustn't take it out and play with it right now."

Hyacinth

Hy's face heated at Shelton's words.

Naturally the irritating man noticed and laughed. "What an adorable, blushing pup you are, Bellamy. Are you sure you don't want Adele to take you into one of the guestrooms and make a real man of you?"

The others laughed.

"No, thank you, my lord, but perhaps she might take *your* seat this next hand and make less of a muck of it than you've been doing," Hy shot back before she could stop herself.

The other players laughed even harder.

Shelton gave Hy a startled glance, the same look a man might give a kitten when he got scratched, but quickly masked it with a lazy chuckle. He leaned the girl back, stroking his hand up her bodice until his fingers came to rest over her breast. His eyes locked with Hy's and then he leaned down and tongued the mounded flesh, his finger dipping beneath the tight crimson satin and pulling a hard nipple above the straining fabric.

Hy's head buzzed at the almost unbearably arousing sight and the room seemed to tilt.

"What will it be, Bellamy?" Delbourne said, his voice impatient.

Hy realized the earl wanted to know if she needed a card.

"I'm out." She pushed away her cards, only recalling at the last moment that she had two jacks.

Blast and damn!

Seething at her own stupidity she looked up to find Shelton grinning at her. She just *knew* that *he* knew what his taunting had done to her concentration. The odious cad.

"Don't be a bore, Shelton," the duke drawled.

The marquess smirked from his cousin to Hy, a supercilious expression on his face that made Hy wish she'd kept her mouth shut and never attracted his attention. Hy knew that she should count herself fortunate that her insult had amused Shelton rather than angered him. What if it hadn't? What if the fool had been offended and had called her out? She could just imagine it: Shot or stabbed to death on Hampstead Heath tomorrow morning. Some good she'd be to her family then.

"I'll tell you what your cousin won't tell you, Shelton," Baron Fowler said, his voice an angry growl. "This room is for cards, not for fucking. Get rid of the tart and shut your mouth or get the hell out."

Everyone's eyes swiveled from the bearlike, rough-spoken merchant to the gorgeous god of a man across from him. With his broken nose, huge hands, and gargantuan body Fowler looked as conspicuous amidst such elegant company as a lump of pig iron tucked in a box of fine chocolates. He eyed Shelton with obvious dislike, his powerful body tense and poised for action.

Shelton hesitated a moment but then shrugged, tucked the prostitute's nipple back beneath her bodice, and said, "It seems you must move along, darling." He gave the woman a gentle push.

Fowler grunted. "And leave the boy alone. I'm more sick and tired of your puerile goading than he is."

Shelton looked from Fowler to Hy, his gaze curious rather than angry. The man seemed impervious to insults. He also seemed far too interested in Hy.

She hastily dropped her gaze to the table, not wanting to attract any more of Shelton's attention than she already had.

The duke scraped up the cards and shuffled, preparing to take his turn dealing.

Hy focused on remaining calm. She couldn't play if she was not calm.

And she *needed* to play.

At first, she'd thought the prostitutes would be the most distracting part of the evening, but that was before Shelton had inexplicably turned his attention her way. After the first hour she hardly noticed the women who were draped over the various men. Instead, she was stunned by what a dreadful player Shelton was. Not only that, but he appeared to be borrowing from the duke, who was covering his vowels even though everyone in the room was giving the marquess derisive looks.

Hy didn't like winning against Shelton when she knew it would be the duke's money that paid her. The thought was irrational. She didn't mind winning directly from the duke, so what difference did it make if she won his money via Shelton?

But it did.

Something brushed Hy's shoulder and she looked up to find one of the half-naked prostitutes beside her, a voluptuous blond woman. She was looking down, her eyes flickering from Hy to the pile of money on the table, and then she smiled and slid a hand around Hy's jaw.

"Oooh, as smooth as a peach."

Hy recoiled so hard she bumped into the duke, who sat on her other side.

Hy turned to the duke, who'd continued dealing as if nothing had happened. "I apologize, Your Grace."

Hyacinth

His mouth—the scarred side of his face was to her—twitched, but he said nothing.

"Come over here, girl," Fowler said, beckoning to the prostitute and yet again coming to Hy's rescue. Hy met the wealthy merchant's probing gaze. Fowler, for all his joviality, had a hard, speculative look in his eyes.

Hy quickly dropped her own attention to her cards.

Play continued.

Hy was not doing her best, but she was still sitting with almost three hundred pounds an hour later when the table broke up for the first of two suppers that Jensen offered his players to keep them from seeking food elsewhere.

She looked up from her money to see that three of the men had drinks and were chatting in front of the fireplace with several of the prostitutes, one man with a woman on each arm. Hy's imagination—always fertile when it came to sexual matters—immediately began to concoct erotic scenarios for the trio and she had to jerk her attention back to the here and now.

Hy knew the trio would be going to one of the rooms on the upper floor that Jensen hired out by the hour. If it had reached that point in the evening, it was probably past time for her to go.

She began to collect her money.

"What? Are you leaving already Bellamy?" Fowler bellowed, looking up from the blond whore, who sat straddling his lap, her skirt pulled up to mid-thighs and exposing black stockings with garters that had roses—complete with thorns—embroidered on them.

Hy wrenched her eyes away from the scandalous, titillating sight. "Yes, my lord."

"I thought you were going to give me back some of my money?"

"No, sir, I said I was going to give you a chance to win the money. You've had several hours to do so, but you've only given me more."

Fowler laughed. And then he lifted the woman up straight up from his lap as if she were as light as a doll and set her on her feet, his massive arms bulging beneath his snugly tailored tailcoat.

Hy goggled; never had she seen such an impressive demonstration of brute strength before. She jerked her gaze away from the baron as he tucked some money into the woman's bodice, her pulse erratic.

Hy had always been this way when it came to the subject of intimate relations. Her imagination, which was dormant most of the time, suddenly sparked to life the instant she was confronted with anything erotic. Her fascination with such taboo matters was one of the reasons her mother believed her to be unnatural and perverted.

Charles had rejected her mother's assessment of her character and put forward one of his own. "You have a sensual nature, Hy, that is all. It is accepted in men, but in women... well, you know better than anyone how our society—and even other women—punish any female who admits to having sexual urges."

A big hand suddenly grabbed Hy's shoulder and she jolted.

"Skittish, aren't ye?" Fowler asked, not waiting for an answer. He squeezed her shoulder and then dropped his hand. "You're the best goddamned card player I've played against in years, Bellamy, maybe ever. Isn't he, Chatham?"

The duke still sat at his place at the table, his expression inscrutable as he tucked away the small stack of vowels his cousin had generated during the evening.

He took a sip from his glass and then looked up, his gaze settling on Hy. "I believe you are correct, Fowler."

Hy felt her face heating for the second time in one evening, albeit for different reasons. First, Shelton's outrageous behavior, and now this unexpected praise. Yes, it had certainly been a night for blushes.

"Thank you, my lord. Thank you, Your Grace."

"Are you going to have some supper?" Fowler asked.

"Thank you, sir, but I'm not hungry." The last thing she needed was to spend more time talking with these men. She had already socialized far more than was—

"*Bellamy?*"

Hy's head jerked up at the sound of her name and she saw that Chatham was staring at her. He wasn't smiling, but his striking brown eyes glittered with humor.

Why was he amused? What had Hy missed? "I beg your pardon, Your Grace, I'm afraid I did not catch that."

"I said that I was leaving and asked if I could give you a ride anywhere?"

A ride with the duke? Hy was torn—she had told Jerry to come for her at two. It was only a quarter past one o'clock and she would have to wait another forty-five minutes. In the meantime—

"Well, I'm off lads," Fowler said in his booming voice, and then turned to prostitute, who'd been loitering, obviously waiting for him. He offered her his arm and then grinned at Hy and the duke. "I'm famished." He winked at Hy. "And I wouldn't mind some supper, either."

The Scot left them alone and the room seemed to shrink, although Hy knew that could only be her imagination. She realized the duke was still looking at her, waiting for an answer, his gaze... intent.

Hy imagined being the focus of that acute gaze all the way home and made up her mind. "Er, thank you for the offer, sir, but I have a carriage coming for me."

The duke nodded and gestured to the door. "Come, I'll walk down with you."

Hy hesitated, wondering if she should mention the fact her carriage would not be there for a while but decided against it as he might then *insist* on giving her a ride. The duke always spoke softly, but she had noticed that nobody—not even his obnoxious cousin—ever directly contradicted him.

"Did you get found out last night, Hiram?" the duke asked as they descended the staircase.

"Found out?" Hy repeated, her breath freezing in her chest.

"Your aunt and uncle—did they catch you coming home late?"

"Oh." Hy exhaled. "Er, no, Your Grace. I got in unnoticed.

The duke shrugged into a cloak—the sort a man wore if he were going to a ball. She'd heard her aunt say at dinner that he would be at the Sheffingdon ball tonight—although Hy had missed exactly *why* her aunt was mentioning it— which is why she'd been surprised when he'd showed up at the Pigeonhole.

"How is your stay in the city so far, Hiram?" the duke asked, handing the servant a generous vail.

"Er, good." Hy wanted to smack herself in the head; was that really all she could manage? *Er, good*? Why the devil was the man talking to her? Why didn't he just *go*? She wished Jerry would decide to show up three-quarters of an hour early but knew there was no chance of it. He was likely sitting in a pub enjoying getting paid for hours when he didn't have to take any fares.

"Tell me, Hiram, how do you entertain yourself all day?"

Hy stared at the duke; why was he asking her these things? This was one question she had never rehearsed an answer for. Men at gambling hells didn't ask each other questions like this. Men at gambling hells drank, played cards, and fondled prostitutes.

Yet again she saw the duke was patiently waiting for an answer while she dithered like a fool. "Er… do?"

The duke chuckled and clamped a hand on Hy's shoulder. "Never mind, *Hiram*, I can imagine. I am not so old that I don't recall the vast array of activities a young man can get up to on his first visit to London."

Hy doubted very much that the duke would be able to guess what she did all day, unless he, too, had toted a farting pug from room to room or ironed the society sections of five different newspapers.

"Your carriage is waiting, Your Grace," a porter said when they came to the club exit. "Mr. Bellamy, sir?"

Hy turned to the porter. "Yes?"

"Jerry, the driver who was to pick you up, had a problem with his coach wheel, sir. He won't be back for you at two o'clock. Should I summon another hackney?"

"You needn't bother," the duke said before Hy could come up with an answer. He flipped the porter another coin. "I will give Mr. Bellamy a ride home."

***

"Are you in a hurry to be somewhere, or would you care for a visit to the Silk Purse, Hiram? It would be my treat."

Hiram Bellamy—or whatever the young woman's name really was—startled at Sylvester's question.

"I beg your pardon, Your Grace? The Silk Purse?"

"Surely you've heard of it?"

The woman shook her head, her face pale beneath the tall beaver hat she wore.

Sylvester knew it was bad of him, but he couldn't help toying with her. "It is an excellent brothel. Only the highest quality girls—very well trained in every kind of pleasure."

It was bloody difficult not to laugh at how wide her eyes went.

"Er, a b-brothel. Oh, I see. Thank you, sir, but I had better not." Her voice was scratchy, like the skittering of dry leaves across cobbles.

"Are you sure?" Sylvester prodded, enjoying himself more than he had in ages. "There is a girl there—Monique, I believe her name is—and she has the most delectable—"

"I'm quite sure," she said firmly.

Hyacinth

"Ah," Sylvester said, nodding and narrowing his eyes, as if he finally understood something. "I see." He leaned across the short distance that separated them and laid a hand on *Hiram's* knee and squeezed gently. "You like something a bit different, do you?"

She pressed back into the far corner of her seat like a lobster in retreat—as far away from Sylvester as the coach would allow.

He'd not believed it when Tackle had told him that his new card-playing companion was a female. But tonight, when he'd entered the gambling house and had seen her sitting there among a bunch of men, Sylvester wondered how he could have ever thought she was a boy.

He suspected most people were fooled by the fact that she was *exceptionally* tall—close to his own above-average six feet. She was also thin to the point of gauntness and—without mincing words—rather plain.

Not that her lack of feminine graces had stopped Sylvester from thinking about her last night after he'd seen her wearing his clothing. Why the devil would such a thing be arousing? He must have something wrong with his head.

It hadn't been just the fact that she was dressed in his clothing, it had also been something in her gaze. For a few moments in that bedchamber her normally opaque stare had given way to something else. Something blazing and intense.

Sylvester would have wagered a pony that she'd looked at him as if she were picturing him without the robe, her heavy-lidded eyes sparking with heat.

Whether that was just his fanciful imagination or not, he'd been erect afterward. He'd remained annoyingly hard until he'd finally been forced to do something about it. The irony of him masturbating while he had a mistress had not been wasted on him.

Sylvester studied her closely as she pondered his lascivious taunt, clearly struggling for an answer. He decided that he'd been hasty to judge her plain. Indeed, there was a certain nobility to her sharp cheekbones, high-bridged nose, and well-formed mouth. She was… distinctive, rather than softly feminine or pretty. Well, except for her lush lower lip, which would do a courtesan proud.

Right now, that lip was thin and taut.

"Well, Bellamy?" he prodded. "Is that your preference? Something different?"

"Er, *different*, Your Grace?" She looked cool enough, but Sylvester saw a flicker of apprehension in her clear aqua green gaze and felt a little guilty for teasing her. He didn't know if she was really twenty-three, or if that had been yet another lie. For all he knew he was taunting a sixteen-year-old.

"Perhaps I am mistaken," he said, deciding to let her off the hook. "Please, accept my apologies." Sylvester moved on before she could respond. "It seems it is a night for apologies as I must offer one for my cousin, Lord Shelton, as well. He appears to have taken an interest in you and I'm afraid he can be something of a pest. I do hope he was not the reason for your early departure this evening. It sounded as if you'd expected to stay a bit later if you'd arranged for a hackney to come at two."

"Oh, no harm done, sir. It was time I was leaving in any case, and I thank you for the ride. I do wonder what happened to my driver. I hope nothing bad has befallen him."

One of Sylvester's servants had befallen the greedy hack driver, paying him a good deal of money to stay away while assuring the man that young *Master Bellamy* would be in good hands.

In Sylvester's hands, as a matter of fact.

As much as his servant had paid the hackney driver, the man had continued to insist he knew nothing of Hiram Bellamy or where he lived, which Sylvester did not really believe. Still, he was in no hurry to find out the truth about the woman or to expose her masquerade; this was more amusement than he'd had in years. He could wait for his answers.

"You never told me where I might drop you?" he said.

She opened her mouth, and then closed it.

Ah, here is a fix, isn't it, pet?

"Perhaps you would like to stop in at my house for a drink and a hand or two of cards since you cut short your evening?"

She blinked across at him, looking very much like a kitten who'd been teased with a piece of string. "Cards?"

"It occurs to me you might play piquet?"

***

Hy was having a very difficult time: breathing, thinking, speaking—pretty much doing anything other than gawking with her mouth open.

The duke had *touched* her knee. True, he'd believed Hy to be a man. Was that a normal way for one man to touch another man? Did the duke *like* her? Thanks to Charles, Hy knew about men liking men. Is that why the duke's cousin had spoken so slyly that first night they'd met?

The first night she'd seen His Grace he'd had a prostitute on his lap. And then there was the suggestion that they visit a brothel together tonight.

Hy considered the implications. Did Chatham like women *and* men?

Instead of the revulsion society would expect her to feel, Hy felt only curiosity.

That's a bloody lie, Hy Bellamy.

All right, all right. She felt a *burning* curiosity and something else, too: something very much like what she'd felt with Charles, but more intense, somehow. It was arousal, and there was no denying it.

Her body felt hot and cold and achy and restless all at once. And there was a nagging, intense awareness in her female parts. And she seemed to be producing far too much saliva, which meant she couldn't stop swallowing.

The duke was watching her, his expression relaxed, tolerant, amused—*lazy*, as if Hy were some form of entertainment. And he had suggested playing piquet. If there was one game Hy could almost admit to *loving*—if she believed that emotion existed—it would be piquet.

And she was good at it. Very good.

Hy's body thrummed with the desire to play piquet with him—to pit her wits against his.

To sit across a table from him, and look your fill, a sly voice taunted.

She couldn't deny the accusation; she found the Duke of Chatham fascinating.

So, what of it? He was an interesting man and she was a woman, after all. Charles had told her this type of thing—infatuation—might eventually happen to her. She had never believed him, but it seemed she'd been wrong.

Hy thought back to what the duke said earlier that evening—about her being one of the best card players he'd ever met. It was pitiful, but those few words from him had touched her. It was so rare that she felt much of *anything* that it had taken her a while to identify her emotional reaction as pleasure.

Was that all it took to make her *feel* something? A few kind words about cards? Is that who she was, who she'd become?

Hy frowned. So what if it was? It was no mean feat to be good at something that might save her family. It was nothing to be ashamed of that she wanted to play cards with him.

But...

If she wasn't in her bed when Selina got home, she would have to endure an interrogation and, to be perfectly honest, she had no mental energy left after dealing with the duke's tiresome cousin all evening. If she played cards with him, it would be a slaughter. The thought of shaming herself in his eyes overpowered even the desire to pit her wits against his.

"As much as I would enjoy that, Your Grace, I'm afraid I must get home."

The duke actually looked *disappointed.*

Hy's chest tightened as his shoulders seemed to slump and he glanced down at his hands, absently straightening the already straight seams of his gloves. Which is when she opened her mouth and said something she knew she shouldn't.

"But I have decided to go to Weller's," she said, making the decision on the spot.

Chatham looked up from his hands and smiled.

His smile reminded her of the taxidermy shark that hung above the bar at the King's Head in Little Sissingdon and attracted curious visitors from miles around. The shark was ancient, dusty, moth-eaten, and missing more than a few teeth, but it still struck fear into the people who came to gawk at it.

And it looked strangely like the Duke of Chatham in that moment.

That's when Hy realized that His Grace hadn't been *sad* or *disconsolate*. He had been sharping her. If not to play tonight, then perhaps to get her to go to Weller's.

Hy didn't know whether she was pleased or worried that he wanted her to go to the club so much that he was willing to manipulate.

The duke's smile grew. "Excellent. We shall have to see if we cannot squeeze in a rubber or two of piquet in one of the private rooms at the club."

"Er, yes."

"If we cannot make time at Weller's, then you must come and play at my house sometime."

"Of course, Your Grace." And Hy knew that she would accept if he asked her again, even though she knew she should avoid the man.

Somehow, Hy realized somewhat dazedly, her schedule seemed to be filling up with the Duke of Chatham.

Chapter 8

"Couldn't I just feign illness?" Hy asked for the third time.

Selina frowned. "Really, Hy. I know you heard me the first two times, and the answer is still *no*."

Hy groaned. "But why not?"

"It is only a picnic, Hy. You have already begged off going to the Manson ball this evening, you cannot reject *every* invitation our aunt makes you. As much as you might wish to, you cannot simply be a hermit here as you are at home." She rested her hands on her hips, her full lips pursed and thin. "I don't think you understand just how much Aunt Ellen wants to help us."

Hy gestured to her *picnic* gown and then pointed to the pink ribbons her aunt's fancy French dresser had insisted on weaving through her hair. "*This* is helping us?"

"It is helping us find husbands, Hy."

"That is rubbish, Linny. First, I don't *want* a husband. Second, Aunt Ellen *knows* no man would ever ask me to marry him. Why can she not simply accept it? Third, she has you to dress up and put on display. Why in the world does she need *me*?" She plucked at her skirt, "I look like a goat in a gown."

Some distant part of Hy's brain told her she was whining.

"Why does she need you?" her sister repeated sharply. "Because you live in her house. Because she feeds and clothes you. And—most importantly—because it will please her if you come out with us this afternoon."

It was unlike Selina to speak so snappishly, so Hy knew she must have been behaving more than just badly. She must have been behaving *insensitively*. Insensitivity was, indeed, her besetting sin.

"Fine. I will go."

"Don't worry, Hy, you will be back in time to sneak out for an evening of cards." Selina hissed the last word.

Hy bristled at her sister's chiding. "You speak as if I am enjoying this, Selina? I am trying to earn enough money so that our family won't be thrown out of our home."

Selina snorted, screwing in an earring and glaring at Hy in the mirror. "Don't lie to me, Hy. You *do* enjoy it. Too much. I can see it on your face when you come back from your—your *adventures*."

"Should I be suffering? Is that what is wrong? I am not suffering while I do this?"

Selina spun around. "I don't want you to suffer, but I also don't want you to do what father did."

Hy's jaw sagged.

"You look so flabbergasted by that. But what would happen if you were to get into debt, too, Hy?"

So, this is why her generally agreeable sister had been so irritable these past weeks. "You are worried I have the same habit as father." It was not a question, but Selina nodded, a deeply unhappy look in her violet blue eyes.

Hy was not given to demonstrations of physical affection, and her entire family knew it. But she could see her sister needed *something* just then—some sign of assurance, some physical, or tangible sign. She put her hands on Selina's shoulders and squeezed. "I am not like father. I do not feel driven." Although she certainly felt *something* when she thought about tonight and her assignation with the duke at Weller's. Anxiety? Anticipation?

Arousal?

Hy hastily pushed that last thought away. She was meeting him because it was the best way to earn the money quickly. Not because she *wanted* to see him.

"Hy?" Selina asked, her furrowed brow telling Hy she'd allowed her attention to drift.

"I do not play if the conditions are not propitious, Linny. I have never come home behind, but always ahead. Well, except for the robbery. And I am *careful* about what I do."

Selina nodded and heaved a sigh. "I know that. I'm sorry for being a shrew to you."

Hy suddenly noticed the lavender circles beneath her sister's eyes. How had she missed such obvious signs of Selina's worry and exhaustion?

Hyacinth

Even before the thought was fully formed, she knew the answer. She'd missed the signs because that was Hy's nature. She watched cards, not people.

"Is that all that is bothering you, Linny? My card playing?"

Her sister's cheeks flushed; Selina even looked beautiful when she was blushing. Unlike Hy—who turned splotchy and red, like a freshly plucked turkey—Selina looked like a rose in bloom.

"What is it, Linny?"

"It's nothing." She smoothed the already smooth skirt of her simple white muslin gown. They wore identical gowns, but her sister looked like an angel in her blue trimmed muslin while Hy resembled a wooden plank wrapped in muslin and mockingly festooned with pink bows.

Hy squeezed her sister's hand. "Please. We should not keep secrets from one another."

"There is a man who"—Selina's tossed her head irritably and grimaced. "It doesn't matter. I don't wish to talk about it."

"You have already met a man who interests you?"

Her sister's golden brows arched, making her look beautiful *and* regal. "Already? Hy, I have been here for weeks and weeks and I have accompanied my aunt to *every* function. That is what people *do* at *ton* functions—meet other people. And it is not as if I have all the time in the world to find a husband. I need—" She bit her lip and gave a small shake of her head, sending guinea-gold curls bouncing.

"I *told* you that you don't need to marry for money, Linny. I will soon have enough to—"

"Enough money for a year? And then what?"

Hy could never tell her sister of her plans. Selina wouldn't understand or approve of the life of an itinerant gambler, of course very few people would. And *none* of her sisters would approve of Hy masquerading as a man.

So, instead, she said, "I want to know about this man. What is his name? When did this happen and why have you not mentioned this before?"

"Do you mention everything you get up to when you are off gallivanting?" Hy gaped and Selina rushed on. "No, you do not. I will start telling *you* what I do and whom I meet when you start telling *me* things."

"I play cards, Selina. Usually with men whose names I don't even know."

"You know the Duke of Chatham's name, don't you?"

Hy blinked. "What—"

Selina crossed her arms. "I want *you* to tell me about playing cards with the Duke of Chatham."

"How do you know I played cards with Chatham?"

"Those clothes you wore—the ones I cleaned and pressed for you?"

"Yes?"

"His *name* was embroidered inside the coat, Hy."

"Oh."

"Is that all you have to say? *Oh*?"

Hy shrugged.

Her sister made a frustrated growling sound and shook her head hard enough to shake a curl lose. "Can you really be so obtuse? You spent the evening with one of the wealthiest bachelors in England—"

"It wasn't only the two of us."

"There were others?"

"Of course there were others there," she said, not telling *all* the truth. "Like you I've been out and about for weeks. I've met plenty of men and gambled with most of them. Why would you ask me a—"

Her sister was relentless. "You've spent an evening with of one of the most eligible, elusive, and scandalous bachelors in Britain—a man who has evaded lures for a decade and who rarely exchanges even five words with a female and you have spent an entire evening with him."

Hy was relieved her sister only knew about the *one* evening.

She shoved a hand through her hair before she remembered the stupid ribbon the maid had woven through. Her fingers became tangled. "Blast and damn."

"Here, don't touch it, Hy. Let me fix it." Hy stood still while her sister repaired the damage.

"Lord, Linny, you make it sound as if Chatham and I danced quadrilles or something. I don't spend my evenings flirting. If you had any idea what went—" she bit her lip, horrified at what she almost disclosed.

"What? What were you going to say?"

"Nothing."

Linny stamped her foot and it was all Hy could do not to smile. Her beautiful sister only looked more beautiful when she became enraged. It made it difficult to take her seriously.

"Why are you so curious about the duke?" Hy asked.

"I'm not," Serena retorted, still fussing. She bit her lip and then stepped back to examine her work. "You'll do."

Hyacinth

"Why are you asking me about Chatham?" Hy repeated.

"Everyone is curious about him, Hy."

"They are?"

"Yes, of course."

"You as well?"

Linny shrugged. "I'm only human, Hy. An elusive man is always of interest. Especially when he is powerful and wealthy."

Hy noticed her sister didn't say *handsome*. "Do you know him?" she couldn't help asking.

"I don't *know* him, but he is often at the functions Aunt and I attend."

Something about her pretty sister with the enigmatic duke made her stomach feel uncomfortably tight.

"Why do you look so startled?" Selina asked.

"I just didn't think you would mix in the same circles. What with him being such a rake and all."

Selina laughed. "You are truly hopeless, Hy. The man is a duke. A *wealthy unmarried* duke who is not in his ninth decade. His raking matters not a jot. He could cut the head off a bishop and still be welcome at Almack's."

Hy's eyebrows rose as she visualized that gruesome spectacle.

Selina continued. "Aunt Ellen believes His Grace is finally seeking a wife this Season and—"

"Yes?" Hy prodded when her sister stopped abruptly.

"Oh, nothing. I don't know how we got off on this subject." She scowled at Hy. "You are trying to distract me from the point."

"Me? What did I do? And what *is* the point?"

"My point is that the more time you spend socializing with the men of the *ton* the more chance one of them will recognize you."

"*That* was the point? Because this is the first you've mentioned it."

"That doesn't mean I haven't been thinking about it. What if somebody asks me to marry him, meets my sister, and realizes that *she* is the same man he's been playing cards with?"

"Has somebody asked you to marry him?" She suddenly recalled her sister's comments a moment earlier. "The duke?"

"What? No! Of course not."

Unwanted images leapt into Hy's mind's eye; specifically, the oddly persistent picture of the duke with a half-naked woman draped across his well-dressed body, his long, elegant fingers absently stroking the prostitute's neck.

"Are you feeling sick, Hy? You have become quite flushed."

This conversation was making her skull tighten and throb with the effort it took to follow along. "I don't understand, Linny. What does any of this have to do with the duke?"

"I merely brought up the duke as an example of a man who is seeking a wife—"

"Did you hear him say that?"

Selina laughed. "Of course not."

"Then how do you know?"

"Aunt Ellen said that Chatham is at odds with his current heir—"

"Who is his current heir?"

Selina's cheeks suddenly flushed. "The Marquess of Shelton," she said in a breathy, hushed voice that made the hair on the back of Hy's neck stand on end.

It was never good when her sister got that dewy-eyed look.

"I did not know Shelton was his heir." Although that explained why Chatham tolerated the man.

"Do you play cards with him too?" Selina asked.

Hy looked into her sister's wide-eyed, curious face and lied, "No."

"Oh," Selina said, looking oddly relieved. "In any case, *everyone* says Chatham will remarry, if only to thwart poor Lord Shelton."

"The duke was married before?"

Selina gave her a scandalized look. "Hy! You've played cards with the man, how is it you don't know such things?"

Hy could hardly believe her sister's naïveté. "We play *cards*, Linny. We don't sit about chattering about wives and courtship and—" she circled her hand in the air, searching for the correct word and failing to find it. "Well, *whatever*." Hy struggled to regain the thread of the conversation. "So, then, about Shelton—"

"I don't want to talk about him." She fiddled absently with one of her earrings. "I hardly know him. I only met him three weeks ago, at Lady Mercer's ball," she said, talking about him despite what she'd just said.

The fact that Selina remembered *exactly* how long ago and where she had met Shelton was not a positive sign. Selina and exactitude were, if not exactly strangers, certainly no more than passing acquaintances. If she recalled Shelton's entrance into her life with such clarity it could only mean one thing: she was infatuated.

Hyacinth

Hy wanted to groan. Of all the men in London, why did she have to choose such an annoying, sponging bounder?

Or maybe Hy was wrong—she often was about such matters. Maybe her sister wasn't smitten by the cad. The subject called for a direct approach.

"Why did you mention Shelton?" Hy demanded.

"It doesn't matter."

"Why did you mention Shelton?" Hy asked again, sounding like their little brother Doddy, who had once repeated a single phrase for two entire months when he'd been a toddler.

"I should never have mentioned his name."

"Linny—"

"Oh, Hy!" Her sister suddenly threw her arms around Hy's shoulders and squeezed her tightly. "I know how you hate discussing such matters."

Hy's head—which had already been pounding—felt like it would explode, even though she knew that was a physical impossibility. Probably.

She took a deep breath, instructed herself to remain calm, and patted her sister's back. "There, there, Linny."

"I am so sorry for being such a shrew to you, Hy. I know you are doing this for all of us. It's just that I'm so worried about home. It has been weeks since I've had an answer from Phoebe."

Hy felt dizzy as the conversation took off on yet another tangent. "But Mama wrote only last week. Surely if anything was wrong, she would have said so." Hy put her sister at arm's length so that she could see her face. "Are you sure something else isn't bothering you?" *Like Shelton?* she wanted to ask but did not because she was a coward and didn't want to set her sister off again.

"No, no. I just don't like being so… cut off from everyone."

Hy nodded, even though she didn't really feel what her sister was feeling. While she missed home, she had already accepted that she would not be returning to Queen's Bower.

"I thought I would have received at least *one* offer by now, but"—Selina wrung her hands, her expression desolate—"I think I must appear too desperate or—"

"Hush. Don't despair, Linny. I shall soon have enough money to buy more time."

"Do you think Aunt will have me back next year if I don't *take* this year?"

"You have *taken*," Hy insisted, although she wasn't really sure what *to take* entailed. "You are the most beautiful, kind, and generous young woman of the Season."

Selina brushed aside her compliment. "No, I am just another impoverished woman scheming for a wealthy husband, which makes me feel positively ill, Hy."

"I keep telling you that you don't *need* to scheme, Linny. Just be *you* and fall in love with whomever you like." *Except Shelton*, Hy wanted to add, but suspected that would not be wise. "There will be offers, don't worry." Hy snorted. "Good Lord, all I hear in these gambling clubs is how every young man in the *ton* has lost his heart to you."

"Men talk of me in gambling hells?" Selina asked, an expression of horror on her pretty face.

"No, no—not in any bad way," Hy hastily said.

"Oh, this is dreadful! To be fodder for men in gambling hells!"

Hy didn't know what to say to calm her sister's nerves. It was the sort of thing that had always evaded her. What difference did it make *where* men spoke of one?

"Linny—"

"I am *fine*," her sister insisted far to vehemently. And then dissolved into tears, sobbing all over Hy's hideous dress.

She patted her sister's shoulder and murmured quietly, as she'd watched her elder sister Aurelia do with their younger siblings times beyond counting.

All the while, she struggled to untangle her sister's words and to understand how Chatham fit into the garbled story.

Chapter 9

Sylvester couldn't help cutting a smirking look from Fowler's scowling face to where a certain angelic female blond head was surrounded by two dozen male heads of varying hair colors.

"Why aren't you over there with all the other young bucks offering obeisance at the alter of your fair Peitho?"

Fowler cut him an irritable look. "I've not the benefit of your fine education, Chatham, but I take it that's some clever classical reference?"

Sylvester prudently smothered his smile at the other man's bellicose response. "Why don't you ask the woman to dance, Fowler?"

"Don't be daft," Fowler snarled, clearly spoiling for an argument that Sylvester had no intention of giving him.

Instead, Sylvester said, "I believe I shall head out."

"You goin' home?"

"No, I'm in the mood for the Devil's books tonight."

Fowler perked up at the thieves' cant for gambling. "I'll accompany you."

The two men took their leave of Mrs. Manson, their hostess, and headed for the cloak room.

Fowler—a mountain of a man with unruly auburn hair that stuck out like a haystack no matter how much pomade the poor fellow slathered on—eschewed fripperies like opera cloaks and collected only his hat, leaving the servant a sizeable vail that wiped the snide smirk from the man's face. Yes, Lord Angus Fowler might look like an ostler from a posting inn, but the man was one of the wealthiest industrialists in Britain. He was also generous to a fault and threw his money about as if it was water, thus putting paid to the cliché that all Scotsmen were clutch fisted.

Fowler's clothing was expensive and conservatively tailored as befitted a man of his massive stature, but it was clear he cared little about his appearance and cut a haphazard figure for all that he'd probably paid more for his toggery than any ten men in Mrs. Manson's ballroom.

As they closed the short distance from the house to Sylvester's carriage, Fowler tugged off his huge white gloves. "Here," he said to the liveried servant who hastened to open the coach door.

The young man caught the expensive gloves—an item he'd doubtless be able to sell—and the coin that came after them and smiled. "Thank you, my lord."

Fowler grunted and climbed into the coach, causing it to tip precariously on its sturdy springs.

"So, what is the problem, my friend?" Sylvester asked as they rolled off, even though he was aware that he was poking a bear by pursuing this subject.

"What problem?" Fowler snapped.

"Lady Selina. Why don't you just court the chit, Fowler? Her family is skint and her father would probably offer her up to you on a platter."

Fowler made a growling noise that sounded remarkably like the animal he resembled and glared at Sylvester. "I should pound you to mince for speaking of that angel in such a disrespectful way."

Undaunted, Sylvester laughed. "I said nothing about *her*, Fowler. It is her father. The Earl of Addiscombe is so far below the hatches he probably doesn't know which direction is up at this point. Why in the world don't you just offer for the woman?"

"A sweet, gentle, and delicate beauty like her with an ugly, brutish, crude bastard like me?" he snorted. "You're barking mad, Chatham."

Sylvester held his tongue and meditated on the folly of his fellow man. It was true that Fowler's father had been a humble cordier and his mother a dairy maid, but he had made a fortune in shipping, not to mention earning a barony for his efforts on Britain's behalf. His manners were less than polished and his speech gruff, but he was more honorable and loyal than anyone Sylvester had ever met. He was also kind, gentle, and generous with women and Selina Bellamy—although a surpassingly lovely chit—would be fortunate to get Fowler for a husband.

But the man simply could not see his own value.

In this instance Sylvester could lead the Scot to the trough, but he could not make him drink.

"So, where are we goin'?" Fowler asked, clearly wishing to leave the subject of Lady Selina behind.

"Weller's."

Fowler rolled his eyes. "Ugh. Bloody hell."

"What is wrong with Weller's?"

Hyacinth

"A more toffy-nosed bunch of hoity-toity aristocratic"—he broke off when Sylvester laughed. "Present company excepted, of course."

"Of course," Sylvester said, still chuckling. "You *do* realize you are an aristocrat yourself, Fowler?"

The baron dismissed the accusation with a snort. "Why not go to the Pigeonhole tonight? Mayhap your scrawny little ginger-headed Captain Sharp will be there and you can chuckle your way through another fleecing."

"As a matter of fact, I invited Bellamy to be my guest tonight at Weller's." And he'd not been able to stop thinking about seeing the damned woman ever since. He was like a bloody ten-year-old boy waiting for Christmas morning. When was the last time Sylvester had been so excited to see somebody? Actually, when had he been excited about *anything*? Not for years.

It was a worrisome thought.

But it was also… invigorating.

Fowler's red brows arched and he grinned. "Ah, I see. Well then, perhaps it might be fun to tag along with you, after all. Young Hiram will set that crew back on their heels, I reckon."

"That's what I'm hoping, Fowler."

Sylvester didn't tell his friend what *else* he was hoping.

***

Hy stared at the entrance to the famed Weller's, surprised it was so unimpressive. For some reason she'd expected red carpets, chandeliers, gold-laced flunkies, and other signs of excess.

But it was just a big house, not even as interesting looking as White's with its bow window or any of the other half-dozen men's clubs she'd made a point to stroll past when she was in her *Hiram* garb.

For all that the building looked so commonplace the factotum who approached her when she stepped inside could have given the Regent some lessons in regal deportment.

He raked Hy's person with a dismissive glare and said, "Perhaps you are lost."

It wasn't a question and the man started ushering Hy back toward the door.

"I'm a guest of the Duke of Chatham." Hy extended the duke's card—which was rather the worse for wear after riding around in her pocket—as grubby proof.

The functionary's brows shot up when he saw the card. "*You* are Mr. Hiram Bellamy?"

"Yes."

The transformation in the man was instant. "Ah, very good, sir. So sorry to keep you standing about. May I take your hat and coat?" he asked, so obsequious he was like another person entirely.

Soon Hy was following the servant through a series of interconnected rooms, where men were eating, talking, arguing, drinking, playing cards, and a few were even trying to read, although why they'd come to such a noisy place to do so was beyond her.

The servant led her to a room on the second floor and opened the door without knocking. Inside was a large round table with only one chair vacant. There were no whores draped over the players and the furniture was plain but of excellent quality, the well-insulated walls giving the small room a hushed feel even though the house below was crowded and raucous.

The duke glanced up from his deal and gave her a faint smile and nod.

Hy took the only seat—right beside Chatham—and watched quietly.

The play was fast and fierce and nobody spoke until after the duke had dealt out the final hand.

"Bloody hell," Fowler grumbled, glaring at the duke. He'd lost for the third time since Hy had been sitting there. When Chatham ignored him, the big Scot turned to scowl at Hy, although she'd not said a word. "Well, look who is here. As if *His Grace* with his revolting string of luck isn't bad enough, now *you've* come to drive in the final coffin nail, eh?"

Once again Hy considered telling the man that luck had nothing to do with it but decided to keep her mouth shut.

The duke ignored Fowler's complaining and said, "Something to drink, Bellamy?"

"Bellamy?" one of the other players—a nattily dressed young man who'd lost spectacularly on every hand thus far—said, scrutinizing Hy. "Any relation to Lady Selina Bellamy?"

"Never heard of her," Hy muttered.

"You live under a stone?" another young buck asked, causing the others—except for the duke and Fowler—to laugh. "She's the most beautiful woman in London."

Hy said nothing, hoping not to prolong the conversation as her sister's reaction to being the subject of gaming hell gossip was still fresh in her mind.

"I had the most astonishing dream about Lady Selina the other—"

The table shook and all the glassware, cards, and counters slid to one end.

Everyone yelled at once, but Fowler's voice was the loudest.

The baron had lunged to his feet—his big body taking the table with him—and his finger was jabbing into the chest of the young man who'd been about to share his dream. "You show some *respect*. That young woman is a *lady*, not some whore whose name is to be bandied about in the telling of your perverted fantasies!"

The room was quiet except for the sound of some broken glass rattling on the wooden floor.

The duke turned to Hy. "Something to drink?" he repeated, as if his friend hadn't just upended the table.

She swallowed and met the wide-eyed waiter's stare. "Er, brandy, please."

***

The players threw in their cards, every single one of them glaring at Hiram Bellamy.

Sylvester would have been irked at how much he'd lost to the woman if he'd not enjoyed watching her thrash the table full of young bucks so soundly. It was a damned shame they would never know they'd been routed by a female.

For his part, he'd enjoyed the thrashing a great deal. Watching her play was better than looking at fine paintings, enjoying a good opera, or listening to the best symphony.

The bell rang for supper and five of the eight players shoved back their chairs and moved toward the door. Only Sylvester, Fowler, and Hiram—or whatever her name was—remained.

The Scot shoved a huge hand through his already wild ginger hair. "Christ that was a bloody slaughter." He narrowed his hard green eyes at

Hiram. "And *you*, you little bastard. I know you're countin' into those decks. How many can you remember?"

Hiram shrugged her narrow shoulders, her eyes wary.

Fowler snorted when she didn't answer. "You'd best stay out of Jensen's place, lad. He'll not be amused by your little parlor trick."

Sylvester had been thinking the very same thing all evening as he'd watched her decimate and dominate the table. She'd received bad cards just like everyone else, but her bidding was always the product of mathematics rather than emotion. She'd lost hands, but she'd never lost big. A compendious memory combined with icy reserve and a genuine understanding of strategy made her the most formidable adversary he'd ever played against.

Fowler shoved up out of his chair. "I'm done in, Chatham."

"You off to Bristol tomorrow?"

"Aye, but it will be a quick visit."

Sylvester knew exactly why the other man didn't care to leave the city at this point in the Season. It was the same reason he'd nearly pounded Viscount Stonebrook into a bloody pulp when the younger man had mentioned having a dream about Lady Selina Bellamy. Poor Fowler was about as smitten as it was possible for a man to be.

The cranky Scot pointed a thick finger at Hiram. "When I return, I'll come lookin' for you and I'll get my money back."

Hiram pushed up her glasses. "You can always try, sir."

Fowler gave a bark of genuinely amused laughter and left them alone.

Chatham turned to the woman who'd fooled at least six men into believing she was a man for the last few hours. He nodded at the counters neatly stacked in front of her. "A good night's work."

She swallowed, her eyes drifting to her loot and then back to Sylvester. "Thank you for inviting me." She cleared her throat and said, "I suppose I should be going."

"But it's not even two o'clock."

"Er—"

"The night is still young. I hope you are not wanting to go home already?"

"Er... What did you have in mind, sir?"

Sylvester knew he was behaving badly, but he couldn't stop himself. Rather than just confront her with what he knew—which would end his enjoyment in an instant—the devil on his shoulder wanted *her* to be the one to confess.

"Come with me," Sylvester said. "I know a place you will enjoy."

Hiram trotted behind him down the stairs and through the main room—where the players at the Macao table were so loud you could probably hear them all the way at the other end of Piccadilly—and she followed him into the foyer where Chance, the pompous, overbearing oaf, was loudly hectoring an unfortunate subordinate but broke off his harangue and came rushing over when he saw Sylvester.

"Your Grace, please let me summon your carriage. I'm afraid nobody told me you'd—"

"I don't need it, Chance. But you could fetch mine and Mr. Bellamy's things, please."

"Oh! Of course, Your Grace." He all but sprinted toward the cloak room.

"Er, Your Grace?" Hiram murmured.

"Yes?"

"I should probably go—"

"Nonsense. You're a strapping lad in his prime. If you can't keep up with an old gaffer like me, I'm going to be concerned about you, Hiram."

Before Hiram could respond to that, Chance arrived laden with hats, cloaks, and Sylvester's walking stick.

Once they were accoutered, Sylvester ushered Hiram out the door. "We'll walk to our destination, it is just ahead at the cross street. Ah, what a lovely evening," he murmured when Hiram opened her mouth—doubtless to beg off again. Sylvester strode ahead briskly so his companion was forced to trot to keep up.

"Your Grace?"

"You are in for a treat, Hiram. It is unfortunate Fowler was in such a *foul* mood or he would have enjoyed joining us."

"I should probably—"

"I'm afraid Fowler isn't nearly as diverted by your ability to count into two decks as I am, Hiram. By the by, how many *can* you remember?"

"Er, I've never tried past four, sir."

Sylvester stopped and turned to stare at her. "Four! Good Lord, but that's impressive."

She shrugged, but her whiskerless cheeks flushed at the compliment.

Sylvester resumed walking and she hurried to keep up. "Um, Your Grace, where are—"

"Ah, here we are," Sylvester said, stopping in front of an unremarkable white house and opening the door. "After you, Hiram."

The masquerading little liar blinked at him through her thick glasses, the lenses magnifying her eyes ludicrously large. She moistened that wicked lower lip of hers and then glanced into the foyer of the house, which was just as unremarkable as the outside, and then back at him. "Is this a brothel, sir?"

"Indeed it is," Sylvester said, relieved that she'd known what sort of place this was and that he'd not been taunting a complete innocent.

And thank God for that, because if she'd been oblivious, then he would have had to cut his amusement short and take her home.

Part of him knew that is what he should do regardless of how experienced she was. *Tell me the truth and we'll turn around*, he silently urged.

But instead of running in the other direction, she gave him a look that was pugnacious rather than terrified and strode confidently into the foyer of the whorehouse, surprising Sylvester yet again.

Not to mention stoking his curiosity to dangerously high levels.

Chapter 10

Hy's body seemed to be in the thrall of some invisible force. She had suspected all along where the duke was taking her—where else would men go at this time of night—and yet she seemed incapable of taking her leave. -

Hy had won a breathtaking amount of money tonight. Not everything she needed, of course, but enough that she'd not need to carry on with her plan for as long as she had formerly believed. Indeed, it would take only five or six more nights at the Pigeonhole and then she could pay off both the interest on her father's *and* afford a cottage and nurse for Charles. There might even be some left over to pay her own expenses for a few months.

She didn't have to go into this brothel. Nor did she need to keep lying to the duke. He couldn't stop her from gambling at public hells in London. She should just take her leave—insist on it—and they could go their separate ways.

But no. Here she was, walking right into a den of iniquity. And now there was a woman coming toward them.

"Good evening, Your Grace," the woman said, her voice and person far more refined than Hy would have expected from a brothel employee.

"Good evening, Mrs. Dryden. As you see, I've brought a friend—Mr. Bellamy—along with me this evening. Hiram, this is Mrs. Dryden, the owner of this establishment.

Hy felt as if she were watching herself from outside her own body as she bowed over the older woman's hand and murmured, "Pleased to make your acquaintance, ma'am."

"Welcome to Avery House, Mr. Bellamy." The madam turned to the duke. "Would you like your usual room and companion, Your Grace?"

His usual room and companion? Hy's mind reeled at the implications of the woman's question. His Grace of Chatham came to this place to engage in sexual relations often enough to have a *usual* room and companion?

Why was that thought so… titillating?

The duke looked at Hy—almost as if he could see into her head—and smiled in a way that only added to the chaos swirling inside her. "Let's get my friend situated before I make any plans, Mrs. Dryden."

"Of course, of course. Right this way, gentlemen."

They followed the elegantly clad madam up a flight of marble stairs and into a drawing room. There were women working at stitchery and reading and one playing an actual spinet.

When Hy, the duke, and Mrs. Dryden entered, they all looked up and smiled.

The duke leaned close and said in a low voice, "Whatever your preference is Hiram, Mrs. Dryden can satisfy it."

"Um, preference?"

"Yes—physical or sexual preference. Do you like your women to be voluptuous? Thin? Light-haired or dark? Aggressive or submissive?"

Hy's gaze flickered over the women who were all turned their way, their smiles pleasant and welcoming. "Er—"

"Or perhaps you'd like Mrs. Dryden to recommend someone for you?" The duke smiled, showing those pointy canine teeth. "Or perhaps *I* might—"

"No."

"I beg your pardon?"

"Er, as it turns out, I'm not feeling particularly, um, energetic this evening." She'd been mad to indulge her curiosity this far. It was time to leave.

The duke's eyebrow arched. "Indeed? So you are looking for something a bit less… strenuous, then?"

Hy opened her mouth to say she was going home, but the smile that slowly spread across the duke's face froze the words in her throat.

"Do you like to watch, Hiram?"

"Watch?" she repeated dumbly.

The duke nodded, as if he were agreeing with something she'd said. "Yes, that might suit me, as well, tonight. Do you mind if I join you, Hiram?"

Things seemed to be moving quickly and in an unexpected direction. "Er, join me?" she repeated, her voice cracking on the second word.

But the duke wasn't looking at her. Instead, he'd turned to the madam. "By chance is there anything of interest in the blue rooms, Mrs. Dryden?"

Hyacinth

"As a matter of fact, tonight is an excellent evening as all five are occupied. I would recommend rooms one and four, Your Grace."

"Your recommendation always ends in my pleasure, Mrs. Dryden."

The two chuckled and then Chatham headed back toward the stairs and tossed over his shoulder, "Come with me, Hiram."

"Where are we going, Your Grace," Hy asked when she caught up with him.

Chatham smirked at her. "I would hate to spoil the surprise, Hiram."

***

Sylvester could scarcely believe the woman. Just what would it take for *Hiram* to confess the truth? What in the world would she do if she ended up in a room with a prostitute?

She'd been so sanguine entering the building that he'd wondered if maybe he and Tackle had been wrong, and Hiram *was* a male.

Or if not wrong, then perhaps he was mistaken about her age. Maybe she was older than what she'd claimed. Maybe her wide-eyed looks were an act and she was a more hardened card sharp who was playing *Sylvester* rather than the other way around.

He had to admit that last thought had rankled.

But her expression of surprise upon seeing all the ladies had put paid to that suspicion. Whoever she was, she was not entirely innocent, nor was she jaded.

Her accent was that of Sylvester's own class, as were her manners. But *ton* ladies did not dress up as men and play cards in dangerous hells.

Who the devil was she? And what was she up to?

If you weren't such a deviant swine you could just ask her, a voice whispered inside his head.

Where would be the fun in that? He smirked as he led the way up the stairs.

Once they reached the uppermost floor Sylvester strode toward the second door on the right. He was not as enamored of watching others engage in sex as some men he knew, but he had no reservations when it came to a bit of consensual voyeurism. And he suspected it would be just the thing to jar some answers out of his mysterious companion.

He raised a finger to his lips in the universal *hush* sign, opened the door, ushered Hiram into the tiny vestibule, and then shut the door, plunging them into utter darkness for a moment before he slid aside a heavy black velvet curtain.

"The curtain is to block the light from the corridor. Go ahead and step inside," he whispered, letting the curtain fall behind them.

Mrs. Dryden had created what punters irreverently called her "peek-a-boo" rooms by partitioning off a narrow slice of each chamber. It was only wide enough for the settee that had been placed in front of a foot high, three-foot-long piece of glass. On the other side of the glass was a bedroom. There was enough light in the other room so that those lurking in the narrow chamber could watch what occurred. But the chamber itself was dark so that the lovers in the other room could not be distracted by movement on the other side of the glass.

Sylvester smirked when he saw the spectacle playing out in the tastefully decorated bedchamber.

Hiram stood rooted to the floor, facing the glass.

"Come and sit down, Hiram."

She jolted slightly at the sound of his whisper but obeyed, never taking her gaze from the scene beyond the glass.

Mrs. Dryden knew Sylvester's tastes well. The man in the other room was clothed in shirtsleeves, breeches, and a loo mask, but the woman was naked. She knelt in the middle of the bed, wrists bound over her head to a hook in the ceiling, her knees spread and bottom canted invitingly.

The man had mounted her from behind and was giving her a vigorous fucking that both parties were vociferously enjoying.

The way the man occasionally glanced toward the glass told Sylvester he was enjoying watching himself perform in the mirror-like reflection. And well he should; he was a handsome male animal, fit, and—from what Sylvester could see—respectably endowed.

But Sylvester wasn't interested in the couple; he was interested in his companion.

Once his eyes had adjusted to the dimness—the room wasn't utterly dark thanks to the light from the larger room—Sylvester studied the woman beside him.

Hiram's lips were parted and she was leaning forward, entranced, rather than revolted or shocked.

Once again, this was not the reaction of a maiden—but neither was it that of a terribly experienced woman, either.

Sylvester was impressed—and not a little frustrated—by her tenacity. What would it take to make her confess her secret?

Perhaps a little more prodding from him…

"Was this what you had in mind, Hiram?" he murmured against her temple, again making her jump. She smelled like pomade and soap and the faintly salty tang of female sweat.

Sylvester was possessed by the strongest desire to lick her sharp jaw.

Instead, he said, "Are you picturing yourself in that room, riding her hard, Hiram?"

Her chest, which had been rising and falling quickly, froze. "Er—"

"It's natural to get excited. There's no rule against mounting a corporal and four, lad."

Hiram visibly wrenched her gaze away from the window to turn to him, her brow furrowed. "I don't—what is a corporal and four, Your Grace?"

Sylvester almost laughed aloud at Hiram's perplexity at a phase that was employed by every schoolboy in the nation at one point or other, no matter their social status.

"You've not heard term that before?"

Hiram shook her head.

If Sylvester had needed any further proof that *he* was a *she*, this was it.

"How about boxing the Jesuit? Fetch mettle?" he paused and then added, "Toss one off?"

Her jaw sagged as she finally encountered a phrase that she knew. It was the first time he'd seen a strong emotion on her normally unreadable face: surprise.

"I'm feeling a bit randy myself," Sylvester whispered, his voice choked with suppressed mirth at her expression of shock. "You don't mind if I"—he deliberately reached for his placket.

She gasped. "Please don't, Your Grace. Please stop." Her voice was not nearly as low as it usually was.

Sylvester lifted his hand off his undeniably tented breeches and hissed in her ear. "I'll stop, but only if you tell me who the devil you are and why you're running about in men's clothing, *Hiram*."

Chapter 11

The duke's accusation was not nearly as shocking as what he'd been about to do.

Mount a corporal and four. Now that Hy knew what the phrase meant, she could visualize it.

Would the duke really have masturbated in that room beside her? She had to grit her teeth against the distracting tightening in her sex that the image caused. Just thinking of such a man pleasuring himself was enough to make her woozy.

"Well?" he demanded quietly.

"Er, you know I'm a woman?" she asked stupidly.

He gave her a withering look and closed a hand around her upper arm. "Come along now."

Hy didn't immediately obey. "Where are we going?"

"I thought we might go somewhere we could converse more normally." He gestured to the window, to where the man was still thrusting into the woman's body, using one of his hands to stroke her clitoris and the other to swat her bottom in between thrusts.

The pair had grown increasingly noisy and Hy was fascinated to discover that people shouted so loudly. She had always been rather quiet, herself.

The duke pulled her closer. "Unless you wanted to stay and watch until they're finished, *Hiram*?"

Her face heated fiercely, even though he couldn't see her in the low light. To own the truth, she'd found the show beyond the glass both arousing and fascinating and would have liked to stay. But even Hy—with her rampant curiosity about sexual matters—would find the situation uncomfortable now that Chatham knew her gender.

Hy stood and the duke all but frog marched her back down to the foyer, where the madam was conversing with a pretty girl who looked nothing like the prostitutes Hy had seen in other parts of the city. Indeed,

Hyacinth

none of the women in the house looked like the desperate creatures who called to men from sordid alleyways outside some of the gambling hells.

If the madam was surprised that they were finished so quickly she didn't show it.

Instead, she dropped another of her graceful curtseys, sent the girl to fetch their things from the cloakroom, and said, "I hope you've enjoyed your time with us, Your Grace, Mr. Bellamy."

"Indeed, we did, Mrs. Dryden," the duke said, his hand heavy on Hy's shoulder, as if he suspected she might run off. "It was most... enlightening. I hate to rush off like this but Mr. Bellamy has just recalled an engagement he'd forgotten."

"Ah, that is unfortunate. Well, I hope we see you both again, soon."

The duke nodded and escorted Hy from the building.

"Don't you have to pay for that sort of thing?" Hy asked.

"I'm not interested in answering your questions about brothel etiquette. Who are you, *Hiram*?"

She cleared her throat and spun the tale she'd hastily concocted in the last few minutes. "Hiram is my brother's name. My name is Mary. Mary Dower."

Dower was the name of the stable master at her aunt's house. He had large quarters above the carriage house and lived there with his ailing wife, and daughter—Mary—who took care of her mother and did odd jobs around her aunt's house.

Chatham frowned. "Mary Dower?"

"Yes." It would take some effort to remember to answer to a strange name, but then she didn't anticipate having to do so for very long as the duke was unlikely to keep playing with her after tonight.

For some reason, she felt a pang of disappointment at that thought.

"How did you discover I wasn't a man?" she asked.

His lips twisted into that feral smile. "Your disguise isn't as good as you think it is."

"What gave me away?"

"I'm not finished with my questions," he said sharply. "Just what the devil are you up to with your masquerade, Miss Mary Dower?"

Hy shrugged. "I like to play cards."

"There are hells in the city that accommodate women players."

"Yes, but they don't play deep. Also, they rarely play the games I like."

"Too many games that rely on chance?" he guessed.

She nodded.

"You say you have a brother—where is he? Why doesn't he accompany you?"

"He is... hiding."

"Hiding?"

"He owes a great deal of money. That is why I've been playing by myself—to pay off his debt." In a way, it was true.

"He could at least escort you about. If he'd been with you the other night, it's unlikely you would have been robbed."

"He cannot be seen; he owes too many people." Hy's father always hid in his study whenever any dunning agents haunted the grounds of their small country home.

"Surely he knows how dangerous this is for you?"

"He does. That's why he's made a bargain with a hackney driver."

He gave a noncommittal snort at that. "Don't you have anyone else to help you? I suppose that story you told me about being raised by your aunt and uncle was just that—a story?"

"No, I am staying with my aunt and uncle at present, taking care of my aunt during the day. My uncle is Viscount Fitzroy's stablemaster."

"Your aunt and uncle are servants?" he repeated in obvious disbelief. "You don't speak like any servant I've ever heard, Mary."

Hy had thought of that, too. "My father was a vicar's son—although his family cast him off when they learned about his gambling—and my mother was a governess before she married my father."

Her parents had once employed a governess who'd spoken with more clipped, crystalline clear accents than anyone in Hy's family.

"A governess," he repeated, sounding bemused.

"Yes. And she was very insistent that we learn to speak properly."

"Where are your parents?"

"They are no longer with us." That was not a lie, exactly.

"Why did you choose the name Bellamy?"

"Lady Selina Bellamy is Lady Fitzroy's niece and she is staying with them, so the name just came to mind."

The duke fixed her with a hard look. "Why do I feel less than convinced by your tale?"

Hy shrugged.

They'd arrived back at Weller's and the duke stopped and gestured to the servant hovering outside the door. The man must have recognized him because he took off at a trot to fetch the carriage.

Hyacinth

Chatham turned to Hy, the damaged half of his face in shadow, and gave her a pensive, rather than skeptical look, his dark gaze too probing to be comfortable. "How much money do you need for your brother?"

"A great deal."

The duke scowled. "How. Much."

Hy had a very slow to rouse temper, but Chatham was beginning to wake it. "That is not your affair, Your Grace."

For a moment, he looked stunned—as if nobody had ever denied him anything—but then he gave a dry chuckle. "I suppose you have the right of it. Still, you seem quite young to be managing all this by yourself. How old are you really."

"I didn't lie about my age. I'll be three-and-twenty on my next birthday. I know I look younger than that, but I promise you that is the truth."

His coach rolled up just then and his footman leapt off the back, flipped down the steps, and opened the door.

The duke nodded for her to go first and Hy settled inside.

"I gather you want to go to Fitzroy's house?" the duke asked before climbing in after her.

"Er, the street behind would be better, Your Grace. My aunt and uncle don't know that I sneak away at night."

"No, I'll wager they don't," the duke muttered.

***

Sylvester had to remind himself that the woman—that *Mary*—had been correct when she'd said her debt and how she chose to settle it was not his affair.

And yet he disliked the thought of her wandering around the seamier parts of the city by herself. After all, she'd already been robbed once.

She doesn't want your help, Sylvester. And you want something more than to be a Good Samaritan. Do not lie to yourself.

The thought startled him and he stared at the woman across from him.

She was certainly… riveting. There was something about her that drew his gaze again and again; it was more than just her appearance.

Her only real claim to beauty were her eyes, which were a striking blue green. But they were not the eyes of a lover—not the sort that were easy or comfortable to gaze into. Rather, her gaze was direct and dispassionate, he'd even go so far as to say emotionless. Not that he thought she was cruel, but she was... removed, distant, and reserved.

And for some inexplicable reason, her air of reserve appealed to him.

She is appealing because you are bored with empty flattery from women who are only interested in your title and wealth.

That was entirely possible.

You do realize you are harboring inappropriate thoughts about the niece of a stablemaster and the daughter of a governess?

Yes, he knew that thought should have shamed him, or at least embarrassed him, but it didn't.

When Sylvester had been a younger man he'd believed—like most of the *ton*—that the lower orders were inferior to his own. His father and mother and the teachers at Eton had inculcated him thoroughly, until he'd believed that his very blood made him superior and suited to ruling.

But then he had spent six years in the army, where many of the soldiers who'd served beneath him had been smart, able, and honorable—oftentimes more so than his fellow officers.

And then there was the fact that his best friend was the son of a dairymaid.

So, no. Sylvester no longer believed he was inherently superior. And certainly not to a woman who was as well-spoken and clever as this one.

"You were not terribly shocked by what went on at Mrs. Dryden's establishment," he said.

She considered his question—and he thought perhaps her cheeks might have pinkened a little—but she did not simper or exhibit outrage. "I have never been inside a brothel but that does not mean that I am ignorant of what goes on between a man and a woman."

She held his gaze in a way that stirred him. Why was he aroused by this woman? Not only was she sitting before him in men's clothing, but she was the antithesis of everything he normally wanted in a female. She was thin to the point of gauntness and uncommunicative to the point of muteness. She did not flirt or laugh or even smile. And yet sitting beside such a seemingly emotionless creature in that dark peek-a-boo room—and watching the effect of the erotic show on her normally impassive features—had been wildly arousing.

And she's not desperate to please you, as is every other woman you encounter.

Hyacinth

Yes, there was certainly truth in that. Sylvester had grown so accustomed to being truckled to, that anyone—male or female—who didn't fawn over him was not only unusual, they were also intriguing.

Sylvester shoved his thoughts aside, not caring to dwell on his body's reaction to her just then. Instead, he asked, "What will you do after you've paid off your brother's debts?"

"What do you mean?"

"Will you continue to play in places like Jensen's?"

"I daresay I will travel—play in various cities."

"Alone?"

"No, with my brother. That was our plan when we were younger."

"You think to make a living off gambling? What makes you believe your brother's luck will be any better somewhere else?"

Her lips twisted slightly and she cut him a look of indulgent scorn. "I don't believe in luck. As for Hiram? He has learned his lesson. He will play with more circumspection in the future."

Sylvester wanted to tell her that gamblers didn't change their ways any more than leopards changed their spots, but he doubted she would listen.

"I can loan you the money you need. It wouldn't be charity," he said. "You would have to pay me back, but you could do it at a more gradual rate."

Rather than answer, she just stared.

Sylvester shifted in his seat under her detached, analytical gaze.

"Why would you do that?"

Her question made him even more uncomfortable, especially as he wasn't sure *why* he'd make such an offer.

"Because it is not safe for you to continue as you are. Even with a driver," he added before she could mention it. "Where was he the other night, when I drove you home?"

"You heard the porter at Jensen's. He had a—"

"No, he did not have a bad wheel. I paid him not to collect you that night."

"You *paid* him?"

"Yes."

"Why?"

"What does it matter?" he asked. "It just goes to show the man will take money to leave you stranded somewhere."

She opened her mouth, but then closed it, her anger shifting to resignation. "You are right," she finally said. "Somebody else might have paid him—somebody with unsavory motives."

Sylvester had the grace to blush a little, even though her words were not pointed. It was true that his motives—while not unsavory—were not precisely innocent, either.

"So, you see, your position is dangerous, Mary. You should take the loan I am offering and then you and your brother should leave London immediately."

"And you would trust me to repay you?"

"I would."

"But you don't know me."

"I think I know enough. You care for your brother. You do not cheat." It was his turn to shrug. "I believe you to be a woman of your word."

He saw some emotion flicker over her face but could not decipher it as it was gone so fast.

"That is generous of you, Your Grace. And kind. But I will continue the way I have—if you will not expose me, that is."

Sylvester almost laughed. Mary Dower was a genius when it came to cards but a babe in the woods when it came to people. She had just given him his trump card without even realizing it.

What are you doing, Sylvester? a voice whispered inside him. *You are bored and looking for someone to alleviate that condition. This is not wise.*

No, it wasn't wise. But neither was it especially *un*wise. Who would care if he was ever discovered to be visiting gambling hells in the presence of a female garbed as a man? It might be cruel to say her reputation did not matter, but it was the truth. She was not of the *ton*. If she faced exposure, the worst that would happen was that she'd be barred from gambling in her old haunts. That would actually be a blessing as Sylvester did not like thinking of her going to places like Cox's or the Pigeonhole alone.

What he was about to say would be a way to protect her.

And to get what you want, as well...

He shrugged off the thought and said, "I will not expose you."

Her lips curved into a faint and rather startled smile. "Then—"

"As long as you agree to only go about in my company," Sylvester heard himself say.

Hyacinth

For once, he could recognize the emotion that seized control of her impassive features. It was surprise.

It was certainly no greater than Sylvester's own.

Chapter 12

Hy pulled the drab grey cloak around herself and stepped from the hackney she'd taken from the hushed streets of Mayfair to the bustle of Bread Street and Cheapside.

It was like stepping into another world and the streets seethed with people and horses and conveyances of all types. Narrow shopfronts jostled with one another, vying for attention: a glover, an horologist, a chandler, a booksellers—all crowded together, tightly packed side-by-side like bolts of fabric in a dressmaker's shop. And, yes, there was one of those, too.

Hy's destination was a brown brick building with gold and black lettering on the front window that said: *Garrett's Bookshop*.

When Hy pulled open the heavy door her senses were immediately narcotized by the smell and sight of books: hundreds and hundreds of books.

The shop was empty, except for Mr. Garrett, who was sitting in the back corner, bent over a small desk on which a fat ledger sat.

"Mr. Garrett?"

His head jerked up and his faded blue eyes told her he'd been somewhere far away. A slow, genuine smile took over his worn features. "Ah, Lady Hyacinth."

"Good afternoon, sir."

The bespectacled old man was a good eight inches shorter than Hy's nearly six feet and his curly gray head came just to her shoulder. They regarded each other through thick glasses, his split to accommodate his vision.

"Charles will be so glad to see you today, my lady."

Hy nodded, wishing to be done with social pleasantries.

He smiled up at her, no doubt reading her mind easily after years spent with his equally reserved grandson, although Charles was far more adept at blending into social situations, than Hy. After all, Charles was the one who'd taught Hy how to *fit in*.

Hyacinth

Mr. Garrett pushed aside the heavy curtain that separated his shop from his storeroom. "Come, I'll take you up."

"You needn't do that—I know where to find him," she said, not wanting to waste any of her precious time with Charles, which is what would happen if his grandfather sat with them.

"Of course, my dear."

"But I wanted to give this to you." She took the paper-wrapped packet from her reticule and handed it to him.

"What is it?"

But Hy could tell by his suspicious expression that he'd already guessed.

"Please," Hy said, when he did not reach out to take it. "You know Charles will not accept it if I offer it to him."

The old man's cheeks flushed and Hy suddenly realized that her abrupt behavior had shamed or embarrassed him. But that could not be helped; Charles was more important than anyone's pride.

"Please," she repeated.

He grimaced but took the packet. "I should not need anyone else's money to take care of my own grandson."

"Please don't allow pride to keep him in London, sir."

Mr. Garrett's flush deepened. "No, of course I won't."

"There should be enough that he can engage a nurse and a small cottage at the seaside." Her face heated under his grateful stare. "A *very* small cottage," she added, but her attempt at humor fell flat, just as they always did.

He took her hand and bowed over it, squeezing it so tightly her bones shifted. "Thank you, my lady. This is most generous."

Hy squirmed at his gratitude. "If it is not enough, I can bring more."

"I'm sure it will be ample. It will take a little time, but I will arrange it."

"How has he been?" she asked, even though she hated to do so. But Charles would lie to her and tell her he was better. He always did.

"He is not better, but neither is he worse. Much."

She nodded, unsurprised by his words. "I will show myself up."

The second floor of the bookshop was given over to more books and a small binding operation and the Garretts lived on the third.

Every tread on the stairs had books piled in stacks along the side, leaving only enough room for one person to walk, and even then, the person could not be very large. As far as Hy was concerned, the house was perfect; she would love to live surrounded by books.

There were three doors on the landing and she went to the farthest one and gave a soft rap.

"Yes?"

Walking into the apartment always made Hy smile—it was almost an extension of the bookshop, with hundreds of books piled on every surface, including the floor.

Charles was balancing one book on his lap and had another open on the table beside his chair and did not look up when Hy entered.

"I'm afraid Grandfather has spilled India ink on another of his coats, Mrs. Hessel. It is in with the other laundry."

Hy felt her mouth pulling into a smile because something about Charles always made her smile.

"Good afternoon, Charles."

His head whipped up and his expression of surprise was rapidly replaced by one of pleasure. "Hy!"

"Please, don't get up, Charles," she said when he began to struggle to his feet.

He grinned and slumped back down, breathing heavily even from that tiny bit of exertion. "What a cad I am, not standing for a lady."

Hy rolled her eyes and lowered herself into the old wingback chair across from him, its worn bottle-green leather as soft as butter.

Charles placed a marker in his book before closing it. "Although I am delighted to see you Hy, you should not have come. If anyone were to see you here it would destroy your reputation. You promised me the last time that—"

"I have met somebody." Hy pulled off her gloves, removed her bonnet, and set aside her reticule while waiting for her friend's reaction.

Charles's jaw dropped in a manner that was both satisfying and insulting. He was so openly *amazed* that she would meet a man. Well, to be honest, it still amazed Hy, as well.

"Is it—er, well, are you going to get married?"

Hy gave a bark of laughter. "You are such a romantic, Charles. There will be no marriage. The man is a peer who believes I am the niece of my Aunt Fitzroy's stablemaster."

Charles snorted. "He must be rather dim-witted if he believes you to be of the servant class—not with *your* accent." While Charles spoke properly, he sounded more like the son of a City banker than anyone you'd meet at a *ton* function.

"Oh, he is clever enough—too clever, in fact. But I am a very inventive liar and I told him that my father was the cast-off son of a vicar and my mother was a governess."

Charles chuckled. "I take it you had that horrid governess of yours in mind when you made up that story." His brow furrowed. "Blast, what was her name again?"

"The aptly named Miss Boil."

"Yes, her—the one who spoke like she was a duchess, but the *royal* kind."

"Just so," Hy said.

"So, a peer, hmm? And how in the world did this come about—don't tell me you met him at a ball?"

"Lord, no. I met him in a gambling hell."

"He saw through your disguise?" Charles guessed with an annoying smirk.

"He is the only one who has."

"Which just goes to prove how stupid a great many men are."

Hy shrugged. "One can scarcely blame them, Charles, since I look more like a man than a woman and I am almost six feet tall."

Charles made an irritated growling sound. "You do *not* look more like a man than a woman. But I can see from the mulish glint in your eyes that you don't wish to hear anything of that nature from me."

"No." Hy had listened to Charles about her appearance too many times. He lacked objectivity on the subject because he liked her. And it was common knowledge that people often grew more attractive upon further acquaintance if you liked them. Conversely, handsome people sometimes grew *less* attractive. The duke's cousin, Shelton, was a prime example of that phenomenon.

"Oh, before I forget," Charles said, gesturing to a familiar green leather book on his desk. "I was going to send that to your aunt's house by messenger"—he pulled an amused face— "suitably wrapped, of course, but now that you are here, you should take it with you."

Hy stared. "But it is yours, Charles."

"I'm giving it to you."

"But—"

"It is my hope that you will get more use out of it than I will—especially now that you have this aristocratic lover."

"I don't *have* him."

"You will, Hy."

She was pleased that one of them was optimistic for her.

"Now, take it," he said. "You will have to find a good hiding place for it."

Hy could not argue with him—not when he looked so... weary.

Instead, she went to fetch the familiar book. When she sat down, she flicked through it, smiling at the memories some of the illustrations evoked.

"I was looking at it the other day and it made me smile, too," Charles said.

Hy paused on one of her favorite plates. "I remember this."

Charles leaned toward her, and she tilted the book so he could see the drawing she meant.

His alabaster cheeks stained with color. "Ah, yes, as do I. Perhaps, one day, you will finish the rest of them."

"But it is *your* book." Hy stared at her friend and erstwhile lover.

"Please, Hy." Charles heaved a sigh. "Don't do what everyone else does. Don't try and reassure me that I shall be my old self again. I am dying, albeit slowly. Arguing about that patently obvious fact only makes me tired. That book is one of my favorite possessions and I want to make sure you have it."

Hy held his sky-blue gaze for a moment, and then nodded. "Thank you. You know I will treasure it."

"It is my *hope* that you will consult it often."

Hy carefully closed the delicate old book. "That is actually part of the reason I've come today, Charles. I need your help."

"You know I'll do anything for you I can." He brushed a stray lock of over-long blond hair from his forehead and sat back in his chair, a spark of interest lighting up his tired eyes.

Even as Hy made a better man, Charles would have made a very pretty woman. Especially now, with his illness making him far more delicate than he'd looked when they'd first met, when he'd still been slim and sleek, but also healthy and vibrant.

"So, tell me, Hy, are you going to take a *lover*?" His full lips pulled into a slow smile, his eyes crinkling at the corners.

The wicked emphasis he put on the word *lover* made her blush. But then Charles was an expert at making her blush, for all that he looked like an angel.

Hyacinth

He laughed when she just narrowed her eyes at his teasing. "Tell me, who is the lucky man—and you know that I *mean* that, Hy."

Yes, she did know Charles meant that. Of all the people in her life, he valued her most. Oh, her sisters and brother cared deeply for her, but only Charles really *knew* her.

"The Duke of Chatham."

His eyes widened until they threatened to pop out of his head. "Chatham?"

"You've heard of him?"

"I'm ill, not dead."

"What have you heard?"

"He is a highly decorated army officer, a vigorous proponent of some rather progressive labor legislation—"

Hy didn't know about that. "Like what?"

"Hour limitations, age restrictions, that sort of thing." He smiled wryly. "Things decent human beings should do without laws being necessary."

"What else," Hy prodded.

Charles gave her an appraising look. "I know *of* him—and not just what I've read in the papers."

"Bad things?"

He snorted. "I would warn you if I knew of anything like that."

"Then *what*?"

"I saw him at one of the places I used to frequent."

"You mean a birching house?"

"Yes."

Well, *that* was interesting. Although Hy wasn't especially surprised to hear that Chatham enjoyed such things, especially given their brief foray to Mrs. Dryden's peek-a-boo room.

"You don't look nearly as surprised as I thought you would. Did you already know about his proclivities?"

Hy felt a rare smile curving her mouth. "Would you like to hear an amusing tale?"

Charles leaned forward in his chair, his eyes lively with curiosity. "Oh dear, what have you done now, Hy?"

Five minutes later Charles was wiping the tears from his eyes. "Mounting a corporal and four," he repeated, chuckling.

"Oh, you can go ahead and laugh," she said, since he was doing exactly that, "but why did you never tell me that silly phrase?"

"I assumed you must have known it from all your association with post boys, grooms, and ostlers at the various inns you've frequented over the years."

"Somehow tossing one off hasn't come up in conversation as often as you seem to think it has."

Charles's laughter turned into coughing.

Hy watched her best friend suffer without offering assistance or fussing over him, neither of which he appreciated.

After a few, agonizing moments he dabbed his lips with a handkerchief, folded it before Hy could see if there was blood, and then tucked it into his pocket and smiled at her.

"Ah, I have not laughed this much since the last time you and I were together."

It made her feel good to give her friend such pleasure, even though she didn't find her own antics nearly so amusing. "Tell me what you know of Chatham?"

"I don't know a great deal other than he is—or was—a frequent visitor to Madam Savoy's."

Charles had told her about the specialized brothel, which he had enjoyed visiting back when he was well enough to do such things.

"Do you know what it is that he does there?" she asked.

"No. It is only by accident that I saw him leaving the building while I was entering." Charles hesitated, an unusual expression on his face.

"What is it, Charles?"

"Are you finally in love, Hy?"

"We have discussed *love* more times than I can count, Charles. I know you don't believe in it—or at least you've stated you've never felt it—why should you think I do?"

"Because as similar as we are, Hy, we are still very different." Charles paused to catch his breath, which seemed to escape him even when he was doing nothing more strenuous than talking.

It sent a chill down her spine: he was worse, so much worse than he'd been the last time she'd seen him—not long after she'd come to London. When he'd told her she must not visit again.

"It is wrong to say you don't believe in love, Hy. You *love* your family and want to save them." He gave her a tired smile. "You want to save me—I daresay you think you *love* me."

"I thought you were asking about romantic love, Charles. Obviously I feel very strongly about those I care about. But this is different." She grimaced. "If I had to name what I feel, it would be infatuation." An emotion she'd always felt superior for not succumbing to.

"That is a first, is it not?"

"It is," she admitted. Even when she and Charles had been lovers, she'd not thought of him as much as she now thought of the duke.

"Tell me a little about you and this duke, Hy. How did you meet?"

"We've been introduced several times at various social functions, but he never remembered me. Yet when he saw me as *Hiram*—"

"*Then* he remembered you," Charles guessed.

"Yes."

"So, how did it come about that he guessed your masquerade?"

Hy bit her lip, wondering if it would upset him too much to hear about the robbery.

"Whatever it is, you can tell me."

Hy snorted and gave him a wry look. "It is terrifying how easily you read me."

Charles just smiled.

"Fine, if you must know, I was robbed one night."

The humorous glint in his eyes faded instantly. "Did they—"

"No, the robbers didn't discover my secret. But they took all my money, my coat and hat, and my spectacles and left me standing in the middle of a dubious area in one of those terrible storms we've been having."

Charles clucked his tongue. "You really must be more careful, Hy."

"Don't worry, I no longer go out alone—but I shall get to that in a moment. That night, the duke saw me and gave me a ride. He insisted that I go to his house to clean my wounds—just some scrapes on my hands and knees," she said before he could ask. "Although His Grace didn't admit it, I'm sure it was his valet who guessed the truth."

"So, how many more times did you see him before the er, *corporal and four evening*?" Charles asked, grinning.

"Just one before he confronted me."

"What did he say?"

"To make a long discussion short, he made me a bargain. He said he'd not expose my secret if I agreed to only go gambling with him."

Charles chuckled. "I'm going to assume you took him up on that offer?"

"I had no other choice," she said, her face inexplicably heating.

Charles just smirked, rather than call out her shamefully weak lie. "So, have you seen him since?"

"Yes, we have gone out to hells three times."

"And nothing happened?"

Hy blinked, confused. "Yes, we played cards."

Charles rolled his eyes. "I meant nothing other than *cards* happened?"

"Oh, no, nothing else."

"You sound disappointed."

Hy scowled at him, but he just smiled.

"This is such progress, Hy."

"I don't see how you've come to that conclusion."

"I don't think you've realized how much you've changed since we first met, Hy. You almost never spoke—certainly not to strangers—you went out of your way to avoid being in situations where you'd be forced to socialize. You believed you'd never want to marry—"

"I still believe that," Hy interrupted.

Charles continued as if she'd not spoken, "—and you were so ashamed and terrified of your *unnatural urges*, as your mother called them, that you never would have welcomed feeling any interest in a man."

That was all true; she had changed a great deal, mostly thanks to Charles.

"I know all that. But what are you saying, Charles?"

"Although you've changed a great deal you still carry guilt, Hy. You need to stop thinking about yourself the way your mother would think. The sorts of things you enjoy—physical pleasure—are things that many men, and yes, even women, enjoy, although a great many of them would never admit to it. Women, especially, are taught to believe such needs or impulses are wicked or immoral."

Hy crossed her arms. "I assume there is a point to all this?"

"This is a new life for you, Hy. You aren't back in Little Sissingdon where everyone already has their opinion of you formed and fixed. This is London, one of the biggest cities in the world. You are mixing with wealthy strangers and beating them at their own game, are you not?"

"Sometimes."

"Approach this new life with an open mind, Hy. I know that as cold and emotionless as others might believe you, that you are capable of deep feeling—perhaps even love, although you refuse to believe that. The fact that you came here today tells me that you want more with Chatham—that you believe he might want more, too."

"I am... interested in him," she admitted. "But as to whether he wants anything from me? That I could not say. I believe he enjoys my company when it comes to playing cards."

"You said that he insisted you only go out with him?"

Hy nodded.

Charles chuckled and gave her a teasing smile. "Then *yes*, Hy, I'd hazard a guess that he likes *you*, not just the card games."

Hy felt a fluttering in her belly at his words but ignored it. "You must help me formulate a plan, Charles. I need to know what I should do. There should be steps." She reached into the oversized reticule she carried—which Selina called hideous and far too large—and brought out a small black book. "If you tell me what to do, I can—" Hy broke off at the sound of chuckling and glared at her friend. "Why are you laughing?"

"Because you think you can *plan* this sort of thing, Hy, and you cannot."

"You planned our meetings—right from the beginning."

"What you and I did—while not *wrong*—was rather, er, unusual, Hy. Don't you think? You can hardly say the things to him that I said to you."

Even Hy could see the humor in such a suggestion. "Clearly I am not going to tell a duke that I will initiate him into the amorous arts."

Charles laughed. "I am relieved I didn't have to explain that to you."

Hy looked down at the small black leather book she still clutched.

She heard the creak of a chair and then Charles's pale, slender fingers settled over her hand. "I am not mocking you, Hy."

"I know that. It's just—well, I feel silly. I am a woman grown and I cannot arrange a—a *tryst* without seeking your advice. You say I've become better over the years, but I feel just as ignorant, tentative, and awkward as ever, Charles."

He squeezed her hand. "When I met you, you could not bear the touch—or even meet the eyes—of another person. And now look at you."

Hy knew Charles was right. She could now bear touching from people and while she might flinch, she never just froze up—or, God forbid—became nauseated and woozy which is what had often happened before she'd begun her *training* with Charles.

Still, she was far from normal. She knew that from watching her sisters and seeing how they behaved.

Charles shifted in his chair and grimaced, as if his entire body ached.

Hy felt a sharp stab of guilt. "I'm sorry, Charles, I should not be bothering you with this when you are—"

"Hush," he murmured. "It is no bother to talk to my best friend."

Hy felt the same warmth in her belly that she'd felt the very first time Charles had said those words to her all those years ago. As strange as she was, Hy had never expected to have a friend, not to mention a *best* friend.

"As for feeling awkward and tentative," Charles continued. "You must realize that *everyone* feels that way when they are attracted to a person and uncertain of whether their regard is returned."

Hy worried her lower lip, trying to imagine her sister Selina being uncertain in such a situation. She couldn't.

"Are you sure about that, Charles?"

"I'm going to go out on a limb and state—without ample empirical data—that I am sure."

Hy smiled at that, which was a gentle dig at her and her need for proof before she was willing to believe something.

She lifted her hands. "So, what should I do?"

"What do you think you should do?"

She *hated* when Charles turned a question back on her. "I don't know."

"Why not simply tell him the truth of how you feel?"

Hy attempted to wrap her mind around that suggestion while studying her hands, which looked like a man's hands with their chewed short nails, calluses, cuts, and scars.

"You don't have to lay everything out all at once, Hy. But you should tell him a little about yourself."

"Tell him about me?" she repeated in disbelief. "So that he will know what a—a *freak* I am?"

Charles gave her a stern look.

"Fine, I'm not a freak," she said, not sure she believed it. "Couldn't I just pretend that I was normal?"

"You can do whatever you like."

Hy stared at her friend, waiting for the rest of it.

"But is that the way you want to commence your first liaison with a lover, Hy—by hiding who you are? By pretending?"

"I don't want to face his horror and disgust if I expose my inner workings to him."

Hyacinth

"I exposed my inner workings to you, not knowing how you would react," he reminded her, cocking an eyebrow. "And did you respond with horror and disgust?"

"No. But you must have had *some* degree of anxiety."

"I was terrified. I know you think I had far more experience than you, but you were my first lover, too—at least the first one I didn't pay."

Charles was right; Hy always thought of her friend as being far more experienced, but he was only a few years older and he'd been almost as shy as Hy when they'd first met.

While he hadn't been more experienced, he'd certainly been *braver* than Hy.

"I'm sorry, Charles. I never thought about how it must have been for you to approach me that first time."

His pale, almost bloodless lips curved into a slight smile and he chuckled. Unfortunately, it turned into a cough. Hy knew better than to hover over him or ask stupid questions while he fought for his breath. When he stopped, his cheeks bore two cherry bright spots. So, she suspected, did the handkerchief he quickly concealed.

"I wasn't just anxious, Hy," Charles continued. "I also had visions of being thrown into some wretched rat-infested gaol for indecency if you'd gone home and reported me to your mother, who would have rallied the villagers and come for me with pitchforks and torches. She wouldn't have been satisfied until I'd been put in stocks and publicly whipped in the Little Sissingdon town square."

Hy's mouth twitched. "But you would have liked that last part, wouldn't you, Charles."

Charles's eyes widened. "Did Hyacinth Bellamy just make a *joke*?"

Hy rolled her eyes and Charles burst out laughing.

His body's punishment for such simple joy was immediate and severe.

The sound of Charles coughing up his insides clawed and tore at Hy's own. She knew the usual response—the ones her sisters would employ—would be to take his hand and soothe him or stroke his brow. But Charles would hate that.

So, instead Hy merely sat and waited, twisting her hands uselessly in her lap and watching quietly while her best friend in the world died before her eyes.

Chapter 13

Hy glanced down at the curt message in her hand: *Midnight. Mrs. Simpson's* and then looked up at the waiting footman. "Thank you, Will," she said, giving him a coin large enough to make him smile.

"Thank you, my lady. Will you be needing Jerry tonight?"

"Yes, tell him to pick me up at the regular place at half-past eleven."

"Very good, my lady," he said, and left her alone in the library.

The duke's system worked well. He sent messages about where they should meet and Hy would show up at the given location if she could get away. Chatham didn't require a response either way, but he was always waiting for her if she could get free.

The duke had—grudgingly—accepted that Hy needed to find her own way *to* whatever hell he'd chosen, but he always insisted on dropping her off near her aunt's house after a night of gambling.

Tonight, would be the fifth time she'd gone gambling with Chatham—and the second time since she'd visited Charles and heard *his* opinion on what Hy should do about her feelings for the duke, which had, in essence, been: *do what you feel like doing, Hy.*

Hy wanted to throttle her friend for his vague, unhelpful advice. As if what she *felt* like doing with the duke wouldn't end with the man calling the constables on her.

Remember that rejection is what Charles worried about, too, when he first approached you.

She knew that, and yet she couldn't make herself *act* on her feelings as Charles had.

And so she had done nothing on her nights with Chatham. Well, nothing except play cards.

With only a few weeks left in the Season it was unlikely that she'd ever gather her courage in time to do something.

Hy had worried that Selina would question her frequent absences—her sister often came home just as Hy was returning—but something was distracting Selina and she seemed far less concerned with Hy's activities of late.

She suspected her pretty sister was in love. She'd seen a similar absentminded behavior in her siblings in the past. What was unusual this time was that Selina was keeping her feelings a secret.

In the past Hy had been driven distracted by having to listen to one sister or another—Selina was the most frequent culprit—agonizing over their love interests. She should be grateful that Selina was sparing her that ordeal, but instead she was worried; it was unlike Selina to hold her own council. She was gregarious and loved to talk even the most mundane and insignificant matters to death. Something was amiss and soon Hy would need to make an effort to find out what.

But not tonight. Tonight was for cards.

The hackney rolled to a stop and Hy peered out the window, surprised at the attractive, dignified house.

They were meeting at a new—at least for Hy—gambling hell tonight.

"You will enjoy the play at Mrs. Simpson's," Chatham had assured her during the ride home on their last evening out.

Hy suspected the real reason His Grace had chosen this club was because it was in a less dangerous part of town. The duke had already made it clear that Hy would no longer be going to Cox's, and not even the Pigeonhole, if he had anything to say about it. Which he did.

Honestly, Hy didn't care where they went as long as the play was deep and she wasn't reduced to games like E.O. or Hazard, both of which she despised.

Hy hopped down from the carriage and nodded up at Jerry, whom she'd already paid.

There was no immediate proof that the house in front of her was a gambling den. From the street it looked like any of its neighbors. But Mrs. Simpson had been operating the club from her home ever since her husband's death nine years earlier. Chatham told her that the banker—whom everyone had believed wealthy—had died leaving his widow drowning in debts.

Hy knocked on the door and it opened so quickly she assumed the large man who stared down at her must have been waiting just inside.

"You got an invitation?" he demanded roughly.

"Er, I am here by invitation of the Duke of Chatham."

"Ah. You must be Mr. 'i-ram Bellamy, then?"

"Yes."

The man opened the door wider. "'is Grace is on the second floor, second door on the right," the doorman said, gesturing to the stairs.

The house looked a great deal like Weller's, with dark, masculine colors, and rich wooden wainscoting that was polished to a shine. The only thing out of place was the doorman, who'd have looked more at home in a boxing ring.

When she opened the door on the second floor the first face she saw was the duke's. He nodded a slight greeting at Hy as a hand was in progress.

His loud Scottish associate wasn't in attendance tonight, but Hy knew that didn't mean Fowler wouldn't show up later as the two seemed inseparable.

At least Shelton had not tagged along again, for which Hy was very grateful.

Hy took the only vacant seat, beside the duke, and watched and waited.

***

Tonight was the first time Sylvester had ever seen Hiram—he still found it difficult to think of her as *Mary*, a name that seemed unsuitable— lose. While she was adept at minimizing her losses—mainly by not throwing more money at bad cards—even she could do nothing when confronted by a string of bad hands.

By the time the table broke for the first supper Mary looked disconsolate, which—given how unreadable she usually looked—was saying something.

"Are you hungry?" Sylvester asked as the room emptied out leaving only the two of them.

"No, thank you," she said, her mouth set in a grim line. "I think I will call it an evening."

When Sylvester stood, she said, "You needn't take me home, Your Grace. This isn't a dangerous location."

"I will take you home."

She opened her mouth, but then sighed and closed it.

"Unless you would like to try someplace else?" Sylvester said, regretting the offer immediately. Damn and blast! Where had that come from? He'd meant to just escort the chit home and then go and visit his mistress.

That's a lie. You'll go home and mount a corporal and four thinking about "the chit."

Sylvester's face heated at his filthy thoughts, as if Mary could somehow see into his head.

But all she did was ask, "You want to go to the Pigeonhole, Your Grace?"

"Somewhere else—a place called Shaw's, which is operated by Barclay Shaw. It's not far from Covent Garden."

She pulled out her pocket watch, glanced at it, and then nodded. "It is not too late. I would like to go."

Within ten minutes they were in his carriage and heading toward Shaw's.

"Mrs. Simpson's is an unusual place," she said.

"How so?"

"It felt almost as if it were somebody's home."

"It is. Mrs. Simpson lives in a small set of rooms with her two nieces, both of whom work at the house."

"And is that… respectable?"

Sylvester shrugged. "A decade ago, when her husband was still alive, Mrs. Simpson was welcome at some of the best houses. But, I'm afraid operating a gambling hell—no matter how genteel in appearance—tends to put one beyond the pale." He smiled at her thoughtful expression. "Would you like to have such a place?"

"No. It looks like it would be rather a demanding endeavor."

"And yet you wish to play cards for a living? Don't you think that will be demanding?"

"Perhaps a little, but it is the most practical option for earning a living."

"You have never considered marrying?"

"Marrying?" she repeated, sounding genuinely startled by the suggestion.

Sylvester couldn't help smiling. "Marriage is a far more traditional choice for a woman than gambling, Mary."

She turned to look out the window. "Not for me."

Sylvester was tempted to pry, but something about the way her shoulders had stiffened made him hold his peace on the subject. Instead, he asked, "You and your brother will be itinerant?"

"Yes."

He waited to see if she'd say more. When she didn't, he asked, "What will he do while you play?"

She turned to stare at him for a long moment before saying, "Why are you asking?"

Sylvester was amused rather than offended by her suspicion. "Just making conversation, Mary."

She made a soft grunting sound and glanced out the window. Sylvester thought she'd decided not to answer him when she said, "It is my hope that my brother will marry his childhood sweetheart and stay here. Her father owns a bookstore and gets on well with my brother. It would be a far more suitable profession for him."

"Ah. But then how would you travel without him?"

She shrugged. "I will address that issue when—"

The carriage suddenly jerked so roughly that Mary was pitched forward off her seat.

Sylvester reached out to catch her, although he wasn't quite fast enough to keep her knees from striking his bench.

The vent slid open and John Coachman's wide-eyed face peered in at them through the slot. "There's a crowd, sir."

Indeed, their voices—male, it seemed—were loud and angry.

"Try to get us to a side street," Sylvester ordered.

The coachman nodded. "I'll try. But I think it's the—Oi!"—he whipped around and the carriage suddenly rocked on its springs. "Get back, you lot!" his servant yelled. "Bloody hell, sir! They're going to—" the rest of what he said was cut off by the shouting of at least a dozen voices, the screaming of springs, and the cracking of wood.

Sylvester pulled Mary tighter as the carriage rocked back and forth with increasing violence.

"Hold on," he said, as he sank down to the floor, pulling her with him, until they were both wedged between the seats.

She pressed against him, her hands digging into his shoulders and her eyes as round as coins behind her spectacles. "What is—"

The carriage gave a deafening screech of wood.

"Close your eyes and cover your face, Mary!" Sylvester shouted against her head just as the world tilted and then slammed onto its side, the sound of men screaming and glass smashing filling the air.

Chapter 14

It was like a sequence in one of Hy's dreams, those garbled, messy montages of images that made no sense. One moment Hy and the duke were engaged in conversation, rolling through the quiet streets, and the next minute somebody picked up the world and shook out the contents, like a willful child upending a box of toys.

Before Hy understood what the duke was doing, he'd wrapped his body around hers and pulled her to the floor.

"Close your eyes, Mary," he said against her temple.

Men shouted and metal and wood shrieked and a high voice cried out. Hy only realized it was hers when the duke said, "It will be alright," and pulled her head against his chest as something sharp cut into her ear and the back of her neck.

There were pistol shots—two—and then the sound of more shouting and many feet running away.

And then silence broken only by the pulsing of blood in her ears.

"Don't open your eyes," Chatham warned, his hold on her loosening. "There are shards of broken window all over."

"My glasses—"

"I will find them," he promised. "Stay here while I climb out and then I'll help you. Alright?"

"Alright," Hy said, cringing at the sound of a horse screaming somewhere nearby. "The horses—"

"Shh, I know it is upsetting but John Coachman will be doing what he can."

Hy swallowed and nodded.

She felt his body pull away and then heard debris shifting. "I've found your glasses and they are all in one piece, although I cannot speak to scratches." Hy felt a hand touch hers. "Here they are."

"Thank you."

"Shake your head before you put them on—try to get rid of the glass and splinters from your hair."

Hy did as he told her, vaguely aware of men shouting, and the creaking of the carriage as the duke pushed open the damaged door, which slammed against the side of the carriage hard enough to break the remaining glass from the window.

While he climbed out Hy tilted her face down and then used her handkerchief to brush the broken glass from her face and then shook again, more vigorously, like a dog throwing off water.

Once she was sure she'd cleared off the skin around her eyes she put on her glasses and looked up to where Chatham was patiently waiting.

Hy winced as she slowly unfolded herself, waving away his hand. "I can lift myself out."

He hesitated, but then nodded and stepped back from the opening.

Hy scrambled clumsily out of the carriage and the duke led her to the nearby streetlamp.

"Look up so I can check your face," he ordered.

He grimaced at whatever he saw. "You've got several cuts and I can see glass in your hair. Just try not to rub it."

Behind them, one of the horses whinnied piteously and they both winced.

"I'm fine. Why don't you go and take care of your horse," Hy said, unhappily aware of what needed to be done.

He nodded and strode to where his two footmen and coachman had cut the traces and managed to free three of the horses, but one was still down.

Hy didn't want to watch and turned her back to the grim scene, staring in the opposite direction.

There were men and women loitering around the opening to a nearby alley, watching the show. There were even more people—mostly men, it looked like—running off down the street, some breaking windows as they went.

Hy flinched at the sound of the pistol shot but didn't turn around.

"Mary?" A hand landed on her shoulder, and she jolted.

"I know it is a foolish question, but are you alright?"

She assumed he meant physically. "Yes. I'll probably have bruises tomorrow, but nothing is broken."

He looked as if he was going to set a hand beneath her elbow but then remembered she was garbed as a man. "Come. My coachman has found a hackney." His eyes flickered over her likely disheveled person. "Can you go home like this?"

Hyacinth

Hy thought of trying to hide this mess from her sister and hesitated.

"Never mind. We'll go somewhere," he said, gesturing toward the hackney cab. "Climb inside," he said, and then turned to driver and gave a familiar address on Piccadilly.

When he closed the door, Hy said, "We are going to Mrs. Dryden's?"

"I know it is not exactly the sort of place to take a young lady, but it is close and she knows how to be discreet. I can't take you back to my house—not with my cousin Shelton there." His mouth flexed into a frown at the mention of his heir.

Hy just nodded and told herself that the sudden quickening of her pulse was due to the accident and not the fact that she'd soon be in a brothel with the duke. It wasn't as if they'd go back to that same room.

Hy knew she should just tell him that he could take her home, but...

Well, she didn't want to tell him that.

She turned her thoughts in another direction. "Who were those men and why did they attack your carriage?"

"I'm not sure who they were, but I'm going to guess they were part of that mob that have been raising the devil at the theater these past few weeks."

Hy had read about the angry patrons who'd protested the price increase by smashing up the newly constructed premises and demanding that ticket prices be lowered.

"I thought they just smashed up the theater, not that they roamed the streets attacking carriages."

"Once the blood it hot it is difficult to calm some men. A mob forms a mind of its own." He scowled, his dark eyebrows pulling down over the bridge of his nose. "While I don't wish to begrudge anyone their enjoyment, I do wish they'd not forced the killing of my animal." He glanced up, his fierce expression softening when he met her gaze. "And I wish they'd not terrorized my gambling companion." He reached out and took her hand, the kind gesture sending her heart into an all-out gallop. "Are you sure you're well?"

"Yes, I am fine," she answered through lips that seemed to have gone numb, intensely aware of his warm, strong hand covering hers. She swallowed and stared down at it. He had lovely hands, shapely and competent. She enjoyed watching him shuffle and deal cards.

She'd enjoyed watching him caress that prostitute's body, as well.

Hy swallowed the moisture flooding her mouth. She wished the erotic images flickering through her mind's eye would just *stop*, but she knew from experience that once she had an idea in her head it was impossible to root it out.

Until she did something about it.

The duke removed his hand and she glanced up to find him regarding her with an unreadable look.

"What is it?" she asked.

He shook his head and turned his face toward the window.

Hy stared at him for a moment long, and then she, too, turned away.

***

Unlike the last time that Chatham brought Hy to Mrs. Dryden's brothel, the duke didn't lead her into the room with all the women. Instead, he spoke quietly to Mrs. Dryden, who nodded and immediately led them to the second floor.

Although the room she took them to was a bedchamber, Hy immediately saw there was no large window across from the four-poster bed, which meant there wouldn't be people watching them.

"I will have hot water and some bandages sent up, Your Grace."

The duke nodded and turned to Hy when the door shut. He gestured to the screen in the corner. "I would have taken two rooms but this is all she had left," he explained. "Go ahead and disrobe behind the screen and we can send your clothing down to be cleaned."

"What about you, Your Grace?"

"What about me?"

"You've glass in your clothing, too. If you don't need to clean up, neither do I. If you will summon a hackney for me, I can just go ho—" Hy broke off when the duke reached for his cravat and tugged on one end, pulling the strip from around his neck and tossing it over the back of a nearby chair. He lifted a challenging eyebrow at her, but didn't speak, instead reaching for the buttons of his coat.

She turned on her heel and fled behind the screen.

As much as she'd scoffed—mentally, at least—at the notion of having her cuts tended and clothes cleaned, she discovered fine shards of glass embedded in the fabric of her coats and cravat. None of the cuts on her hands or person were deep, but there were many.

Hyacinth

She'd just stripped down to her drawers and chest bindings when there was a light knock on the door.

"Come in," the duke said.

"Mrs. Dryden thought you might need some refreshment, Your Grace," a breathy female voice said.

"And I have brought extra hot water and another basin, Your Grace," a second voice added.

"You can set both on the table in front of the fireplace."

Hy heard the faint clatter of crockery.

"Mrs. Dryden also said I was to collect your clothing, Your Grace."

"Mine are on the chair. Hiram, have you your garments?"

"Er, yes," she said, hastily draping her clothing over the screen.

The garments disappeared and one of the maids asked, "May I fetch you anything else, Your Grace?"

"No, that will be all, thank you."

The door shut softly and Hy slipped on the robe she'd found hanging on the hook, fastened the large toggle at the top of the shawl collar and tied the sash tightly around her waist before taking a deep breath and stepping out from behind the screen.

***

Sylvester smiled at the sight of Hiram—*Mary*, he mentally corrected—wearing the over-large banyan. It wasn't too long for her, but she was so slender it looked like it could wrap around her twice.

Her magnified eyes moved slowly over his person and although she didn't show it by so much as a flicker of an eyelid, Sylvester knew that his brave card sharp was relieved that he was covered from calves to neck by one of the heavy brocade robes.

Sylvester gestured to the tray that held tea, biscuits, a bottle of sherry, a stack of clean cloths, bandages, and a tin of some sort of unguent. "Sit and let me tend to your wounds."

She lifted her hands and glanced at them, her brow furrowing. "Oh, that's not—"

"Mary."

Her head jerked up, her expression almost perplexed.

"Sit, please."

She sighed but obeyed. "Shall I start the tea steeping? Or do you prefer"—she squinted at the decanter, but there was no label.

"It is sherry," he said. No doubt Diana Dryden was wondering why in the world he'd requested tea and sherry, but she was a woman who was too discreet to ever say anything. Besides, if Tackle had guessed Mary's gender, then the canny madam had likely done so, as well.

"I'd rather have whiskey, if there is any?"

Sylvester smiled; he should have guessed. "I will pour us some." He went to the three decanters on a nearby table. "How are you feeling?"

"You keep asking me that, but I am fine."

"Most women would be feeling a bit out of sorts after such an experience," Sylvester said as he handed her a glass. He smiled and added, "Actually, *I'm* feeling a bit out of sorts."

"I am fine."

Sylvester sat down beside her, placed his glass on the table, and took one of the cloths and wet it. "Let's see your hands."

She hesitated only a second before holding out her right hand.

Sylvester examined the myriad small cuts before carefully dabbing away the dried blood. "Does this hurt?"

"No."

He glanced up at her flat, monosyllabic answer, but her expression was impassive, her gaze on her hand rather than him.

"None of these are deep," he said after he'd finished washing the second hand. "You've got some cuts on your face, I'm afraid." Sylvester took her chin and tilted her face upward, aware of how she stiffened at his touch.

"I'll use a new cloth," he murmured, his gaze lingering on her lips. Christ but the woman had a mouth made for sin.

He looked away and took a fresh cloth, frowning when he lifted her hair to tend to the cuts on her forehead. "There is still glass in your hair—tiny, but lots of it."

When she didn't answer, he met her gaze.

Her spectacles magnified her eyes so hugely that Sylvester could see the individual striations of her irises. Her eyes were a truly magnificent blending of blue and green, the overall effect almost turquoise.

Had he believed her to be skinny to the point of gauntness before? Looking at her now, he saw that she was finely boned instead of too thin. Her freckled cheeks were full rather than hollow.

No, she was not gaunt; she was delicate.

Sylvester felt a sudden stirring in his groin and realized that he was staring—and she was looking right back at him. He released her, both amused and annoyed by his body's inappropriate reaction. "I think you should wash your hair—that is the only way to get it all. There is water in the pitcher by that basin."

"What about your hair?" she retorted, as direct as ever.

"Will you check for glass?"

She nodded solemnly, her face as smooth and emotionless as the surface of a frozen pond as she leaned toward him and lifted the hair from his brow, her fingers moving lightly and briskly over his scalp. She was touching him as impersonally as Tackle did, and yet his prick—which was already half-hard—stiffened the rest of the way.

"You don't seem to have any," she murmured. "Why did I get so much?"

"My hat was on while yours got knocked off," he said gruffly. "Come, let's rinse your hair."

When she stood and turned away Sylvester exhaled the breath he'd been holding and adjusted his robe—not that he could do much to conceal his arousal—and stood.

Good Lord. What was wrong with him?

***

What was wrong with her? Why was she so hot and shaky?

Hy could hear her blood pumping as she rose from the settee on wobbly legs. The skin on her hands, which he'd cleaned with a gentle thoroughness that nobody—certainly not her mother or even her loving childhood nurse—had ever used on her, tingled from his care.

Her chin felt branded where he'd lightly touched her with his thumb.

Normally she disliked other people touching her, only tolerating casual embraces from her family, but never seeking them out. And yet she was increasingly desperate for the duke's touches.

Her own desires unnerved her. Why did she like the feel of his hands on her?

Why did she want more?

This is your chance, a voice that sounded a great deal like Charles's whispered in her head.

Hy thrust away her distracting thoughts and set aside her spectacles before she filled the basin halfway.

Do something...

Hy gritted her teeth against the insidious voice and dunked her head. The water in the pitcher had cooled and it felt good on her hot skin.

She didn't scrub as she would shampooing, but just submerged her head until her hair was soaked, allowing the water to carry off the crushed glass.

"Let me help," the duke's voice came from right behind her.

When Hy jumped, he set a hand on her shoulder. "I'm sorry, I didn't mean to startle you, but the back of your head is still dry. Let me pour some over the part you missed." Cool water flowed over her neck and nape as his fingers gently parted the hair. She shivered and closed her eyes at his touch, biting her lip to catch the grunt of desire that tried to slip out.

"Is that too cold?" he asked. Before she could answer, he said, "Just a moment and I will get the hot tea water and add it to the pitcher."

Hy dunked her head twice more before he returned, hoping to shock her brain back to normal.

It worked.

Until one touch of the duke's fingers on the back of her neck sent her temperature soaring yet again. "This will be warmer," he said.

She stood motionless while he poured the water, her body humming with awareness when his hip brushed against hers.

Once he'd emptied the pitcher, he said, "Let me just see if we got all of it." He gently parted her hair to the scalp in several places. "I can't see any in your hair, but there is plenty sparkling at the bottom of the basin. Let's just rinse once more. Can you dip down a bit?"

Hy did so and he used his hands as a cup.

"There," he said. "You can stand, I've got a towel." Firm hands draped the cloth over her dripping hair while Hy stood like a child and he carefully pressed the water from her hair, careful not to rub too hard on her scalp just in case there was a shard they might have missed.

Once he was finished, his hands landed lightly on her shoulders and he turned her, removing the towel when she was facing him.

Hy looked up, aware that her hair would be sticking out like the spines on a hedgehog.

The duke picked up her spectacles and carefully lowered them over her nose.

His expression as he stared at her was so stern that she wondered if she'd done something to anger him.

She also wondered why such sternness made her heart drum hard and fast, as if she had a woodpecker trapped in her chest.

Hyacinth

He gave a wry, self-mocking smile and shook his head slightly, but his gaze never left hers. "Mary, Mary, Mary."

"Hy," she corrected without thinking, her normally trustworthy brain pushing the word out before she knew what she was saying.

One of his dark eyebrows arched.

"It is better you call me that even when we are alone," she explained, "so that you don't forget and call me Mary at the card table."

He looked doubtful. "You want me to call you… Hy?"

She nodded, holding his searching gaze even though it was becoming uncomfortable.

"Very well… Hy." He lowered his hands from her shoulders and would have taken a step back but Hy's hands shot out and grabbed his upper arms to stop him.

The duke's eyes widened, but he could not have been more shocked than she was. Hy stared at her hands as if they belonged to somebody else.

Never had she initiated contact with anyone other than Charles, and rarely with him.

As if she'd summoned her friend, his voice whispered in her head: *Do what you feel like doing, Hy. That is how matters of the heart* should *progress.*

Hy had to open her mouth to get enough air, and even that didn't seem to help.

She had *grabbed* another person and was still attached to him.

And he felt *good*. Shockingly, astoundingly good.

Hy flexed her fingers and they tightened around hard, warm muscle. His biceps were surprisingly muscular beneath her hands. She suspected that she was squeezing him hard—probably hard enough to be uncomfortable—but she couldn't make herself let him go.

"Mary? Er, Hy?"

She looked up from her hands at the sound of his voice.

He was staring at her as if she were a mad woman.

She *felt* mad. Or at least she didn't feel like herself.

"What is it? You look… I don't know what you look like. What is wrong?"

"I want to touch you."

Hy heard the wonder in her voice but doubted that the duke would guess what her words truly meant and how unprecedented her actions were.

"Is that unusual?"

Hy's lips parted and she nodded, surprised and pleased that he'd understood what she meant. "Is it—may I continue?"

His eyelids lowered slightly and he nodded. "Do what you want," he said, his voice slightly raspy.

She felt as if she were caught in a magical spell, and that if she moved too quickly or spoke too loudly, that she would shatter the spell.

But he had given his permission to touch and feel and explore and she would not miss this opportunity.

She loosened her grip on his upper arms and allowed her hands to slide up to his shoulders. His robe was just like hers, the expensive silk brocade thin enough that she could feel the rounded cap of muscle that connected arm to shoulder.

Hy explored the fascinating bulge, yet again surprised by how substantial he felt. He didn't look big, but he must lead an active life to have such a hard, toned body.

She pulled her gaze away from her hands and forced herself to meet his gaze.

He looked faintly puzzled, but not angry or revolted. Nor did he seem eager to stop her exploration. Instead, he appeared patient and a little curious.

Hy's hands resumed their trek, her fingers lightly grazing over the doubled material of the robe's lapel, moving inexorably toward his bare throat.

A soft sigh escaped her when skin met skin for the first time and the sensory jolt travelled through her body like the sinuous ripple of a serpent.

She was vaguely aware of her labored breathing as the pads of her fingers met the rough prickles of his night beard. The taut cords of his throat flexed as he swallowed and she caressed a finger over his Adam's apple.

Up and up she went, gliding over his firm, chiseled jaw to his cheeks. One side of his face was smooth perfection while the other was a puckered, hairless whorl of skin. Only when his eyelids fluttered shut did the full impact of what Hy was doing descend on her.

If somebody touched her face—or any part of her, really—in such an intimate way, she'd probably jerk away at best or slap their hand at worst.

This was *rude, intrusive* behavior.

Some part of her felt shame at invading his person in such a way, but he felt so good—so *right*—that she couldn't make herself stop.

Hyacinth

Ever so gently she caressed the thick fan of lashes that rested against his cheeks before lightly grazing the bony hardness of his nose, the velvety softness of his eyebrow, and the pulsing blue veins beneath the thin skin of his temples, not stopping until her fingers carded the fine, soft hairs near his ears. She was interested to discover that the gray hairs were slightly rougher than the glossy brown ones.

Hy saved the scar until last, careful not to touch the baby-soft skin too roughly.

She tried to imagine what he must have looked like before the injury but found that she could not picture him without the scar. It seemed so much a part of who he was. Had it changed him as much inside as it had externally?

How could you ever ask a person such an intimate question?

He opened his eyes when her hands made their return journey back to his shoulders. She told herself to release him, but her fingers refused to obey.

"Mary—"

"No. Hy," she insisted roughly.

His lips curled up and his eyes crinkled at the corners as he nodded. "Hy."

Before she could stop herself, she leaned forward and licked the fine wrinkles that fanned out from the corner of his right eye.

The duke sucked in a lungful of air but did not flinch or back away.

He was salty and warm and Hy desperately wanted to lick him again, but she forced herself to pull away and meet his gaze.

His eyes had gone almost black, his nostrils flared. "I want to kiss you."

Hy nodded. "Yes."

He gave a soft, wry snort. "I must be honest; I want to do more than kiss you. A great deal more."

Again, she nodded.

He raised his hand to her face, but stopped short of touching her, his eyes locking with hers, a question in his brown gaze.

Hy—who struggled to read even the most basic of human emotions on most people's faces—somehow knew the duke was asking permission to touch her.

Her answer was to lean closer. She exhaled a shaky breath when the pad of his forefinger delicately grazed the line of her jaw, caressed her cheek, and came to rest on her lower lip, which he tapped lightly.

"Your mouth has been tormenting me and giving me… ideas."

Hy wanted to beg him to describe those ideas, but she couldn't make herself speak.

"I want to do unspeakable things to you… Hy."

She made a noise that should have embarrassed her, but the duke's pupils flared even more at the low, raw sound.

"Yes," she said, the word scarcely a whisper.

Yet still he hesitated.

Hy's memory flickered back to the last time they were at this house of ill repute—to the scene he'd chosen to show her—a scene that hinted at what this powerful, fascinating man enjoyed in the bedchamber.

The recollection of what they had—far too briefly—watched together in that darkened room was one that Hy used nightly to pleasure herself.

And Chatham wanted to do that. With her?

Do what you want to do, Charles whispered.

And so, for once, she said exactly the words she wanted to say, "Do you want to tie me up and fuck me, Your Grace?"

Chapter 15

Her question—the unexpected use of the word *fuck*, not to mention the images her words conjured—struck Sylvester like a wicked uppercut to the jaw.

Mary—or Hiram or Hy or whatever the hell she called herself—was adept at doing and saying the most astoundingly unexpected things, and not just when it came to cards.

Sylvester stared into her pupils, which had blown wide, leaving only the thinnest green-blue rind hugging the swollen black.

"Yes, tying up my lovers is one of the things I enjoy. It does not frighten you or repulse you?"

"No," she said, not hesitating for so much as a second. "It excites me."

His cock, which had already been engorged and aching, throbbed so hard it hurt.

Her lips parted and her mesmerizing eyes lowered to his mouth. "I want you to do whatever you wish to me, Your Grace."

Sylvester's threadbare control snapped and he claimed her mouth with a savagery that shamed him, but he couldn't stop—nor did she appear to want him to stop. Instead, she groaned and her mouth opened wide beneath his.

He plunged into her with all the finesse of a pirate pillaging a foreign shore, maddened by his need for her—a need that had been slowly, inexorably building for weeks.

Her strong fingers dug into his back like claws and she melted against him, their tongues jousting and thrusting as one of her legs wrapped around his hip.

Sylvester grunted explosively when she rocked her cleft against his shaft. "Bloody hell," he muttered, pulling away to catch his breath.

Her hands went to his sash and Sylvester reacted in kind.

Tearing, hurried fingers made a mull of the easy task and he gave a huff of laughter when she pulled off the heavy ivory toggle at the neck of his robe and then tossed it to the floor with a clatter.

The look on her face when she bared his chest was everything a man could ever want to see reflected in a lover's eyes.

Her lips parted in a hungry expression, and questing fingers slid over his chest, the soft pads grazing his hardened nipples.

"What is this from?" she asked, leaning closer to study the scar beneath his right nipple.

He smiled at her blunt curiosity. "Bayonet," he said, finally getting the damned toggle on her robe unbuttoned—without tearing the garment—and then staring in perplexity at what he discovered beneath. "What the devil...?"

Her lips pulled into a rare smile. "It is just strips of sheeting. My breasts are not large, but it seemed prudent to bind them," she explained in her practical way, not embarrassed or shy—a reaction which made his cock throb even harder.

When she reached for the strips he stopped her. "No. I want to unwrap you," he said, his voice harsh with desire.

Her answer was to shrug off her robe, leaving her standing in an outfit that should have been ludicrous at best and unattractive at worst but somehow managed to be more arousing than any lace negligee Sylvester had ever seen.

"You wear drawers," he said rather stupidly. How the devil could *drawers* look so bloody sensual?

She reached for the tape holding up her undergarment and gave it a tug. The fine muslin slid to the floor, exposing her flaming red bush.

She was slender, her hips boyishly narrow, but her long, long legs were feminine and shapely.

When Sylvester could pull his gaze away from her lower body he discovered she was watching him with a curious, but not embarrassed, expression. Indeed, there was not a hint of shyness in her eyes. This was a woman who was arousingly comfortable in her own skin.

Sylvester wanted to drop to his knees, part her private curls, and see if he could shake that calm, confident expression from her face, but he wanted her naked, first.

He gestured to her bound chest. "Where do I start?"

She shoved two slender fingers into the cloth beneath one arm and pulled out a tattered end, offering it to him.

Hyacinth

Sylvester stepped closer and then gave an unmanly squawk when her hand closed around his shaft.

She smirked at him—their eyes on the same level—and the bold expression was so unprecedented—so shocking—that Sylvester's hand frozen in mid-unwrap as he gaped at the sly, sensuous grin that transformed her normally emotionless face into that of a teasing temptress.

"Are my hands cold?" she taunted, and then she pumped him from root to tip, her touch firm and confident and *experienced.*

Who *was* this woman?

***

Hy had imagined what Chatham would look like naked and aroused dozens of times, but reality was proving far more satisfying than her fantasies had been.

He looked nothing like Charles, who, even when he'd been healthy, had been slim and fine boned.

Nor was the duke thick and bulky like some of the shirtless farm laborers Hy had made a point of spying on over the years. He was somewhere in between, all hard muscled masculinity—his elegant body toned and chiseled.

And then there were the scars on him…

Why did Hy like such evidence of pain in his past? What was it about damage that aroused her so?

Was it just more evidence of her flawed character?

Charles had always told her to accept her awkward desires.

What would he make of her new attraction to scars?

"Stroke me again… Hy," the duke ordered, reminding her that there was a living, breathing man attached to the thick shaft in her fist.

Hy instantly obeyed, pumping him firmly and wetting her palm with his body's excitement, her actions earning a guttural but approving groan.

"You have a skilled touch," he said, his hips rolling and thrusting his erection into her tight fist as he slowly unwrapped the layers of bandaging around her breasts.

Hy knew she should be ashamed by his words and what they implied: that she must have stroked many cocks—or at least one cock many times—to have become so skilled. But instead of shame, a warm wave of pride, not to mention arousal, washed over her; giving pleasure to a man like Chatham was erotic in and of itself.

He groaned and for a moment she thought it was from her ministrations, but then she realized he'd dropped the bandage and was staring at her chest, his expression flatteringly hungry and appreciative.

"You are so damned lovely," he muttered, raising his palms and cupping breasts that she'd always believed insignificant.

His dark gaze lifted to meet hers. "What a delightful body you've been hiding beneath your coats and breeches, Hiram." His lips pulled into that feral smirk that she had come to adore and he lightly massaged her breasts, gently pinching her already peaked nipples. "Do you like this—are they sensitive?"

"Yes, that feels good. And yes, they are."

She shivered when the next pinch was harder still, causing a sharp throb of arousal to shoot directly to her sex.

"You like it hard," he murmured when Hy pressed herself against his palms after one especially cruel pinch.

"Yes," she whispered, mesmerized by the sight of his elegant fingers stroking her.

Hy stroked his shaft slowly as he alternately soothed and punished her nipples, until she was breathing roughly, her thighs slick with desire.

Chatham groaned. "You are entirely too skilled, my dear. I shan't last long if you continue on this way. Let go."

Hy ignored him; he felt too good, too—

The duke's hand closed over hers and he stilled the movement. "Get on the bed," he ordered, his quietly commanding tone causing her inner muscles to tighten in a delicious way.

Was he going to tie and blindfold her, like the woman they'd seen that night?

She wanted to ask, but her heart was already palpitating too fast, her skin was sheened with sweat, all of which told her that she was far too stimulated. She'd already stunned herself by taking the first step. The next one would have to be his.

Hy scrambled onto the bed and reclined on her back, pushing up onto her elbows to watch the duke, who went to lock the door before coming to join her, his thick cock bobbing in front of him in a taunting way that made her want to grab it again.

He gave her what could only be described as a smirk when he realized she was watching him.

"You are remarkably comfortable with naked bodies and unvarnished sexual conversation," he observed, climbing up onto the bed and pushing her legs wide in a way that caused yet more clenching of her internal muscles.

"So are you."

He laughed. "Touché. Do you know what I want to do to you?" he asked, a lock of dark hair falling over his forehead as he lowered to his elbows between her thighs and cut a glance at her exposed sex.

"Pleasure me with your mouth?" she asked, unable to keep the hopeful tone from her voice.

He looked genuinely pleased rather than horrified that she would know such a thing. "What a delightful surprise you are turning out to be," he muttered.

Hy might have said the same thing if she'd been as easy about expressing her thoughts as the duke appeared to be. She never would have guessed that such a forbidding looking man could be so playful and teasing in the bedchamber.

He lightly trailed a finger over her private curls, his gaze locked with hers, the intensity in his brown eyes causing her breathing to hitch. "I can stop right now—you need only say the word—and we can put on our robes and ring for our clothing. You don't have to do this."

"I know I don't have to do this." She cocked her head. "You don't have to do this, either."

"I don't want to stop."

"I don't *want* you to stop."

He smiled, his sharp canine teeth making him look wolfish, and then he dropped his gaze, parted her nether lips with his thumbs, and made a gruff, approving growl in his chest. "So pretty," he said, and then lowered his mouth over the swollen bundle of nerves.

Hy hissed in a breath, her eyes never leaving his as he sucked and tongued, his actions sending rapturous bolts straight to her womb.

She bit her lower lip and spread her thighs wider, earning a crinkle-eyed smile from him as he used one hand to stroke her, slicking his thumb before probing the entrance to her body, his lips tightening around the source of her pleasure.

Hy's climax came fast and hard, and she caught her lower lip with her teeth to bite back her cry of passion as she thrust her fingers into his thick, glossy hair and pulled his head down while raising her hips, grinding her sex against his hot, wet mouth.

Her eyes rolled back in her head as a second, more intense wave of pleasure chased the first orgasm, her body curling in on itself as every muscle clenched.

Hy drifted in a haze of bliss, luxuriating in pure sensation. Only when she realized that his mouth had moved—his slick, hot tongue no longer teasing her bud but was thrusting inside her—did she force open her heavy-lidded eyes.

His hair looked like somebody had tried to tear it from his scalp and when she lifted her hand, a few dark strands fluttered between her fingers.

Rather than feel shame at her uninhibited behavior, she thrilled at the sight of the dark head still between her thighs. *This is the Duke of Chatham*, a voice inside her head whispered, as if she wasn't perfectly aware of that miraculous fact.

His eyes lifted to hers and whatever he saw on her face made him smile and lift off her sex, the lower half of his handsome face slick with her juices.

"What is it?" he asked in a raspy voice and then extended a wickedly long tongue and laved from her entrance to just shy of her too sensitive clitoris.

"I like looking at you while you pleasure me," Hy answered truthfully.

His eyelids lowered and an approving growl emanated from his chest. "You don't speak much, but when you do… well, it is always something worth hearing."

Hy smiled at that. "What sort of amusing street cant do you have for cunnilingus?"

He chuckled. "Hmmm, let me think." He pondered for a moment, his fingers absently stroking her lower lips and sending shivers of pleasure through her. "I'm ashamed to admit all I can call to mind is the rather ancient term *larking*."

"Larking? What does that even mean?"

He shrugged.

"That is not nearly as amusing as mounting a corporal and four."

"No, it isn't," he admitted, then his eyes narrowed slyly. "I prefer the less humorous but more evocative term *cunt licking*."

Hy gasped at the filthy word, her breathing suddenly ragged.

He gave an evil chuckle at whatever he saw on her face.

"What?" she asked.

But he merely shook his head and said, "You are delightful."

Hyacinth

Whatever *that* meant.

He pushed up onto his hands and knees and climbed up her body. When they were face-to-face his gaze dropped to her mouth and he claimed her with a deep, slow kiss, the taste of her own arousal flooding her senses.

Hy and Charles had spent a great deal of time kissing over the years—probably entire days if you added it all up—but there was something far more primitive about kissing the duke, which was odd considering he was such a civilized, urbane man.

At least when he was clothed.

But naked, he appeared to be somebody else entirely...

His kiss was a slow, thorough claiming. The scent and taste of Hy and whisky on his breath, the faintly salty tang of clean male sweat, and the lingering echo of expensive cologne and fine wool more of an aphrodisiac than Hy would have imagined possible.

"I want to be inside you," he whispered before pulling back to meet her gaze. "I will withdraw before ejaculating, but there is always a possibility of pregnancy."

"I know." Hy slid a hand over his strong jaw—choosing the scarred side of his face—her fingers lightly tracing the oddly circular scar.

His nostrils flared as she explored the old wound, his gaze once again locked with hers.

"I want you to fuck me, Your Grace."

His eyelids fluttered at her crude words, the skin over his unscarred side darkening. "You like to say naughty things, don't you, Hy?"

"Yes."

He shook his head, a marveling expression on his face. "Do you even realize how utterly enchanting you are?"

Hy blinked.

"You look so astonished. Has nobody ever called you enchanting?"

"No. I usually hear *frustrating*."

He laughed. "Well, I could see how that might apply—but one does not negate the other, you know." His hand moved between their bodies and Hy spread her thighs wider without being asked, placing her feet flat on the bed and tilting her hips to accommodate him. "And you have a delectable little pussy," he said, sliding two fingers between her slick folds and very gently squeezing her swollen bud.

Her body clenched at the filthy words coming out of such a proper mouth.

"You liked that—I felt you clench… *here*." He pushed a finger into her.

"Yes," she said in a breathless voice. "I like it. A lot."

"What a filthy girl you are," he said approvingly, pushing a second finger in to join the first, the stretch almost painful. "Mmm, so soft and tight and wet for me," he praised as he slowly pumped her.

Hy slid her hands over his chest, her fingers mimicking his earlier actions on her own nipples.

"Ungh," he grunted, his eyelids drooping and his hips jerking, jamming his slick crown against her thigh.

"You like that," she whispered, her words an echo of his as she pinched the tiny nubs hard.

"Yesssss," he hissed through clenched teeth. "Harder. Make it hur—*ah*! Christ, yes!" His fingers withdrew from her body but were quickly replaced by something far bigger and hotter. "Ready?"

"Yes."

His gaze pinned her as his cock pushed into her body, stretching her inch by delicious inch.

Hy leaned forward, licking the nipple she'd just pinched, latching on and sucking hard as his pelvis came to rest on hers as he buried himself to the root.

"My God you feel good." His eyes closed as he took a moment to allow her to adjust, the pulse at the base of his throat throbbing so hard she couldn't resist tonguing it.

He groaned as she licked him again and again. Hy lowered her mouth over the thin skin and sucked.

He gave a low chuckle. "Are you going to leave your mark on me?"

She nodded, using her teeth to graze the skin. When she pulled away, she smiled at the purpled, swollen skin.

"Proud of yourself?"

"Yes."

He withdrew slowly the action making them both gasp softly, and then sank back in, faster and harder this time.

Hy tightened her muscles in the way she'd learned, earning an approving hiss. "Yes, just like that." His strong body worked her with slow, thorough thrusts. His gaze was intense, but his lips curled into an unexpectedly sweet smile. "I want you to come for me one more time," he said, lowering his weight to one elbow and reaching between them, his finger lightly stroking her bud as his hips pumped.

Hyacinth

"I shan't last much longer," he warned in a strained voice, his hips thrusting harder, faster, and with less control.

Hy tilted her pelvis and tightened around him, earning an almost agonized groan.

"Now!" he shouted in a guttural voice. "Come with me, Hy."

His words as much as his touch pushed her over the edge and Hy was only vaguely aware when he suddenly withdrew, the splash of hot spend on her belly surprising her—making her grateful that he had remembered, even if she had not.

Chapter 16

Sylvester slipped on his discarded robe and fetched a cloth before returning to the bed.

He paused to admire the sight of his uninhibited lover. Hy was sprawled out on her back, lazily moving a finger through the cooling spend on her belly.

His cock, which was exhausted, twitched at the erotic sight.

Her eyes lifted to meet his. Although she gave him that flat, opaque stare that seemed to be her specialty—along with thrashing the men of the *ton* at cards—he suspected she was privately amused by his slack-jawed expression.

Hell, Sylvester was amused by the woman's ability to shock him time and again.

As if reading his mind, she lifted her slick finger to her mouth and licked the tip of it clean.

"Bloody hell!" His empty ballocks clenched in a way that said the spirit was willing but the flesh was too damned weak. He snorted and shook his head. "That was very wicked, but I suspect you know that."

She smirked, but it was a mere shadow of the almost blinding smile she'd given him earlier. Sylvester couldn't help noticing the dark smudges beneath her eyes and wondered if she ever managed to get any sleep. He felt a pang of guilt at keeping her out so late, but he could not regret it.

"Is that for me?" she asked, gesturing to the cloth, the question jolting him out of his fugue.

"Allow me," he said, not giving her a chance to cheat him out of such a pleasurable task.

Sylvester's mind raced as he cleaned her belly. He still could not believe that the sensual creature who'd just licked his spend from her finger was the same detached card sharp who'd lightened his wallet weekly for the past month.

He also couldn't believe that he'd allowed his cock to dictate his actions tonight and that he had absolutely no regrets on the matter.

Indeed, he wanted to ensure that he could have her again. And again. And soon.

He tossed the cloth aside. "Do you want something to drink?"

"I would have another whiskey."

Sylvester snorted at the incongruous request coming from her kiss-swollen lips.

She was… well, she was something, that was certain.

By the time he'd poured two glasses and returned to the bed she had pushed the cushions up against the headboard, propped herself against them, and pulled the blankets up to her waist. Unlike every other woman Sylvester had ever bedded, she'd not bothered to cover up her delectable breasts.

He was not about to point that out.

"Here you are," he said, handing her a glass, forcing his eyes to meet hers rather than lecherously gorge on her tits.

He hooked his foot around a nearby chair and dragged it close to the bed before sitting and taking a sip from his glass, regarding her thoughtfully.

"Why are you looking at me that way?" she asked after a few moments of silence.

"I am surprised."

"Because I am not a maiden?"

"I'd assumed you weren't based on your reaction the first time we came here. No, right now I'm surprised by the fact that you do not appear shocked by any of my suggestions."

"You mean because you like to bind your lovers?" She cocked her head. "Or would *you* rather be bound?"

Sylvester felt his face grow hot and could scarcely believe the reaction. Blushing? At his age?!

For her part, she looked as cool and untouched as if she'd just asked him about the weather.

"Are either of those things that you have done before?" he asked, somehow not surprised when she nodded.

"And did you enjoy it?" he asked when she seemed disinclined to say more.

"Yes."

Sylvester stared. Was there a person in England—man or woman—more laconic than the one across from him?

"Oh," she said, as if suddenly reading his thoughts. "You are wondering what I liked—being bound or doing the binding? Or are you wondering how I know about it all?"

"Yes," he said, giving her a dose of her own terse medicine.

She blinked at that. "Er, which one?"

"Both. Either. All."

Rather than look annoyed, she merely nodded. "I have a book."

It was not the answer he'd expected. But then he should expect the unexpected from her by now. "A book?"

"Yes. It is a book with illustrations of, er, well, I suppose there is no other way to describe it than erotic acts. A sort of primer."

Sylvester wasn't accustomed to conversations like this—ones where he had *no* idea of what came next. He was almost afraid to ask, but… "A primer?"

She nodded and took another sip.

"Where did you get this book?"

She swallowed and—for the first time that he could recall—her gaze slid away, a shadow passing over her.

What was this?

"Should I not have asked?"

"I don't think you'll like the answer."

"Why don't you let me decide that?" Sylvester said.

"The book belonged to a friend of mine. We used to look through the illustrations and practice the ones we liked."

"A friend?" Sylvester knew he sounded like a witless twit, but he was too bloody befuddled to come up with anything better.

"Yes, a friend. I suppose you could call him my lover although not in any conventional sense."

Not surprising as nothing about this woman was conventional. "If you don't mind, could you explain?"

She inhaled deeply and let it out, the action doing distracting things to her lovely chest.

"You will think me odd if I tell you."

Sylvester couldn't help it; he laughed.

***

"I'm sorry, I should not have laughed," the duke said. "It's just—well—"

Hyacinth

"You already think me odd."

"Odd is a harsh word. I would rather use the word, er, *original*."

Hy had heard that word used among the *ton*. She suspected it was just a polite word for *odd*, not that either word offended her.

"You are certainly unusual," he added when she didn't respond. "But that is not a bad thing, Mary—er, Hy."

Hy had heard the same weak reassurance times beyond counting from her sisters. While the comment didn't hurt, it was rather disappointing that here was another person who viewed her as an oddity.

If she told the duke about Charles, he would think she was even stranger—even *she* knew that much.

But, as Charles had said, did she really want to build their association on a lie? That was assuming there was anything to *be* built, of course.

Hy looked up from her musing to find him patiently waiting, his rich brown eyes curious and warm, a tentative smile curving his lips.

That expression was what decided her; anyone who could behave so courteously and kindly, even when confronted with her oddity, was worth trusting.

"His name is Charles, and we met at a card game," Hy left out the part about Charles having been her brother Doddy's math tutor. After all, how could she explain that? The family she'd concocted for herself was unlikely to be able to afford such things as tutors.

"What sort of card game?"

"Just a country game, the kind that some inns allow on their premises after they close."

The duke nodded, obviously familiar.

Hy took another sip of the whiskey, savoring the way it burned on the way down.

"Charles is the only son of a bookseller. His father managed to send him to Cambridge, but Charles's ill health made staying at university too difficult. He'd been studying mathematics, a subject I have always been intensely curious about, but, because of my sex, was not allowed to learn." She could still recall her elation that she'd met somebody who could finally answer all her questions—and more.

"He taught you mathematics?" the duke asked.

"Yes, along with card strategy."

He hesitated, and then asked, "And mathematics led to physical intimacy?"

"I had…" Hy paused, trying to think of way to describe her curiosity without making her sound like the depraved pervert her mother accused her of being.

"Yes?" Chatham prodded.

"I knew I'd never marry," she said, leaving behind the too uncomfortable confession until later, or never.

"Why is that?"

"Most young men I meet don't look *at* me so much as past me. Charles saw things in me that I'd not realized existed. He understood"— she chewed the inside of her cheek.

Once again, she could not bring herself to share such intimate details.

Instead, she said, "Charles will never marry, either. He suffers from a lung ailment the doctors cannot cure. Their only solutions are cupping and sea air. And he refused the former and cannot afford the latter." Well, he could *now*, but she kept that information to herself.

The duke lifted his empty glass and gestured at hers and Hy nodded and handed it to him.

"We became friends, good friends. And it occurred to both of us that we could explore our curiosity together, without societal expectations or strictures." It sounded rather cold and emotionless when spoken out loud, but it had seemed like a sensible decision at the time—when would she have another chance to learn about physical intimacy with somebody she liked and trusted?

"I don't regret the decision," she said more sharply than she'd intended, meeting his gaze directly. And she didn't regret it, even though it was yet another nail in the coffin when it came to how *odd* she was.

"I did not say that you should," the duke said mildly.

"But you must be thinking it is scandalous behavior and that I am immoral."

"Must I?"

Hy blinked at his response, not sure what to say.

"I don't think you immoral, Hy. Every man I know, me included, has *experimented* sexually." He chuckled. "You could say some of us are *still* experimenting."

Hy was so surprised by his easy acceptance of what she'd done that she had no words.

"You've had just the one lover?" he asked.

"Two, now."

He smiled. "Yes, two, now."

"I daresay you've had more."

"That is true."

"Do you keep a mistress?"

His eyebrows shot up and the skin over his cheekbones—at least the unscarred side—flushed.

"Should I not have asked that?"

"No, no, you must ask anything you like," he said, snorting softly. "I certainly have."

Hy sipped her drink and waited for his answer.

"I do have a mistress."

She felt an unpleasant tightening in her chest at his confession, a reaction that left her slightly off balance. Why should she care if he kept a mistress? It had never bothered her when Charles had taken other lovers.

"Do you still see your lover—Charles?"

"Yes, but not often," Hy said, but then realized what he was asking. "Oh—are you asking if we engage in our experiments?"

Chatham nodded.

"No. It has been quite some time since he has been well enough to engage in such activities. He is…" She swallowed. "He is dying."

The humorous light that had been twinkling in his eyes disappeared. "I'm sorry to hear that. Would it upset him to know you've been with somebody else?"

"No, we were lovers, but not in love."

"Ah." Chatham raised his glass, the wide gold ring he wore on his thumb glinting in the light.

"I've never seen anyone with a ring on their thumb before," she said.

He glanced down at it, as if he'd forgotten that he was wearing it. His lips curved into a fond smile and he slipped it off and handed it to her. It was heavier than it looked and still warm from the heat of his body. There was writing inscribed on the band, but not any sort she recognized.

"It's Nordic," he said. "A friend gave it to me."

Hy looked up at the change in his tone to find his smile was now grim. She waited for more, but that seemed to be all he was willing to say on the matter.

She handed it back to him and he slipped it onto his thumb. "You never told me your preferences—I distracted you with questions about your, er, primer," he said.

Did she have sexual preferences? Hy thought about his startled but aroused expression from earlier, from when she'd surprised him in a way that he'd obviously liked. *That* was her preference: doing what pleased her partner.

But that would probably be another *odd* answer, so instead she ignored his question and said, "I would like to do this again."

His eyes widened slightly.

"Should I not have said that?"

"No."

Hy frowned, confused.

"I meant *no* that you said nothing wrong. I just wasn't expecting you to be so… direct." He chuckled. "Although I *should* expect directness from you at this point."

Hy knew many *ton* women carried on affairs—she'd heard the gossip—but wasn't at all sure of the accepted conventions. Did the women choose their lovers or wait to be chosen?

"I like your directness," the duke said. "And I want to see you again, as well."

Hy nodded, relieved that he felt the same. She glanced around the room. "Would it be possible to meet here again?"

"I think it could be arranged quite easily."

"Then that is what I would like."

He smiled. "Then that is what we shall do."

Hy realized, with a jolt of pleasure and pride, that she had successfully negotiated exactly what she wanted with exactly the man she wanted.

For the first time in a long, long while, Hy had something to look forward to other than cards.

Chapter 17

"Just what the devil is your cousin about, Chatham?"

The words—more of a growl, really—came from behind Sylvester's left shoulder. He turned to find Fowler glowering at the dancefloor, where Shelton and Lady Selina were currently engaged in a quadrille.

"Nice to see you, too, Fowler," Fowler teased. "I thought you weren't coming tonight. Didn't you have an engagement at Carlton House? Please tell me you did not snub the Regent?"

Fowler snarled a vulgar word, his eyes fastened on the vision in white. "I don't know whether to thank you for introducing me to Prinny or call you out, Chatham. The bastard kept me hanging about for almost three hours before granting me an audience that took less than five minutes."

"It might be advisable to lower your voice when you are calling our future king a *bastard*."

Fowler gave a dismissive grunt. "So, is he dangling for her?"

Sylvester didn't need to ask which *he* or *her* Fowler meant. "You would have to ask Shelton that. And if you *did* ask my cousin such a question, I would probably then have to choose between the two of you as to whom I'd second."

Fowler scowled. "And that would be a difficult decision?"

Sylvester gave the bigger man a mocking pat on the shoulder. "You would always be my heart's choice, darling."

Fowler snorted, his grim look easing. "Very droll," he said, still staring at Lady Selina. "Why aren't *you* interested in her?"

"Who said I'm not?" Sylvester couldn't help teasing.

"You've a bloody odd way of showing it!"

Before Sylvester could reply, the bigger man said, "Fucking aristocrats!" causing a nearby chaperone to hurriedly hustle her charges away.

"I take it you are referring to me?" Sylvester asked lightly.

"You don't make any sense, Chatham. You are going to remarry—even *I* know you won't allow everything to go to that bloody bounder Shelton when you die, and yet you are refusing to pursue the sweetest, loveliest goddess to have stepped foot into London in years. You could have her for the snap of your fingers and yet you do nothing!"

"First of all, why are you so eager to kill me off? Who is to say that Shelton won't predecease me?"

Fowler's mouth curved into a genuine smile. "Good point."

"Second, if you are not after her then why are you so curious about who is or is not courting the chit?"

Sylvester already knew the answer to that question, but the other man enjoyed goading him, so it only seemed fair that Fowler should tolerate some goading in return.

The Scot's fair, freckled skin flared like a torch, and he lifted his massive shoulders as if he were shrugging away something unpleasant. "She's a sweet, innocent thing, and you can see her aunt is ready to sell her to the highest bidder."

"Then why aren't *you* bidding, Fowler? After all, when it comes to wealth you could buy and sell me several times over."

"That's an exaggeration," Fowler said. "I could probably only buy and sell you twice."

Sylvester laughed.

"As to your question," Fowler said, giving him an incredulous look. "Surely you can't be suggesting that somebody like her would marry somebody like *me*?"

"What the devil would be so strange about that?"

Fowler ignored his question, instead gazing across the room to where Shelton was currently promenading Lady Selina in a circle.

"Good God," he muttered, visibly anguished. "Just *look* at them."

"They do make a pretty pair—two examples of golden perfection," Sylvester agreed.

"He might look like an angel but he's nothing but a rotter," Fowler said with uncharacteristic viciousness. And then cut Sylvester a quick glance. "Beggin' your pardon, Chatham. I know he is your cousin and heir, but—"

"You have not offended me. Shelton does have a good bit of the rotter in him, but familial loyalty compels me to point out his service record is impeccable."

Fowler made an irritable gesture with one huge paw. "Oh yes, yes, I know all about that," he said, his eyes never moving from his quarry. "But he's been bloody useless since returning from the war, hasn't he?"

"He's certainly had his... problems."

Sylvester experienced an odd pang of regret as he watched his golden cousin dancing. Once, long ago, they had been as close as brothers.

Until Mariah had come between them.

"Shelton wasn't always this way."

"What changed him?"

I married the woman he loved.

Sylvester ignored Fowler's question and glanced again at his watch.

"What is the matter with you tonight, you're as nervous as a cat. Why do you keep looking at your watch?"

"No particular reason," he lied.

"Why don't you ask the lass to dance."

Sylvester squinted up at the towering man. "I'm sorry, but ask *whom*?"

"Who the devil do you think I mean? The Bellamy chit!"

He laughed. "Thanks to *you*, I've already danced with her once more than I wished to do."

"Not tonight."

"You *do* realize what will happen if I ask the same woman to dance twice in a Season?"

"People will say you are courting her and that will warn your cousin off her. Dammit! The man is a dog. He's just sniffing around her because he knows everyone else is mad about her—he's not really interested in *her*. He loves himself too much to love anyone else."

Sylvester laughed at that assessment, which he honestly believed was not true, as much as Shelton did everything in his power to perpetuate the belief.

"Why don't *you* ask her to dance, Fowler?"

"I *have* danced with her, Chatham—as often as she'll let me, as a matter of fact. Unfortunately, I am just another member of her huge court of admirers so it doesn't have the same effect as *you* dancing with her, and you know it."

"I think that me asking the woman to dance will incite Shelton rather than deter him."

"It's just a dance. One dance." Fowler heaved a put-upon sigh. "Can you do this thing for me, Chatham? Can you? I've been a good friend to you and I've never asked you for anything before, have I?"

That was certainly true. "But…"

"Yes?" Fowler prodded.

"What if by dancing with her I give her… expectations? Wouldn't that be a bit cruel?"

Fowler looked struck by that idea, as if it hadn't occurred to him. But he quickly shook the worry off. "You're too old for her to ever look at you that way."

Sylvester had to laugh.

Fowler, who only then realized what he'd said, blushed an amusing shade of red. "Sorry. I didn't mean that like it sounded. I just meant—"

"I know what you meant."

"You could still dance with her, Chatham. Just don't be all… loverlike or flirtatious."

Sylvester stared at the man.

"What? Why are you looking at me that way? If you don't want to help, then just forget I asked anything of you."

Sylvester sighed. "Any particular dance?"

"No. Just do it quickly—I know you want to leave."

"She is probably engaged for every dance already." He snorted. "Probably for the rest of the Season."

"You are a *dook*. Just give them that look you've perfected and the bloke—any bloke—will step aside for you."

"Fine. One dance, but I draw the line about saying anything to Shelton to warn him off. It would only have the exact opposite effect—you must know that."

"Aye, aye, fine. Where are you off to tonight?"

"I fancy some cards."

"With your little Captain Sharp?" Fowler asked slyly.

"Hiram might be there, I don't know," Sylvester lied. It disturbed him how just thinking that name—which wasn't even hers and was *male*—made his cock swell.

"I might go with you," Fowler said, fixing Sylvester with a too-piercing look. "Unless you don't want me along?"

"Don't be daft. Of course, I want you along," Sylvester lied yet again. "But I still believe your time would be better spent soliciting Lady Selina's hand for one dance before you go."

"I'm sure all her dances are taken tonight."

"You won't know unless you ask. You should seize every opportunity, my friend. The Season is hurtling toward its end."

Fowler shrugged irritably. "Go and ask her now, this set is ending."

"Fine. But you will now owe me. I've spent years dampening rumors of my impending nuptials and dancing with a newly out chit *twice* in one Season will have them all on guard." He gestured to a corner of the ballroom that was thick with chaperones. In the middle of the group sat Lady Selina's aunt, Lady Fitzroy. "Just look at them all—look what I'm about to wade into, just for you."

Fowler looked at the thicket of females and cringed. "Bloody hell, it looks like a poorly concealed duck blind." He squinted. "Is that a fowling piece Lady Portsmouth has tucked in her skirts?"

Sylvester laughed. "Yes, you have the right of it, my friend. And we, I'm afraid, are the ducks."

***

Hy stepped out of the hackney in front of Weller's and paid the driver, gathering her strangely scattered thoughts.

It had been four days since her scandalous evening with the duke. Between one thing and another she'd not been able to get away. She knew that was probably for the best—indeed, she should avoid him entirely and forever—but, for once, prudence evaded her.

Her desire to see Chatham had become painfully distracting. All day long, in between carrying out various tasks for the dowager Lady Fitzroy, her mind had returned to the other night.

In addition to their pleasurable sexual interlude, she couldn't help thinking about his reaction—or lack of one, rather—to her story about Charles. She'd been expecting disgust or shock, but instead he'd looked... thoughtful.

They'd ended by agreeing to meet again after their next evening of cards.

It had been past three when the hackney had dropped her off and Hy had feared she'd need to run the *Selina Gauntlet* when she entered the house, but her sister's room had been quiet and dark, so she must have returned early from the ball she'd attended that night.

Over the past four days she had endeavored to spend more time with Selina, but her sister had been distant. When Hy had asked if anything was amiss, Selina had given her a vague answer about missing their sisters and little brother, which had made Hy feel guilty as she'd scarcely thought of anyone but the duke.

All in all, it had been an exceedingly unrestful week and Hy hoped that cards tonight would help sooth her frazzled nerves.

Not to mention seeing the duke after *cards,* a teasing voice whispered in her head.

Hy ignored the taunting thought and nodded to the servant who opened the front door to Weller's. Thankfully, Chance—the oppressive majordomo—was away from the foyer. Indeed, there was only a young lad taking hats and coats.

The rooms she passed through were quieter tonight and Hy suspected that as because of an important ball that evening at the Duchess of Worth's house. She'd been surprised that the duke would be able to get away so early. Her aunt and Selina had both been in a flutter about the event because the Regent was rumored to make an appearance.

Hy paused outside the door to the cardroom, straightened her cuffs, and took a deep breath. While she was looking forward to seeing Chatham, she was also… agitated. She had never suffered from any nervousness when it came to her evenings with Charles, so why was this so much different?

She shoved aside her jitters and opened the door, pausing when six heads turned toward her from the green baize covered table.

And none of those heads belonged to the Duke of Chatham.

***

Sylvester wanted to throttle Fowler. The man seemed determined to do everything possible to cock up an evening that he had very much looked forward to.

First, Fowler had taken his advice and asked Lady Selina to dance. Amazingly, she'd still had the supper waltz free. The Scot had been elated and had begged Sylvester to dine with them.

"Christ, Chatham—if you don't stay, I'll not have a word to say to her! I'm tongue-tied enough when I dance with her, Lord knows how bad it will be sitting at a table."

The huge, powerful, wealthy lord had looked so terrified by the prospect of a meal with a debutante in her first Season that Sylvester had capitulated to his begging, which had meant staying on for supper.

Hyacinth

It had also meant Sylvester had needed to dance twice in one evening.

What had followed had been the most insipid hour in recent memory. While Lady Selina offered intelligent enough conversation, Sylvester's supper dance partner—a pretty young brunette chosen by Lady Fitzroy—had hardly stopped chattering long enough to draw breath.

By the time the meal was over Sylvester was on the verge of puncturing his own eardrums with a fork.

He'd hoped to leave the Scotsman behind at that point, but Fowler attached himself to Sylvester like a limpet. They arrived at Weller's an hour and a half *after* he'd told Hy to meet him. He'd feared that she'd be gone when he opened the door and had smiled like a fool when he'd seen her familiar red head bent over her cards.

If he'd expected a smile in return—or any acknowledgement of what they'd shared at Mrs. Dryden's establishment—he would have been disappointed. Gone was the sensual vixen and in her place was the phlegmatic, nearly pulseless, Hiram Bellamy.

Fowler had ribbed her mercilessly about the diminished pile of counters in front of her, teasing her that she'd lost her touch.

Indeed, the cards did not seem to fall for Hy over the course of the hour that had followed. Even her impassive mask had slipped and irritation had shown through by the time she rose from the table just after one o'clock.

"Leaving already?" Fowler taunted.

"Yes, I've had enough for tonight," Hy said quietly, and Sylvester could hear the truth in her voice.

He shoved away from the table. "I'll walk out with you, Hiram."

"You're leaving too?" Fowler asked, his blunt features creased into a confused frown. "But we only just arrived."

Sylvester mock yawned. "I believe I'll call it a night."

"Give me a moment to cash in all these counters and I'll come along. I could do with an early night."

Sylvester and Hy had exchanged a speaking look.

"We'll meet you downstairs," Sylvester said.

The corridor outside the cardroom was crowded from all the arrivals from the Worth ball, and Sylvester couldn't speak to her until they'd passed through the noisy Hazard room.

"I apologize for being late. I unashamedly place the blame on Fowler's shoulders," he added, only partly in jest. "The man has been clinging to me like a kitten all bloody night long."

Hy laughed, the sound endearingly low and squawky.

"What?" she asked when Sylvester just stared.

"I've not heard you laugh before."

"Imagining Lord Fowler as a kitten is enough to make anyone laugh."

Sylvester couldn't help smiling at the image, even though he still wanted to strangle the man for tampering with his evening.

"So, then… some other night?" she asked in a low voice.

"Good God, no. Tonight."

The slow, sensual smile that spread across her face went straight to his balls. "Somebody is… eager, Your Grace."

Sylvester laughed, delighted by this side of her. "You're damned right I am. We'll have to say that you want to go to Dryden's and I've decided to tag along."

As ever, she took his suggestion in stride. "I take it Mrs. Dryden will know what to do?"

"I already reserved two rooms—adjoining, but with separate entrances."

Her eyelids lowered slightly at that.

Good God but the woman could teach courtesans something about sultry looks.

She opened her mouth but before she could speak Fowler joined them.

"Change of plans," Sylvester said before the other man could commence talking. "Hiram wishes to indulge at Mrs. Dryden's."

Fowler's eyes went round, and he turned to Hy, who merely looked resigned, no doubt anticipating a great deal of teasing. "Why, young Hiram! I'm shocked, I am. Hoping to change your dismal luck with a bit of *free-and-easy?*"

Sylvester could see by the faint wrinkle that formed between her eyes that Hy wasn't familiar with the cant term for *prostitute*.

"I don't believe in luck," she said.

Fowler hooted. "I can understand why you wouldn't after tonight. How much did you lose up there, Bellamy?"

She scowled.

Hyacinth

The Scot just grinned, undaunted by her glare. "I believe I'll join you two lads for a bit of *nature's tufted treasure*."

That term for pussy was one that Hy could guess, even if she'd never heard it before, and her cheeks tinged an amusingly bright shade of red, which Fowler thought was hilarious. He continued to chaff the poor woman mercilessly on the short walk to Dryden's.

Thankfully, the clever madam immediately saw the way matters were and made haste to separate Fowler and lure him off to make his selection.

"You will take the first door on the right," Sylvester murmured as he and Hy climbed the stairs.

Once he'd shut and locked the door behind him, he moved to the connecting door and opened it to find her waiting, her cravat already dangling from her fingers.

Sylvester grinned. "Who is the eager one, now?"

"I want you," she said, tossing aside her cravat and stepping close enough to slide a hand over his erection and grip him hard.

He sucked in a noisy breath. "Oh?" he taunted. "And what do you want with me?"

"What will you let me do?"

Blood roared in his ears at the wicked look on her face. "Whatever you want to do."

Chapter 18

Hy pushed off the high mattress and strode to the collection of decanters that seemed to have multiplied since her last visit. Indeed, there were several new additions in the room—a tray of food, more pillows, and other luxuries that she assumed the duke had arranged for.

She sniffed three of the bottles before finding the one she wanted. After she'd poured a healthy portion of whiskey and took a sip she returned to Chatham.

"I thought you were going to just leave me here," the duke said, not looking especially worried even though his hands and feet were bound to the corners of the big four poster bed.

"Is that something you'd like me to do—leave you here?"

He laughed. "No, thank you."

"Tilt your head up and I'll give you a sip," she ordered.

"You could just untie one of my hands," he suggested, but lifted his head anyway.

"I could do anything I wanted," she corrected mildly, making him laugh, which is what she had hoped to do.

"Yes, that is true. Terrifyingly true."

Hy had developed something of a mania for Chatham's laughter. Not only was the sound exceedingly pleasurable, but she'd grown very fond of the way his eyes lit up and his lips curled at the corners.

She tilted the glass to his mouth and he took a deep swallow and then sighed and dropped his head back. "Thank you. If you are going to keep me prisoner, will you put a cushion beneath my head, please?"

Hy placed the glass on one of the nightstands, gave him not one, but two cushions, and climbed up on the bed.

She knelt between his spread thighs, her gaze resting on his cock, which was rigid and leaking.

"I get to do whatever I want to do?" she confirmed.

"As long as it doesn't end in permanent injury."

"But temporary injuries would be acceptable?"

His jaw dropped.

"I am only teasing."

The duke gave a breathless, relieved laugh. "I suppose I deserve to be teased for allowing you to do this to me."

"You are very trusting," she agreed. She'd been more than a little amazed that he'd given her what she asked for without demur.

"You had better be nice to me because next time it is my turn," he reminded her.

Hy felt a shiver of excitement in her belly when she met his hard, hungry gaze. Curiosity was not an emotion that often plagued her, but she was eager to find out what he wanted.

But that was for next time. Right now, she had him exactly where she wanted: naked and bound and spread eagle.

She slid her hands up his tantalizingly muscled thighs, lingering over the part where his hairs had been worn away by riding.

He groaned. "Mmm, that feels good," he said, flexing his legs as she rubbed the knots from his muscles. "Harder," he muttered, giving a low moan of pleasure when she complied.

"I see my mark on your throat has almost faded," she said, kneading the tight sinews of his hamstrings.

He stared at her through slitted eyes. "Not before it earned me a great deal of ribbing."

"Your *valet* teases you?"

"No, Tackle merely gave me a pained look. I'm speaking of the men at Gentleman Jackson's. They were all quite curious as to what had happened, especially as the word had already spread that I'd let Julia go."

"Julia? That is your mistress?"

"*Was* my mistress."

"Why did you discharge your mistress?"

He cocked his head at her. "Why do you think?"

Her hands stilled. "Because of me?"

"Yes." He frowned. "Why do you look upset about that, Hy?"

"I feel guilty that I'm responsible for somebody losing their job."

His eyes widened and then he laughed. "Oh, sweetheart, don't worry about that—although it speaks of a kind heart. Julia is well taken care of. She doesn't need to work again, although I suspect she will."

Hy *did* feel relief at his admission. She also felt something else—an emotion she couldn't readily identify. She shrugged the thought aside and asked, "You said other men knew about you discharging your mistress—why is that?"

"There was some, er, competition for her."

"Men fight over mistresses?"

"Sometimes."

Hy's brain raced at what it was that made this woman so much in demand. She was tempted to ask, but then wasn't sure she wanted to hear the answer.

Instead, she said, "And that is what men talk about when they are alone? Mistresses?"

"Women or horses, that about sums it up."

Hy snorted. "How charming of you to group women with cattle."

He smiled at her arch tone. "Yes, as a species we men can be quite shallow and vile."

"You don't talk about wives?"

"Not unless you want to end up at twenty paces at dawn."

"So, will you tell the men about me?" she asked, moving to his calves.

The smile that had been curving his lips fled. "No. You are private."

Hy was pleased by his answer, but decided it was probably time to leave the subject behind. "Do you ride a great deal?"

"Most days," he said with a groan, his eyes closing and big body going limp as she massaged the muscle that ran along the shin bone. "My God that feels delicious."

Hy moved to his other leg, amused by his groaning and squirming.

"What else does a duke do with his day?"

He pulled an annoyed face. "If I'm not at Westminster then my time is spent with my secretary or answering correspondence."

"You have a grand country estate?" she asked, even though she knew he did. Indeed, she had seen illustrations in one of the guidebooks in her aunt and uncle's library.

"I do," he said, sounding cautious. Why? Did it shame him to be bedding the daughter of a governess and gambler? The niece of a stablemaster? She wouldn't have guessed he was the sort to care. After all, dukes comprised such a tiny, elevated group of men that all but a few dozen people in Britain were their social inferiors.

"When will you go to the country?" she asked, moving her hands up over the smooth, hairless skin stretched taut over his pelvis, avoiding his

Hyacinth

erect organ—which jerked and jumped as she stroked the skin around it—and settling on the fascinating musculature of his lower abdomen.

He hissed in a breath as she dug her fingers into the tightly woven ridges. "At the end of the month," he said, his voice sounding strained as he flexed the muscles of his belly beneath her vigorous massaging. "How about you?" he asked, "Does Lady Fitzroy close her house here and leave for her country estate? What is it called—Highly?"

Hy shrugged, not wishing to talk about the end of the Season and what would happen.

As usual, he chuckled at her rudeness. The only other person who thought her brusque ways were amusing was Charles and, on occasion, her older sister Aurelia, who understood her best of all her siblings. Probably because Aurelia, too, felt more comfortable with her own company.

And yet for a change Hy was enjoying being around another person more than she enjoyed being alone. She wanted to savor the moment and enjoy the man beneath her fingers for as long as possible, loath for the evening to end.

The duke was a fine physical specimen, his body perfectly proportioned and well-tended for all that he had so many battle scars.

"How long were you in the army?"

"Almost seven years."

"Isn't it unusual for a duke's heir to go to war?"

He didn't immediately answer, and she looked up to find him watching her, his gaze once again wary.

"Should I not ask you personal questions?" she asked, her hands stilling on the hard, slabbed muscles of his chest.

"You can ask me anything you like," he said, his eyes locking with hers in the way he had—when he seemed to exert almost a magnetic pull on her. "I had an elder brother—two, actually—but they both died, Nicholas when I was twenty-four. And then there was Ivo, who was only a year older than me." Sorrow spasmed across his face. "He was my favorite brother and died right before I joined up." He hesitated, and then added, "He hanged himself."

"That is dreadful," Hy said, struggling for something better—more profound to say—and failing.

"It was. He was of a melancholy disposition." Yet again he hesitated. "My father also killed himself. But at least he did not make his exit so... obvious. That did not stop speculation about his hunting *accident*."

"I—I didn't know."

He gave her an absentminded smile. "No, it was kept from all the newspapers, but among certain members of the *ton* it is common knowledge."

Selina had said nothing about it, but then her family was no longer *haute ton*, so it wasn't surprising that Hy had never heard the rumor. "Does—do you suffer from melancholia?"

His lips twisted into a bitter smile. "I am of a pessimistic turn of mind."

"How can one not be?"

His eyebrows lifted. "You do not seem melancholic."

"Oh, I'm not, but I do think there is very little reason to be optimistic when one looks around. Poverty, cruelty, war, and more. Human beings are not the most attractive of creatures when one looks at their behavior."

"No, indeed."

"Your cousin—er, Lord Shelton, he was in the army as well?"

"Yes, he joined a few years after me and we served together." He snorted softly. "Shelton and I were very close back then, if you can believe it."

"Really?"

He cut her an amused look.

"Er, I just mean he seems very hostile toward you now. At least the few times I've met him."

Something that looked like sadness clouded his gaze but then he shrugged. "People change."

"Did you change? Or did he?"

"Oh, both of us, I am sure."

Hy didn't like the subject of Shelton—or the way it made the duke look—and was sorry she'd raised it.

She lowered one hand to his cock, which had softened.

He gave her a wry look as she stroked him. "Shelton is one of those topics best avoided in the bedchamber."

Hy snorted. "So I see." She teased one of his nipples and stroked his quickly hardening cock from root to tip, her gaze riveted to his face as his expression shifted from wry amusement to desire to naked need.

Just when his body became sheened with sweat and his thrusting less controlled, Hy relaxed her grip, her fingers far too loose to provide him with satisfactory friction.

He growled, his hips thrusting harder. "Dammit, Hy..."

She ignored both his warning tone and insistent bucking. Instead, she traced the curved scar beneath his nipple with her tongue and then sucked the tiny bud into her mouth.

His body jolted beneath her, his back arching, hips ramming his hard organ into her unclenched fist.

"Please," Chatham groaned when she continued to torment his nipples but avoided his erection. "I can feel you *smiling* against me," he said, his plaintive tone making her grin even more. "You like hearing me beg, don't you?" he accused, shaking the bed with the violence of his thrusting.

Hy released the nipple she'd been sucking and sat up on her knees, holding his gaze as she tightened her hand around his silky shaft. "Yes, I like hearing you beg." She pumped him slowly, drinking in his need and frustration, his jaws clenching tighter as his hips rolled. "Beg," she ordered.

He gave another of his primitive growls and she could see he had to force the word between his clenched jaws. "*Please*."

"Please, what?"

He glared at her so fiercely she couldn't believe he didn't leave scorch marks. "Please let me *come*."

The combination of angry begging and crudity caused an almost unbearable tightness in her own body. The desire to please him warred with the urge to torment him just a little bit more…

She loosened her grip, admiring the way the muscles in his torso and legs flexed with each frustrated buck of his body. "You can still move your arms and legs too much," she mused. "Next time I will tie you tighter."

Passion flared in his dark eyes as his hips slammed into her fist. "You *witch*."

Hy gave him a squeeze and then released him, earning another groan, this one pained.

"Are you trying to kill me?" he muttered.

She ignored his complaining. "Tell me about this," she said when she'd crawled her way up his torso and could cup the damaged side of his face.

"*Aaargh*! You need to know that *now*?"

She nodded, amused by his infuriated, whiney tone.

He inhaled deeply, lifting her bodily with his expanding chest, and then sighed. "It happened when I'd been in the army five years. It is a gruesome tale, are you sure you want to hear it?"

She nodded.

"We'd taken over a small village and set up our temporary command in the mayor's house. Something about the ease with which we'd just marched in, without meeting any resistance, hadn't felt right to many of us, but the general in charge was satisfied—or he was hungry for his dinner—either way, all that mattered were his orders. To make a long, violent story short, it was a trap."

Hy stilled her hands, staring into his eyes, which had become distant.

"They'd set up artillery on one side of the village and…" He trailed off and then shrugged. "There weren't many buildings left standing an hour later. When our house was shelled, I was thrown toward the hearth and landed on a hot andiron. Hence the distinctive scarring." His gaze sharpened and he smiled at her. "Shelton used to jest that I was fortunate I didn't end up with some French blacksmith's mark permanently burnt into my face."

Hy stared at the scar, trying to imagine how he must have felt. Empathy was not her strong suit, but she'd suffered injuries in her life and knew it must have been excruciating.

She kissed the scar, released him, and then backed down his body, holding his gaze.

"Where are you going *now*?" he demanded, his eyes following her.

Hy stopped over his hips. His cock was still hard, despite the story.

His breathing quickened when she lowered her mouth, but still did not touch him. Hy smiled at his reaction, amused when his cock jumped, just from being stared at.

His lifted his hips, the gesture humorously pleading, and Hy met his gaze while she took his shaft in her fist.

He hissed, his jaws clenching and nostrils flaring as his eyes lowered to her lips. "I've dreamed about your mouth," he said, his voice hoarse with desire.

Hy lowered her head until she could reach the slit in his crown with her tongue.

His body shook as she probed the tiny opening with the pointed tip of her tongue, teasing him until several vulgar, desperate words slipped from his lips.

Not until he whispered, "*Please*," one more time did she take the fat head in her mouth and commence to wreck him.

***

Hyacinth

The instant Hy released the last of Sylvester's bindings he grabbed her by the waist and rolled her onto her back, smirking at her squeak of surprise.

"You are not just a temptress," he said, kissing her hard. "You are a torment-tress."

"I don't believe that is a word," she protested, her voice pleasingly breathless.

"The next time it is my turn," he reminded her. "And I shall tell you right now that I am looking forward to hearing *you* beg."

She smirked.

"What? You don't think it will happen?"

"You are welcome to try."

He growled and claimed her mouth again, stabbing deeply and suggestively with his tongue to warn her what she'd be getting.

They were both breathless when he pulled away.

"When *is* the next time?" he demanded, sitting up on his knees and taking the opportunity of having his hands back under his control to fondle her gorgeous tits.

"I don't know." She hissed and her back arched when he pinched her nipples as she'd done to his a short time earlier. "It all depends on my aunt and whether she needs me."

Sylvester grunted, displeased by her answer, but not surprised. Finding time to be together was annoyingly difficult. He was spoiled by having had a mistress at his beck and call for most of his adult life, and that was the way he liked it. Between Hy caring for her aunt and accumulating money for her brother she simply did not have much time left for *him*.

"You didn't win much tonight, did you?" he asked, giving her nipples one last tweak before sitting back.

"Not much," she agreed, clasping her hands beneath her head and staring up at him, evidently unaware of how fetching she appeared in such a traditionally masculine pose. "But I am getting closer."

Sylvester scowled. "Why don't you just—"

"Thank you, but no," she said quietly, her eyes sliding toward the clock. "And I really should be going soon."

He should know better than to offer her money. But this entire situation was… well, he was too accustomed to having things his way. For years he had done nothing but complain about how people catered to his every whim and now he was whining because the only person who did not leap to obey was not leaping to obey.

Sylvester knew he was unreasonable to expect to have whatever he wanted whenever he wanted it, but it was frustrating to see a problem he could easily fix and yet be prevented from helping.

He wished like hell that she would accept his money and help, but he could not imagine her being satisfied if he set her up in a house like his former mistresses.

No, his new lover was a contrary woman who did things her own way.

Sylvester leaned down to steal one last, lingering kiss, pleased when she slid her arms around him, her hands wandering to his buttocks, which she squeezed and kneaded.

He groaned and reluctantly pulled away. "I supposed we'd best get you home."

"Do you think Fowler is still here?" she asked as she rolled from the bed and commenced to dress in a matter-of-fact way that held him riveted.

If you enjoy watching a woman pull on stockings, small clothes, and breeches then you are obviously smitten, Sylvester.

He knew he was smitten and he didn't care. He'd spent far too many of the last few years dangerously bored. He'd take smitten over crushing ennui every time.

"Chatham?"

"Hmm?" he asked, fully aware that he was lounging and watching her dress rather than readying himself.

"I asked if Fowler will be out there?"

"No, he will find his own way home. But just in case I will leave first, and you come down a few minutes later."

She nodded and picked up the torn sheets she used to bind her chest.

"Here, let me help you," he said, getting off the bed.

She gave him an arch look. "I don't know… Can you remember that we are supposed to be putting them back on and not taking them off?"

He laughed at her dry humor. "I think you left a few of my wits unscrambled."

Chapter 19

As things turned out, Hy had not only the next day completely free, but also the next evening because the Dowager went to visit an acquaintance of hers in Richmond for the night.

"She is an old school friend, and it has been years since I've seen her." She pulled a face. "If this were *my* home, I could invite her *here*. But least said on that subject, the better."

Hy thought so, too. The dowager's dislike of her daughter-in-law was both unfair and irrational.

"In any case, I shan't need you Hyacinth, so you may catch up on your sleep while I am away."

Of course, Hy planned to do no such thing.

It was her hope the duke would send word that evening and she could meet him. If he did not, she would have to venture out on her own. After last night's dismal performance she needed to recoup some of her losses.

But she had hours until evening came and so she went to look for Selina, not surprised when she found her in the music room, practicing on their aunt's superlative instrument.

Her sister was the most talented pianist in her family, so it was nice that she was able to play on a piano that was better than the old castoff at Queen's Bower.

Hy waited until Selina finished the nocturne and then clapped softly, so as not to startle her.

Selina spun around on the bench, her distant gaze quickly sharpening.

"That was very good," Hy said.

"Anyone could sound good on this." She gently stroked the black shiny case.

"I'll wager I could make it howl like an alley cat."

Selina snorted. "That is because you don't *practice*."

Hy didn't argue.

Selina narrowed her gaze. "How is it that you are so chipper and amusing with so little rest? I heard you come in, you know."

"I didn't come here to account for my evening, Linny. I came to ask if you wanted to go to Hatchard's and perhaps stuff your face with some of those cream buns from that tea shop just around the corner?"

Selina clapped her hands. "You have a day free?"

"I do," she said, not sharing the information that her evening was also free.

"I have a few errands I must run," Selina warned, cutting Hy a nervous look.

"Modiste? Milliner?"

"Er, both, I'm afraid."

Hy was a good sister and bit back her agonized groan. "I will do them with you."

Selina gave her a look of mock astonishment and laid a hand on her brow. "Are you ill? Should I summon a doctor?"

"Very droll. Come along," Hy said. "Let us get going before Aunt comes up with more *errands*."

***

"Why is this new gown so important?" Hy asked a few hours later as they left the modiste's, where her sister tried on a rather magnificent white and silver gown.

Selina pursed her lips and walked for a few moments without answering.

"Linny?" Hy prodded.

"Aunt has a ridiculous notion in her head."

Their flighty aunt *always* had at least a dozen ridiculous notions floating around in her head, but Hy didn't point that out.

"What notion?"

Selina's cheeks darkened. "It's foolish."

"Selina."

"The Duke of Chatham has asked me to dance twice."

Hy was grateful that her sister was looking straight ahead rather than at her when she heard that name.

"Oh?" she finally managed. "Does that mean something?"

"Oh, Hy!" Selina clucked her tongue.

Hyacinth

"Why are you *oh, Hy*ing me? Don't you dance twice with lots of men?"

"Yes, I do, but the duke almost never dances."

"Then why does he go to all those balls?"

Selina laughed. "You are hopeless."

"So I've been told. Often."

"Aunt believes I need at least two new gowns. One for Lady Norridge's ball next week and then one for Castleford ball. As you know, that will be the unofficial end of the Season."

Hy hadn't known but kept that to herself. "So, there are not even two weeks remaining?"

"I thought you would be grateful, but you sound almost sad, Hy."

In two weeks, the duke would leave for his country house and it was likely that Hy would never see him again.

"What happened to his wife?" Hy asked just as they reached the bookstore.

"Whose wife?" Selina asked.

"The duke's—you said *re*married."

"Why do you care? Have you played cards with him again? I noticed his clothing isn't in the trunk."

"No, I haven't seen him again," Hy lied. "I sent Will to return the clothing. As to why I'm asking—you brought his name up."

"His wife died in childbed with their first child. They'd not been married long. It is a tragic story. She was exquisitely beautiful and had been sought after by half the men that Season. But then the duke came back from the war and it was love at first sight." She gave Hy a cutting look. "Yes, Hy—I said *love*, that blissful state you do not believe in."

Hy smiled faintly, still digesting her sister's words. Why should she be surprised that he'd been married to a beautiful woman? After all, he was handsome, rich, and a duke.

Still, it was… surprising considering that he seemed to like Hy. Or at least he liked having sex with her. As bad as she was at reading people, she would have needed to have a wooden block for a brain not to notice he'd enjoyed their time in bed. A great deal.

"What are you smiling at, Hy?"

"Hmm? Oh, nothing," she murmured. "Let's cross the street now," she said before her sister could persist.

They were almost at the bookstore door when a young man saw them—or Selina, rather—and rushed forward to open the door for them.

"Thank you," Selina murmured primly and sailed into the shop, head held high to discourage any inappropriate overtures from the visibly smitten young man.

Hy was going to thank him, too, but then she realized he had not even noticed her.

***

By eight o'clock that evening Hy had not received a message from the duke.

Whether he was busy or just didn't think she'd be able to get away two nights running, she didn't know.

Hy briefly considered staying home. After all, she had made a bargain with him. To go out without him would be breaking her word, wouldn't it?

After some reflection, she decided that she couldn't be blamed for not accompanying him if he wasn't available. Besides, last night had been dreadful. She still needed another nine hundred pounds and had barely two weeks to get it.

And so she summoned Will to the library. "I'll need Jerry's services for the evening."

"Very good, my lady. When should he collect you?"

"As soon as possible." Why not? There were always people at Jensen's, no matter the hour. "Tell Jerry I will need him for the *entire* evening, Will. I won't have another way home tonight."

"Aye, my lady. The whole evening." The fact that he blushed told her that he knew that his brother had—on that one occasion—taken money from the duke to leave her. "You can count on him, my lady."

Hy nodded. She could only hope that Jerry would not leave her stranded again.

***

If last night had been one of Hy's worst evenings, tonight was one of her very best.

Although there had not been any open seats in the private room where she usually played, there was a table in the main room that offered the same game, albeit in a far, far noisier environment. Also, the players did not take turns at bank. Rather, one of Jensen's men dealt every hand.

Hyacinth

"Mr. Jensen sent this over for you, sir."

Hy looked up from her cards to find the waiter handing her a glass. "I didn't ask for this."

"On the house, sir."

The other players were looking irritably at her, waiting for her to play, so she just nodded and said, "Thank you."

Once the hand was over, Hy glanced at her pile of counters and then took out her watch. It was barely past midnight and she was already up four hundred pounds.

"Not leaving yet, are you lad?" the older man on her right side asked, grinning at her as he stacked his counters. "You're my good luck, you are."

"There's no such thing as luck," Hy said absently, before she could catch herself.

But the old man laughed rather than look offended.

"You in?" the dealer asked her.

Before she could answer, the old man pushed forward a counter. "He's in. Why, he's not even finished his drink." He shoved the untouched brandy toward Hy. "You don't want to offend Mr. Jensen now, do you?" He jerked his chin at a man in an ill-fitting suit who was leaning against the far wall, his gaze on Hy.

She picked up the glass and drank fully half, needing to struggle not to gag as the brandy was cheap and rough.

Fifteen minutes later Hy was beginning to wonder what had been in that glass. She was also wondering if she could make it out of the building—or if she could even manage to stand.

"You in?" the dealer asked, except there were now two identical men where there had only been one before.

Hy's tongue felt like it was made of lead and coated in fur. She swallowed repeatedly, but the heavy, fuzzy feeling wouldn't go away.

"I think our lad's had a bit too much to drink," the man sitting next to Hy said, leaning in close and leering. "What he needs is a breath of fresh air. Come with me, my boy. Help me take him outside, Roy."

The room spun around her as at least two men all but dragged her from the room since her feet had stopped working.

"Where—where you taking me?" she slurred.

"You're a lucky, lucky lad and you get to meet Mr. Jensen," the man on her right said.

The old man smiled down at Hy, his expression no longer benevolent, but avid and cruel. "See, *there* is luck after all!"

Hy's vision blurred, and just kept getting blurrier, no matter how much she blinked.

When the men shoved her against the brick wall in the alley, her legs simply slid out from under her and she slumped to the ground, landing in something cold.

"Pick him up," a new voice snapped.

Even in her dizzy state Hy could guess who was speaking.

Her captors jerked her to her feet and held her upright, and then an ugly face looked up at her. "I don't like people countin' cards," the newcomer hissed. When Hy didn't answer, he snarled, "Wake up, you!" And then he slapped her so hard that white lights exploded behind her eyelids, which slid closed.

"I *said* wake up." He slapped her again and Hy forced her eyes open before he knocked her head right off her neck.

"I'm awake," she croaked, the pain in her temple causing her vision to fragment so badly there were two identical men standing in front of her.

"You know what I do to Captain Sharps, eh? Do ye?" Huge fists grabbed her coat and shook her so hard that Hy bit her tongue. "I'm gonna make an—"

"What in God's name is going on here?" a familiar voice thundered, although Hy had never heard him sound so cold and furious before.

The hands holding her coat let go and she slid back down the wall into the puddle again.

"Oh, Yer Grace. Er, wot'cher doin' back here, sir?" Hy's persecutor asked, his rough tone suddenly diffident and fawning.

Hy felt movement beside her and a gloved, gentle hand took her chin and tilted her face toward the light overhead.

The duke hissed. "Hy, can you hear me?"

Her tongue was even more leaden and furry, but she could nod, even though it made the world spin.

The duke released her and stood. "You've drugged him—what did you give him?"

"I'm sorry, Yer Grace! I didn't know he was one of yer mates," Jensen squawked, sounding terrified, even though he probably had three stone on the duke.

"I asked you what you gave him?" Chatham's voice oozed so much menace that even Hy shivered.

Hyacinth

"Nuffing that will 'urt 'im. "Ee'll be all right and tight in a few hours."

"His lip is bleeding. Did you strike him?"

"I just gave 'im a wee—*urgh*! *Aghh*! Yer choking'—" his voice broke off with a gurgle.

"He's not even eight bloody stone, you fucking brute!" the duke yelled.

Somebody gave a pained grunt.

"You want to hit somebody, hit *me*, you bully bastard!"

Hy was vaguely aware of more grunting, hitting, and begging, but couldn't have said how long it all went on. Eventually, there was a sound much like she'd made when she slid to the cobbles, but this time the body sounded far heavier.

"Go fetch the carriage!" the duke barked, and then, once again, he was crouched in front of her—him and an identical friend.

"You little fool," he muttered, and then slid an arm beneath her legs and another behind her back and lifted her without so much as a huff.

"I'm—I'm thorry, Your Grathe," Hy whispered.

"Hush." Firm lips pressed against the top of her head and suddenly Hy felt warm.

And safe.

She closed her eyes and let the darkness take her.

Chapter 20

Sylvester glanced at his watch and saw it was less than five minutes later than the last time he'd checked.

He slipped it back in his pocket and turned to Hy—for some reason he simply could not think of her as Mary—wincing yet again at the sight of her cut lip and swollen cheek. The rage in his belly flared hot just looking at her mouth and he briefly wished he'd kept hitting Jensen even after the man had gone down.

Sylvester was generally even tempered, but he'd genuinely seen red when he'd come around that corner and saw Hy between two of Jensen's bully boys, with the ex-boxer's big, meaty fist poised to strike her.

All the anger he'd been feeling at her for slipping out after giving Sylvester her word that she would only go to gambling hells with him—especially dangerous ones like the Pigeonhole—had dissipated in the blink of an eye when he'd seen her bruised and battered face.

"What am I going to do with you, Hy?" he murmured, picking up her hand and holding it in his. It was not the hand of a lady, not even the hand of a female. The nails were chewed to the quick, her knuckles were grazed, and there were various scrapes and cuts that demonstrated she did more than spend her days eating sweetmeats and stitching samplers.

Sylvester tried to picture her garbed in a dress and nursing a sick relative and simply did not possess ample imagination. He could only see her two ways: cool and merciless at a card table or naked and merciless in a bed.

There was a light tap on the door and Sylvester released Hy's hand and stood when Mrs. Dryden entered.

He joined her on the far side of the room so they could talk above a whisper.

"Has she woken up yet?" the madam asked.

"No. But her breathing seems to have become less labored. The emetic you gave her has obviously had a positive effect." He hesitated and then added, "Thank you for insisting on that. I'm sorry if I shouted at you at the time."

Mrs. Dryden gave him a surprisingly warm smile. "I know it seemed like a cruel thing to do, but it was better to purge everything from her system. Would you like some tea, Your Grace."

"Yes, tea is an excellent idea." He smiled at her. "Thank you for all your help. I apologize for turning your establishment into a field hospital—not to mention the other, er, services you've recently provided." Although he'd paid her very well for the use of her rooms, he knew she was only accommodating him because of who he was.

"You have certainly kept things interesting," she said, smiling. "One of the maids is cleaning and mending her clothing. Are you still insistent on taking her home? She is welcome to stay here—nobody will see her but me and one very trustworthy servant."

Sylvester hesitated. "I'm not sure what I'll do if she is still sleeping when dawn approaches. Your offer is kind, but I believe she—"

"Your Grace?" a voice said behind him.

Sylvester turned. "I'm right here, Hy."

"I will leave you now," Mrs. Dryden said.

He nodded and strode toward the bed. "Ah, the sleeper has awakened."

"Where am I?" she asked, squinted up at him, which made him recall her spectacles.

"Here," he said, lifting the glasses off the nightstand and lowering them onto her face. "I'm afraid they got scratched during your scuffle."

"Thank you." She adjusted the frames slightly and then glanced around.

"It was the only place I could think of to bring you," Sylvester said when she did not speak.

She nodded. "Thank you for rescuing me from my predicament. I'm sorry I didn't listen to you and Fowler when you warned me about Jensen."

"Hmm." He took her hand and gave it a light squeeze. "You know how to take the wind out of a good scolding, don't you? *I'm sorry that I didn't send you a message as I promised to do. I was unavoidably delayed, and when I finally received word that you weren't at home—that you'd indeed gone out—it was late. Fortunately, the servant who usually relays the messages was able to discover where you'd gone and so I went directly to Jensen's." He lightly brushed her cheek with the back of his knuckles. "Would that I had arrived even five minutes sooner."

"Do I look bad?" she asked, sounding more interested than concerned.

"Jensen looks worse."

Her mouth pulled into a faint smile. "Ah, yes—I remember that now. I could hear you thrash him, but unfortunately my eyes weren't working well enough to watch. Did you give him a proper roughing up?"

He barked a laugh. "Bloodthirsty little thing, aren't you."

"I'm glad you beat him," she said, her pupils flaring slightly as they flickered over Sylvester's body, the heat and unexpected admiration in her gaze causing an entirely inappropriate response in his breeches.

"How does your head feel?"

She lifted a hand and felt her jaw and lip. "I've got a headache, but I don't think it is from being struck." She moved her jaw from side to side experimentally and gave a slight shrug. "There is not much damage. But they drugged me while I was playing." Her lips pulled into a moue of disgust. "My mouth tastes dreadful."

"That could be the drugs or the fact that Mrs. Dryden gave you something to purge your stomach of whatever he'd given you." He hesitated and then said, "She knows about you." Sylvester gestured to Hy's torso, which was bare beneath the sheet. "I thought Jensen might have hit you somewhere other than your face, so Mrs. Dryden stripped you and looked for signs of internal damage."

She lifted the sheet and glanced down at herself. "I don't recall him hitting me anywhere else."

"No, you seem fine, thank God."

Hy lowered the sheet and looked at the clock, grimacing when she saw the time. "I have to get dressed and get home, Your Grace."

Sylvester wanted to argue—she looked so beaten and exhausted—but instead he nodded. "I'll ring for your clothing and some hot water."

***

"Oh, my goodness, Hyacinth! What happened to your poor face?" Aunt Ellen demanded when Hy entered the sitting room the following afternoon.

"I caught my hem with my heel and fell down the stairs." In fact, she rather felt as if she'd fallen down several flights of stairs. Hy hurt all over.

Hyacinth

She hurt so much that she'd checked her body in the looking glass after she'd stripped off her *Hiram* outfit at five o'clock that morning. But other than a few more scrapes on her hands and calves she was unmarked.

"You must be more *careful* my dear. I had hoped that you would come to the Norriston ball with your sister and I, but"—she broke off and bit her lip, her brow deeply furrowed— "I don't think that swelling will have abated by then. And it is already turning into a dark bruise. I will send Wallace to you with some cosmetics to conceal some of the damage, but I'm not sure you should go."

Hy curbed the urge to cheer. "No, I think you are correct. I should stay home and rest."

"Yes, I suppose you should," her aunt said.

"Lady Fitzroy wanted to know if you had any blue to match this." Hy held up a strand of embroidery floss.

"Let me check and see, my dear."

Hy's gaze slid to Selina while her aunt riffled through her needlework basket, but her sister refused to look at her. She'd seen Hy's face first thing—over breakfast—and had been furious when she'd heard the—highly abridged—story of her evening.

Now she was giving Hy *The Silent Treatment*—as their brother Doddy termed it—because Hy had refused to promise to stop going out in the evenings and Selina was no longer placated by the promise of having Jerry drive her. Of course, Hy could hardly tell Selina that she would *only* go out in the company of the duke from now on, so her sister was justifiably furious.

As much as Hy wanted to ease the tension between them, she refused to give up her few remaining evenings with the duke—why lie to herself that it was only about cards?

Hy glanced down at her aunt, who was still digging through her needlework basket. "Have you received any word from our mother lately, Aunt Ellen?"

"Nothing for almost a week. It is unlike her to be so quiet. And of course your father could not lift his hand to write a letter if his life were hanging in the balance."

Hy knew that her aunt greatly disapproved of Hy's father, who was her younger brother. She didn't think her aunt approved of Hy's mother, either, but at least the two had always corresponded regularly. Whatever was happening in Little Sissingdon had certainly ceased the flow of letters from not only the countess, but also her sister Phoebe, who'd always been a faithful letter writer.

Hy took after their father when it came to writing letters. Or writing of any kind, which was abhorrent to her. It was bad enough putting one's thoughts into words; putting them into words *on paper* was ten-fold worse.

"Ah, here you go, Hyacinth." Her aunt held up the embroidery thread. "These two shades are very close, I think." She pulled a face. "Of course, *Mama* is unlikely to be pleased."

Aunt Ellen was probably right. Even though the colors looked identical to Hy's admittedly unskilled eyes, the dowager seemed to take pleasure in persecuting her mild-mannered daughter-in-law simply *because* the younger Lady Fitzroy was so sweet-natured.

Hy was halfway to the dowager's apartment when she heard footsteps behind her.

She turned to find her sister.

"I thought you weren't speaking to me."

"Very droll," her sister retorted. "You'd better not be thinking about going out just because aunt has released you from attending the ball tonight."

Hy turned her back on Selina and resumed her trek.

"I shall tell her what you are doing, Hy," Selina called after her.

Hy stopped and spun on her heel. "Why would you make such a stupid threat?"

Selina recoiled at her uncharacteristic anger. "Because what you are doing is *dangerous*, Hy. Just look at your face! What would have happened if—"

"I won't play those pointless *what if* games, Selina. I am *fine*. I am also nearly at my goal. There is barely enough time left to get the rest of the money. If you just stay out of my affairs for a little longer then you—we," she amended hastily, "can return home and have a year's reprieve."

"And what *then*?" her sister hissed.

"Aunt Ellen will want you back—you can come for another Season and not be in such a hurry to—"

"I have had five offers of marriage."

"*What*? You told me just the other day you'd had none."

"I lied," she said, her cheeks flaming.

Hy was so confused she didn't know where to start. "So—who were these men?"

Hyacinth

"It doesn't matter. They were all well off, but I told aunt to politely decline on my behalf. My point in telling you is that I *can* get the money we need without you putting your life in danger, Hy."

"I don't understand, Linny. Why haven't you told me about any of this?"

Selina opened her mouth and then closed it.

Hy stared at her normally honest sister, who looked more miserable by the second. Finally, it hit her. "You haven't told me because you feel guilty for not accepting any of them."

"Of course I feel guilty—just look at you! Your poor, poor face."

Hy winced at her sister's wailing and glanced around.

Selina lowered her voice. "I know we are in terrible peril, and yet"—she broke off and bit her lip. "And yet I did not accept offers that would rescue all of us. *Five. Times.* I am wicked and selfish and—"

"Hush! We all promised not to sacrifice ourselves—do you remember that, Selina?"

"Yes, but—"

"No *buts*. You are not to sacrifice yourself to save the rest of us."

"But that is what *you* are doing."

"I *like* what I am doing. You would not *like* being married for the rest of your life to a man you did not love. You did the right thing rejecting those offers. And besides," she added when Selina looked determined to argue, "marrying somebody doesn't just last a few weeks like my gambling, it will last the rest of your life." She paused and then asked, "Is there somebody you are hoping will ask you to marry?"

Selina hesitated and then nodded, her cheeks once again turning pink.

"Who is it?"

"I'm not saying."

"Why not? You've cried on my shoulder about every boy you've ever lost your heart over and yet—"

"This is *different*."

"Different how?"

"Stop bullying me!"

"Is it the Duke of Chatham?" Hy blurted before she could stop herself. "Is that who it is?"

Selina looked away for a moment, and then looked back. Her mouth pursed tightly and her eyes narrowed in a way that would have been threatening if her sister wasn't so beautiful and feminine that it robbed a person of breath. "I will tell you who it is if you promise not to go out to any more horrid clubs."

Good God. Was her sister in love with Chatham?

Was the duke in love with her sister?

Why did the thought leave her so breathless? Why did her chest feel so… hollow? Selina and the duke would be a magnificent couple. It would be like one of those nauseating romantic novels all her sisters enjoyed reading so much—a handsome, but wounded duke who falls in love with a lovely but penniless heroine.

"Will you promise, Hy?"

You can promise and learn the truth right now, her cool inner voice whispered.

Hy looked at her beautiful sister—the woman every man in London seemed to have fallen in love with, perhaps even the one who was currently Hy's bed partner—and suddenly knew that she didn't want the truth.

"No, I won't promise."

And then she turned her back on Selina and walked away.

Chapter 21

Sylvester flung open the door to the connecting room and then grabbed Hy, who was in the process of shrugging out of her coat, by the upper arms and pinned her against the wall.

He claimed her mouth like a starving man falling on a banquet, more than a little pleased when she responded with equal hunger. She shoved her fingers into his hair, knocking off his hat and tightened her hands into fists.

"Mmmm," he groaned, relishing the oddly pleasurable pain as she flexed her fingers, tugging hard enough to pull out more than a few hairs. "I thought the evening would *never* end," he said when he came up for air.

"I noticed your playing was off tonight, Your Grace. Were you distracted by something?"

He nipped her lower lip. "You find that amusing, do you?"

She gave a throaty chuckle as Sylvester bit her chin.

"I thought bloody Fowler would never let us leave the table," he muttered as he cupped her buttocks with both hands and ground his aching erection against her.

A muffled, primitive noise vibrated in her chest, and she bit his lower lip, sucking it into her mouth hard enough to pull a yelp from him.

She released him and smirked at him. "Did that hurt, Your Grace?"

"You are a vixen." He thrust his hips hard enough to abrade the sensitive skin of his cock, the dull pain only adding to his desire.

"It is your turn tonight," she said in a breathless voice, speaking the words between savage kisses that were more like bites. "What do you want to do with me?"

Sylvester groaned. God. The thoughts that had tormented him these past few days. But as experienced as she appeared and as accepting as she had been, Sylvester could not bring himself to ask for what he craved. Not tonight. Maybe not ever as they had only mere days remaining before he would need to go home to Chatham for the summer.

No, it was better that he not risk disgusting her, not when he could recall Mariah's revulsion even a decade later.

"I give my choice to you," he whispered, and then closed his mouth on the thin skin of her throat, not sucking hard enough to mark her as he knew she'd not be able to hide a love bite behind a cravat as he had. But tonight he was determined to leave his mark somewhere on her body—somewhere only he would see it.

She pulled back just enough so she could meet his gaze. "You will allow me to choose—again?"

He nodded, his fingers massaging the prominent bones of her pelvis, wishing he'd already stripped her so it was skin, rather than clothing he was touching.

Her lips curved into a smile so slow that it was like watching the sun rise. But if her smile was like a sunrise then her eyes were more like sunset, her pupils swelling until the black swallowed the tropical green.

"That is very generous of you, Chatham," she said, her tone almost teasing.

"I can be a very generous man, Hiram," he teased right back.

Her eyelids lowered and she stroked her hand over the scar on his face that nobody but he, himself, ever touched. "I know what you want, Your Grace."

It was suddenly difficult to draw enough air into his lungs and he pressed his cheek into her palm, his fingers moving to the catches of her breeches, tugging and pulling so roughly he thought he tore off one of the buttons in his haste. He pulled on the tape that held her drawers, shoved his hand beneath the fine linen, and cupped her sex. "Sylvester."

She merely stared at him, her fingers lightly caressing, her expression as maddeningly unreadable as ever.

"Say it," he ordered, and curled his middle finger into the soft petals of her sex, hissing at the wet heat he encountered.

"Sylvester."

He thrust a finger inside her hard enough to bring her up onto her toes. "I like the sound of that," he muttered, pressing his thumb beneath her tiny bundle of nerves. "Say it again."

"Sylvester."

He growled, withdrew his hand, sucked his finger clean, and then steered her backward toward the massive bed.

She gave a startled half-gasp, half-laugh. "I thought *I* was going to choose."

Hyacinth

"You can do whatever you want after—but first I need to get inside you. Now *strip*."

***

All night long at the gambling hell the duke had looked harried and distracted. And if Hy had noticed it, that meant everyone else had. Especially his friend Fowler, who had taunted him mercilessly all evening.

Hy's own distraction had led to some of the stupidest wagers she'd ever made. Her brain had been fuzzy—a unique phenomenon in her experience—and her body had been feverish since receiving Chatham's curt message earlier that day: *Weller's tonight.*

Thank *God* she had been able to get away.

No thanks to her wretched sister, who'd engineered tasks and duties for Hy every single evening for the last five days, until Hy's difficult-to-rouse temper had reared its ugly head and she'd snapped at her sister.

Selina had desperately lobbied their aunt to press Hy's attendance at the miserable Norridge ball tonight.

Interestingly, it had been the dowager who'd saved Hy from a fate worse than public stoning—at least in Hy's opinion. The old lady had demanded her attendance at a crony's card party tonight, only to change her mind at the last moment—after Selina and her aunt had already left for the ball—giving Hy her liberty for the evening.

And so here she was *finally*, with the duke all but tearing off her boots, stockings, and breeches while Hy fumbled with her coats and shirt.

"Leave the wrapping for me," the duke ordered, pulling hard on one of Hy's boots.

Hy might not have much of a sense of humor, but even she could see the absurdity in using a duke as her bootjack.

Chatham had dropped to his haunches to pull off her stocking, which he tossed aside and then lifted her bare foot to his mouth, his eyes never leaving hers as he trailed kisses over the arch and down to her big toe and then beneath to the sole. Hy shivered at the pleasurable feeling of slick heat as his tongue moved over the remarkably sensitive skin. She never would have imagined that having her foot licked could be so erotic.

He kissed the spot he'd licked and then lowered her foot onto the tented front of his breeches.

Hy pushed down and he groaned and slid to his knees, thrusting his hard ridge against her.

Something about seeing such a powerful man on his knees sent a sharp thrill of arousal to her already stimulated sex. Her mind was racing with possibilities when the duke suddenly surged to his feet, grabbed her by the hips, and tossed her onto the bed.

Not until he was kneeling between her spread thighs did she realize he'd not removed a single article of clothing.

That, too, sent pleasurable shivers through her.

"I've thought of you often these past five, interminable days—far too much for my sanity," he said, the words almost an accusation as his hands went to the front of his tight satin breeches.

"What have you thought?" she asked, genuinely curious.

He laughed. "I'm not sure I should tell you—it might go to your head." He shoved his breeches and drawers down his thighs, exposing his thick, ruddy cock. Something about the combination of his elegantly clothed torso coupled with his pulsing erection and bare thighs was obscene.

Not to mention unbearably erotic.

"Tell me, Chatham."

He ignored her and stroked himself from root to tip, using the copious moisture on his crown to slick his shaft. "Do you like watching me touch myself?"

"Yes," she said without hesitation. Hy actually *adored* watching him pleasure himself but was too dizzy with desire to articulate that fact just then.

He worked himself slowly, performing for her. "I fisted myself every single night—sometimes twice—thinking about you."

Her lips parted in shock as she visualized Chatham alone in his bed—it would be some grand, ancient thing fit for a duke—stroking himself to thoughts of *Hy*.

"You like that, don't you—thinking of me hard and wanting… for you."

Hy couldn't help smiling. "Yes. I like that very much."

He snorted. "Do you want this inside you?" he asked, circling his hand around his root and pushing his hips forward, until he appeared twice as long.

She nodded, enrapt and unable to look away. "Yes."

"I'll give it to you, but first show me that pretty cunt of yours," he ordered, his fist moving faster.

Hyacinth

A shudder wracked her at his crude command and Hy slid her hands down to her sex, parting her lower lips and exposing the most private part of her to his hot gaze.

The duke's nostrils flaring. "Bloody hell that's a gorgeous sight. Keep yourself nice and open for me," he muttered, lowering his body over hers. He reached between them and dipped a finger inside her, pumping her several times. "So wet," he hissed, removing his finger and replacing it with something larger. "Are you ready?"

"Yes, I want you... please," Hy said in a strained, desperate voice.

The last word was hardly out of her mouth when he hilted himself with one long, hard stroke.

They both groaned.

"This is heaven," he said as he held her full of cock, his breath hot against her temple. "Did you think of me, Hy?" he asked, withdrawing slowly.

"Every night."

He gave a breathy chuckle and then slammed back in.

"Did you touch yourself when you thought about me?"

"Every night."

He raised up onto one elbow, until they were nose to nose, his free hand moving to her clitoris. "One day I will want to see that."

She sucked in a breath when he pressed his thumb in exactly the right spot and began to rub her in tight circles while his hips pumped, his thrusting slow and deep.

Hy pushed her hands up beneath his shirt to his chest.

His eyelids flickered when she tugged on his nipples. "Good Lord that feels good," he said, his hips drumming faster.

Hy set her feet on the backs of his calves and tilted her hips to welcome him as deeply as he could go.

"Yesss," he hissed, his thumb rubbing harder and faster while he worked her with increasingly punishing strokes.

Hy's orgasm came fast and hard, every single muscle in her body clenching for one impossibly long moment before bliss exploded.

The duke gasped when she convulsed around him, his thrusting became more savage and less controlled.

"You have captivated me," he whispered just before he gave an anguished groan and then withdrew from her body.

Hy was ready for him this time and she reached out and pushed his hand away, closing her fist around his slick cock. "Come for me,

Chatham." She pumped him twice more before he threw his head back and spent in hot ribbons on her belly.

***

Sylvester woke to the exquisite feel of a skilled hand caressing his balls.

He lifted heavy eyelids and looked directly into an intense pair of green-blue eyes.

"Oh good, you're awake," Hy said, staring at him with that disconcertingly direct gaze.

He gave a sleepy chuckle. "I apologize—how long was I asleep?"

"Only eleven minutes."

"You *timed* me?"

She nodded. "You started to shift and move when I began to touch you."

"I'm surprised I didn't wake immediately." Bloody hell but her hand felt good. Sylvester shamelessly spread his thighs to give her more room to ply her remarkable skills.

"I've been touching you for three minutes."

He couldn't help laughing.

She cocked her head. "What is so amusing?"

"Nothing."

Her hand stilled and her brow furrowed. "You should tell me if I'm doing something that is odd."

"There is that word again—*odd*." Sylvester rolled onto his side and slid a hand over her breast and kissed it, teasing the nipple until it was a hard point. Once he'd sucked its partner into a similar turgid state, he met her gaze. "Somebody has obviously told you that you are *odd*. Who was it?"

"It is all I've heard my whole life."

"Ah," Sylvester said, carefully considering his next words as he stroked from her delectable breasts to her hips, and then back up, not stopping until he reached her face this time, which he cupped. "You are not odd. In my opinion, which is the only one that matters when the two of us are together, you are utterly enchanting." Sylvester frowned when she failed to look convinced. "Why don't you believe me?"

"You are only saying that because you want me to feel more… comfortable," she said. "Charles said similar things."

Hyacinth

Sylvester was amused that she'd bring up her lover's name while in bed with *another* lover. But then the man was also her closest friend. Sylvester had always paid women to warm his bed and had never had a lover who was also his friend—although he supposed Hy might be close. Not that he knew enough about her to call her a friend, but then he hardly knew Fowler's inner workings, either.

"Have you ever noticed how most people believe negative comments or criticism more readily than they will accept a compliment?" Sylvester asked.

Her eyes grew distant as she considered his question. She pondered it for such a long time he thought she might not answer. But that was fine because Sylvester took the time to drink his fill of her.

Somewhere along the way she'd gone from being a skinny young boy to an attractive young woman to a bewitching lover. How he had ever believed her to be plain he could not understand. From her delicate, high-bridged nose to her large, heavy-lidded blue-green eyes, to her expressive, sensual lips, she was the most attractive woman he had ever met. Just thinking of her was enough to make him hard these days—not even thoughts of her naked, but memories of her keen gaze at the card table or her wry smirk when she mocked Fowler for believing in *luck*.

Earlier in the evening Sylvester had, yet again, danced with Lady Selina Bellamy, a woman who was undeniably lovely.

Yet as beautiful as she was, Sylvester had not felt the bone-deep pleasure in her company that he did with the woman now lying beside him.

Sylvester had always sought out beautiful, accomplished lovers—what man didn't—but never had he experienced the combination of excitement and utter contentment that he felt with this mysterious, reserved, card-counting governess's daughter.

"Yes, I have."

Sylvester shook himself at the sound of her voice. "I'm sorry?"

"You asked if I'd noticed that people tend to believe criticism more readily than praise. And I have noticed that. I have a—a friend, a woman who is an illustrator. She is as skilled as any man, but she allowed her mother's criticism to make her believe otherwise for a long, long time. Recently I learned that she has taken a job as an illustrator for a famous naturalist."

"What happened that suddenly made her believe in her talent?"

Hy's gaze sharpened as she came back from wherever she'd gone. "Financial exigency forced her to seek work. Once she saw how potential employers viewed her drawings, she accepted that her sisters hadn't exaggerated her skills."

"Or her friends."

Hy frowned. "I'm sorry?"

"You said she is your friend and you believed in her work too, didn't you?"

"Ah, yes. And her friends."

"So, then," Sylvester said, sliding his hand back down to her waist and pulling her closer so he could kiss her. "Will you believe what I say about you—and what your friend and lover Charles also said? Because I cannot be happy at the thought of you, er, demonstrating your skills to prospective employers as your illustrator friend did."

Her eyes widened for a moment, and then she laughed, the rare sound was gruff and low, more of a squawk, really.

And the sound was oddly familiar…

"What is it?" she asked.

"Your laughter just reminded me of somebody, but I can't recall who." Sylvester shook off the thought and turned his attention back to his lover. "How long can you stay tonight?"

She met his gaze with that opaque look of hers—the one that was beginning to drive him wild—and cocked her head. "Hmm, I don't know. Do I still get to choose what we do next?"

Chapter 22

"I'm sensing something of a theme," the duke said as Hy tied the soft rope around his wrists and made a double knot.

"This is nice rope," Hy said.

The duke chuckled and the low, masculine sound settled low in her belly, sweet like honey. Although she and Charles had been comfortable with each other, they had rarely laughed together while engaging in their sexual experiments.

Hy had to admit that she liked it.

Once his wrists were secure, she pulled on the other end of the rolled velvet rope, which wasn't just soft, but also strong.

The rope ran through an iron loop embedded in the ceiling. She had noticed it the last time and had guessed its purpose.

She pulled the rope until Chatham's arms were stretched high over his head.

"Is that too tight?" she asked.

When he didn't answer, she lowered her eyes from the rope to meet his gaze. As bad as she was when it came to reading people's expressions, she could easily read his at that moment. The word *smolder*, which she'd always believed to be an exaggeration, came to mind.

Hy glanced down at his penis—which was hard, pointed straight up, and leaking profusely.

His Grace was aroused. *Very* aroused.

She held his burning gaze as she secured the rope in place with a bowline knot, which Doddy had taught her when he was going through his knot-tying phase.

"There, tug on that, Your Grace."

The duke tugged, frowned when the rope didn't move, and tugged again. "Good Lord. Were you a pirate before becoming a gambler?"

She ignored his jest and stepped behind him, sliding her arms around his waist and closing one hand over his shaft while tightening her fingers around his root.

He sucked in a breath and held it while she pumped him, his body rigid with expectation. Hy hissed in his ear. "I could do anything to you that I wanted. *Any*thing."

His chest rose and fell rapidly, his cock leaking in her hand.

"I know what you want… Sylvester." She squeezed him hard enough to make him grunt, the sound half gasp, half groan. "Do I have to restrain your legs, or will you behave and stand still?"

He huffed out the breath he'd been holding. "I'll stand still."

Hy released his pulsing erection, lightly kissed his neck, and then shrugged out of the robe she'd donned to prepare him.

She had turned him so that his back was to the large armoire that stood against one wall. Hy had investigated the contents of the armoire the first time they'd used the room and she'd found many interesting things inside.

She took the object she wanted and then stood motionless for a second, assailed by a rare moment of indecision. If she'd guessed wrongly, she would look like a fool.

But if she were right?

Hy took a deep breath, exhaled, and then crossed the room to her lover.

She watched his face more closely than she'd ever watched anything in her life. His darkened eyes met hers for a moment and then lowered to the object she held in her hand.

His body flexed and he gasped softly, his lips going slack as his gaze fastened to the crop.

Hy savored the expression of pure, unselfconscious arousal while it lasted, which wasn't long before his eyes jumped up to meet hers.

She recognized the flash of raw hope and amazement—as if he could not believe what he was seeing—and chose to read that as a positive response. Hy dragged the stiff leather keeper on the crop across his chest, allowing it to scrape his nipples.

His body shuddered but his jaws clenched tight, holding in any sounds.

She lightly tapped the sensitive crown of his erection with the whip, pleased when his throat flexed and his Adam's apple bobbed.

"I can make it hurt," she said, lightly flicking the tightly ridged muscles of his abdomen. "If that is what you want?"

Hyacinth

His eyes blazed into hers and the moment stretched and stretched. And then he gave a curt nod, and said, "On my back. As hard as you are able."

***

Sylvester was beyond grateful that Hy was willing to do something that pleased him, but his tastes were… extreme, and he did not hold out much hope that he would get what he wanted.

What he needed.

He should have remembered what sort of woman he was dealing with: one who did nothing unless she could do it well.

"Very well," Hy said after a long pause. "You must tell me if it is too hard."

Before Sylvester could open his mouth—and tell her that was unlikely—she stepped behind him and brought the crop down with a savagery that made him bite his tongue hard enough to draw blood.

"Hard enough?" she asked as her hand caressed the spot she'd just whipped. Even though her touch was gentle it still sent jagged bolts of pain through the blazing hot lash. "You mark nicely," she murmured.

Sylvester shuddered at her praise, desperately wishing he could see her face while she admired her work.

"That was perfect," he said, once he was sure he could speak without squeaking like a mouse in a trap.

"I was thinking ten," she said, her hand disappearing from his back.

Saints preserve me, he prayed, thankfully silently.

Aloud, he said, "As you wish."

Suddenly her hot breath was on his ear. "Not a sound, now—not even a peep. Or you will get twenty."

Sylvester lost himself to the pain somewhere around the sixth or seventh stroke, but he obeyed her to the letter, not making so much as a hiss until she was finished.

If she was surprised or shocked that he'd ejaculated while she'd whipped him, she did not say.

Instead, she kissed his neck and pressed her naked body against his flaming back. "You were very good for me," she praised, licking the sweat from his throat as her hand curled around his spent shaft.

Sylvester chewed his lower lip ragged to keep from cursing as she stroked his too-sensitive cock, working him cruelly.

A low, evil chuckle vibrated from her body to his, telling him she was perfectly aware of how much discomfort she was causing.

He heaved a—silent—sigh of relief when she finally unbound him.

"Go and lie on the bed," she ordered quietly.

Sylvester's legs were so weak and watery could barely lift his feet for his short walk. He flopped down gratefully—on his front—and sighed, with contentment this time.

"Here."

Sylvester opened his eyes and saw that Hy was holding a glass of amber liquid to his lips.

He swallowed a mouthful and said, "Thank you."

Hy set the glass on the nightstand and stretched out beside him.

Sylvester rested his head on his crossed arms and met her gaze, waiting for the inevitable questions to start: why did he like such a thing? Had he ever consulted a physician? Or a vicar?

Instead, she studied his back. "May I touch you?"

It was a typically *Hiram* response—as if Sylvester was an interesting pair of cards she was planning to split.

"You didn't bother asking so nicely earlier," he reminded her.

She shrugged.

"I would like you to touch me."

Sylvester should have known she'd show no mercy, and her fingers went immediately to what had to be the largest of the welts, the one that had landed just across the top of his buttocks. He'd almost bit through his tongue with that one.

"My aim was not precise," she said.

Sylvester laughed at her clinical comment. "Your aim was perfect, Hy. *You* are perfect."

Not until he'd spoken the words did Sylvester realize that what he really should have said was: *you are perfect... for me.*

Hy lifted her pale eyebrows at him, yet again looking unconvinced by his words.

Sylvester had the urge to laugh—not joyously, but with frustration and disbelief.

And yet he could hardly blame her for not believing him when he was flabbergasted, himself.

It had taken almost thirty-six years for it to happen, but Sylvester had finally done what he'd believed impossible: he had fallen in love.

Hyacinth

What he'd felt for Mariah all those years ago had never been love, but a combination of adoration, lust, and infatuation. He had wanted the illusion of Mariah—her beautiful, poised exterior—but he'd not cared who she really was or what *she* had wanted.

Only after meeting Hy could Sylvester admit that he had done Mariah as great a disservice—if not greater—than she had done him.

The difference between mere lust and love was astounding—like the difference between the crepuscular light of dawn and a blazingly blue summer sky.

Sylvester had never wanted to laugh with Mariah or learn the way her mind worked or pit his wits against hers or discover how to please her—both in and out of bed—all he'd wanted was to *have* her, to use her body to satisfy his selfish desire, uncaring of what she liked or needed.

It was more than a decade too late, but Sylvester felt shame for the way he'd treated his long dead wife.

And his cousin.

He suddenly felt sick to his stomach at the possibility that Shelton really *had* loved Mariah. If he had, then what Sylvester had done was beyond cruel.

He could not think about that. Not now. Not when his precious seconds with Hy were ticking away.

Sylvester studied her from beneath lowered lashes, a sudden ball of anxiety pulsing in his belly.

She was clever, resourceful, loyal, sensual, adventurous—and more.

She *was* perfect for him—not just the perfect lover or companion, but the perfect person to share the rest of his life.

Perfect except for one, single, insurmountable obstacle: she was a stablemaster's niece.

Chapter 23

Sylvester was in the library sorting through the daunting pile of correspondence that had accumulated over the past few days when the door opened.

He didn't even need to look up. There was only one person who would just come striding into his private room without bothering to knock.

Sylvester took off his spectacles and looked up. "Why, Shelton—what a surprise."

His cousin—who was garbed only in slippers and a gaudy red silk robe—flopped into the chair across from Sylvester's desk, sighed, and shoved his guinea gold curls off his forehead.

"My dear, dear Sylvester—how nice to have a chance to chat with you. You have been so… elusive these past few weeks. You are rarely at home anymore and you pop up at some ball or other—usually only long enough to dance with Lady Selina, and of course a few other nonentities in a pitiful attempt to throw the match-making mama's off your very obvious scent—and then you hare off with your pet barbarian to Weller's, where I understand you've played deep four nights out of the last seven, and then you go sate your baser needs on one of the lovelies in Mrs. Dryden's stable of goods."

Sylvester experienced a slight chill at how closely Shelton had been monitoring his behavior.

"I'm pleased that my activities are of such interest to you, Shelton," he lied. "Did you just come here to tell me what I already know, or was there something else?"

"Oh, come now, can't we simply have a friendly chat, Syl… vester," he added with an impish look that made Sylvester smile, even though he didn't wish to. It also reminded him of the cousin Shelton used to be—his best friend and the man he'd relied on during those grueling years in the army.

Of course, Shelton quickly ruined that pleasant recollection.

Hyacinth

"So, will you come up to scratch on the Bellamy chit, my dear coz? I've a hefty wager riding on the question."

"I've warned you against putting my names in any betting books, Shelton."

"Don't fly into a pucker—it wasn't me who entered the wager at Brooks. And you *know* I don't belong to White's. Unlike *some* people, I can neither afford to do such a frivolous thing, nor do I have any inclination to hobnob with all your tory chums."

It was true that Sylvester held memberships at both clubs. He also paid Shelton's fees at Brooks, a fact that had apparently slipped his cousin's selective memory.

He'd not been aware there was a bet concerning him and Lady Selina, but it did not surprise him. Bored aristocrats would bet on anything, he should know that as he'd been one of them up until a few weeks ago.

"I will do what I can to see that both wagers are removed," Sylvester fixed his cousin with a glare. "As you've not hesitated to show your interest in the Bellamy girl, I would have thought you'd not encourage the dragging of her name and reputation through the mud, but I suppose that is hoping for too much from you."

Shelton clapped. "Bravo, Sylvester! Bravo! You are as lethal with your barbs as you are with your fives—or so I hear, not having enough money to frequent Jackson's as you do."

Sylvester sighed. "How much do you need, Shelton?"

"I'm offended that you think I am here for money."

"If you don't tell me what you want in the next"—Sylvester pulled out his watch and glanced at it—"five seconds, you can show yourself—"

"Five hundred should hold me over, my dear coz."

Sylvester didn't bother asking how *long* it would hold him over. "Fine. And you might as well give me your bills while you are at it."

A look of genuine surprise flickered over Shelton's face. "Why, Sylvester! No quibbling? No lectures? Are you ill?" He paused and grinned hopefully before adding, "Dying?"

Sylvester barked a laugh. "You should be so fortunate." He unlocked the bottom drawer on his desk and drew out the small cash box he kept on hand for emergencies. Or for Shelton. Or for emergencies precipitated by Shelton.

"Oh, there *is* one more tiny thing."

The hairs on Sylvester's neck stood up before his lifted his gaze to meet his cousin's. He forced an insouciant smirk he wasn't feeling, cast a pointed look at Shelton's barely covered crotch, and lifted an eyebrow. "Dear me. Have you contracted something nasty at one of the brothels you fancy? Or are we talking about some other *tiny* thing?"

Shelton gave a genuine belly laugh. When he could stop, he nodded. "Very good, Sylvester. No, it's not my tiny prick I'm talking about, but where *you* have been putting your prick."

Sylvester just stared.

"I know about *Hiram*." Shelton laughed. "At first, I thought you'd lost your head over a lad. But then I really *looked* at her." He snorted. "Good God. She really has made fools of us all, hasn't she?" When Sylvester didn't answer, he went on, "I followed the two of you after you left Dryden's place." He clucked his tongue. "It was you who really gave her away—handing her into the carriage as if she were the queen, old boy."

Sylvester inhaled deeply, held it, and then let it out. "What do you want to keep your knowledge to yourself?"

"Who *is* she? I tried to follow her after you dropped her off, but she scurried through the rubbish alleys and mews like a bloody wharf rat and I lost her."

"How much?"

"Why do you care if I expose her or not?"

Sylvester decided to tell him the truth and hope there was some shred of humanity left in him. "She is saving up her winnings to pay her brother's gambling debts. He is in danger from some unsavory people."

Shelton's brow furrowed. "Why don't you just give her the money?"

"Unlike some people, she doesn't want charity."

Shelton's cheeks flushed, but he laughed. "What a fool. I'll take another five hundred to keep mum," he added, his eyes hard and no longer laughing.

Sylvester counted out more notes and then held them toward his cousin. "Send one of the servants back with your bills—all of them you want paid—within the hour, Shelton."

Shelton stood and sauntered over to the desk. But when he reached for the money, Sylvester did an obnoxious thing and held on to it.

His cousin snorted. "Very droll."

"I also have one *tiny* thing."

Shelton smirked. "What can I do for you?"

Hyacinth

"You can stay the hell away from Lady Selina Bellamy."

Shelton stared for a long moment, as if he were trying to see into Sylvester's head. Finally, he laughed and gave him an angelic smile. "She is too poor for me, so I will be happy to leave her for you, dear coz."

Sylvester handed him the money and watched until the door closed behind Shelton before putting on his glasses and turning back to the daunting pile of bills—which would soon be even more daunting when Shelton sent down his.

He knew that giving his cousin a thousand pounds and paying his likely exorbitant bills wasn't enough to keep Shelton from haunting him on his evenings with Hy *or* stop his pointless pursuit of poor Selina Bellamy. At least not for very long. But there was only a week left in the Season and she would soon be safely ensconced either in the country or—if Fowler could quit behaving like a spineless ninny—betrothed to one of the wealthiest, and most infatuated, men in all of Britain.

Sylvester had bought some time for his friend; it was now up to Fowler to make use of it.

As for protecting Hy's secret from his cousin… Well, he'd need to give that some thought. A great deal more thought.

***

"Oh, *do* quit pouting, Hy," Selina chided as she regarded herself in the triple looking glass, which reflected triple perfect images. "This is the last gown you shall have to sit for. And it is making Aunt Ellen so happy."

Hy thought her aunt must have suffered some sort of head trauma to find forcing other women to purchase ballgowns a satisfying experience.

"I would not need another gown if you would stop encouraging our aunt to include me on these junkets," she grumbled in an under voice.

"What did you say, Hy?"

"Nothing." Hy turned her attention back to the book she was reading—or at least trying to read, if Selina didn't bother her every ten seconds.

"Well?" Selina asked.

Hy sighed and looked up to find her sister standing in front of her. "What?"

Selina held out her arms. "What do you think? This one or the pink one?"

"This one," Hy said without hesitation.

Selina's eyes narrowed. "You're only saying that because you don't recall the pink one."

Well, that was true.

"Oh, never mind," Selina said, "I don't know why I bother asking." Neither did Hy.

"You *must* choose material for your new gown, Hy."

"You pick one for me."

The bell over the door tinkled, heralding the entry of another customer.

Selina looked over Hy's shoulder and her face pinkened at whomever had just entered. "Lord Shelton," she said in a breathless voice.

"Why, you were correct Horton," Shelton's irritating voice boomed. "It *is* Lady Selina. and here I thought I was witnessing an angel come to earth!"

Hy sank down lower on the settee, opened her book, and raised it until it was covering her face.

Selina laughed, her sudden animation making her breathtakingly lovely. "You are so silly, Lord Shelton." She waved a chiding finger at the men—or probably just Shelton. "It is very naughty of you to be peering into dress shop windows, my lords."

"No! Is it?" Shelton exclaimed, his voice coming nearer.

Hy surreptitiously slid off her glasses and tugged down her cap.

When Selina's eyes darted to hers, Hy saw the question in them clearly and shook her head and mouthed *no introduction*.

Selina's lips tightened slightly in disapproval, but quickly turned back to Shelton and smiled.

"Is that delightful confection you are wearing for the Castleford ball, my lady?" Shelton asked.

Before Selina could answer him, the bell tinkled again. A lightning-fast look of consternation flickered across her sister's face before she said, "Oh, you are back already, Aunt Ellen."

"I'm afraid the hat is not ready, Selina," their aunt said. "Have you both selected your gowns?"

"Not yet, Aunt. But look who came to say hello."

There was a long, pregnant pause, and then, "Ah, yes."

Hy smirked at Aunt Ellen's voice, which was so frosty that for a moment Hy almost didn't recognize her flighty aunt.

"Good afternoon, Lord Horton, Lord Shelton. Are you here dress shopping?" she asked in an uncharacteristically arch tone.

Hyacinth

Shelton took it all in stride, of course. He chuckled. "No, my lady. We were just passing by when I chanced a glance into the shop and saw your niece. I'm afraid I was naughty enough to force my way into this feminine bower to tell her how exquisite she looks. I also wanted to claim a waltz—if they have not already been snapped up weeks ago."

Hy rolled her eyes. How could such an idiot possibly be related to a man like Chatham?

"I trust you've done both?" Lady Fitzroy asked, her tone cool enough to leave the two men in no doubt that their presence was *de trop*. "Hyacinth? Have you tried anything on yet?"

Hy took a deep breath, closed her book, and forced herself to stand, meeting Selina's worried gaze before she turned to her aunt.

"This is my other niece, Lady Hyacinth," her aunt said.

Any fear that Hy had entertained about being recognized immediately dissipated when both men nodded and murmured greetings in her direction but didn't bother to pull their adoring gazes away from Selina.

"I'll go and try on the gowns now, Aunt Ellen," Hy said, making her exit speedily in the unlikely event either of the men looked her way.

The shop assistant gave Hy a blank look when she stepped into the dressing room. "I'm sorry, my lady, was there a gown here for you to—"

Selina pushed in behind Hy and smiled at the confused woman. "My sister would like to try on that deep rose silk and the teal."

Hy pulled a face. "I really don't—"

"Don't you think she should try the more vivid shades, Aunt Ellen?" Selina asked loudly, cutting Hy a significant look before stepping aside to reveal their aunt, whom Hy hadn't realized had come with her.

Her aunt's brow furrowed deeply, as if she were considering calculus rather than a ball gown. "Both those colors are a bit, er, *mature* for a girl who is only one-and-twenty—"

"Hy will be twenty-three in less than two months," Selina pointed out helpfully.

Aunt Ellen's eyes widened. "Oh, is that right? Well, then, perhaps you *might* try them on…" she said, her sentence trailing off rather than ending in any definitive way, which was a habit of hers that Hy found distracting.

"Will you please fetch them," Selina asked the hovering salesclerk.

When the woman left the room Aunt Ellen leaned closer to Selina. "My dear Selina, I really wish you wouldn't encourage Shelton. You *know* he doesn't have a feather to fly with and—well, have you heard about that poor, unfortunate creature he—" She bit her lip. "But I really should not repeat such a shameful tale."

Hy wanted to shake the story out of her aunt. If Shelton had done something heinous to a woman, shouldn't *all* other young women be warned? Shouldn't he be forced to wear a scarlet R on his chest for reprobate?

"I've heard the story you are speaking of, Aunt," Selina said. "And I really do not encourage him, I promise you. He is just… amusing."

Her aunt gave Selina one of her vague smiles. "I am *so* glad to hear it. You know your dear Mama entrusted you to my care. I should never forgive myself if you were to fall into the clutches of some sort of…"

Again she trailed off.

Hy glared at her sister and finished her aunt's sentence for her. "I think the word you are searching for is *rake*, Aunt Ellen."

Selina refused to meet her glare.

"Hyacinth is right, my dear. I'm afraid that if you encourage Shelton you risk insulting Chatham—and I know you don't wish to alienate *his* affections, not when matters are so…" She adjusted one of her gloves and stared vaguely at the far wall.

Hy wanted to grab and shake the rest of her sentence out of her. *Matters were so… what? What were matters?*

Selina's mouth tightened and her skin darkened even more. "No, of course I don't, Aunt Ellen."

Hy looked from her aunt to her sister. "Has Chatham offered for you?"

"No," Selina murmured.

"No," her aunt admitted with obvious reluctance. "But there is every indication that he…"

Hy waited. And waited. And then said, "What—"

"Here you are, my lady. I believe this rose will be most lovely on you," the clerk said, effectively putting an end to any chance for a private conversation.

Chapter 24

Hy reached her monetary goal—earning enough for both the loan *and* two hundred pounds to start her on her new life—the following evening, after she'd only been playing for an hour and a half.

They were at Mrs. Simpson's, where Chatham had arrived earlier than expected and without either his annoying cousin or the nosy Scotsman in tow.

Although the duke had said nothing to her about leaving London, she knew everyone who was anyone would flee the City shortly after Castleton's ball.

That ball was only four nights away.

Thanks to Selina's machinations, Hy was going to be forced to attend both Castleton's horrendous squeeze and also a less august ball tomorrow night at Lady Duckworth's.

Her sister had also been remarkably evasive on the subject of Chatham and his alleged *affections*.

"That is only Aunt Ellen's wishful thinking," she'd insisted when Hy had pressed her on the issue, and then she'd narrowed her eyes at Hy and asked, "Why are you so interested all of a sudden?"

Of course, Hy hadn't had a response for *that* question.

"Hiram?"

Hy's head whipped up.

The duke was looking at her, his eyebrows raised. "Do you want another?"

Hy blinked and then followed his gaze to the cards sitting in front of her—neither of which she'd looked at because she'd been so busy gathering wool.

How mortifying.

"I'm out," she said, her face no doubt a glaring shade of red.

The duke nodded and the play moved to the man on Hy's left.

Sylvester smirked to himself as he and Hy climbed into his waiting coach. "Somebody is eager tonight," he teased, his words a mocking echo of *her* mocking words.

His laconic companion had no response other than to flip the louvered blinds shut and snuff the lantern.

"Hy? What are you—" he broke off at the sound of two thumps and then the feel of her hands shoving his thighs wide.

"Unbutton your breeches."

Sylvester chuckled. "Oh, is it your turn again tonight?"

She shoved his hands aside. "You're too slow," she muttered, her fingers tearing at his fall.

He heard the sound of a button hitting the metal heating grate before her cool fist and hot mouth closed around his cock.

Sylvester groaned as she swallowed him down to the root, her mouth like hot, tight silk. "God, yes," he muttered, "suck me."

She growled approvingly at his crude command, the vibration rolling up his prick to his tight, aching balls and testing the limits of his restraint.

Sylvester fisted the soft leather seat to keep from burying his hands in her hair and thrusting into her throat, using her like a back-alley tart. "I brought myself off this morning thinking about this," he confessed, smirking to himself when a shudder racked her body. "You like the thought of that, don't you—you filthy girl?"

She nodded as vigorously as she could with a mouth full of cock.

"Is this what you were thinking about tonight when you were supposed to be playing cards, Hy?" he taunted as she filled the small space with the sound of her erotic labors.

Her answer was another wet growl and she grabbed his wrist and shoved his hand into her hair, her message clear.

"If I take you this way, I won't be kind, darling."

Her nod was brief but undeniable and she took him deeper.

Sylvester tightened his fingers in her silky curls as he forced her head lower and pumped his hips, the sound of her moan assuring him he'd not mistaken her wordless command.

He closed his eyes as he used her, wishing like hell that she'd not snuffed the light, imagining that wicked mouth of hers stretched around him, tears running down her cheeks, her challenging green gaze wrecking him while she took him apart piece by piece.

"Yes," he hissed, his hips rolling. "Such a good girl taking all of me."

She shivered beneath his cruel hands and then took him so deeply she choked herself.

"Like that, Hy… Just. Like. That." Sylvester punctuated each word with a sharp thrust, reveling in the feel of her pliant body in his hands, his own muscles shaking with the effort of restraining himself.

And then she swallowed around him and his control snapped.

"Coming," he warned. But when he tried to lift her head, she resisted.

Sylvester gave up without much of a struggle and took what she offered, emptying himself inside her in wrenching spasms that felt like they'd snap his spine.

Rather than retreat, she swallowed every drop, milking him dry but stopping before her touch became painful. Soft lips pressed against his thigh in a kiss and then she roughly yanked up his breeches and small clothes.

Sylvester chuckled weakly at her savage ministrations. "You are a brutal valet."

He heard a soft chuckle in the darkness as her deft fingers buttoned his breeches.

Once she was finished, she flicked the louvered blinds open a crack. "We're almost there."

Sylvester snorted. "You'd better summon my footmen because I'll need to be carried into the building."

Sylvester knew he was hopelessly lost when he realized her low, squawky snort of laughter had somehow become more precious to him than gold.

***

"I'm leaving London next week," the duke said.

They were lying in bed after a long, thorough session of making love. There had been no whips or ropes tonight and Hy knew that both were thinking this might very well be the last time they saw each other.

"Oh?" she said, because… what else was there?

"I want you to go with me."

Hy pulled her attention from her study of the duke's endlessly fascinating body. She'd been happily exploring his chiseled abdomen, which was so hard she couldn't push a finger into it, and not for a lack of trying. She'd enjoyed Chatham's affronted gasps and yelps almost as much as she'd enjoyed touching him.

When she forced herself to meet his gaze, she saw that his brown eyes looked stern. Hy was aware that he'd used his *ducal* voice on her, but she could see that—for once—he was not confident in its effectiveness.

It amazed her that she'd learned to read him so quickly. She'd spent all her life with her siblings and still had no idea what her sister Aurelia was thinking most of the time. She was slightly better when it came to reading Selina and Phoebe, but not much.

Only Doddy, her little brother, was easy to read, and that was because he thought about three things: his pet squirrel Silas, horses—any horses—and evading their mother's notice.

And yet somehow Hy could understand the workings of a complex man like the Duke of Chatham after only a little over a month.

"Hy?" he asked, and then muttered beneath his breath. "I can't believe I keep calling you that."

She smiled slightly. "I like it better than Mary." That much was true.

"Come with me to the country."

"You want me to live in your *house*?"

"Only if you wanted to—or you could have own establishment, there is a lovely manor on the grounds of Chatham."

"And do what?"

"Whatever you want."

She snorted.

"What?" he demanded, pushing up onto his elbows to better fix her with his ducal glare.

"You wouldn't mind if I nipped down to your local village inn for an after-hours card game, Your Grace?"

He frowned. "I would be there—you could play cards with me."

Hy smiled at that. "If you move me into your house or put me somewhere on your estate people will talk. What will you tell them about me? That I am your whore?"

He flinched, as though she had slapped him, and his frown shifted into a scowl and the skin over his undamaged cheekbone darkened, along with his gaze. Hy could have told him that his stern look aroused, rather than intimidated her, but she was enjoying it too much to put a stop to it.

"I won't allow anyone to call you that—not even you."

Hyacinth

Hy rolled over onto her side and propped her head on her hand, truly intrigued as to what sort of plan he had in mind. "What would I do there? Work in your house? I'm not pretty enough for a parlor maid, but then I suppose a chambermaid would be more convenient for what you have in mind."

He sat up, his eyes no longer a warm brown, but throwing hot sparks. "Is that all you think I want from you? A body to warm my bed?"

"No. I think you like to play cards with me," she admitted.

There were limits to how well Hy could read him, and she had no idea what he was struggling with at that moment, but whatever it was, he was clearly unhappy.

He sighed. "I'll think of something." His hand closed over hers.

She merely nodded. Why argue? They had so little time left, the last thing she wanted to do was spend it arguing.

"I don't suppose you know if you can come out tomorrow night?" he asked a moment later.

Hy scowled as she recalled what she had on her plate tomorrow night. "No, I can't. But the night after I will come." She would make *sure* of it, regardless of what Selina might come up with to keep her at home.

"I want to meet you here, Hy. I don't want to waste any of our evening at a card table."

"I don't need to play cards again."

The duke frowned. "What do you mean?"

"I mean that I have saved up the money I need."

"You've paid your brother's creditors?"

"I will do so, soon."

He took her hand and pulled her closer. "Come lie beside me."

Hy inched up the bed until they were lying face to face.

"You're not going to go haring off as soon as you've paid his debt, are you?"

"No."

"Are you still determined to leave London?"

"Yes."

"When?"

"Not for another week."

"I thought your brother had a girl—didn't you mention a bookseller who might wish to hire him?"

Hy was amazed that he'd recalled such a detail. "Yes. It's possible he might stay."

"You wouldn't consider remaining in London if he did?"

"No."

He gave an exasperated snort. "Why not?"

"I know what you are asking."

"Oh?"

"You want to set me up in a house here—give me money and servants and keep me as your mistress."

He opened his mouth, hesitated, and then said, "Would that really be so bad?" He hurried on before she could answer. "I promise you that it would be a much less rigid arrangement than what you are probably thinking."

Hy didn't share what she was thinking, which was that the offer was remarkably attractive—far more enticing than the thought of being a duchess—which is what he'd feel compelled to offer if he ever found out who she really was. Thank *God* he would never, ever find out.

Her mind returned to his suggestion, which was more appealing by the minute. She would not mind the social ostracism of being a man's mistress because she hated the *ton*. She could have card parties—like the Simpson woman gave at her house, but for a much more exclusive group of players. The duke could visit her when he was in London and they would not have to hide their arrangement.

Chatham would leave in the summer and Hy would have weeks to herself when she could explore the city. He would probably give her enough money to hire a bodyguard to take with her when she played at the various hells.

It would be an ideal life in many respects.

Hy looked up from her thoughts to see him watching her, waiting. "It is more appealing than moving to the country," she admitted.

His lips parted and hope blossomed in his eyes. "Then you would consider it?"

If she did such a thing, she would be cast beyond the pale—she could never socialize with her sisters again, at least not publicly.

Chatham would be generous with her; she knew that instinctively. And when he tired of her—which he inevitably would—Hy would be comfortably positioned and could do whatever she wanted.

"It is worth considering," she said, pleased that her answer didn't commit her and yet was enough to ease the tension in his gaze. "I will give you my answer the next time we see each other."

Hyacinth

He didn't look happy about having to wait but nodded. "What time do you need to leave tonight?"

She knew Selina would be out late tonight—probably until first light—because her aunt had mentioned it over dinner.

Is that where Chatham had been earlier tonight? Hy had heard her aunt musing about his possible attendance at the ball. When she'd looked at Selina to see her reaction to the duke's name, her sister had merely stared fixedly at her plate.

Hy's gaze wandered to Chatham's face. He was looking at one of her bare breasts, which he was stroking with his lovely, skilled fingers.

"Did you go to"—Hy stumbled, suddenly realizing that a governess's daughter probably wouldn't know the name of the person who'd hosted tonight's ball—"er, to some sort of function tonight?"

The duke's hand stilled and he raised puzzled eyes to hers. "Why do you ask?"

"You are dressed very nicely."

His lips curled into a slow smile. "You mean those breeches you ripped off me in the carriage?"

"Sorry about the button."

He snorted. "Are you saying I'm not usually dressed nicely?"

Before she could come up with a suitable retort, he said, "Yes, I went to a ball." He pulled a face.

"Do you like going to balls?" she asked, not sure why she was persisting. Based on his perplexed look, he wasn't either.

"Not especially."

"Then why do you go?"

Again, he paused his stroking and she could see he was struggling to find the right words. No doubt he was thinking that she—a woman who was essentially a servant—wouldn't understand the motivations of a peer.

Hy decided to help him along. "Isn't that what toffs do to find a wife? Go to balls?"

He laughed. "*Toffs?*"

She shrugged. "You know what I mean."

"I think I do. It's just amusing to hear the word coming from a woman who sounds quite like a *toff* herself."

"I told you about my mother," she reminded him. "But I live above a carriage house and my uncle is a stablemaster. Just because I sound like a toff, doesn't mean I am one." Hy sounded so convincing that *she* almost believed the words. She briefly wondered if that was how actors felt when onstage, as if they were somebody else.

"Yes, that is what toffs do to get married," he said.

"Are you going to marry?"

His eyes narrowed. "Why are you asking me about this?"

"You said that I might ask whatever questions I wanted," she reminded him.

His smile, when it finally came, was different somehow. But she couldn't decide *how*.

"Yes, I did say that, didn't I?"

Hy nodded.

"Yes, I will likely marry."

Hy nodded again. It was the answer she had expected. Even so, it left her slightly unsettled.

"Why have you waited so long to marry?" Hy asked, feeling more than a little guilty for prying answers out of him in such an underhanded way.

He held her gaze for a long, uncomfortable moment, during which time Hy's face heated until she knew she'd be red.

"I was married before."

"Oh." Hy couldn't bring herself to ask more, but it turned out she didn't need to.

"My wife died a little over ten years ago."

Hearing the words *my wife* from his mouth felt even stranger than hearing him admit to having a mistress had felt.

Selina had said his wife had been beautiful. She'd likely been accomplished and sophisticated. Somebody like Chatham.

"How long were you married?"

He sighed and reached for the glass on the nightstand. "Less than two years." He took a hearty swallow.

"What was she like?"

"Why are you asking me these questions?"

"I told you all about Charles."

He sighed, but said, "Mariah was beautiful, vibrant, charming. Everyone loved her."

Hy was not surprised. What *did* surprise her was that he did not sound especially happy about all that bounty.

His gaze slid from the glass back to Hy. "She died in childbed." The pain in his eyes was that of an old, but still raw, wound.

Hyacinth

Hy wasn't an affectionate person and rarely wanted to embrace or touch others, but at that moment, she felt a strong—almost overpowering—urge to offer him comfort.

She struggled to come up with the right words or actions to ease his pain but drew a blank.

And so Hy did the only thing that she could be sure would not make matters worse: she did nothing.

Chapter 25

It was positively horrific. Hy had never felt so miserably crushed and crowded in her entire life.

"Hyacinth?" the dowager said, the whites of her eyes showing as she stared at the crush of humanity.

"I'm right here, my lady," Hy all but shouted.

The older woman's skin was pale beneath its thick layer of powder.

So, even somebody who'd probably seen seventy Seasons was intimidated by the sheer number of people. Somehow that made Hy feel better.

"Hyacinth?" her Aunt Ellen said.

Hy had to bend down almost in half to hear her aunt, who was not quite five feet tall. "Yes, Aunt Ellen?"

"I think you should take Lady Fitzroy to the cardroom."

"Of course." Hy bit back a smile of relief. This was going to be far easier than she thought. Once she was in the cardroom she would—

"But I want you to come *right* back after you have made her comfortable, my dear."

Hy wanted to groan. "Yes, Aunt Ellen."

It took her more than fifteen minutes to escort the dowager to the room that had been set aside for cards, not because of the crowd, but because Lady Fitzroy seemed to know every person they passed and needed to stop and chat with each and every one of them.

By the time Hy settled her at a table with three of her cronies, the older woman had recovered from her earlier bout of confusion and seemed quite happy.

Hy wished she could stay, but her aunt had, for once, looked adamant.

"Aunt Ellen asked me to return to her, my lady."

The dowager nodded absently. "Yes, yes, you go and dance."

Hy's solo journey toward the dancefloor was far faster than the one to the cardroom as nobody stopped *her* to greet her.

Hyacinth

Although she recognized several men from various card games around the city, none of them gave her a second glance.

Selina was already dancing, and with a man Hy had never seen before. Evidently Hy had not played cards with every male member of the aristocracy quite yet.

Her aunt was in the middle of a group of chaperones and Hy was about to make her way toward her when a pair of familiar figures approached the women.

Even without her glasses Hy recognized the duke and Fowler.

Chatham moved with a lazy confidence that was no doubt bolstered by the knowledge that he would be welcome anywhere, because he would.

Hy hadn't seen him in this milieu for weeks, not since she'd played cards with him that first time. It felt strange to see him in a ballroom, and she didn't care for the uncomfortable tightness in her chest. Yet she could not look away. Instead, she edged closer, insinuating herself in with the wallflowers who inevitably clustered together at every *ton* function she'd ever attended. She went as close as she dared, until she could make out the details of his face and person, even without her spectacles.

Chatham mingled effortlessly, cutting through the crowds with his head at an arrogant angle, master of all he surveyed.

Unlike most of the other men in the ballroom he was garbed in the newer, less colorful style which the Prince of Wale's intimate—Mr. Brummel—had recently made popular.

The black and white raiment should have dimmed his light among so many turquoises, pinks, and golds, but Chatham stood out from the others. Hy supposed it must be something about being a duke that caused him to emanate such an aura of power.

He bowed over various hands and exchanged greetings with the chaperones, all of whom had perked up when he'd ventured near to them. He stopped beside her Aunt Ellen and the two chatted like old friends.

Her aunt gestured to the dancefloor, to where Selina was dancing, and the duke turned to watch Hy's sister.

Hy swallowed down a mixture of frustration, disappointment, and resignation as she watched the duke watch Selina.

Well, what man in the room *wasn't* attracted by her beautiful, vivacious sister?

The duke was not alone in worshipping at Selina's alter and Hy saw Fowler and a collection of young men hovering on the outskirts of the dancefloor, their heads swiveling to follow her movements.

She couldn't blame them, her sister seemed to draw light from the chandeliers, her beauty enhanced by her smiling face and spontaneous laughter at whatever her dance partner had just said.

Hy took a glass of champagne from a harried servant and settled in to watch.

This was the first time she'd ever had any interest in *ton* proceedings. She decided not to examine the reasons for that interest.

When Selina left the dance floor the collection of men moved in her direction like a single, multi-legged organism. Her sister laughed and smiled and plied her fan at her court. And then the duke took a step toward her.

Even from this distance Hy could see the change in her sister's posture: she stood taller and prouder at the distinction his attention bestowed upon her.

Chatham's attention might have made her sister blossom, but it had the opposite effect on Selina's court of admirers, who fell back like a receding wave.

The next set began to assemble and the duke led Hy's sister onto the floor.

It was a waltz.

***

Sylvester suspected Lady Selina Bellamy was concerned by his attention, even though she was too polite to show it.

For some reason, he didn't think it was his scar that made her nervous, but that might have just been wishful thinking.

He'd not wanted to single her out for another dance—he'd not wanted to be at this bloody ball, full stop—but as his attention had attracted Shelton's notice Sylvester felt he owed the girl a warning.

According to Fowler, Sylvester's five hundred pounds hadn't even purchased a week of good behavior from his cousin and Shelton had amplified, rather than diminished his attentions toward the girl.

Sylvester knew that Shelton wasn't seriously considering marrying Lady Selina—his cousin could not settle for anyone less than an heiress—and was only toying for her, either for his own amusement or to annoy Sylvester or Fowler or all three.

"The Season is all but over, Lady Selina, do you have any plans for the summer?"

She smiled, and it appeared genuine and free of restraint. "I will probably return home, Your Grace."

"No house parties or a trip to Brighton?"

"No. I miss my family."

She was a genuinely sweet girl—a great deal too sweet for Sylvester—and he hoped that he'd not encouraged false hopes in her breast, as he had certainly done with her aunt.

Lady Selina couldn't be too disappointed given the huge group of men who were currently watching Sylvester with intense dislike. He'd heard of at least three men who'd offered her marriage, so she was not desperate to marry.

"I see your court has trebled since the last time we danced." He said, rousing himself to make conversation with the beautiful woman in his arms. "Look at the way they are glaring," he urged. "I fancy they would all like me dead. If my body is found floating in the Thames tomorrow, with a knife in my back, there will be no shortage of suspects."

Instead of a delicate titter Lady Selina gave a rather surprising squawk of laughter.

The sound sent a slight shock through him. It was remarkably like Hy's rare laugh—a sound he'd only ever heard once.

How… interesting.

"They are quite foolish."

"Who is foolish?" Sylvester asked.

She gave him an odd look he cursed his inattention. "The men you just mentioned, Your Grace."

"You think them foolish for admiring you?"

"No, but I think them foolish for ignoring all the other girls who are sitting unpartnered."

Sylvester was impressed that she would spare some thought for the less well-endowed members of her sex. She was easily the most beautiful girl he had seen in years—if ever. But it wasn't just her appearance, she was also delightfully unspoiled. Sylvester knew her family was in desperate need of money, and she would accept an offer from him regardless of their age disparity, his reputation, his disfigurement—or her unwise attraction to Shelton.

He shoved the grim thought from his head and said, "I knew your father and recall you have several sisters. Do they all live in the country?"

"I have four sisters and one brother." Her soft cheeks flamed suddenly, and her gaze slid off to the side, her eyes widening briefly before snapping back to Sylvester.

Sylvester cut a look in the same direction, but could see nothing to evoke a blush, merely a clutch of neglected wallflowers watching the dancefloor with yearning plain in their postures.

Sylvester suddenly felt tired. He was creeping toward forty years of age and he was still doing the same thing he'd been doing at twenty: engaging in pointless socializing while unhappily contemplating the prospect of remarriage, when all he *really* wanted to be doing was spending his time with one of the least marriageable women in Britain.

Lady Selina's violet-blue eyes slid to somebody over Sylvester's other shoulder, her flush deepening and her eyes sparkling.

This time when he followed her gaze, he saw it rested on none other than his cousin.

He turned away from Shelton's triumphant gaze to meet Lady's Selina's embarrassed one.

Sylvester decided not to mince around the subject. "You are acquainted with my cousin?"

"Yes, Your Grace."

"He is charming and very handsome."

She nodded hesitantly at his pronouncement.

"He is also rather… wild. Not to mention poor."

Her lips parted and the shyness she'd been exhibiting was replaced by another emotion: indignation.

"Lord Shelton told me the two of you have had your differences."

Sylvester wanted to groan. This was *not* good. If Shelton had got to the point of confiding private matters in this chit, then he was clearly seeking to overcome her reservations.

At least Sylvester *hoped* the woman had some reservations about his cousin. Every woman in the *ton* should know what his feckless relative had done to Sir John Creighton's daughter two years earlier.

Sir John had been powerless to avenge his daughter's deflowering at Shelton's hands, so Sylvester had thrown money and a suitable bridegroom at the problem, but it had been too late to salvage the poor woman's reputation. Sarah Creighton had been fortunate to find a country squire willing to marry her and she would spend the rest of her life buried in the country, too ashamed to ever show her face in London, thanks to Shelton.

Hyacinth

Sylvester did not want to see the same thing happen to Lady Selina.

If only the woman would give Fowler a fraction as much attention as she gave Shelton. But the heart wanted what it wanted, as Sylvester was only now learning.

The thought of his own impossible obsession made him feel kindlier towards her. But feeling kindly didn't mean he would help her into marriage with his cousin. Any woman who married Shelton would suffer. He was reckless and selfish in the extreme and would make his wife's life hell.

Sylvester could not come out directly and tell her that his cousin was only toying with her in the hopes of getting under his skin.

No, but he could say all that and more to Shelton.

And he would.

Unfortunately, he would also have to give his cousin more than just a few thousand pounds to stop. Shelton had come to London looking for money for his idiotic stud venture and he'd badger Sylvester until he got it.

Sylvester would give him the money and hope it would keep his cousin occupied for at least a year until the next hairbrained scheme.

Sylvester opened his mouth to utter some suitable platitude and steer the conversation away from Shelton when he saw Lady Selina staring, once again at the same group of wallflowers.

He was about to turn away when one of the women—a pale brunette who was bent almost in half listening to something Lady Fitzroy said—straightened up and nodded.

Time seemed to slow—the dance, the music, the movement of the crowds—as Sylvester's brain struggled to put a name to the face.

"Will you be going to Brighton, Your Grace? Or do you return to Chatham for the summer?"

He knew it was terribly rude, but he was unable to wrench his gaze from the woman in rose colored silk. She had left Lady Fitzroy's side and was now headed in the direction of the cardroom.

"I'm sorry?" he said when she disappeared behind a group of young bucks and he could finally turn away.

Lady Selina was regarding him quizzically. "I wondered what your plans for the summer were, Your Grace?"

"Ah, my plans," he repeated, his mind reeling drunkenly from what he'd just seen. He gave a laugh that sounded slightly hysterical even to his own ears. "My plans have changed recently—very recently."

Hy was worn to a nub trying to please her Aunt Ellen—who *still* insisted on introducing her to potential dance partners—while also avoiding both the duke, his fool of a cousin, and Fowler, all three of whom appeared to be everywhere at once.

And all three of them had danced at least one set with her sister.

She'd been startled to see Linny with the massive Baron Fowler, even more so when her sister had been the one chattering and laughing while Fowler—a man whose mouth never stopped moving—was visibly tongue tied, not to mention a more awkward dancer even than Hy.

Something about Fowler's lack of polish and awkward social skills made Hy like the bluff Scot even more than she already did. But she pitied him if he had fallen in love with her sister. With a man as handsome as Shelton skulking around Selina the rich but unprepossessing baron would not have a chance to shine.

And now Selina was dancing with Chatham.

Hy's feet were rooted to the spot as she watched her lover dance with her ethereally beautiful sister. While they did not make nearly so handsome a pair as Selina and Shelton, Hy thought Chatham both a superior dancer not to mention a more dignified and elegant partner. Any woman would look better for being in his arms and even her sister shone brighter by association.

Although Hy wasn't wearing her glasses tonight she could see well enough to notice when Selina turned in Hy's direction but quickly turned away.

She also noticed that the duke turned to see what his partner had been looking at.

Hy's breath froze in her lungs as he surveyed Hy and the other women around her—all wallflowers who sat up straighter when a man like Chatham so much as glanced in their direction.

Although she could not see his eyes, she saw that he merely turned away once he'd satisfied his curiosity.

He does not know me.

Hy didn't know why his lack of recognition caused such an unpleasant twisting sensation in her belly. She was garbed in a dress—a shade of dusty rose that her sister and aunt seemed to like but which Hy found faintly nauseating—her hair was a dull brown, thanks to the temporary dye, and she was not wearing her glasses.

Hyacinth

Not to mention he thought she was a servant and the last person he should expect to see at a *ton* function.

"Hyacinth?"

Hy forced her gaze away from the duke and turned to her aunt. "Yes, Aunt Ellen?"

"Young Lord DeVere is very interested in dancing with you, but the poor boy is shy." She gestured to a spotty young man a good four inches shorter than Hy who was, indeed, looking at Hy with an openly admiring look. Well, would wonders never cease?

"Perhaps in a little while, Aunt." Or never. "My shoe is pinching me dreadfully." That was not a lie, the shoes Selina had chosen for her had impossibly narrow toes. "I believe I should go and check on Lady Fitzroy. She was not feeling well earlier."

Her aunt pursed her lips. "Very well. But don't allow her to trap you into playing cards all night, my dear."

Hy only wished that might happen.

"Of course not, Aunt Ellen."

Hy stole one last, quick look at Chatham and Selina, yet again wishing she had her spectacles—and then removed herself from her aunt's orbit to the relative safety of the cardroom. She knew it was the one place in the huge house she didn't need to fear encountering Chatham or Shelton as only chicken stakes were ever allowed in such an environment. To wager real money would be to insult the hostess by treating her house as a gambling den.

It turned out that Hy had arrived not a moment too soon.

Lady Fitzroy's table had already broken for supper and the old woman looked up at Hy as if she were a savior. "I am so glad you have come, Hyacinth. I'm afraid I'm suffering something of a recurrence of my indisposition."

Hy knew what the old woman did not wish to say: she needed to get home immediately, where she could be alone with her chamber pot.

"I will summon the carriage right away, my lady. Shall I escort you to the retiring room to wait for me?" she asked with as much subtlety as she was capable of.

The old lady's look of gratitude was answer enough.

After depositing Lady Fitzroy in the relative calm of the retiring room she surveyed the thinning ballroom for any sign of her aunt. She could not see either Lady Ellen or Selina anywhere; they must have already gone into supper.

Hy approached a nearby servant. "Will you please find Lady Fitzroy and let her know that her niece is escorting the dowager Lady Fitzroy home early."

The footman bowed. "Very good, ma'am."

Hy hurried to the cloakroom, where she sent another servant to bring their carriage around and also collected Lady Fitzroy's heavy velvet cloak.

She tried not to take pleasure in her employer's indisposition, but leaving before her sister and aunt meant she could go home, wash the unpleasantly heavy brown dye from her hair, and get a full night's sleep and be fresh for tomorrow night's meeting with Chatham.

Hy had thought of little else but the duke's offer and she'd finally settled on an answer. It was not everything Chatham had asked for, but she believed she had come up with a decent compromise.

A smile curved her lips as she contemplated the plan she had mapped out, which would yield a future that was both rewarding and exciting.

Chapter 26

Hy was so eager to get to her room at Mrs. Dryden's that she took the stairs two steps at a time, her heart pounding with more than physical exertion as she hurried to see her lover.

Her fingers were already tugging off her cravat as she flung open the door to the room, her mind on what the duke would want to—

"Oh!" she yelped when Chatham rose from the armchair where he'd obviously been waiting for her, rather than in the adjoining room as he usually did.

"You got here before me," Hy said foolishly, her mouth no doubt curved into an equally foolish smile. "Have you been waiting long?"

"No, only a few minutes... Hy."

She flung her cravat onto a chair and threw her hat to join it, tugging off her gloves while closing the distance between them. "I have been thinking about this all day," she confessed, dropping her gloves where she stood and then sliding her hands up the front of the duke's elegantly coated body. "You are wearing far too many clothes, Your Grace."

Chatham smiled, but Hy couldn't help noticing the expression didn't reach his eyes. Indeed, if she'd been a fanciful sort of person, she would have said that his usually warm brown irises looked decidedly... cool.

But a person's eyes didn't really change color with their moods, they just *appeared* to darken or lighten depending on the size of their pupils.

The duke's pupils were pinpricks.

Hy removed her hands from his body and took a step back. "Is aught amiss, Your Grace?"

"Not at all, why would you say that?"

"You look... different."

"I am just lamenting that this is our last night together here."

A smile pulled at her lips. "As to that, I have given your offer some thought."

He arched an eyebrow. "Have you indeed?"

"Yes. I have come up with a counteroffer."

He gave a bark of laughter and his expression shifted into more relaxed lines. "And what is that?"

"I will live in a house you provide and will allow you to spoil me with servants and such—but only during those months of the year when you live in London, too."

Rather than look pleased, as she'd hoped, he looked... Actually, Hy didn't know what he looked.

"And what will you do the rest of the year? Oh wait—I know," he said before she could answer, "You and your brother will travel about as you'd planned, fleecing unsuspecting gamblers?"

Hy nodded, relieved that he understood. "Is that not a practical plan?"

He smiled at her and finally, *finally*, touched her, although only her hand. "It is very practical." He raised her palm to his mouth and kissed it before saying, "I have a plan of my own."

"Oh?" she asked, her eyes riveted to where his lips caressed her skin, the tip of his tongue poking out to lick at her palm.

"We never did play piquet, did we?"

Her eyes jumped up to meet his. "Er, what?"

"Piquet. Would you like to play?"

She frowned. "Right now?"

He shrugged. "If you'd rather not—"

"No, no, I just thought..."

"What did you think?"

Hy could scarcely believe that he didn't know what she thought. She'd hoped he would be thinking the *same thing*, and for once it wasn't cards on her mind. She met his gaze, more than a little bit... disgruntled.

They had this room for the next few hours and he wanted to play *cards*?

"Don't you want to play?" The duke smiled, his gaze strangely opaque.

"Of course, I would like to play." A thought struck. "It is too bad we don't have any cards."

Chatham gestured to a small table Hy had not noticed before. On it was a pack of cards, a sheet of parchment, and a pencil.

"Oh, you have everything ready."

Chatham wanted to play cards more than engage in sexual experimentation? Had she been wrong about him and his attraction to her? Was his interest in her already waning?

Hyacinth

Something nagged at her, some emotion that was so rare it took her a moment to identify it: Hy felt offended.

"Is something wrong?" Chatham asked.

She glanced at the card table and forced herself to look on the positive side of things. While Hy would have much rather stripped the duke naked and tied him up again, pitting her wits against him at her favorite game was probably the next best thing.

"No. Nothing is wrong. Let's play."

"Excellent. Have a seat."

Hy sat and the duke did likewise. He shuffled the cards and then fanned them out. "Cut for the deal?"

Hy drew a four and Chatham drew a king.

Not an auspicious omen, if one were the sort of person to believe in such things.

Chatham shuffled the cards and Hy watched his long-fingered hands, which were dexterous and oddly mesmerizing.

He had beautiful hands, and she couldn't help remembering how they'd looked moving up and down his erect cock and stroking her sex, his elegant fingers slick with both their juices…

Hy swallowed and looked away; those sorts of thoughts were hardly conducive to concentrating on the game.

"Stakes?" Chatham asked.

"Er, five shillings a point?"

The duke gave a derisive laugh. "Come, I thought you sneered at chicken stakes."

Hy's face grew hot even though the room had a distinct chill. "Ten?"

"Let us say twenty, shall we? Just to keep things interesting."

Good Lord. Twenty?

Chatham continued to stare, a faint smile pulling his lips up on one side and exposing that pointy canine tooth she found so attractive.

Hy cleared her throat. "Twenty is fine."

The duke nodded. "Twenty it is."

And thence began the most unpleasant hour and a half in Hy's memory.

***

Sylvester knew he should feel guilty about fleecing Lady Hyacinth, but he didn't. Or if he did feel any guilt, it was buried so deeply beneath his anger that it didn't matter.

Lady Hyacinth's ability to count cards wasn't nearly so helpful in piquet as it was in double pack vingt-et-un.

Although she appeared to know the game quite well, Sylvester had played piquet almost nightly for years when he'd been in the army, and those hundreds of hours of experience meant poor Lady Hyacinth didn't stand a chance against him.

Midway through the first rubber he could see the truth beginning to dawn on her. He should have eased up on her then—he'd not come to Madam Dryden's to thrash her at cards, after all—but he was too furious to be merciful.

Now that he knew who she really was he was astounded by his own idiocy. Daughter of a governess, indeed! Oh, she was not as proper as her sister Selina, but she carried herself like a lady, her manners were exquisite, and he was a bloody fool not to have put the pieces together long ago.

He was *such* a fool.

Instead of seeing through her ridiculous façade, he had sat in this very room and offered a carte blanche to the daughter of an earl.

How she must have laughed at him.

Hell, she must have been laughing for weeks to have convinced him that she was an over-educated servant.

Sylvester was perfectly aware that it wasn't just his pride that had been damaged. He had not only enjoyed her company, he'd believed that she'd honestly enjoyed *his*. He'd almost believed that she'd liked him for who he was, rather than *what* he was.

He hated how painful it was to realize he was nothing but some twisted amusement for her. The truth was that he was far angrier at himself than at her. He loathed himself for exhibiting such weakness. He would have thought he'd learned his lesson after Mariah, but it appeared not: Sylvester was a sentimental idiot through and through.

So, no, he refused to show mercy to the woman currently looking miserable as her money slipped through her fingers. And it was nobody's fault but Lady Hyacinth's that she'd found herself in such a situation.

By the end of the second rubber, she was down eight hundred pounds. Sylvester could scarcely believe how recklessly she was wagering.

Hyacinth

He'd never seen her throw good money after bad before. She was plunging deep when it was clear she didn't have either the cards or the skill.

"Well, Hy?" Sylvester asked as he gathered up the cards after a particularly brutal game.

Hyacinth—a name he found strangely fitting for the young woman dressed in men's clothing—looked dazed, as if she were in the grip of some sort of mental reorganization, and it took her a moment before she turned her blue-green gaze in his direction.

"Er, I beg your pardon, Your Grace?"

"I asked if we were finished for the evening."

She fixed Sylvester with her disconcertingly direct stare. "No."

Sylvester shrugged. "As you wish. It is your deal."

***

Hy wanted to kick herself.

The duke had given her a way out of this mess. Why on earth had she insisted on continuing? This was a slaughter. Not only were the cards falling unreasonably kindly for Chatham, but he was a far cagier player than anyone she had ever encountered.

Eight. Hundred. Pounds.

Hy was beyond mortified to realize that she felt tears prickling in her eyes. All these weeks of painstakingly saving up money only to lose a great whacking chunk of it in less than two hours.

Instead of shuffling the cards she should be running from the room—running from London—and looking for a rock to hide under. This was a disaster.

"I believe you are going to shuffle the pips right off those cards," the duke said, his deep, velvety voice yanking Hy from her miserable musing. "Are you sure you want to continue playing, Hyacinth?"

Now is your chance! You can tell him no. You can tell him you've changed your mind.

Hy opened her mouth to do just that when his last word slapped her in the face: *Hyacinth.*

The cards fluttered from Hy's nerveless fingers and she looked up to find Chatham watching her with the same avid, almost harsh, expression he'd worn since she'd walked into the room an hour and a half earlier.

"You know," she said foolishly.

"Yes, I know, *Lady Hyacinth.*"

On his tongue the ridiculous name sounded... quite nice, actually.

"What are you going to do?" she asked.

"I invited you here so we could discuss what *we* are going to do."

"That will be a short discussion, then, because I don't think *we* need to do anything. Who I am is none of your affair, Your Grace."

"You can't really believe that."

No, she didn't, but it had been worth a try. "If you are worried that people will find out about us and what we've done here, you needn't be concerned, Your Grace."

"That is the least of my worries, Lady Hyacinth."

She recoiled at his icy tone and heated glare. "What would be the, er, most of your worries?"

"Did it amuse you to make a fool of me?"

Her jaw sagged. "A fool? What are—I mean"—Hy bit her lip, swallowed, and tried again. "I don't know what you mean, Your Grace?"

"You've known who I was all along. Not just my name, but you've known *about me*."

Hy shrugged, not sure where this was leading. "You are the Duke of Chatham; everyone knows about you."

Rather than be appeased by her comment, he looked incensed. "You knew that I was married, that I am widowed, *why* I am widowed, and probably more. Admit it."

An unpleasant lump began to form in her belly. "Yes."

"And yet you enjoyed toying with me."

"But—how?"

"*How?*" he repeated, an ugly gleam in his eyes. "What about the other night—after we'd finished *fucking* and were lying in bed and you became chatty for the first time since I met you. I wondered why you'd suddenly developed such an interest in me. Asking if I would marry and what ball I had gone to. Tell me, what was the point of all that?"

Hy closed her eyes briefly, suddenly horrified by how those questions must now appear to the most hunted man in the *ton*. When she opened them, she found him waiting. "You are right that I asked some questions that I already knew the answers to. But it is not how it seems."

"Tell me how it *is*, Lady Hyacinth?"

"I know you must think I've been playing some elaborate game to trap you"—he gave a bitter bark of laughter— "But trust me, Your Grace, that is *not* what I've been doing." Hy met his skeptical, angry gaze and couldn't help laughing at the irony of it all. "I don't want to marry anyone,

Hyacinth

especially not you." Only after the words left her mouth did she realize how unkind they sounded. "I didn't mean it that way, I meant—"

"Please, don't apologize; I appreciate your honesty." His nostrils flared and his face had suddenly paled.

"Chatham, please. I'm not good at this sort of thing. I—"

"What sort of thing? Telling the truth?" He smiled, but there was no amusement in it. "Yes, I've noticed that."

"No, I meant—"

"Why do you risk your safety and your reputation to play cards? Just what the hell is this all about?" he demanded, talking right over her, as if she hadn't been speaking.

Hy stared at him for a long moment, considered persisting with her apology, but could see by his cold gaze that he would not hear her.

Instead of trying to explain herself to a man who would not listen she scraped up the scattered cards, put them to rights, and then split the pack in half and shuffled, the familiar action helping a little to calm her frazzled nerves.

"I do it to win money."

"Yes, but *why* do you need to win money?"

"How do you know I don't just like money?"

He gave her a withering look. "Don't lie to me. You looked as if you'd just lost your best friend in the entire world when you went down eight hundred pounds."

Hy heaved a sigh. "Are you going to tell my aunt about this?"

"Yes," he said without hesitation.

Hy could only stare, her lips tightening as she struggled to contain her mounting anger. Not just at the fact that he knew the truth, but at her own inarticulateness when it came to her feelings. She *hated* arguing and she *hated* being put on the spot. Her mind always became as torpid as a tortoise and she never thought of the right things to say. Only later, when she was alone, and everything was over and done could she finally think of the words she had been struggling for. Of course, by then it was always too late.

"What game are you playing with this masquerade, my lady?" the duke demanded.

"I'm not playing any game—nothing except cards."

"I don't believe you."

"I don't care if you believe me. You were perfectly happy to play cards with me—to *fuck* me—when you believed I was a mere governess's daughter. You didn't think I was playing a game then, did you?"

"That was different and you know it."

"Whether I am a stableman's niece or an earl's daughter should not make any difference."

He scowled. "There is the way things should be and the way things *are*."

It was Hy's turn to scowl because he was right.

"You have a brother, my lady."

Hy blinked, nonplussed by the sudden change of topic. "Yes, but what—"

"I know your brother is young but imagine he was twenty-one and was discovered to have been gallivanting about London with an earl's daughter. Not only are the two seen playing cards together in dubious hells, but they've also spent evenings at a brothel."

Hy stopped shuffling the cards and dealt them out with shaking fingers. "I know what you are getting at. You want me to admit that the only decent thing for my brother to do in that situation would be to marry the woman in question."

"I shall make you an offer, my lady. If you can honestly tell me that you would advise your brother to abandon the woman then you may get up and walk out of this room right now with my blessing."

Hy ignored him. Instead, she studied the cards she'd just dealt. She snorted; it was the first decent hand she'd had all night.

"Well?" the duke prodded.

Hy counted her suit cards and then organized her hand.

"That is a very interesting habit you employ—ignoring any question you don't wish to answer. Does it always work for you, my lady?"

"It doesn't appear to be working tonight."

"Put down the cards, Hyacinth."

Hy wanted to defy him—to tell him to go to the devil—but apparently her respect for authority ran deeper than she knew.

She tossed her cards onto the table and folded her arms across her chest. "What do you want, Your Grace?"

"I want you to answer my question, please."

"I would vigorously counsel my brother to do the proper, gentlemanly thing and marry the woman whose reputation he'd destroyed. There, are you pleased?"

He ignored her taunt. "Why do you think I should behave any less honorably?"

"Because the situations are not analogous."

"You are an earl's daughter, I am—"

"I am no virginal maiden, Chatham. You did not debauch me or rob me of my innocence."

"When word of what we've been doing gets out, your reputation will be destroyed—regardless of whether you were a virgin or not."

"Word *won't* get out. I have been careful and there is—"

"My cousin knows you are a woman."

Hy stared. "Shelton *knows* who I am?"

"He knows you are a female masquerading as a man, but he doesn't know *which* female. It is only a matter of time before he finds out."

"Why would he care about such a thing?"

"Because shaming me is Shelton's *raison d'être*, my lady. And there would be no greater shame than to prove I have debauched the daughter of a peer."

"How did he find out?"

"Does it matter?"

Hy exhaled a shaky breath. "No, it doesn't."

"I can see by your reaction that you understand my position, now."

Hy did understand his position, and it was an unenviable one. He was an honorable man and didn't wish to be lumped in with Shelton, a scoundrel who'd infamously ruined an innocent young woman just to win a wager.

By associating with the duke—and tricking him into believing she was a servant—Hy had effectively forced his hand. To anyone with half a brain it would look as if a dowdy wallflower had conceived of a perfect way to trap the biggest matrimonial prize in London.

The dowager Lady Fitzroy's face and words came back to her—her gloating expression when she'd confessed to trapping her husband into marriage.

Chatham had danced with Selina—singled her out to give her attention. Had he been planning to ask her to marry him? Her Aunt Ellen certainly thought so.

Hy suddenly felt ill.

Although he'd not said the *M* word yet, Hy knew what Chatham was moving toward.

There had to be some other way out of this trouble.

The *ton* loved a scandal and it would truly enjoy dragging a duke's name through the mud. But would it really be a scandal if the woman in question was nowhere to be found? Did not the maxim *out of sight, out of mind* apply when it came to gossip?

She looked up. "I have an idea."

He sighed.

"I will leave London immediately. I know you probably won't believe me, but going out on my own and earning my way playing cards has been my plan for years, so leaving would not be ruining my life." She paused, waiting for a response, but the duke just stared. "If I am gone from London then surely any gossip your cousin tries to spread will lack teeth? After all, if I am not here, then you can deny whatever Shelton alleges and he will have no proof."

"I know you don't need the money for your brother—he is only fourteen and lives with your parents in Hampshire. What *do* you need it for? What is it that sends you out into the most dangerous parts of London, my lady?"

Hy gave a disbelieving laugh. "Did you not listen to what I said at all, Your Grace? I have a *plan* that will—"

"What kind of trouble are you in?" he persisted. "Just tell me what is wrong and I will help you."

"I don't *want* your help," she snapped. "I *want* you to forget you ever met me, Your Grace."

Once again Hy regretted her angry words, but she could see by the duke's coldly shuttered expression there was no point in trying to take them back.

"Unfortunately, I cannot pretend I never met you, my lady. Nor can I allow you to wander off on your merry way and play cards."

"Why *not*?"

"Because it makes no difference whether you are in London or not. When people find out—and they *always* find out—I will be branded a cad whether you are here or not. And then there is the matter of honor."

Hy sneered. "Ah, yes. I was wondering when we would get to the sacred notion of *male honor*."

"I am relieved to hear it is no surprise to you, my lady," he retorted icily.

"So, we will ruin both our lives to satisfy your *honor*."

Hy had not believed that brown eyes could look so very cold.

"I deeply apologize for ruining your life, my lady."

Hyacinth

"You know I didn't mean that as an insult."

"Oh, I should be flattered?"

"I just—"

"When I look at you," the duke said, talking over her as if she'd not been speaking, "all I can think is what I would feel if some other man did what I've done to you, to my sister or daughter. I'm not just talking about the *fucking,* Hyacinth." His mouth tightened and he leaned closer, his face so stern that Hy didn't even recognize him as her playful lover. "I'm also talking about the fact that I knew your gender weeks ago and still allowed you to go about your business—an action which ended with you being drugged and beaten by a vicious ruffian. What happened was bad enough, but have you ever thought of what might have happened if I hadn't shown up? Or if Jensen had realized you were a female? I cannot apologize enough to your parents for my part in your treatment. If *my* daughter had been robbed by highwaymen and stripped of her coat and left in the rain in the dark in the middle of the most dangerous part of London, or manhandled by an angry ex-boxer I would want one of my peers to do the right thing and bring her home to me and put a stop to such foolishness."

Hy's head buzzed she was so angry. But she hugged that anger close and met his cold hard stare with one of her own, her jaws tightly clamped to keep from saying one more stupid or cruel thing that she would regret.

"What do you need the money for, Hyacinth?"

"That is not your concern," she said through clenched jaws, her hands fisted so hard they hurt.

"Very well." He stood up and offered her his arm. "Shall we go?"

Hy's brow creased. "Go where?"

"I am taking you home and we shall wait for your aunt to return from the Castleford ball. We shall tell her everything and I will try to start making matters right by asking your aunt for your hand in marriage."

There it was, what she'd been expecting and dreading. "Marriage."

"You must know it is the only way."

Hy knew that he believed that—and so would her aunt and family and anyone else she might ask.

"I don't suppose it matters to you that I do not *wish* to marry you?"

The duke flinched slightly and something flickered in his eyes, something too quick for her to identify.

"I'm sorry to hear that," he said in a cool tone. "But I'm afraid we lost our right to choose otherwise. I am just as much to blame as you are—"

"No. No, you are not just as much to blame, Your Grace. Don't try to shoulder my blame. You never would have done any of this—played cards with me or come to this place—if you'd known who I really was."

He did not deny it. If he'd discovered her identity that first night, he'd have done exactly what he was doing right now: his duty.

Duty. That was what she was, now.

Hy didn't know why that hurt so much, but it did.

"Can't you just forget what you learned tonight?" she begged. "I absolve you of any responsibility you might feel. I will leave London and do as I always planned to do. You will not—"

"Do you imagine I can let you wander off on your own—into any sort of danger—and live with myself? Don't you realize that I would wonder each and every day if you were safe? What would I feel if you were robbed on some road? But this time raped, or perhaps killed? Do you think that is the sort of thought I wish to carry with me?" He shook his head. "I will *not* have that on my conscience."

"For reasons beyond my ken, you have appointed yourself my keeper and seem determined to interfere where you are neither needed nor *wanted*." Hy had never in her life spoken with such undisguised venom, and she felt more than a little shame at doing so now. He was obviously concerned for her welfare, and she was reacting like a shrew, but the thought that he would sacrifice himself out of duty sickened her. "Do you think I am protesting marriage to you to be coy, Your Grace? Because believe me, I am not. I do not want to be a duchess. Indeed, there is no worse fate that I can imagine. I would rather be transported than marry you, sir."

His smile was chilling. "Direct, as ever. You may not care about your reputation or prospects, my lady, but I daresay your sisters do not feel the same way."

Hy felt like he had slapped her. She opened her mouth, but then closed it.

"Yes, I can see you know what I mean. Lady Selina, no matter how beautiful and engaging she is, will have a difficult time managing another Season with a scandal of this magnitude hanging over your family name."

He was correct. If his wretched cousin made his knowledge about her public, it would make any alliance with her already beleaguered family unpalatable to any respectable man.

In effect, it would make marriage impossible for those of her sisters who might want it.

Hyacinth

Hy suddenly felt tired, so tired she could curl up in the big, undisturbed bed in the other room and simply go to sleep.

"How long have you been dressing in men's clothing?"

Hy sighed. "Why?"

"Please answer my question."

"I began when I was thirteen."

"Why?"

"Because I could hardly play cards as a woman—I've told you that before."

"Yes, but why would a young woman—"

"Because I like it. Because it is easier for me to be a man."

"What do you mean *easier*?"

Hy gritted her teeth at his startled look. Why hadn't she just kept her mouth shut? She was not normally so talkative, so impulsive. Of course, this was not a normal day, not by any stretch.

"How can it be easier? You are a young lady, you are—"

"I make a better man than woman."

His jaw sagged. "What… rubbish."

"You have played cards with me many times. How many men have questioned my gender, Your Grace?"

"My cousin knows."

"Fine, that is one out of hundreds."

"I know."

"You only knew because your valet told you. If he had not walked in when I'd been without a cravat, we'd probably be sitting across from each other in some gambling hell as we speak."

His jaw clenched, but he couldn't deny it was the truth. "I might not have guessed so quickly, but I would have known sooner rather than later."

"Yes, keep telling yourself that. You wouldn't want to admit that you were anything less than clever, would you, Your Grace?"

His lips pressed into a scowl.

"You have met my sister—even danced with her."

The duke's face reddened, his annoyance replaced by embarrassment. "Yes, what of it?"

"Selina is a great beauty, is she not?"

His jaws flexed. "Yes."

"My other three sisters are all very attractive, as well. Even my brother was blessed with a face which will bring members of the opposite sex to their knees. Meanwhile, I am just shy of six feet, bespeckled, and bespectacled, not to mention so awkward that I can barely speak in a social situation."

"You've spoken many times and been fine," he said.

"When I was dressed as a man. You've not seen what I am as a woman."

He gave a snort of disbelief. "You cannot be so different."

It was Hy's turn to snort, but she left his comment unanswered for the moment, instead continuing with her point. "From my earliest days my mother made it clear what my role would be in our family: that of maiden aunt. She did not say it to be cruel, but to save me from false expectations—to keep me from hoping. She said, and I quote, *A wealthy man might marry a poor beauty, but he would never take a poor, ugly woman as his wife.*"

"Why would any mother say such a thing to her daughter?" the duke asked, visibly disturbed by her words. He shook his head, "She was *wrong*, Hyacinth," he added before she could argue.

Hy waved dismissively, so very, very tired of this very, very tiresome topic. "If my mother hadn't said anything I would have discovered the truth quickly enough when I was forced to attend our local assemblies. Being on display in some hideous gown rendered me all but mute and even more clumsy than usual. I was so unappealing that the only men who asked me to dance were either forced to do so by their female relatives or they were social aspirants who hoped that dancing with an earl's daughter would somehow improve their stock."

The duke looked more and more unhappy the longer she spoke.

"I am not telling you this to garner sympathy, Your Grace. I am happy with my lot in life. I have accepted my future and planned accordingly. Dressing as man and mixing with men might have its share of dangers—as I've discovered twice during my stay in London—but those risks are worth it if I can support myself. You might see what I do as some sort of punishment, but I find masquerading as a man to be restful—yes, *restful*," she repeated at his disbelieving look. "When I am Hiram, I am not constantly reminded of my shortcomings as a female."

"It so happens that I find you very attractive, Hyacinth—or haven't you realized that these past weeks?"

Hy would have been inhuman—something her sisters and brother *had* accused her of on occasion—if she hadn't appreciated his words and felt warmed by them. They'd been lovers and yes, she had seen the desire blazing in his eyes when they were in bed, so she knew he spoke at least some version of the truth.

"I believe you enjoy bedding me, Your Grace. But wanting me as your wife—as your duchess—is something else entirely." He opened his mouth, but Hy talked over him. "The truth is that I am the last woman you'd have sought to marry if you had a choice, and you know it. You would not have noticed me in a thousand years in a ballroom."

"You can't know that—"

"Actually, I *can* know that because you met me on at least three occasions before I played cards with you at Jensen's that first time: Lady Singleton's ball, the dreadful Venetian Breakfast at Mrs. Mowbray's, and the Countess of Claymore's ball. All three times my aunt introduced us—because *you* had forgotten that you'd met me before."

His stunned expression should have been satisfying, but it was not. After all, reaffirming one's general invisibility to men—especially a man she esteemed—was hardly something Hy enjoyed.

Chatham swallowed but did not speak.

That was fine; Hy didn't need him to speak. She could see the truth on his face.

***

"I don't remember ever having felt like such a cad," Sylvester said. "I am deeply, terribly sorry that I treated you as if you were... invisible."

She shrugged off his apology. "You did not do it on purpose. It was apparent each time we were reintroduced that you didn't want to meet me or any of the half-dozen wallflowers around me." She gave a soft snort. "Plain women are especially familiar with the wary, hunted expression that attractive men get when faced with the prospect of being forced to dance with us."

Sylvester's face became even hotter. "So, not only have I been a heel, but I've been a rude, vain, and arrogant one, to boot." When she merely shrugged, he continued. "I'm afraid that my lamentable behavior in the past does not change our current situation, Hyacinth."

"You are adamant that we must marry," she said tonelessly.

"Yes, we must marry. And I'm afraid we must do so quickly—before Shelton can cause any mischief."

She stared blankly at the table.

"I can see you are not pleased."

If he'd been hoping for her to deny it, he was to be disappointed. She looked so distant at that moment that Sylvester doubted she was even aware of his presence.

As he studied her miserable expression it occurred to him that he was—for the second time in his life—about to marry a woman who did not wish to marry him. He swallowed down an almost hysterical urge to laugh.

She looked at him. "Is there anything I can say that will change your mind?"

"No, there isn't," he said with more heat than he would have liked. "I'm afraid that even if the thought of becoming my wife makes you physically ill, I would still have to insist on doing my duty."

By God Sylvester regretted those self-pitying words the instant they were out of his mouth.

He should have known that the woman across from him—who had never responded in a predictable fashion—would surprise him yet again.

"Your duty," she repeated, not accusingly or mockingly, but thoughtfully. "Duty is something I understand, Your Grace." She nodded, as if coming to some decision, and then stood. "Can you give me tonight to explain our situation to my aunt and sister? Tomorrow you can come and discuss the particulars with my aunt, who will no doubt know what to do."

Sylvester was so startled by her sudden acquiescence that it took him a moment to realize she'd asked a question. "Yes, yes of course you can have tonight to explain." It shamed him how relieved he felt not to be faced with the initial explanation to Lady Fitzroy.

He took a step toward her and took her hand, feeling as if he were approaching a stranger, not the adventurous lover or canny cardplaying companion of the past weeks.

She lifted her eyes to his and gave him the blank, opaque stare that she had not turned on him since the early days of their acquaintance.

"I know this is not your choice, Hyacinth, but I promise you that I will strive to be a good husband."

"Thank you."

He waited for something more, but that was, evidently, all she had to say on the matter.

Sylvester released her hand.

"Will you summon a hackney for me, Your Grace?"

"I will take you home in my carriage, Hyacinth."

An emotion flickered across her face then—too fast and too subtle for him to decipher.

Hyacinth

"Thank you, Your Grace."

Sylvester rang for a servant, and they waited in silence, just like two strangers who had nothing at all to say to each other.

Chapter 27

The following afternoon the door to Fitzroy house opened before Sylvester even touched the knocker and a black-suited domestic filled the doorway.

"Welcome, Your Grace, Lady Fitzroy is expecting you," the butler said.

Sylvester nodded and handed over his hat, gloves, and walking stick.

He'd been to the house in the past, of course, but it had been years and he'd come to call on the viscount, who was apparently busy with some diplomatic mission on the Continent rather than doing his duty as uncle and making sure his adventurous niece wasn't masquerading as a man in gaming houses and brothels all over London.

Lady Fitzroy wasn't alone when Sylvester entered an elegant, entirely feminine sitting room a few moments later.

"Ah, Your Grace, what a pleasure to see you," the tiny viscountess chirped as she held out her small hands.

Sylvester took them in his own hands and bowed. "The pleasure is mine, my lady."

"This is my mother-in-law, the Dowager Lady Fitzroy."

Sylvester turned to the room's other occupant—or other human occupant, rather, as there was also an ancient, white-jowled pug curled on a cushion beside the old woman.

"Chatham and I are old rivals at the whist tables," the old woman bellowed, holding out her beringed, claw-like hand for kissing while grasping an enormous ear trumpet with her other hand.

"And even partners on one infamous occasion," Sylvester reminded her, speaking loudly enough so that she wouldn't need to keep the heavy instrument pressed to her head.

She cackled at that. "Yes, that was a quite a grand *occasion*. I believe we thrashed your father and that silly sister of his quite savagely. How is Leticia, by the way?"

"Er, my aunt passed away four years ago, my lady."

"Ah, did she?" the dowager said, looking neither saddened nor surprised. "She always was a fragile little thing."

The younger Lady Fitzroy made a nervous tittering sound at her mother-in-law's insensitive pronouncement, her hands fluttering like moths. "Would you like tea, Your Grace?"

Sylvester opened his mouth to decline, but the dowager beat him to the mark.

"Lord, he doesn't want *tea* to maudle his insides, Ellen! He's a man, for pity's sake." She cut Sylvester a leering look that almost put him to blush. "A *real* man by what I've heard."

"Oh, *Mama*," her daughter-in-law moaned, her face redder than the strawberry pink divan she was sitting on.

"I understand you've come to call on my great niece," the dowager plowed on, undaunted by her daughter-in-law's chiding.

Sylvester was trying to puzzle out their relationship—he had believed Hyacinth's father and Lady Fitzroy were siblings—when the vilest stench imaginable suddenly flooded his nostrils.

Although he tried to control his expression, he must not have been entirely successful.

"I am terribly sorry," the younger Lady Fitzroy blurted, her face dangerously red.

Sylvester was trying not to breathe, when the dowager gave another of her earthy cackles. "It's not my daughter-in-law if you are wondering, Your Grace."

Only Lady Fitzroy's mortified face stopped Sylvester from laughing.

"It's poor pug, I'm afraid." The old woman's face softened so much she was scarcely recognizable as she stared at the bony little creature snoring audibly on the velvet cushion.

It was difficult to believe that such a small animal could produce a stench of such truly horrific proportions.

"Well, don't just sit there swooning; open a window, you ninny," the dowager barked at her daughter-in-law.

But it was Sylvester who sprang to his feet. "Allow me," he choked out, grateful for a reason to get away from the miasmic cloud, which only seemed to be getting stronger.

He opened not one, but two windows.

He was deliberating crawling out of one the windows rather than returning to his seat when the door opened.

Lady Fitzroy, who was holding a delicately embroidered handkerchief to her face, gave a whimper and said, "Ah, there you are, my dear. Don't leave just yet, William," she said as the footman began to back away from the door he'd just opened for Lady Selina. "Please take pug to Lady Fitzroy's room."

With a pained expression that spoke of a long and intimate association with *pug*, the footman approached the dozing hound with a scrunched up face, casting apprehensive glances at its mistress.

"Oh, go ahead and take him," the dowager ordered with a scowl, and then turned to Lady Selina. "It's not *you* the duke wants, missy. It is your sister."

"*Mama!*" Lady Fitzroy shrieked, and then turned to Sylvester. "I apologize, duke. She does not know what she is saying."

"Oh, yes I do, Ellen." The dowager twisted around until she could pin Sylvester with her surprisingly sharp old eyes. "Tell her, Chatham. Tell her it's the other one you want, that disastrous long Meg with the atrocious hair and spectacles, isn't it?"

Sylvester stared from one woman to the other, and then looked at Lady Selina, who's face had lost every bit of color.

He hastened toward her, suddenly ashamed by his amused reaction to the abrasive old crone. "You look as if you need to sit down, my lady."

But when he tried to escort her to a chair, she thrust a sheet of parchment at him. "Your Grace, I'm afraid something terrible has happened."

"What is going on, Selina?" The younger Lady Fitzroy demanded, glancing from her niece to Sylvester to the letter in his hand.

Before Lady Selina could answer the dowager threw her head back and laughed.

Everyone turned to watch as she cackled until tears ran down her cheeks.

Sylvester let her mirth run its course and turned to the letter.

Dearest Linny:

If you are reading this then that means the Duke of Chatham has come to call and William has just handed you this letter.

I am sorry I could not be the one to tell you myself, but I knew how you would argue, dear Linny.

I lied when I told you that nobody recognized me on my nights out.

The duke learned my sex weeks ago. His cousin, Shelton, is poised to discover my identity and will use it to shame the duke.

Hyacinth

Chatham blames himself for the damage to my reputation that his cousin's action will likely cause.

His Grace is the best of men and he deserves a duchess as lovely and clever and kind as he is. In his way, he has courted you this Season and he knows that you are a perfect choice for the role of wife.

Sylvester snorted and shook his head in disbelief. She was graciously giving him to her sister to marry—as if he were an old bonnet or pair of gloves she no longer wanted. A man had to laugh—or throttle her. Lady Hyacinth really was the most unpredictable woman he'd ever met.

He sighed, almost afraid to read the rest.

But because he is a good, honorable man, he is prepared to do the good, honorable thing and make a disastrous—for both of us—marriage to rescue my reputation.

I cannot allow that to happen.

I have left the money for Queen's Bower in my trunk. Eight hundred of it belongs to the duke, but once you are betrothed you might presume on him to forgive the debt.

Sylvester laughed. "You little scoundrel," he muttered beneath his breath. To Lady Selina, he said, "What does she mean, *money for queen's bower?*"

"My father's gambling debt," she said in an under voice. "We will be evicted if it is not paid."

So. That was why she risked herself: to rescue her family.

Sylvester sighed heavily and turned back to the letter.

Nothing good can come of continuing a relationship with me Selina—I know that. But I'm not so selfless that I can give up my beloved brother and sisters, so I will contact you from time-to-time to let you know I am well.

Don't fret about me or search for me Linny, just know that I am finally going to live the life I have always wanted.

Your sister,

Hy

The duke looked up to discover that only Lady Selina was paying him any attention. The two lady Fitzroy's were engaged in a half-hushed—on the younger woman's side—and half-shouted disagreement.

Sylvester stepped closer to his lover's sister and asked in a low voice. "When do you think she left?"

"She left just after three o'clock this morning," the dowager bellowed from across the room.

Sylvester glanced from the settee—where the ear trumpet lay unused—to the old lady on the other side of the room. He lifted one eyebrow.

She gave him an impish grin that told him her hearing loss was selective.

"How do you know that?" he asked.

"Because I saw her leave. And I saw her leaving and coming back time after time over the last weeks." She chortled. "Oh, she thought she was so clever—that she looked like a boy—but I knew who she was the first time I saw her sneaking away." She gave Sylvester a penetrating look. "How long before *you* knew?"

"Too long," he admitted, and turned back to Lady Selina. "I need to speak to William—the one whose brother is a hackney driver."

Rather than ask pointless questions, Lady Selina nodded and pulled the servant cord.

"Do you have *any* idea where she might have gone?" he asked her.

Selina glanced at her aunt—who'd resumed bickering with the dowager—and shook her head. "I can't think of anywhere except home. We simply don't know anyone she might visit." Her forehead puckered. "Surely she would not go someplace where she didn't know anyone?"

Sylvester didn't think Lady Selina knew her sister very well if she believed that.

"She mentioned a friend named Charles—do you know him?"

"Charles?" She looked genuinely perplexed.

Sylvester stood silently while she pondered, his own mind reeling at how stupid he had been last night when she'd suddenly stopped protesting and had accepted matters far too readily.

At her request, he'd had his driver drop her in the same place as always. He'd not expected her to so much as look at him when she left—he'd seen how angry and disappointed she was—but she had taken his face in both hands and said, "I would have liked to be your mistress, Sylvester." She'd then kissed him fiercely before hopping out and hurrying off. Sylvester had watched her until she had disappeared. She had not turned back.

And now she was gone.

"I can think of four Charleses," Lady Selina finally said. "The local sexton is Charles Hayes, but he is eighty-five."

Hyacinth

"It's not him," Sylvester said without hesitation. Or at least he hoped to God it wasn't.

"Charles Dolan is the butcher in Little Sissingdon and he is married and has seven children."

Sylvester reluctantly left Dolan's name on his mental list and said, "Next."

"Charles Martin is eleven and—"

"Not him. Who is the last?"

"That would be Charles Garrett. He was my brother's mathematics tutor for several years when he came to Little Sissingdon to recuperate."

"How old is he?"

"I don't know, but I should think he was somewhere around my age."

"Recuperate from what?"

"I don't know that, either. I just know he stayed with his uncle—Mr. Petersham is our vicar—and that he'd needed to leave university because of his illness. He lived in the area for four, maybe five years, so I suppose Hy might have known him, although I don't recall seeing them together."

That was the one, Sylvester knew it. "Do you know where he went after leaving Little Sissingdon?"

"I believe he came back here, to London. His grandfather owns a bookshop and he works with him."

"Do you know the name of the bookstore?"

"I'm afraid I don't know."

No, that would be too simple. How many booksellers were there in London? Hundreds, at least. Sylvester ignored the sharp stab of hopelessness. He would just need to make a comprehensive list and go to each and every—

"I'm sure the vicar would know."

"I beg your pardon?"

"The vicar—Mr. Petersham, he will know the name. Charles is his nephew, after all."

He felt like an idiot. "Of course, thank you."

The door opened and the same footman as earlier entered.

Lady Selina gestured him closer. "Ah, Will, His Grace wishes to speak with you."

The footman's eyes went round and his terrified gaze slid to his employer, who'd stopped arguing long enough to stare at the young man questioningly.

Sylvester turned to his hostess. "Is there somewhere I might speak to your servant in private, my lady?"

"Of course, Your Grace—but—might I know what this is all about?"

He forced himself to smile. "I will tell you everything after I speak to your footman." *Or at least everything that you need to know*, he mentally amended.

Chapter 28

After more than twenty hours in a stagecoach—in the middle seat—the first thing Hy purchased when she crawled out of the coach in York was a horse.

Although she had not ridden regularly for several years—not since her father sold the last of their hacking horses to cover yet another of his gambling debts—Hy knew enough about horseflesh that she was able to choose a mount that was, if not exactly handsome, at least sturdy.

Her purse was considerably lighter by the time she purchased some third-hand tack, but at least she was no longer at the mercy of coach drivers whose goal was to stuff as many bodies as possible into their conveyances.

The journey from York to Skipley took an additional four hours. She could have spent the night in York—slept in a bed rather than on some stranger's shoulder—but she was suddenly desperate to get to her destination.

Although it was the beginning of summer, the area between York and the coast was said to be one of the coldest in the country and Hy was chilled to the bone by the time she approached the tiny village on the southern edge of the bay.

After she'd taken care of her weary mount and hired a room at the town's only inn, she walked to the cottage that sat overlooking the water.

An older woman answered the door, her eyes going comically wide when she saw her well-dressed visitor.

"Are you lost, sir?" she asked.

"I hope not. I'm looking for Charles Garrett."

***

Sylvester and Tackle sipped pints of homebrew on adjacent barstools in Little Sissingdon's only taproom, which was amusingly called the Prince and Weasel.

The two men had made a lightning-fast journey from London on horseback. Sylvester preferred riding not only because it was faster, but also because he could evade all the pomp and ceremony that attended any journey in his ducal coach or even his curricle, which was recognized on most of the major thoroughfares in England.

Reverend Petersham had proven endlessly helpful to Sylvester, who'd presented himself as Mr. Sylvester Derrick, a gentleman scholar from Oxford looking for a London bookseller whose name had been evading him.

During his visit to the vicarage, he'd heard the extremely interesting news that one of the daughters of the local lord—the Earl of Addiscombe—had a few weeks earlier married the son of the infamous iron magnate John "Iron Mad" Needham.

Sylvester knew of Needham, of course. The man had been raised to the peerage for his support of a prior Hanoverian monarch and his son. The second Viscount Needham was proving every bit as useful to the current king in the endless war on the Continent.

Sylvester had been stunned to hear of the match and wondered why he'd heard no news of the union in London. If Needham had married one of the earl's daughters, then surely he would have settled the debt Hyacinth was working so diligently—and dangerously—to pay off?

Clearly something else was afoot and Sylvester decided to visit the best place in any village to gain information: the local taproom.

When the barman came to see if they wanted a refill on their pints, Sylvester nodded and said—just loudly enough to be heard by those other patrons propping up the heavy oak bar in midafternoon— "I understand you had a big wedding here not long ago."

"Aye, the Earl of Addiscombe's daughter caught herself the new master of Wych House."

"I thought Wych House was Addiscombe's country seat?" the duke asked, knowing full well it was, but willing to dissemble a bit to get the locals talking.

"Aye, it is," an aged man on Sylvester's right side piped up. "But he's not lived there in ages. He leases it."

"Ain't nobody lived there for almost two years," said another man, who drifted up to the bar and set down an empty glass, nodding to the innkeeper. "The earl and all his children live in the old dower house—Queen's Bower it be called."

Hyacinth

"Queen Elizabeth is said to have slept there," the barman offered, placing a pint before Sylvester.

"It must be quite grand," Sylvester said.

"T'ain't grand," a fourth man countered, sidling up to stand on the old gimmer's other side.

The duke gestured for the barman to refill the glasses of the men around the bar—a number which had trebled in only a few minutes.

"Much obliged," the man next to him said, the others murmuring their thanks as well.

Properly lubricated now, the conversation rolled on with only slight prodding from Sylvester.

"The earl and his wife won't be moving into Wych House now that their daughter is married?"

"Ha!" another snorted. "You know it will be puttin' Herself's nose out of joint to see Lady Phoebe mistress of the big house."

"She's *Viscountess* Phoebe, now," a third man inaccurately, but proudly, announced.

"The new Viscountess Needham is Addiscombe's daughter, I take it?" Sylvester asked.

"Aye, and what a sweet lass she is."

"The earl has several children, doesn't he?"

"A right gaggle," another old man said as he joined the throng.

"And all of 'em too good for their parents," somebody said in a stage whisper.

The others *shushed* him down, but not with much conviction.

"The earl and countess are not well-liked?" Sylvester asked.

"*He's* easy enough—"

"Especially if you're a handsome, young lass," a newly arrived barmaid added archly, earning a great deal of laughter all around.

"Can you blame him with a wife like *that*?"

A half-dozen groans filled the air and a half-dozen more men winced at the reference to the countess.

"Lady Addiscombe is a tartar, is she?" Sylvester asked.

"Proud as a queen," one said.

"Prouder," another corrected.

"And *cold*," said a third.

"Cold enough to freeze off a man's pump handle before she'd ever polish it," the old fellow beside Sylvester announced, to the hilarity of his listeners.

Well, there was one thing that Sylvester and Hyacinth had in common. His own mother had despised Sylvester's father until the day he died—she probably still did—and had never made any attempt to hide it.

"Can't quite understand why Needham married Lady Phoebe when her sister still be on the loose."

"Oh? Which sister is that?" Sylvester couldn't resist asking, although he could guess.

"Ah, Lady Selina," a man who'd not yet spoken said, his eyes going soft and dreamy. Somebody else lifted his pint and all the others raised theirs.

"To Lady Selina, an angel on earth," the old man said, breaking the worshipful silence that had descended over the men.

"That one'll marry a duke, you mark my words—she's too good for the likes of anyone like Iron Mad Needham."

"Needham has been right generous to folks around here," the barman said in a sharp voice, giving the speaker an equally sharp look. "I'll hear nothing against him in my establishment. He's done more for the people in these parts in a few weeks than Addiscombe has done in thirty years."

Once again, the pints were raised, and Needham toasted.

"Is the family in residence now?" Sylvester asked.

"Not a one," his righthand neighbor said. "The oldest girl went somewhere up north to be a companion or such. The two middle ones are in London to catch husbands—"

"Can you imagine the sort of husband that gangly, plain as a pikestaff Lady Hy finds to take her?" one of the men asked.

His companions laughed uproariously.

"It would have to be a right desperate toff who liked his women to look more like—"

Sylvester pushed his barstool back across the floor with a deafening *screech* of wood on wood and got to his feet, his hand white-fingered around the pint glass.

Every eye turned to him.

A throat cleared. "I should remind you that it's time we be off, Mr. Derrick," Tackle said.

The haze of red in front of Sylvester's eyes hung on.

"Derrick?" the old man beside him said, breaking the awkward silence. "Any relation to old Thomas Derrick?"

Several others at the bar chuckled uneasily, clearly aware something was amiss.

Hyacinth

Sylvester wanted to thrash each and every one of them. But he wanted to thrash himself even more for looking through Hyacinth three times in one Season. In his way, he was no better than these men, only noticing a pretty face.

He released his death-grip on the pint before tossing enough money onto the bar to pay for the drinks he'd ordered and saying, "No. I'm no relation to the infamous hangman, I'm afraid."

Sylvester was suddenly desperate to leave not only the bar, but also this village, which was yet another place the woman he loved had been not only undervalued, but likely shamed and ignored.

He had the information he'd come to get—the name of the bookstore—he and Tackle would ride straight back to London.

Sylvester hoped to God that Hyacinth's former lover and friend would know where to find her.

Chapter 29

Hy propped the tray on her hip and opened the door to Charles's room.

"Ah, you are up," she said, surprised that her friend was sitting in front of the fire rather than lying down.

"You were hoping to catch me in bed, were you?" Charles waggled his eyebrows in what was supposed to be a lascivious manner but looked adorable, instead.

Hy snorted, but she was secretly pleased that he seemed so much better than he had when she'd first seen him yesterday evening.

That was the nature of his illness; one day he'd look almost healthy and normal and the next he would hardly be able to move.

"I know you just serve me so I will make your tea for you," he teased, sitting forward to take charge of the tray she set down on the table in front of him. "Or have your tea making skills improved in the past year?"

"No," she admitted, dropping into the chair across from him. "They are as execrable as ever."

"How was your sleep—was the inn comfortable? I really do wish I had room for you here."

"It is very comfortable and the stable is convenient. I was a bit shocked by how cold it was this morning on my brief walk over here."

"It will warm up by midday—and then it is quite lovely. You will see."

"I was too exhausted to ask you this last night, but why in the world did you pick the only seaside town where it is *cold*, Charles?"

He smiled as he rinsed the pot with hot water and then added the precise spoonful of tea. "I am not fond of the bustle of places like Brighton. Besides, Skipley reminds me of my mother."

"Ah, that's right—she was from somewhere around here, wasn't she?"

Hyacinth

"Yes, she grew up in York and always loved this area even after she moved to London with my father. They brought me here a few times when I was a child." Charles put the lid on the pot and sat back with a sigh. "So, are you ready to tell me what happened to bring you all the way here, Hy? Did you have a falling out with your duke? The last time we spoke I felt so optimistic for you."

She turned to look out the window. "He's not my duke, Charles. And our... association, such as it was, was temporary." Hy shrugged. "The Season is now over so I left. I earned enough money to keep the wolves from Queen's Bower for another year and now I am finally going to do what you and I always talked about doing." Hy turned back to her friend when he didn't answer. "What is it, Charles? You look almost... disappointed."

He chuckled softly and it turned into the dreaded cough.

Hy waited patiently. Although he was still coughing, it sounded less severe than it had in London, so perhaps the sea air might be helping.

Or perhaps that was wishful thinking.

He cleared his throat and then sighed heavily before saying, "I'm sorry that is what you think my look means, Hy. What I am really thinking is that you seemed almost happy the last time I saw you. I thought perhaps you'd found somebody you enjoyed being with."

"I do—*did*—enjoy being with him. But now it is over. I have the money we need, and he has his life to get back to." She paused and then reluctantly added, "And he learned who I was and became tiresome."

"By tiresome you mean he asked to marry you?"

"*Insisted* would be more accurate."

Charles clucked his tongue. "And so you fled."

Before he could delve into the matter she plucked at her buckskin breeches, wanting to change the subject. "Thank you for these, by the way."

"You are welcome. It is convenient we are so similarly sized. You may keep them, Hy. I've held onto them for far too long thinking I'd ride again, but the last time I tried—well, I don't need them."

Hy felt a deep, painful stab at his words. Charles was a graceful and skilled rider, and it was tragic that he could no longer engage in an activity that brough him so much joy. She probably should argue with him—tell him that he'd come about—but that was disrespectful to her friend, who knew his own body better than anyone else.

And so, she said, "Thank you, Charles, they are a gift I will enjoy using."

"Are you really going to do this alone, Hy? I've not tried to dissuade you before, but it is dangerous for a person—even a man—to travel alone. These are lean times and the roads abound with desperate people."

"I thought I might find a place in York for now, rather than traveling."

"I am glad to hear that," he said, looking relieved. "And you know I would adore having you nearby. You are my only friend who does not fuss over me endlessly."

Hy smiled, deeply pleased by his words. "I could say the same about you."

He grinned and gave her hand a squeeze before turning back to the tea tray.

"Do you like it here?" she asked. "Is it not a bit… quiet?"

"I do like it. I know it will be different come winter, but… well, it is possible I will stay." He poured out two cups. "I am not much help to Grandfather any longer and he really could use that spare room for somebody who would ease his burdens. The money you gave me—and yes, I *know* it was you, although Grandfather denied it—will pay for this cozy little cottage for a long time. Far longer than I will probably need it."

Hy felt a dull ache at his words, which she suspected were true.

"Here you are, my dear."

"Thank you," she said, leaning forward to take the cup and saucer from him.

"I'm afraid there is not much to entertain you around here," Charles said, once he'd settled back with his own cup.

"I have had my fill of entertainment," Hy said, sighing with contentment after taking a sip of perfectly brewed tea. "I just need a few days to… think, and then I will explore York." She cocked her head at him. "Did you ever have the opportunity to play there?"

"I have not, but there is a fellow at the inn—Jed, is his name and he works in the taproom—and he will be able to tell you some of the best places." His gaze drifted over her. "You had no problems at the inn last night?"

Hy snorted. "No. The one constant in my life appears to be the fact that I am a convincing man."

"But your duke knew."

She frowned at her friend. "He was *not*—"

Hyacinth

"—your duke," Charles finished for her. "Yes, you've said that already. Quite emphatically, in fact. Especially for you—a woman whose temper is usually so difficult to rouse I once doubted its existence. But the fact remains that *he* found out you were a woman."

"Only because his valet did."

Charles gave a dismissive flick of his hand. "You came to me in London asking for my advice about him—and what to do about your... interest in him. Are you trying to tell me nothing happened?"

Hy felt her face heating and wondered at both her embarrassment and reticence to share the details about her experience with Chatham. She and Charles had always exchanged and compared information of every sort without shame or hesitation. Why was she so shy now?

"Something happened," she finally admitted.

"I've never seen you turn that shade of pink before, Hy. It suits you."

"Oh, *do* shut up."

Charles chuckled. "I can't help but notice that you seem slightly distracted. It is very unlike you, my friend."

Hy felt *extremely* distracted and she loathed the sensation.

She forced herself to meet Charles's too sharp gaze. "He wanted me as his mistress until he learned who I was. Then it was marriage."

"That is... interesting."

"I told him I'd be his mistress." Hy recalled the elation she'd felt when she made that decision. "It was a way to see each other that could have been beneficial to both of us. But then... well, archaic aristocratic male honor overrode everything else, including what I wanted—or what he wanted, for that matter."

"So, what did you do?"

She shrugged. "I left."

"You mean he asked you to marry him, and you said *no* and he had nothing to say to that?"

Hy chewed her lip. "I may have given him reason to believe that I accepted his offer."

Charles groaned. "Oh, Hy. What did you do?"

Five minutes later Charles was still shaking his head at her. "I can't believe you think he would show up at your aunt's house and offer for Selina merely because *you* weren't there! Are you mad?"

"That is the third time you've asked me that, Charles. I *know* you can't believe it. But just *think* about what I've told you—not as my friend, but as a man. He could marry Selina—kind, sweet, caring, *beautiful*

Selina, whom he'd already sought out and danced with, so he *is* interested in her—or he could marry *me*. A woman he met three times as a woman and never noticed. A woman who is more comfortable as a man. A woman whose nickname growing up was *walking stick*. A woman who is no virgin and better suited to be a man's whore than his duchess. Do you think that is a difficult choice for him to make?"

"*Yes, I do!*" Charles all but shouted back at her.

Hy recoiled, stunned by his anger.

"I cannot believe you value yourself so little. Don't all our years as friends—and lovers—mean anything to you? How is it that I never managed to convince you that you really *are* some people's first choice, Hy?"

She opened her mouth, but he wasn't finished.

"I know your mother made you believe that nobody would ever want you, but if this man—this *duke*—accompanied you all over London playing cards with you and spending his evenings with you—then it is likely that *you* are his choice." Charles was breathing heavily by the time he reached the last word and Hy felt terrible for working him into a state. Especially over something that no longer mattered. Hy had all but stitched Selina and Chatham together with her actions. Her aunt had probably already dragged her sister to shop for her wedding gown.

"Hy?" Charles said.

Hy ignored him, her thoughts on her mother and father. They would be delighted by such a magnificent match for their daughter. The countess would be thrilled at the connection to a duke and her father would be over the moon to have a wealthy son-in-law who could pay his debts.

"*Hy?*" Charles snapped his fingers an inch from her nose.

She startled and glared at her friend. "What?"

"Is it possible—and I know you don't believe the emotion exists—but is it at all possible the duke has grown to care for you? Dare I say… love you?"

"How can you ask me such a thing when you don't believe in the emotion, yourself?"

"Just because I don't believe in love doesn't mean many other people—both men and women—do."

"The duke is far too logical a man to fancy himself in such a state."

But then Hy recalled Chatham's face when he'd spoken of his wife. Whatever emotion he'd felt at that moment, it had been strong. But surely what she'd seen had been grief—which she most certainly believed existed—and not *love*. Hadn't it?

Hy closed her eyes and rubbed her pounding temples. "I cannot think about matters I simply don't understand, Charles. Love, romance—"

"Do you really need to understand them to let yourself be happy, Hy?"

She opened her eyes and pushed to her feet. "I—I can't talk about this right now."

"Oh, Hy! I don't mean to drive you away with my probing. Sit and let us talk of other things."

"You're not driving me away. I just need to be alone for a while—to think and sort out my mind so that I am decent company for you, Charles."

He smiled, knowing her so well he didn't really need the explanation. "Of course. There is a path along the shore that is lovely and a person can go for hours without being interrupted."

Hy nodded. "Thank you."

Charles nodded. He knew what she was thanking him for—not directions for a walk—but for being the only person who'd ever taken the time or made an effort to understand her.

"Tell Mrs. Nelson you are going for a walk and she will give you a scarf and an apple."

Hy smiled at his fussing. "She is here to be *your* nurse, not mine."

"I suspect you could use a little care and pampering, too, my friend."

***

Sylvester looked at the little house and then handed the reins to his valet. "This is the place, Tackle. Take the horses back to that inn we passed and see they get decent forage."

"Very good, sir. Shall I hire rooms for the night, Your Grace?" Tackle asked, his expression as unreadable as ever, but the slight emphasis he put on the word *night* made Sylvester smiled.

"Yes, Tackle. Hire rooms. We shall stay regardless of what I discover in there." He gestured to the cottage.

"*Thank you*, Your Grace."

He couldn't help chuckling at his servant's subtle rebuke. Sylvester deserved rebuking and more after how hard he'd used poor Tackle. They'd not been out of the saddle for longer than a few hours since the morning he'd gone haring down to Little Sissingdon.

He'd not done so much riding since his time in the army and he ached in every joint and sinew. But his chest ached even more, the conversation with the old man who owned Garrett's Bookshop ringing in his head the whole headlong ride up the Great North Road from London.

"My grandson is very ill and he is at the cottage alone, Your Grace—except for the presence of his nurse, that is. I have not seen Lady Hyacinth in months, not since Charles moved to London. I'm sure you are wrong believing that she would have run off with him."

Sylvester had persisted—not believing the old man, no matter how sincere he had looked—and had finally managed to badger his grandson's address out of him.

He had no idea what he would do if the old bookseller had actually told the truth—if Hy really *wasn't* with the man's grandson. Because if she had ridden off by herself then Sylvester knew it would be impossible to find her.

He had needed to shove that fear from his mind or risk going mad as he'd ridden non-stop to Skipley.

Instead of engaging in endless worrying, he'd thought about his time with Hyacinth—both in bed and out—and had relived every moment and memory.

He'd been a fool that last night with her. Instead of yammering on about duty and shame and responsibility he should have dropped to his knees—said a prayer of thanks to a God who'd finally given him something worth having—and *begged* her to marry him. He should have confessed his love and promised her anything and everything she wanted.

But he'd allowed his bruised pride to dictate his behavior. He'd acted like a thwarted lover rather than a man who'd just been given the very thing he wanted most: a legitimate reason to marry the only woman he'd ever loved.

He would not make that same mistake twice.

Sylvester waited until his servant rode away and then strode up to the little cottage and knocked on the door. When nobody answered, he knocked a second time, harder.

He was just beginning to feel sick to his stomach that he'd come to the wrong house—or that the pair had already run somewhere else—when the door opened.

Rather than a servant, the person in the entrance wore an elegant dressing gown with fluffy sheepskin slippers. The younger man was tall, pale, and unhealthily thin. He also bore a striking resemblance to various paintings of angels that Sylvester had seen over the years.

His cheeks were pale with feverish spots over knife-sharp cheekbones and he clung to the door handle like a man who required the support.

"Mr. Charles Garrett?"

The younger man's look of surprise gave way to a truly beautiful smile. "Yes, and you are the Duke of Chatham." He stepped back and opened the door wider. "Please, come inside."

Sylvester was momentarily stunned by the warm welcome. He gestured to his mud-spattered boots and leathers. "I'm afraid I just arrived and have not had time to clean off my dirt."

Garrett's smile broadened at that information. "Ah, so you came directly here."

Sylvester's face heated at the knowing look in the other man's eyes. "Yes."

"Come in. Please. I care not about a little dirt."

Sylvester stepped into a tiny, dimly lighted vestibule.

"Will it offend your sensibilities if we sit in the kitchen?" Garrett asked. "I'm reading in there because it really is the warmest room in the house."

"A warm kitchen sounds most welcoming," Sylvester assured him.

Garrett took his hat and gloves and set them on a small console table. "You can hang up your coat there," he said, gesturing casually to an already overburdened coat tree.

Once Sylvester had hung up his coat, he followed the other man down a narrow hallway.

"Have a seat," Garrett said when they entered the kitchen. There was a small table in front of the hearth, the surface strewn with books and parchment.

Sylvester sat while his host slowly bustled about the tiny kitchen. A glance at the work showed him mathematical calculations far beyond anything he had ever done.

"It is The Calculus," Garrett said, carrying the kettle over to the hearth and hooking it in the tripod.

"I gathered as much, although I've never personally studied it," Sylvester admitted. "You were a student of mathematics at Oxford I understand."

Garrett sank into one of the chairs with a heavy sigh and nodded, taking a moment to catch his breath before answering. "Only briefly before my health forced me to leave." He pulled a wry face. "Truth be told I doubt I would have liked the life of an Oxford don, no matter how much I dearly loved the university itself." He cocked his head, his smile returning, but less exuberant this time and more cautious. "I must admit I am surprised to find you here, Your Grace."

"Why is that?"

"I wasn't sure Hy had told you about me—about who I was to her."

Sylvester was ashamed, but not surprised, at the hot stab of jealousy he felt at the other man's words. Even ill, Charles Garrett was an extremely attractive man. He must have been magnificent looking when he'd been healthy, the sort to turn any woman's head.

And he'd been Hy's lover.

Even more painful was the fact that Garrett was also her friend—far closer to her than Sylvester had ever managed to get.

"She told me that you were lovers. And also that you are her closest friend."

Garrett nodded. "As she is mine." He cleared his throat and shifted in his chair, a spasm of pain marring his handsome features before he settled into a more comfortable position. "In fact, it is safe to say that Hy is my favorite person."

Sylvester nodded, so envious of this man's history with the woman he loved that it was a struggle to sit civilly in his kitchen. "You are in love with her," he said, the words causing bile to rise in his throat.

Garrett smiled. "No, I'm not in love with her, but I do love her." His smile drained away and his sapphire blue eyes hardened, making him look far older. "And I will do anything to keep her from getting hurt."

"I don't wish to hurt her." Sylvester swallowed down his jealousy and pride and spoke the words he'd hoped to say to Hy first, but something told him that Garrett would not help him if he could not be honest. "I love her, and I am also *in* love with her."

The other man's smile returned. "Ah, yes—they are two different things, aren't they? Made better together. Or so I understand."

Sylvester snorted. "Right now both feelings are mainly causing me pain, but I have hopes of taking pleasure from my emotions at some point—soon."

Garrett laughed. "I knew I would like you. Hy cares for so few people and her taste is always impeccable, of course." He grinned impishly and stood to lift the steaming kettle from the tripod. "I know what Hy and I had—the fact we could be intimate with each other without falling in love—is unusual," he said as he went through the familiar rituals of making tea, his gaze somewhere else rather than on the crockery. "Hy *is* unusual—not to mention more intimidating than she will ever admit to being. It took me several months before I got up the nerve to even talk to her."

"Will you tell me how you met?"

"I was tutoring in the village and saw her family every Sunday at church. Later I would tutor her brother, but back then the only way we would have met was church or the afterhours card games at The Weasel, which is the—"

"I know the place; I've been there," Sylvester said.

"You have?"

"I went to Little Sissingdon to ask about the name of your grandfather's bookshop. Lady Selina did not know it, but she knew enough to point me in the right direction."

Garrett smiled and Sylvester once again flushed under his knowing gaze.

"I would have been here sooner if I'd not had to take that detour," Sylvester confessed, refusing to be embarrassed for the lengths to which he'd gone.

Garrett chuckled. "It's just as well you didn't as Hy only arrived last evening. She took the stage up from London."

Sylvester grimaced. "Lord, I'll bet she won't do that again."

"Oh, I wouldn't be too sure about that. She can be very… stubborn."

"Yes, I've noticed."

"I'll wager you have, Your Grace." Garrett laughed and after a moment Sylvester joined him, suddenly feeling lighter than he'd done in days.

"How do you take your tea?" Garrett asked.

"Black, please."

"Ah, another aesthete like Hy."

"Thank you," Sylvester said, taking a sip and sighing. "This is good."

Garrett put two spoons of sugar and a dollop of milk into his own cup. "You must have ridden straight through to get here so fast—or at least I assume you rode?"

"Yes. Just me and my valet." He took another swallow of tea and considered what he was about to say. Like it or not, he needed the other man's help—he knew that without even seeing Hyacinth again. He suspected he would only have this last chance with Hy and he wasn't about to cock things up a second time.

He looked up from his cup and met Garrett's gaze. "I lived in terror that she wouldn't be here. Even though I've found her, I know I don't have much hope of changing her mind, not if she was willing to run away to escape marriage with me."

Garrett stared at him for a long, long moment and Sylvester knew the other man was taking his measure.

It was one of the most uncomfortable experiences of his adult life.

Finally, Garrett curled his hands around the cup, inhaled the steam, and said, "Did Hy ever tell you about what her mother did to her when she was thirteen?"

Chapter 30

It took two hours of walking before Hy's mind stopped racing.

When she was finally calm, she found a sheltered spot on the bluff overlooking the ocean, laid down, and promptly fell asleep.

When she woke up—refreshed if slightly disoriented—her pocket watch told her she'd slept for almost two hours.

Unfortunately, it wasn't only her body that was rested; her mind, too, was rested and ready to race.

The thought that occupied her all the way back to Charles's cottage was the last thing her friend had said to her as she was putting on her coat.

"Just because you don't believe in love doesn't mean that somebody won't fall in love with you, Hy."

She'd merely frowned at the statement, determined to shove it from her mind. But it had come back to tease her again and again.

What did he mean? Did he think the duke was in love with her? But how could Charles know when he'd never even met the man?

It was an asinine thing to say—to anyone, but especially to Hy. It was her belief that if she'd not *fallen in love* with Charles—who was kind, caring, and her best friend—then she was incapable of experiencing that mythical emotion. Not once had she ever felt compelled to throw herself on her sisters' shoulders and weep over Charles—even when she'd missed him greatly or worried for his health.

The same was true for the duke. Yes, she missed him greatly, an uncomfortable amount, in fact. But throwing herself onto Charles's shoulder and weeping would not make her miss the duke less. Nor would it make her forget what a disaster she had avoided by saving him from his male sense of duty and honor.

After listening to Charles—and seeing his horrified reaction to her letter to Selina—Hy had been forced to admit that perhaps what she'd done might not make sense to some people. After all, not everyone believed in rational behavior in all matters. While Chatham had shown himself to be admirably rational in most ways, she could not forget that he had once asked her to be his mistress at his country estate. That had been an exceedingly foolish offer. Anyone who'd spent as much time in the country as the duke would have done should know that housing one's mistress beneath one's roof would attract more attention than shooting off fireworks while riding naked through Hyde Park.

Their situation would have been different if he'd never learned who she was.

But now that he had? There was no future for them when it came to marriage. The last thing in the world she wanted was to be a duchess.

She knew the duties the wife of such a man must shoulder. Duchess wasn't just a title; it was a profession in and of itself. The woman who married Chatham would have every minute of her days and evenings taken with duty, duty, duty.

If Chatham were poor and socially isolated like her father, there might have been a chance for them. After all, it drove her mother distracted that they lived an impoverished existence with no entertaining, no London Season, no hunt balls, no house parties, nothing but the eight of them all crowded together in a too-small house.

Personally, Hy had loved living at Queen's Bower. The only unpleasant part about it had been listening to her parents squabble and her mother bemoan the loss of Wych House.

But Chatham was *not* a poor country lord like her father. He was wealthy—obscenely so, with at least six estates, according to her Aunt Fitzroy, who'd taken to extolling his financial graces over every meal.

And he was active in Parliament. After talking with Charles about the duke's political views Hy had made a point to read the newspapers and had even read the text of one of Chatham's speeches. He was brilliant and articulate and the wife of such a man would need to host dinner parties and attend state functions and dine with the Regent and on and on and on.

If Hy had to construct the perfect nightmare future for herself, being a duchess would be *it*.

Chatham would hate her before they'd been married a week. Probably long before that—before the ceremony, even, when he discovered what a tongue-tied lump she was in any social milieu other than a gambling hell or bedchamber.

She sighed. She'd done the right thing by leaving. Although she had to admit that trying to put Chatham and Linny together had probably been a mistake. For one thing, it would have been difficult to ever visit with her sister if she'd been married to Chatham.

Hyacinth

Hy shook her head, tired of mulling over what she'd done.

The best she could do now was stay away from London entirely and hope she would forget about the duke as time passed. It wouldn't be easy to sift thoughts of him from her mind—especially the wicked ideas she'd considered in the privacy of her own bed, the ways to make him laugh, to make him shiver, to make him shout out her name when he ejaculated.

No, those thoughts would take some time to eradicate, but Hy could do it. *Would* do it.

Eventually.

Forgetting was not a perfect solution, but it was the best she could contrive.

So she told herself, over and over and over again as she trudged back to Charles's cottage.

By the time Hy pushed open the cheery blue door to the little house she was so tired of her own thoughts she could finally understand why people became gin addicts.

"Charles?" she called as she removed her gloves, hat, and coat. "Mrs. Nelson?" she asked, although she knew the nurse did not work on Saturday and Sunday, except briefly to deliver meals.

"Come into the kitchen, Hy!" Charles called out.

She turned to set her hat on the narrow console table and saw another hat and gloves already there. Charles had a guest?

"Hyacinth?"

She spun on her heel and stared. "Your Grace! What are you doing here?" Her eyes darted over his shoulder to where Charles stood. "Charles? What is going on?"

Her friend smiled, the dark smudges under his eyes more pronounced in the low light. "Talk to him, Hy. Better yet, *listen* to him. You can have the kitchen; I am going to lie down for a bit before dinner." He turned and walked to the narrow stairs that led to the second floor, pain evident in every step. Not until he'd disappeared into the gloom did she turn to the duke.

"Will you sit with me?" He gestured to the kitchen—as if Hy didn't know the way.

Evidence of tea sat on the table, jumbled in with Charles's books.

Hy looked up and found Chatham staring at her. "What?"

His smile was sheepish—almost *shy*. "I'm glad to see you—relieved that you are actually here."

His open, kind words startled her. Hy had expected chastisement, recriminations, not... Well, not *this*.

"Did you want more tea?" she asked, for lack of anything intelligent to say.

"I am about to float away, but you've been out a long time, you must—"

"I know where there is a bottle of whiskey."

The duke smiled. "Thank God. I couldn't bear another cup of tea."

Hy fetched the bottle and poured two generous portions.

"Thank you," he said, waiting for her to sit before taking a seat himself.

Hy took a hefty sip and set the glass down with a hand that only shook a little. "Why are you here, Your Grace?"

"Perhaps you might call me Sylvester."

She flexed her hand around the glass but did not allow herself another drink so soon.

"Do you know who else has called me by my Christian name?" he asked when she remained quiet. "Other than you that night at Mrs. Dryden's?"

Hy shrugged. "Your mother?"

"No."

Hy was not surprised to hear his mother did not use his name—her own mother called Doddy nothing but Bellamy, which was his courtesy title. Indeed, she could not recall her mother ever calling her father anything other than *sir* or *my lord* or *Addiscombe*.

"Your wife?"

"No."

"Not even in private?" she asked, more curious about his wife—and his relationship with her—than she liked to admit.

"Not even in private." His lips pulled into an unhappy smile, and he took a second drink, not bothering to pace himself as Hy was doing. "My mother never called me anything but *Shelton* after I became my father's heir. Before then, she rarely spoke to me at all. As her fourth son, I had no real value and was generally not worth speaking to."

His words were painful, but it was the lack of inflection in his voice that was worse. His mother was yet another woman who did not care for her child. For some reason Hy hadn't believed that sort of thing happened to male offspring.

Hyacinth

"My wife never used my Christian name, either. She used my title to remind herself—and me—of the only reason she'd married me."

His wife had not wanted to marry him? But… wait. That wasn't what Selina had said.

"I don't understand?" Hy said.

"Mariah had been betrothed to my elder brother, Nicholas—the one who died when I was in the army. Nicky was the sort of man whom everyone liked, men and women. He was handsome and charming and Mariah had been delighted with the match. And then he died and her father and mother, who were not well off, insisted she marry me. We had met each other only once, years before when we were scarcely more than children. I recalled her, of course. Shelton—who was not Shelton back then, but mere Cousin Andrew—and I had been instantly smitten when we saw Mariah that first time, but she'd only had eyes for Nicky and my golden brother had fallen hard for her, as well." He gave Hy a wry glance. "Mariah looked a great deal like your sister—ethereally beautiful, the sort of woman who drew every eye in a room."

Hy nodded; she'd seen hundreds of men fall at Selina's feet.

"I believe she genuinely loved Nicky and I knew she didn't want to marry me. But she was a dutiful daughter and agreed to take me as a replacement. Nobody saw fit to tell her of the injury I'd suffered, so when I returned home"—he snorted and gestured to his cheek with a flick of his hand. "I'm sure you can imagine her reaction when she saw me." He sipped his drink, his eyes gazing into the past. "She hid her revulsion well—at first—but I could see the thoughts in her head as she stole looks at me. She knew the way our lives would be—we'd rarely see one another for most of the year and she'd only have to bed me long enough to give me two sons. I watched as she talked herself into accepting her role—her future. I knew I should have done something—or said something—to end the betrothal. I knew that to marry a woman who was repulsed by me would be… unpleasant."

Hy stood and poured him more whiskey without being asked.

"And then, to make matters worse, Andrew came home perhaps a month before our wedding. He'd been injured and had received a commendation for bravery. And—well, you've seen my cousin, I'm sure you can imagine what happened when he met my beautiful, reluctant fiancé."

Hy bristled at that. "I've seen your cousin and I would no more swoon at his feet than I would split a pair of knaves, Your Grace."

The duke laughed, his gaze suddenly warm again, his eyes wrinkling attractively at the corners. "No, it is difficult to imagine you swooning for Andrew. Or any man, truth be told."

"He is a bounder and a cad and I do hope you've dissuaded him from pursuing my sister," Hy said, while the thought was upon her.

"I tried—with both of them. But, at the end of the day, they are of age and can do as they wish." He tilted his chin down and raised his eyebrows. "I'm sure Lady Selina would not welcome me telling her what to do any more than you did."

It was Hy's turn to snort. "No, you are correct. Selina gives the appearance of yielding softness, but she is fierce when provoked. But I interrupted your story, and I want to know what happened."

"It's not a particularly surprising story: Mariah and Andrew fell in love. He begged me to release her, no matter that men do *not* jilt their fiancées. He argued that I had to do it, regardless of the shame I would face, because her parents would never allow her to do it. They needed the money that would come from their daughter's marriage." He swirled the liquid in his glass. "When I refused, Andrew sent Mariah to beg on their behalf. I was angry—and hurt—but I knew I should have done what they wanted, regardless of how it would reflect on me. After all, my position would protect me from any real damage. And when I eventually inherited my title, nobody would even remember what I'd done."

"Selina said you could cut off a bishop's head and nobody would call you to account."

Again, she earned a delicious ripple of laughter. "I had no idea Lady Selina was so bloodthirsty. I doubt that even I could get away with *that*, but your sister makes a fair point. Any scandal would have washed away without leaving damage. But I was... stubborn. And selfish. I realized that... afterward."

He sighed and threw back the rest of his glass. "I refused to jilt her. I married her and she hated me for it. And so did—does—Andrew. To make a long, sordid, tedious story shorter, I went to her bed only a handful of times and only during our first month of marriage. It was... unpleasant, not only for Mariah, but for me. And for Andrew... well, I now know it must have been a living hell to think of the woman he loved with another man." He paused, his gaze heavy as it rested on Hy. "And so Andrew did the only thing he could think of: he discredited me to her so thoroughly—painted me in such *vile* terms—that if I wanted to bed her, it would feel more like rape."

Hyacinth

"What did he say about you?" Hy asked, although she could guess.

"He told her that I was addicted to the perversions offered in birch houses. That I liked to be bound and whipped, among other things."

Hy was momentarily distracted by those last three words—*among other things*—and it was a struggle not to indulge her sudden, burning curiosity and demand what those *other things* were. But even she was not so socially maladjusted as to not realize that *now* was not the time for that conversation.

"Mariah said if I wanted to bed her that I would need to force her. She said I sickened her, that I was a pervert and could do her one kindness by never touching her. She asked me to stay away—to use whores to satisfy my needs." Chatham gave a mirthless chuckle. "One thing she *didn't* tell me was that she'd planned to fill my nursery with my cousin's bastards."

"Are you saying—"

"I'm saying the child she died having was Andrew's, not mine." He shook himself and met her gaze. "I'm sorry, but I wandered off the subject with that story. The reason I brought it up was to make a point. Won't you please use my Christian name, Hy?"

"Why have you come here… Sylvester?"

"I will tell you that, soon. But first—Mr. Garrett told me I should ask you about something."

"Charles's grandfather wanted you to ask me something?"

He smiled. "No, *Charles*."

"Oh."

"He said something happened to you when you were thirteen, but he would not tell me—he said that was for you to do. Do you know what he meant?"

Rather than answer him, Hy stared at her clasped hands as she pondered what her friend meant by bringing up such a subject. She knew Charles would never hurt her, so he must think that sharing this particular story, the most shameful in her life, would somehow benefit her.

Well, the event—no matter how shameful—had brought her Charles, hadn't it?

She sighed and looked up. "I know the story he meant." Hy threw back the contents of her glass and refilled it. She would need it for this tale.

Chapter 31

Sylvester gave Hy all the time she needed to prepare for what was obviously an unpleasant subject. He was content just to sit and stare at her like the unashamedly lovesick man he was.

Although it had only been a few days since he'd last seen her, he felt like he'd been wandering in a desert for years and had finally found an oasis. She looked so damned good to him that he wanted to grab and squeeze her, hold her tightly and never let her go.

He also wanted to tell her the thoughts that had been assaulting him from the moment he'd realized she was gone, no matter how vulnerable such a confession would leave him.

But he believed her friend Charles knew her better than anyone. So... if Charles thought Sylvester should hear this story, then he should hear it.

She poured them both more whiskey and then sat. "As I'm sure you can imagine, I was a strange child. I didn't start talking until I was eight. My parents believed I'd been born a mute, but then one day, I suddenly spoke. Not to either my mother or father, but to our old nurse, Nanny Fletcher, who'd been trying to teach me to read, even though my parents had long ago told her not to bother. My first words were to ask for a different book—a book written for adults, rather than children. You see, she *had* taught me to read and I'd been doing it for some time."

"You did not speak until you saw the point," Sylvester said, not surprised to hear that.

Hy looked startled. "Yes, that was exactly it. Unfortunately, my mother did not see it that way. She believed that I'd willfully ignored her all that time."

She sipped her drink, her expression pensive.

"What I didn't understand until much later was that my behavior had shamed my mother. At first because everyone in the area believed she'd given birth to a damaged child. But after I began to speak the embarrassment was almost worse because then people believed she'd given birth to a disobedient, stubborn, and unnatural child who didn't *want* to speak to her own family." She met his gaze briefly. "Embarrassment is something my mother will never forgive. When I was growing up, she showed her displeasure by speaking to me as little as possible, choosing to communicate through my elder sister, Aurelia, if she had anything to say to me. My mother is not... maternal. She believes that to nurture one's child is a sign of low birth." She snorted softly. "She is a shopkeeper's daughter, a fact which she has always taken great pains to hide, but I don't think she understands how much her background has influenced her thinking."

"What do you mean?" he asked.

"My mother has given all her children values, much like a shopkeeper puts prices on his commodities. Her most valuable child is her only son and heir. Doddy is priceless in her eyes, not because he is sweet and clever and charming, but because he can be used to further the family's fortunes through marriage. Next is her eldest daughter, my sister Aurelia, who is beautiful, accomplished, and compassionate. For years Aurelia was worth a great deal to my mother, but her value recently plummeted when she refused to barter herself for a husband. Then there is Selina. My mother sees only her beautiful face and ignores the person behind it. She is certain Selina was put on earth solely to make a magnificent marriage and rescue the family fortunes. Then there is my sister Phoebe. My mother views her as a convenient and useful tool because she manages the household, thereby sparing my mother from having to engage in such mundane tasks. Then there is Katie." Her lips curved into a smile. "Katie is beautiful and lively and intelligent, but she is probably my mother's second least favorite child because she refuses to do the one thing my mother absolutely demands: conform. Lastly, there is me, her second eldest daughter and least valuable child.

Hy's expression was one Sylvester had never seen on her face before: bitterness.

"I don't just lack value; I actually *detract* value from the rest of my family. I am like mealworms in the flour or the moths eating the shopkeeper's wool. My mother could not eliminate me, of course, but she decided I should be... mitigated. When company called—which they still did when we resided at Wych House—I was never allowed to meet our guests. On the rare occasions when we visited anyone else, I was left at home. That suited me as I became tongue-tied, clumsy, and stupid when I was among anyone other than my siblings. I liked my own company best, not because it is superior, but because I didn't have to constantly apologize or watch everything I said or did."

"You don't seem tongue-tied or clumsy now," Sylvester said, thinking back to how cool and competent she appeared at the card table. Or how confident and sensual she'd been when tying him up and whipping him to orgasm.

Sylvester quickly batted away that second thought. Getting hard while she was confessing her childhood trauma was hardly appropriate.

"You've only seen me in my chosen milieu, Sylvester. Trust me when I tell you I am a different person entirely when all six feet of me is forced into a frilly gown and dropped into the middle of some ballroom."

The jolt of pleasure he felt hearing his name on her tongue was overborne by sadness at the rest of her words.

"Many people—both men and women—become anxious at *ton* functions, Hy. The entire business is unnatural and quite frankly cruel." He shook his head in disgust. "Parading young women about as if they are cattle at Tatt's. It is no wonder you were uncomfortable and nervous."

"It goes beyond that with me. I'm not just nervous, I… freeze. I'm—well, I'm not normal."

"And you think *I* am, Hy? I'm not sure any of us is *normal*. If you"—Sylvester broke off and shook his head. "I want to come back to this subject later. But first I want to hear your story."

She cleared her throat and continued. "I put myself beyond redemption when I was thirteen."

"That was when you started to dress as a man?" he asked, recalling what she'd said the night he'd confronted her with the truth.

She nodded. "Yes, that began after the event I'm about to tell you about. It was an event which changed my life and—but I am getting ahead of myself. I've already told you that I spent a great deal of time by myself?"

Sylvester nodded.

Hy chewed her lip, clearly struggling with something. "Oh, stuff it," she muttered, looking up and meeting his gaze. "I got myself into trouble when I discovered that I could bring myself intense physical pleasure."

"You discovered masturbation," Sylvester said.

She looked both surprised and relieved. "Yes. I liked it. A great deal."

Sylvester smiled. "I discovered the same thing, but perhaps a few years earlier. Trust me, you were not alone when it comes to liking it. If you had gone away to school as most young men of our class do, you would be more surprised to meet somebody who *hadn't* discovered masturbation by that age. Rather than something to be ashamed of, a good many boys did not bother to hide what they were doing. Indeed, I cannot count the number of times I walked in on another lad, er, mounting a corporal and four."

That reference to their first night at Mrs. Dryden's pulled a faint smile from her, but it was fleeting. "I understand that… now. But back then, I was terrified that there was something wrong with me. I didn't just touch myself, I also had vivid fantasies of touching somebody else, of *being* touched." She swallowed hard, her delicate throat flexing. "Sexual thoughts."

"Again, that is natural, Hy." He smiled. "I can personally attest to the fact that adolescent males think about touching and being touched—and all matters sexual—perhaps as often as every thirty seconds."

"But that is boys, Sylvester. You know the standard is different for girls."

He sighed and nodded. "Yes, I know."

"In my parents' house—a house with two people who hated each other fiercely—touching, or affection of any sort, was viewed as vulgar. But my mother was especially adamant that physical intimacy in the bedchamber was for one purpose only: procreation. Anything else was a base bodily function that was the purview of men like my father, who took their needs elsewhere."

Sylvester did not know what to say. His mother held similar opinions about men and their *needs* and how they were best satisfied by the sorts of women who were paid to endure such things—*not* decent, moral wives.

"Being left to myself so often I became accustomed to doing as I pleased." She pulled a rueful face. "I'm afraid I was doing exactly *that*—in one of the many linen cupboards at Wych House—when my mother found me."

Sylvester groaned. "Oh, dear."

Hy nodded. "*Oh, dear* is correct. It would have been bad enough if she'd been the only one to catch me with my hand up my skirt, knees spread, and abandoned to my pleasure. But, to make matters many times worse, our housekeeper was with her."

Sylvester briefly closed his eyes, afraid to hear what happened. But such cowardice was beneath him. If she could live through it then surely he was brave enough to hear it?

"What happened, Hyacinth?"

"If you are imagining beatings and starvation, you needn't fear I was physically damaged. My mother is far more devious and subtle. She took me aside—just the two of us—and gave me her thoughts... unvarnished. I'd always known she did not like me—that she resented me, in fact—but that day she told me something that chilled me. She said the only reason she hadn't sent me somewhere that would treat sick perverts like me was because there wasn't enough money to do so."

Sylvester jolted at the familiar words—*sick pervert*—an echo of his wife's accusation from all those years ago.

"She said that if the day ever came when there were ample funds, she would see to it that I was locked up."

Sylvester reached out and took her hand. "You must have been so frightened."

Rather than pull away, she squeezed his hand so tightly the bones ground against each other. "Yes, I was terrified because I knew she was in deadly earnest. I began to plan my escape that very day." She inhaled deeply and then let her breath out slowly before continuing. "As punishment, she had my head shorn and moved me to the south wing of Wych House, to an area that hadn't been occupied for decades. The room where she put me was not unsafe, but it was isolated. It was to be my gaol. I slept there, took my meals there, did my lessons there, and generally lived my life in those rooms."

"My God, Hyacinth, how long did that last?"

"The punishment was to last—in my mother's words—until I could behave normally."

Sylvester could only shake his head.

She lightly squeezed his hand. "I can see that you are imagining the worst, Sylvester. My mother could try and shame me and isolate me, but she underestimated my sisters. Aurelia organized the campaign of rebellion and Selina and Phoebe were loyal foot soldiers. Katie and Doddy were just babies, then, so they don't know what happened. One of my sisters always stayed with me at night, even though I wasn't scared." She chuckled softly. "I think all three of *them* were more terrified to be spending the night in the haunted south wing. They smuggled in books and shared their lessons with me so that I would not fall behind. They told me the village gossip. We circulated letters and shared diaries and staged nighttime feasts and revels and generally thwarted my mother's will in a dozen other ways." A slow, sly smile slid across her face. "That wasn't the

Hyacinth

only part of her punishment that backfired. Shaving my head was supposed to shame me and ensure I could not hold up my head among decent people. Instead, it made me realize that I no longer had to be a too-tall, gangly, unattractive girl. Instead, I made an excellent tall, gangly boy, something I *never* would have been able to do with a head full of hair down to my bottom."

"So you began your masquerading then—going to card games?"

"Yes. I honed my skills wherever there were games, earning more and more money as time passed. It was easy to sneak out of the south wing whenever I wanted and I grew accustomed to my freedom and liked it."

She paused, and then snorted softly. "Ironically, my liberation from *gaol*—which happened when we were forced to leave Wych House and move into the much smaller dower house—actually meant *less* freedom as it was far more difficult to sneak out of a crowded manor. Not only that, but there weren't enough rooms at Queen's Bower to isolate me any longer. All five of us girls were forced to share two rooms. I shared with my older sister, who already knew of my nocturnal activities. If she didn't approve of what I did, at least she didn't pester me to stop." She chewed her lip for a moment. "Aurelia knew I played cards, but she knew nothing about Charles." Her mouth curved into a fond smile that made him burn with jealousy, followed immediately by shame for begrudging an isolated young woman a friend and lover.

Sylvester shoved his jealousy back where it came from and asked, "Will you tell me how you met?"

"I'd noticed him long before we ever spoke. My mother didn't keep me from attending church—even she didn't want to jeopardize my immortal soul. Charles's uncle is the vicar, so he sat beside his aunt in church and I saw him every week. I didn't know that he saw *me* until he approached me at one of the games." Her gaze turned inward. "You've seen him—you know how handsome he is. I never thought he'd be interested in someone like me. But he saw something in me—something he recognized." She looked up. "Charles was the only other person I met who was like me."

"What do you mean?"

"He's rational, not emotional. He is reserved and happier alone, most of the time." She shrugged. "He's an *odd* bird, as people like to call our sort."

Sylvester felt a pang of guilt; he'd thought of Hy that way when they had first met.

"It bothered Charles when he learned how my mother was treating me. He was especially displeased by how she tried to shame me—not to mention her threat to lock me away."

Sylvester thought the countess's reaction would bother any decent person, but he kept that to himself.

"It might be difficult to believe, but I was far more awkward before he came along." She smiled to herself. "He has smoothed off a great many of my rough edges over the years, mainly just by discussing matters in a rational way."

"Can you give me an example?" he asked.

She pondered for a second and then said, "I find touching others... uncomfortable."

"But...you touch me."

Her lips twitched into a slight smile that made heat pool low in his belly. "Well, you are obviously different. Very different."

For once, it was Sylvester who was tongue-tied.

"Charles taught me how to manage my... aversion. He suffers from the same sensitivity, but to a lesser degree. His advice was actually very simple and common sense. He told me to initiate touch with somebody I felt comfortable with. With my sisters, for example. Just a pat on a shoulder or a light touch on their hands, small things to accustom myself. He told me to think hard about how that touch felt—to *think* rather than just react." She shrugged. "It is hard to describe, and I know it sounds silly, but it somehow helped over time. I still find it jarring to be handled by strangers, but I no longer react so strongly."

Sylvester nodded. Even though he didn't understand *what* she meant, he knew that having another person to share one's trauma, for lack of a better word, could be soothing. It was something all soldiers knew after they'd lived through battle and war.

Hy gave him a vaguely amused look. "No doubt you are confused how that led to becoming lovers—but that didn't happen until after we'd known each other for several years.

"At first, we just played cards when we sneaked out to meet each other. Then he began to teach me what he calls number theory. I was woefully ignorant, so he had to teach me basic mathematics, first. I was ignorant, but not stupid, and I caught on quickly." She cut him a rueful look. "My life really would have been easier if I'd been born a boy. I love numbers and would have done as Charles did and gone to university. As it is?" She shrugged. "A woman who loves mathematics is about as useful as a horse that loves needlework."

Sylvester hated that she was right about that. Clever women, he was ashamed to realize for the first time, did not have an easy time of it.

"You are probably wondering about the... other things he taught me," she said, a wry smile on her face.

"How did you guess?"

"He had a book—the one I mentioned to you—and I saw it one day. Instead of trying to hide it, as almost anyone else would do, he told me to look my fill." She swallowed, a slight flush coloring her cheeks as she stared down at her laced fingers. "Once I'd seen those illustrations... well, I could not get them out of my mind." She looked up. "I told him I wanted to do those things. Men—or boys—can go to brothels, but for women?" She shrugged. "I told him I didn't want to marry, but that I didn't want to forego physical intimacy, either. I couldn't imagine doing such things with a stranger—or somebody I didn't know or like—but with Charles it seemed not only natural, but right, somehow."

Sylvester nodded, still struggling with rampant jealousy thinking of her with another man. To begrudge her of her one lover was hypocrisy given how many dozens of women he'd had over the years but realizing that did not make him any less jealous.

She gave him one of the direct looks that seemed to see right into his soul. "I refuse to regret what I did, Sylvester. That time with Charles not only kept me sane, but it made me realize I might not be normal, but that didn't mean I couldn't find happiness." She sighed. "I had such high hopes for our future together. Charles always said he'd come with me when I made my escape from Queen's Bower, but I think we both knew that his illness would never allow that to happen."

"And is that what you are doing now—making your escape, Hyacinth?"

She nodded. "Yes. Selina will make sure the money I saved gets to my father's creditors." She slid a slightly embarrassed look his way. "I *will* pay you the eight hundred I lost to you—you know I pay my debts—but it will take a while. The money for my family will only buy a year's respite, but I can earn more for the next payment."

Sylvester contemplated telling her about her new, wealthy brother-in-law, but—selfishly—he wasn't sure that would aid him in the argument he was about to make. And he needed every advantage he could get, no matter how underhanded.

With that thought in mind, he decided now was as good a time as any to put forward his case. "You asked earlier why I was here?"

She nodded.

"I came to ask you to marry me—and to do it the right way this time."

"You did nothing wrong in the way—"

"Yes, Hy, I did." Sylvester kissed the back of her hand, which she'd not yet pulled away. "I should have prefaced my offer with several important details. First, I adore spending my evenings with you—and not just the time we are in bed. I don't think you understand how much I enjoyed seeing you, whether you were Hiram or Hyacinth or Mary or by any other name. You gave me something to look forward to—a reason to get up in the morning, other than just duty. I like everything that I've learned about you, Hy—everything. I only wish that I'd learned more."

Her cheeks had turned a fiery red at his words, and he kissed her hand again. "I'm sorry if I'm embarrassing you, but you'd better prepare for more."

She snorted but didn't pull away.

"Second, when I think of life without you, I—well, let me just say it does not just make me unhappy—it makes me miserable and hopeless. Do you know how rare it is for two people to get on as we do? Or at least it is rare in my experience. Never before have I wanted to spend both my nights *and* days with somebody."

She swallowed hard but remained silent.

"Third—and I probably should have started with this—I love you, Hy." He chuckled when he saw the way her jaw dropped. "Thanks to Charles, I know your views on that particular emotion, so I don't expect a return declaration, my love. To be honest, I'd stopped believing it existed until I met you. Before my marriage, I fancied myself in love with Mariah, but now, with the clarity of hindsight, I know that was a pale imitation of love—infatuation and lust."

He squeezed her hand. "I love you and *want* to marry you. It was never about duty, Hy. I'm sorry I lashed out at you the other night and behaved like an arse. And I especially regret the way I made you believe I was *forced* to offer for you. Can you forgive me for being an angry idiot?"

"Yes, of course I forgive you. But—but that wasn't why I left, Sylvester."

"Then *why* did you leave, sweetheart? I want you to explain why you don't want to marry me. Tell me what I can do to change your mind. Please."

Her mouth twisted into a miserable frown, and she pulled her hand away and lurched to her feet, striding to one end of the small room, and then walking back, pacing.

Sylvester let her do what she needed, watching her quietly and waiting.

She suddenly turned on him. "You are dangling something in front of me that is simply not possible, Your Grace."

He flinched from her anger.

"Look at me!" she demanded, sweeping a hand over herself. "Am I really the duchess your family needs? An ill-favored hermit who would rather dress as a man? Can you see me presiding over your dinner table? On your arm at *ton* functions?"

He stood and quickly closed the distance between them, taking her face in his hands and forcing her to look at him. "You are the duchess *I* need, Hy. To hell with my family. I married the first time to please my mother and father. I married the *perfect* woman according to them, and we made each other's lives hell. I've spent the last ten years of my life regretting my marriage and dreading the need to do it again. And then suddenly, I met you and I *want* to marry again—do you know how much that shocks me and thrills me? This time, I'll marry to suit *me*. And you, sweetheart, are the only woman I've met in ten long years that I want to see every single day for the rest of my life. You have made these past weeks the best I've ever had."

"That is because these past weeks have been a—a holiday from life, don't you see?"

"No, I don't see. Why can't we be this happy all the time?" He paused and studied her face. "*Have* you been happy, Hy? Or am I terribly wrong?"

"Of course, I have been happy! Happier than I can ever remember being. And yes, I, too, looked forward to those evenings with you. But if we marry everything will change."

"How?" he demanded, his voice rising with frustration.

"Your life is a series of duties. Duty to your family, your tenants, servants, and the country. I've read your speeches in the paper, Sylvester. You are the sort of man who needs a wife who will host dinner parties and say clever things. I can barely *attend* a public dinner and you've seen how much I speak when I am among strangers. The life of a duchess would be *hell* for me. Seasons and balls and house parties and—Ugh!" She pulled away from him and turned to the wall, her back heaving with the force of her emotions.

"Hyacinth," Sylvester set a hand on her shoulder but she shrugged it off.

"No, don't ask me to turn and look at you. I can't. Because when I look at you, I want you more than I have ever wanted anything in my life. And it isn't *logical* to want somebody whom you know you will never ever be able to please. You might not think so now, but you will grow to hate me when my odd ways cease to be entertaining and become an embarrassment to you. I have lived the first part of my life as a disappointment, Sylvester. I cannot live the rest of it that way."

Sylvester slid his arms around her and this time she didn't shrug him off. This time, she leaned back into him and allowed him to hold her.

"I understand your fears, Hy." He kissed her temple and pulled her tighter. "But you don't understand my determination or my commitment to you. I've lived for a decade without a hostess at my dinner parties. And I've attended ball after tedious bloody ball without a woman on my arm. I'm not seeking the perfect dance partner or social ornament to stand by my side. If that is what I'd wanted I would have remarried years ago. I have a wizard of a secretary to organize house parties and draw up dinner menus and seating charts. But what I *don't* have is a companion and a friend and a lover. You just said that you don't think my love for you will be enough—that I will grow grudging and blame you for not filling the role of duchess in the way society expects? But I am no green boy, Hy. I'm a grown man who has found the woman he didn't even dare hope existed. You are a miracle to me, and I refuse to let anything stand in the way of our happiness. Trust me, I have enough faith in our future happiness for the both of us."

He kissed her again and inhaled the now familiar Hy scent of her: pomade and leather and whiskey with a hint of salty sweetness that was pure *her*.

Sylvester squeezed her tight and murmured against her curly red head, "The question you need to ask yourself—the logic you need to apply—is simple, darling. Will you be happier living with me, or will you be happier without me. If you tell me that you don't want me, I will leave here, and you will not see me again. I will not hound you or follow you or tell your family where you've gone or what you're doing. I will respect your wishes." Sylvester swallowed hard. "But think carefully, my love, because you hold not just my happiness, but also my heart in your hands."

Sylvester heard a sniff and felt something wet on his hand. When he tried to turn her, she stopped him.

"What is the matter, Hy? Why are you crying?"

"Because that was the loveliest thing anyone has ever said to me."

He smiled and tightened his embrace. "That's good, isn't it?"

A choked sniffle was his only answer.

"I love you so much, Hyacinth," he whispered. "Please don't break my heart, darling." He kissed the delicate pink shell of her ear. "Not when you have just put it back together again."

Chapter 32

Hy twisted around in his arms, uncaring of how hideous she must look from blubbering like a baby, and claimed his lips with a hungry need that frightened her.

They feasted on each other like starving people. She felt as if she'd not touched him for a year rather than only a few nights.

It was the duke who finally pulled away, both of them gasping like landed fishes. "Please tell me that was a *yes*, sweetheart?"

"Oh, Sylvester! Your question is easy to answer—yes, I was unhappy without you, miserable, in fact. But that doesn't mean I would feel *right* about accepting your offer of marriage." She chewed her lip, horrified by what he'd think when he finally saw the *real* Hyacinth. "It would not be fair to you, not when you've *no* idea of just how awkward I am, or—"

"Look at me, Hy."

"No." She shook her head.

His warm, firm fingers closed on her chin, and he tilted her until she was forced to meet his gaze. "If you agreed to become my wife, would you play cards with me?"

She snorted. "Yes, of course, I would play—"

"Would you make love to me?"

"*Yes*, you *know* I would be overjoyed to—"

"Will you show me that book you mentioned?" His voice dropped to a whisper. "The one with the naughty drawings, and will you agree to reenact every single one of them with me?"

Hy laughed. "You might be careful about asking for *all* of them, Sylvester. But, *yes* to that, too."

"Will you listen to me bore on about Catholic Emancipation and expansion of the franchise and a dozen other dull subjects that are dear to my heart?"

"Yes, yes, and yes."

Hyacinth

"Will you protect me from my mother who—I'm sorry to say—sounds a great deal like yours and, unfortunately, will live at least part of the year with us at Chatham?"

Hy cut him a horrified look that was only partly feigned. "She will live with us? But you are a duke. Surely you can just snap your ducal fingers and banish anyone who displeases you."

He chuckled, but there was no amusement in the sound. "Believe me, I've considered it." He held her gaze. "Is that what you would do to your mother? Banish her?"

"Yes," she said without hesitation. "Not for my sake, but for my younger sister and brother—they are still young and under her dominion for years to come."

"I can't snap my fingers and banish her," Sylvester said, "but I *can* help your siblings. And they can come and stay with us whenever they wish."

Hy cupped the scarred half of his face with her hand and gave him a kiss. "Of all the wonderful things you've said, I think that is one of the loveliest."

He smiled and kissed her. "It is the first of many, I promise. *Will* you marry me, Hy?"

"You are very persistent."

"I haven't even begun to be persistent."

"Are you sure, Sylvester? Truly?"

"I've never been surer of anything in my life, darling."

Hy exhaled heavily and said, "If you are *sure*, then ye—"

His mouth crashed down over hers and he pushed her up against the wall.

Hy moaned at the hard ridge of flesh that pressed against her pelvis. She shoved a hand between them and—

A throat cleared behind them and they sprang apart like thieves apprehended in the act.

"I'm terribly sorry to interrupt," Charles said when Hy turned and glared at him. "But I thought I should remind you that Mrs. Nelson will be here any moment to deliver our evening meal. Perhaps you might both like to step into the parlor?"

Hy turned to the duke. "Can you stay a bit longer?"

"As long as you like."

"I'm sure we can stretch dinner for three," Charles said, smirking in the most odiously self-satisfied way at them.

"Thank you, I'd love to stay," Chatham said.

Charles winked at Hy and mouthed *you are welcome*, and then left them.

"Come with me," she said, leading the duke to the tiny parlor at the back of the house and then shutting the door behind them.

Once they were alone, she hovered beside the door, suddenly experiencing an uncharacteristic bout of shyness. "When did you get here?"

"Why are you all the way over there?" the duke asked, and then took the matter out of her hands by stepping close enough to put his arms around her waist. "There, that is better." He kissed her soundly. "To answer your question, we arrived just a few hours ago. Tackle went to hire rooms for us at the inn."

"Oh, that is where I am staying."

"I thought you'd be staying here?"

"No, it is too small and Charles needs lots of rest. He enjoys my visits, but he tires quickly."

Sylvester stroked her jaw with his knuckles, his brow furrowing. "And there is nothing that can be done for him?"

Hy shook her head. "There is no treatment, but I believe he is better here than in London."

"Yes, London is hardly a healthy place." He kissed her again, this time long and lingering. By the time he pulled away, Hy felt like her legs had turned to water. "There," he murmured. "Now I feel better." He cocked his head. "What is wrong? You've suddenly developed a line right *here*." He gently brushed the bridge of her nose.

"I suppose we have to return to London soon? My aunt must be beside herself."

"She is," he admitted. "But I thought we might stay a day or two before we have to return."

Hy brightened. "Really?"

"You've only just got here, and I know you'd like to visit with Charles a bit longer."

"I would like that." Hy stared into his lovely brown eyes. "That is very considerate of you. I know not every man would be as tolerant of such a friendship."

"Oh, I am jealous enough."

"You *are*?"

"Mmm-hmm," he murmured, tracing her lip with one finger, his pupils large. "Very. You will just have to be extra affectionate and tender to me to soothe my wounded feelings."

Hy laughed and he kissed her soundly. "I love hearing you laugh, Hy," he said when he pulled away.

Her face heated at the raw affection in his gaze. Even Charles, whom she knew cared deeply for her, had never looked at her the way Sylvester did: as if she were the most wonderful thing he'd ever seen.

"Oh, there is one other small matter." He reached into his inner coat pocket and drew out a folded parchment.

When Hy opened it, her eyes bulged slightly. "Goodness, I've never seen one of these before. How did you get it so quickly?"

"One of the perks of being a duke, my dear."

"So... do you wish to get married *here*?"

He nodded. "I was thinking it might help to soothe your aunt's ruffled feathers."

"Ah, yes." Like the bad niece she was, Hy kept forgetting about her poor aunt. "While it will be more respectable if you bring me back as your wife, I'm sure she will be most displeased not to have a grand wedding." She couldn't help smiling. "Personally, I'll be delighted to marry here rather than St. George's." She grimaced. "But I'm afraid I don't have any clothing other than this"—she gestured to her breeches and boots.

"There is a full outfit of clothing for you in my valise, although I daresay it is a bit wrinkled. But Tackle will see to that."

Hy goggled at him. "You didn't just get a special license; you also bought me a *gown*?"

"Er, not quite. It is one of yours that your sister packed for me when I told her I was coming after you."

"Ah. Did my aunt say whether she was taking Selina home?"

"They are staying in London until I return. I told her that if anyone asked about you, she should just say you'd gone to a house party somewhere."

"Nobody would ask about me—except the Dowager Lady Fitzroy."

"Oh, she already knows about you—*and* us."

"*What?*"

"Your nightly jaunts were not nearly as stealthy as you believed. The old lady watched you coming and going."

"No! And she never said a word."

"She said plenty to me when I arrived at your aunt's house."

"What do you mean—was she there when you arrived?"

He nodded, giving her a grim look that said he had not yet forgiven her for *everything*. "Her and her exceedingly smelly pug."

Hy grimaced. "Oh no! Lily was there? Was it awful?"

"Only the worst olfactory experience of my life." He pulled a face. "You were companion to that woman? How could you bear the beast?"

Hy couldn't help laughing imagining the duke, the dowager, and the pug in the same room.

The duke rolled his eyes. "Finally, I see what you find humorous, and it turns out to be a gaseous hound. I shall have to cast my mind back twenty years and dredge up the multitude of fart jokes that were bandied about at Eton."

Hy had to wipe tears from her eyes. "Oh, please do. I can tell them all to Doddy and be his hero as that is favorite sort of humor."

"That reminds me of something—not about vulgar jokes for your brother, but it *is* about your family."

Hy's laughter fled. "What about them? Has something happened?"

"It's nothing bad," he soothed. "At least I wouldn't think so. Your sister Phoebe married several weeks ago."

"*What*? To *whom*?"

"Viscount Needham."

Hy could scarcely believe her ears. "Phoebe married Iron Bad Needham?"

"You've heard of him."

"Who hasn't? Do you know him?"

"He briefly mixed in society a few years ago and we met, but he was even less social than I am. I daresay his reception was a great deal like Fowler's. He would be welcome everywhere because of his wealth, but you know how people sneer at new peers."

Hy could imagine. "I cannot believe my mother did not say anything in her letters." A sudden thought struck her, and she scowled. "What a muttonhead I am! Of course she wouldn't mention it. She'd believe that marriage to a man like Needham might harm Selina's chance at making a fine match." Hy gave a snort of disgust. "How could she keep such a thing from us?"

Chatham's gaze was sympathetic. "I'm sorry you were not allowed to be there." He cleared his throat, and his expression became uncomfortable. "I felt you should know because your worries about the payment on your family's home are likely no longer an issue."

Hyacinth

Hy suspected he was right; Phoebe would have made sure of that.

"Why are you looking at me that way?" she asked the duke when he continued to look uncomfortable.

"You don't need to marry me to save your family, Hy."

She was often slow when it came to such subtleties, but she instantly caught his meaning. "I hope you don't think that is the reason I changed my mind and accepted your offer, Sylvester?"

The duke slid his arms around her and jerked her close, kissing her on the tip of the nose. "I *do* love hearing you say my name. And no, I am fully aware that you could manage the money issues yourself. I just felt it was something you should know."

"I hope Phoebe is happy." Hy and her sisters had made a pact not to do something rash or self-sacrificing for the rest of their siblings, but Phoebe was the most selfless of her sisters.

"I heard nothing on that score, but Needham is very popular in the village and surrounding area. He has leased Wych House—"

"He *has*?"

"Yes, and he has apparently begun improvements on both the tenant farms as well as the house itself."

"I am very grateful to hear that. My sisters and I have often lamented that there would be nothing left for my brother Doddy to inherit." She frowned. "Isn't it unusual for a lessee to make such improvements?"

"Yes, very much so. I'd say Needham is clearly committed to your family. You should also know that he and your sister have come up north—they might even be in Yorkshire somewhere nearby, although I'm not sure where his houses are. Also, your other siblings and parents are not at Queen's Bower."

"I cannot believe you know all this! What else do you know?" Hy said. "Where did everyone go?"

"*That* I do not know, I'm afraid. But don't fret, darling. We'll get to the bottom of everything."

"Did you mention any of this to Selina?"

"I'm sorry, but I did not. I was in something of a… a state when I called at your aunt's house."

Hy couldn't help teasing him a little. "Were you worried about me, Sylvester?"

"You know I was, you little witch!"

"You were very cruel to me that last night in London."

"I know I was, darling. I'm sorry I made you believe I would only marry you because of duty."

"I'm not talking about that. I'm talking about how horridly you thrashed me at piquet."

He laughed. "Oh, that."

"Yes... *that*," she said, poking him hard in the belly.

"Ow!" He rubbed his stomach. "You should have seen your face when you realized how outmatched you were." He grinned and then kissed her. "Don't worry, sweetheart, I'll give you a chance to win some of it back."

"I'm not sure I want to experience a repeat of that evening," she grumped.

"Have I mentioned how utterly adorable I find you?"

Hy pursed her lips to keep from smiling. "I don't think so."

"Are you sure?" he asked, trailing kisses across the bridge of her nose and cheeks and even down to her chin, completely bypassing her lips.

"I am sure I would have remembered," Hy assured him, losing the battle not to grin like an idiot. She lifted her mouth to him so that he might give it some attention, as well.

"You are utterly adorable," he murmured, and then proceeded to give her lips all the attention they could manage.

Chapter 33

"Welcome to your bridal suite, Mrs. Derrick," Sylvester said as he carried his wife of less than six hours over the threshold of the same room she'd been occupying as Mr. Hiram Bellamy a mere day earlier.

"Thank you, Mr. Derrick." Hy kissed him chastely on the cheek and Sylvester carefully lowered her to her feet. "I cannot believe Charles insisted you carry me over the threshold. I never would have imagined him coming up with such a romantic notion." She flopped into a chair and heaved a sigh.

"Tired?" he asked.

"No, I'm just… happy."

He smiled. "I'd say that's an excellent start to married life."

"Thank you for the small wedding, Sylvester. I know you would normally be married in St. George's with three-quarters of the *ton* in attendance."

"It would be more like seven-eighths of the *ton*," he corrected. "And I have already done that once in my life, thank you very much." He hesitated and then added, "You know I cannot protect you from *everything,* darling? Some events, like your presentation, you will have to endure."

"Strangely, I'm not terribly worried about it as everyone I've seen in court finery looks awkward, so for once I shall fit in."

He laughed.

She cut him a sly look. "And all the annoyance will be worth it to see you in ermine and strawberry leaves, Your Grace."

"Ha! You have been grossly misinformed. I'm afraid you'll have to wait for a coronation for that event, my dear."

"Really?"

"Really. That is the only time those motheaten robes come out for an airing. Thank God."

"Well, I would hate to wish an early demise on our monarch. Perhaps you might wear your coronet for me in private. Along with your court robes. And nothing else."

Sylvester laughed. "I can think of nothing less erotic than a fusty ermine cape." He reached out and took her hand, the need to touch her—even in such a simple way—almost overwhelming. "Are you sure you are ready to return to London tomorrow? We might stay a few more days."

"I would like not to go back at all, but I feel too guilty to put it off. I must apologize to my aunt." She smirked. "Although I think she will be easily placated when she learns I have caught the prize of the decade."

Amazingly, Sylvester felt himself blush at her teasing.

She squeezed his hand. "Thank you so much for inviting Charles to come stay at Chatham."

"It is my pleasure. I'm happy that he agreed to move there once the summer is over," he said, speaking truthfully. He was greatly taken by her best friend. And if he suffered the occasional twinge—or twenty—of jealousy when he thought of them as lovers, well, it was not enough to withhold kindness to a person his wife cared for.

"It will be delightful to have him nearby," Hy said.

"I think he will like the cottage," Sylvester said. "And it is barely ten minutes from Chatham. I want you to know that all your siblings are welcome to make their homes with us, Hy. Chatham has for too long been empty. The same goes for the London house, which only Shelton and I have stayed in for the past decade."

Her lips wrinkled into a moue of distaste at the sound of his cousin's name. "I know he is your family, but I cannot promise civility if he behaves as obnoxiously toward you as he did these past weeks. It drove me to distraction to watch him playing like a reckless fool and expecting you to cover his debts."

Sylvester glanced at the ring on his thumb. "He wasn't always like he is now," he said. "During our time in the army he saved my life." He smiled. "And then I saved his. We exchanged these"—he gestured to the ring. "They are called *life* rings and Viking warriors wore one for every man they saved. The ring means you will always bear some responsibility for that man's soul afterward." Sylvester still wore his ring and had Shelton's at home in his desk drawer, where it had been since his cousin threw it in his face a decade ago when he'd come to beg him to release Mariah from their betrothal. He'd also thrown the some very ugly words that day. "*I wish I'd let you die, Sylvester!*"

Hyacinth

He met his new wife's gaze. "Now that I am in love, I deeply regret the pain I must have caused Shelton when I married Mariah. I will have to apologize to him." Shelton would probably throw that in his face, too, but he needed to say it.

She considered his declaration in silence for a moment. "That is for you to decide. But for my part," she went on to say, "if I were a man I would have—well, not called him out, perhaps, but certainly given him a proper thrashing."

Sylvester stood and tugged her to her feet, sliding his arms around her. "That is one of the nicest things anyone has ever said to me."

"It is?"

"Mmm-hmm," he murmured, kissing that delectable lower lip of hers. "You're defending my honor. Nobody has ever done that before."

"I'll wager Fowler gave it serious thought. He doesn't like Shelton much, either."

Sylvester smiled. "Very well, you are right. He threatened to defend my honor several times, but mostly because it would have afforded him a great deal of pleasure to do so." He lowered his lips over hers, which tasted like strawberries and vanilla cake, and gave himself up to a slow, thorough exploration of her mouth.

When she slid her fingers around to the front of his hips and squeezed his hard shaft, Sylvester had to pull away to catch his breath.

Her gaze was heavy lidded, her lips slick and parted and hungry. "I want you, Sylvester."

"That is my favorite sentence in the entire English language."

"Are you sure?" She gave him a lazy, taunting grin. "How about this one, *I want to suck your cock, Sylvester.*"

He growled. "I think I might like that sentence even better."

"What about this one"—she gave a yelp of surprise when he picked her up and tossed her onto the bed.

"Quit teasing me, vixen," he ordered. "Enough talking and get on your hands and knees, pull up your skirt, and show me what is mine."

Sylvester smirked at her hasty obedience.

"Good girl, now turn this way," he murmured, positioning her kneeling form at more of an angle so they were facing the looking glass over the dressing table. Their eyes met in the mirror, and he nodded. "Shoulders down, bottom up, and eyes on me."

He bit back a desperate groan when she complied, baring her swollen sex to his pillaging gaze.

"Knees wider," he said. "Mm, yes, that is lovely," he praised, opening his fall and pulling out his swollen, leaking prick, stroking himself so that she could see him in the glass. He reached out with his free hand and ran a finger through her soaked petals. "I wish you could see how lovely you are."

She hissed in a breath when he lightly flicked her engorged bud.

"Does that feel good?" he asked, his eyes never leaving hers.

"Yes, Sylvester," her lips curved ever so slightly, telling him that she knew what using his name did to him.

"What a dirty thing you are," he muttered, thrusting a finger into her tight, slick body. "My God you feel delicious, Hy." He pumped her deeply and slowly, until the room was filled with the sounds of wet flesh and soft grunts. "Fuck yourself with my hand," he ordered.

She caught her lower lip with her teeth and groaned at his vulgar command, ramming her hips back against him.

"So beautiful." He teased her stiff little nub as her thrusts became less and less controlled. He'd never a met a woman who climaxed so quickly at his touch, and it was unbearably erotic. "Come apart for me, Hy—I want to watch you."

Sylvester knew she was already close, but to watch her orgasm as if on demand was one of the headiest experiences of his life. Only when she gave herself up to *la petite mort* did she truly lower her guard, her sinuous body bucking and writhing as the contractions rippled through her in waves.

When she was boneless with bliss, he parted her cheeks, spreading her wide before lowering his mouth over her and licking up her juices. He chuckled when she canted her bottom for more.

"So greedy," he praised, laving her slowly and thoroughly with the flat of his tongue. Once he'd cleaned her to his satisfaction, he kissed her pink rosette, holding her heated, surprised gaze in the looking glass. "Have you been taken here?" he asked, lightly stroking that most taboo part of a person's body.

***

Hy shook her head, not really shocked by his question—she'd seen many drawings of such things, after all—but titillated and pleased that he'd ask for what he wanted so directly. "No, that is only for you… Your Grace"

Hyacinth

The flare of heat in his gaze told Hy there *were* times when her husband appreciated a more formal address.

"We will save that until we are in our own home, when we have hours to play and nobody listening at the wall beside us."

Hy chuckled. The tiny inn was full to capacity and the story of a wedding—with somebody important enough to have a special license!—had drawn people like ants to a picnic. None of the villagers knew it was a duke who'd married in their tiny church as the special license was for Sylvester Derrick and made no mention of his title.

Sylvester had bought several rounds for the patrons and guests earlier as they'd hosted their informal wedding breakfast in the taproom. Oh, how her mother would shudder when she learned of their humble ceremony.

For once, Hy no longer had to fear the countess's ire. She outranked the countess by several orders of magnitude.

"What are you smirking about?" Chatham demanded. He knelt on the bed behind her and used his slick crown to stroke her already stimulated sex, teasing her mercilessly.

"I am just happy," she said, which was no more than the truth.

"As am I. Some part of me cannot believe we are really here—that I found you and you've given yourself to me."

The gratitude in his gaze was both humbling and thrilling, but before she could reflect more on his words he pressed against her, breaching her with agonizing slowness.

When Hy tried to push back, to take more, his fingers bit into the flesh of her hips. "You will take what I give you, however I wish to give it… *Your Grace.*"

Hy shivered under his stern gaze and relaxed her body, giving control of her pleasure to her lover.

Chatham pulsed his hips, giving her only his crown, over and over, using her for his pleasure.

"Please," she begged, frustrated and aroused by her need to be filled by him.

"Please, *what?*"

"I need you—all of you—"

"You beg so prettily, and here I thought you never would."

Hy groaned, maddened by the smug smirk on his lips and his barely moving hips.

"Again," he said.

"*Please*... Sylvester. I need—"

He slammed into her, filling her with one long, hard thrust, until they were fully and completely joined.

His eyelids fluttered shut and Hy drank in the sight of his pleasure while her body slowly accommodated to being stretched and filled.

He began to move as he opened his eyes, one hand sliding up her back and neck into her hair, fingers closing in an almost painful hold.

He worked her with deep, powerful strokes and Hy arched her back and lifted her hips in silent supplication.

Sylvester took her offering, pumping into her harder and tightening his grip on her hair, pulling until her throat was exposed and her neck was almost painfully arched.

His lips curled back in a feral snarl as his hips snapped and he rode her with erotic abandon.

"Going to come," he hissed. Rather than withdrawing as he'd always done in the past, this time he drove himself deep and shouted her name as his shaft swelled and Hy felt jet after jet of heat inside her for the very first time.

She drank in his reflection in the glass—an expression of unselfconscious bliss on a man who was usually so controlled—and warmth pooled in her belly at the realization that *she* had done that to him.

Hy might not believe in love, but she believed in happiness, and she had never been so happy in her life as when she was with this man.

She was still shamelessly gorging on Chatham when he lifted his heavy eyelids and smiled at her a few moments later. "You look deep in thought, no doubt regretting marrying a man who selfishly takes his pleasure and leaves you wanting."

"My new husband took care of me very nicely once already." Hy allowed herself a tiny smile. "And he will do so several more times before our wedding eve is through."

An expression of surprised delight spread across his face and he laughed, his body still deep inside hers. "I will attempt to *rise* to the challenge, my love." He gave a low groan of regret and slowly withdrew from her. Hy missed the heat and weight and fullness immediately.

She watched as he pulled up his breeches and buttoned his fall.

"Are you leaving?" she asked when he strode toward the connecting door.

He gestured to the basin and pitcher on the dresser. "I'm only going far enough to fetch you a cloth.

Hy nodded, bemused by her sudden, intense, need for him.

He returned a moment later with a damp cloth and Hy reached for it.

He pushed away her hand. "No, this is my job," he murmured, nudging her thigh.

Hy opened wide for him, pleased at the way his pupils flared as he carefully tended to her.

"Will you sleep with me tonight?" she asked.

"Do you want me to?" he asked, cutting her a startled glance.

Hy nodded. "I have never slept with anyone, have you?"

"Not often. A few times when I was on campaign."

"You found time for lovers?"

He suddenly grinned and shook his head.

"What?"

"It feels strange to discuss my previous lovers with my wife."

"Does it bother you?"

"No. Does it bother *you*?"

"What do you mean?"

"I mean do you get jealous?"

Hy considered his question and was surprised to find that she felt *something* that wasn't entirely pleasant, although she wasn't sure if it was jealousy. "I don't like to think of you with another woman but it happened before I met you so it would scarcely be rational to hold such a thing against you." She couldn't help smiling. "After all, ten years ago I was barely thirteen."

He groaned and tossed aside the cloth. "Don't remind me of what a child you are."

She grabbed his hand and placed it over her sex, pressing his thumb over her still engorged clitoris. "Does this feel like a child?"

"No, thankfully." He lazily thumbed her bud while sliding a finger into her. "Mmm, so silky and slick. I like the feel of my spend inside you."

Hy's inner muscles tightened and he chuckled. "Such a naughty girl you are, wife," he said, looking and sounding immensely pleased with himself as he added a second finger.

She gently pulsed her hips, meeting each stroke. "Do you think we have made a child?"

"I don't know. I have heard that for some it can happen after only one time and for others it takes ten years." He tilted his head, his gaze flickering between her eyes and what his hand was doing. "Are you eager for children?"

"I never thought I was, but I would like to have your baby."

His eyes kindled. "And I look forward to making every effort to putting one inside you. Can you take one more?" he asked, pausing his thrusting.

"Mmm, yes please," she said, letting her knees fall open wider.

"Such a good girl, spreading your legs for your lord and master," Sylvester murmured, easing a third finger in beside the other two and resuming his erotic caressing.

Hy thrilled at his words and heated look. "And will you be a benevolent lord and master, Your Grace?"

He gave her a haughty look. "It depends."

She snorted. "Indeed?"

"Mmm hmmm."

"On what?"

"On whether you please me," he said, inching down the bed to get a better angle for his mesmerizing fondling.

"And if I don't?"

A wicked smile twisted his lips. "Ah, then I shall have to punish you."

Hy groaned, her imagination running in several directions.

"You never answered my question," Sylvester said.

"What question?" she murmured.

"About whether you feel jealous?"

"I don't *think* I have ever felt jealous. How would I know?"

"Oh, trust me—you would know if you felt it. Your head gets hot, your skin feels too tight, and you want to break something." He frowned at her, his hand stopping. "What is it?"

Hy didn't think he needed to know that she'd felt all those things and more when she'd written that self-sacrificing letter to Selina, essentially presenting her sister with the man *she* wanted.

And so she lifted her hips. "Don't stop," she ordered.

He chuckled and resumed his measured thrusting.

"You said before that you are jealous of my experience with Charles," she murmured. "Is that something that will be a problem?"

"I *am* jealous, but that is the sort of jealousy I can manage," he said. Then his eyes narrowed and his expression turned fierce. "But I would not be so sanguine if you ever took a lover, Hyacinth."

"No, I don't believe I would like it if you did, either. Will you be keeping a mistress?"

Hyacinth

"No, my love. I discharged my last mistress not long after meeting a certain red-headed card sharp siren."

"Card sharp?" she demanded. "I never cheated."

"Some would call counting cards cheating."

"That is ridiculous. I am only using my brain, not marking cards or weighting dice."

"Yes, ridiculous," he agreed, inching down the bed, ever closer to her sex.

"You are still fully clothed, Sylvester." As was Hy, her gown hiked up around her hips.

"No... Am I?" he murmured, lifting his glistening fingers to his mouth and licking them clean slowly, his gaze holding hers.

Every muscle in her body tightened at the erotic sight. "Why do I feel you have lost interest in this conversation?" she asked in a breathless voice as he parted her lower lips and gave a grunt of approval at what he saw.

"I couldn't imagine why you'd think that." He lowered his mouth, bathing her with wet heat.

"Urgh." Hy let her head fall back and closed her eyes as her husband commenced to shatter her wits into a thousand pieces.

Suddenly, Hy had no great interest in talking, either.

Chapter 34

"I thought you said you had a real horse, my love, not old Dobbin here." Sylvester gestured with his crop to the nag currently yanking a mouthful of flowers out of the pot the innkeeper had misguidedly placed in the inn courtyard. "He won't make it ten miles without wheezing up his lungs."

Hy took a step toward him and tapped his thigh with *her* whip, hard enough to make it sting.

Sylvester hissed in a breath and his cock responded in a way that would make riding very unpleasant. "Darling," he chided in a low voice, his gaze sliding toward the groom holding the reins, "not in front of the help."

"For your information, *Mr. Derrick*, I rode Thunder all the way from York and he was barely winded," his wife shot back.

He choked on a laugh. "Thunder?"

His beloved's eyes narrowed and Sylvester lifted his palm in a supplicating gesture. "Very well, but he looks like he has the gait of an ox."

Sylvester couldn't stop admiring his wife, who was beyond delectable in her closely fitted clawhammer coat and snug leather breeches, her glossy top boots—the shine courtesy of Tackle's vigorous buffing—making her already long legs appear twice as long.

The villagers were more than a little startled by her radical changes of clothing and he was sure the legend of the unusual *Mrs. Derrick* would spread far and wide. How long it would take for somebody to connect Mrs. Derrick to the Duchess of Chatham, he didn't know. Fortunately, one of the many perks of being wealthy and titled was not having to care about such matters overly much. Certainly not out in the hinterlands, although they would be wise to behave with more discretion in London.

"Well?" Hy said, cutting him a challenging look that sped his pulse.

Hyacinth

"Ride *Thunder* if you must." He leaned close to his new wife and whispered, "It is your arse that will suffer the pounding. Just know I will be riding *you* later tonight, regardless of how sore you are."

She sneered at him. "Worry about your own arse, Your Grace, I shall be fine."

He laughed. "Very well. But tomorrow we shall engage a post chaise. While London will have begun emptying out for the summer, we still can't be sure we won't encounter somebody we know."

She nodded. "That makes sense."

When he cupped his hands to offer her help, she snorted and mounted up with no help from Sylvester, thank you very much.

While the next seven hours were spent riding at a bruising pace and hardly luxurious, Sylvester couldn't imagine a better initiation into his newly wedded state.

He quickly discovered that his wife was an excellent rider with a hearty disposition to match his own.

Rather than fall into bed fatigued when they reached their inn, she convinced Sylvester to have several pints in the taproom, where they learned about a card game that would commence after the innkeeper had closed for the night. Not surprisingly, his brand-new duchess won enough money from their defenseless guests to pay for their evening's lodgings.

"I could have done it," she mused the next afternoon as their hired chaise approached one of the last towns before they reached the sprawling metropolis that was London.

"I'm sorry, my dear. You could have done what?" Sylvester looked up from the book he'd been reading.

"I could have earned my way, couldn't I?"

He placed the marker between the pages and set the book aside. "There was never any doubt in my mind about your abilities, Hyacinth."

"Can we do this from time to time, Sylvester?" she asked, a faint yearning in her normally level voice.

"You mean can you dress up like a bloke and the two of us sneak off and play cards at an inn or gambling hell?"

She nodded.

He took her hand and kissed her palm. "For you, I would never give that up."

She graced him with one of her truly rare, beautiful smiles. "Thank you."

Sylvester was leaning in to kiss her properly—or improperly if he could convince her to do more than kiss—when the post chaise began to slow.

He frowned and looked out the window. They were in the middle of nowhere—no toll booth and no posting inn—so he had no idea why they were stopping.

A familiar red-headed figure rode up to the window.

"What the devil," Sylvester muttered, lowering the glass as the postilion brought the carriage to a clumsy stop. "Good Lord, Fowler, what is the matter?" he asked when he saw how frantic, sweaty, and muddy the other man looked.

The baron's wide green gaze slid to Hy and then back to Sylvester, and then back to Hy, and then his jaw sagged. "What on earth—"

"It is a long story," Sylvester assured him. "But before we go into anything, let us get out and allow the postilion to move the carriage from the middle of the road."

Fowler nodded and wheeled his sweaty horse around, sliding clumsily off it when Sylvester and Hy joined him on the grassy verge.

"Now, what in the world are you doing out here?" Sylvester asked. "And for that matter, how did you find me?"

"I went to your house to call on you just as Tackle returned. He said he'd ridden ahead but that I would encounter you if I came this way—which is the way I was coming in any event."

"What is going on?" he asked again.

"Your bastard of a cousin eloped with Lady Selina!"

Hy gasped. "*What?*"

Fowler turned on her and demanded. "Just who the devil *are* you, Bellamy?"

Sylvester took a deep breath. "I will keep this short. This is Lady Hyacinth—née Bellamy and now my wife, the Duchess of Chatham." He turned to Hy. "Darling, I believe you know Baron Fowler."

"When did they leave?" Hy asked, ignoring his attempt at humor.

"Er," Fowler glanced from Hy to Sylvester, who nodded encouraging at his obviously betwattled friend. "Sometime last night or early this morning. Lady Fitzroy—er, your aunt, I suppose—was not sure."

Hy set a hand on Sylvester's arm. "Selina would never do this, Chatham. She wouldn't shame our family by eloping and I simply cannot believe she would be so dizzy witted as to marry a man like your cousin."

"My thoughts exactly," the baron said, nodding vehemently.

"What are you saying?" he asked his wife. "That Shelton *kidnapped* Lady Selina?"

"No, of course not. But I think he might have lured her on false pretenses."

"I think that as well," Fowler agreed.

Sylvester ignored his friend—Fowler would agree to anything rather than admit the woman he was smitten with had run off willingly. "You are a devotee of logic," he reminded Hy. "Yet you are saying this with no evidence."

Her cheeks flushed slightly at his gentle chiding, but she gave him a mulish look. "Sometimes a person must rely on instinct."

Sylvester snorted, more than a little amused at what was—for her—a shocking admission. "We shall have to talk more about your changing attitudes later, my dear. But for now, you should return to your aunt's house and Fowler and I will—"

"No!"

"Why are you saying *no*? Don't you want her back?" Fowler demanded.

"Of course I want her back," Hy snapped. "But I don't want Chatham to go off without me."

"Oh." Fowler said, clearly at a loss for words.

"While I'm grateful for the news you brought, my lord, why would *you* go after her?" Hy demanded.

"Er, well—"

"You want to marry my sister, don't you?" Hy said, cutting off Fowler's hemming and hawing.

A rather hunted expression slid over Fowler's blunt features. "Er, yes?"

"That sounds like a question, my lord."

"No, it's not! I *do* want to marry her."

"What makes you think she will want to marry you?"

Sylvester winced at his wife's callous question, but Fowler didn't appear to find it offensive.

"Under normal circumstance she probably wouldn't want me," the big Scot admitted. "But I'm afraid she will have to marry *somebody* after what has happened."

Sylvester groaned, afraid to ask what his friend meant.

Fortunately, he didn't have to. "What do you mean?" Hy asked.

"They were seen at the *Swan with Two Necks*," Fowler said, naming a posting inn at the head of the Great North Road.

"Seen by *whom*?" Sylvester asked.

"Lady Portman."

Sylvester grimaced.

"Who is Lady Portman?" Hy asked.

"You've heard of the *London Times*?" Sylvester asked.

Hy frowned. "Yes, of course."

"Lady Portman can spread news even faster."

Fowler nodded grimly. "Lady Portman wasn't the only one. Lord Jessup and his brother also caught a glimpse of Lady Selina inside a hired post chaise." He sighed. "You know how it is at this time of year, everyone heading out of the city."

"Shelton would have known they were bound to be seen," Hy said, "which means he *wanted* them to be seen, but why?"

Guilt flooded him. "Because Shelton believed it was your sister I was courting. He has done this to get back at me."

"And it is *my* fault," Fowler all but wailed.

"How is it your fault?" Hy asked.

"Because I asked Chatham to dance with her—to pay attention to her—believing it would keep Shelton under control. Instead, it has incited him."

Hy turned to Sylvester. "You danced with Selina because he asked you to?"

Sylvester blinked at the question. "Er, yes."

"So, you really weren't pursuing her?"

He gave an exasperated sigh. "I've already told you that I wasn't interested in courting anyone—not your sister or any other woman. Isn't that true, Fowler?"

"Er, is now really the time to—"

"Tell her," Sylvester insisted.

Fowler turned to Hy. "I've known this bastard"—he jolted when Sylvester cleared his throat. "Oh, er, apologies, Your Grace," he said to Hy. "But I've known Chatham for seven years. He befriended me my first Season, when my title was so new it still pinched like a pair of new boots. Every single bloo—er, every year women have flocked to him like sheep to a salt lick." Sylvester snorted and even Hy's lips twitched. "But not once has he even looked twice at any of them." Fowler's cheeks darkened suddenly. "Truth be told, I'd noticed Chatham seemed to have a particular interest in *you, Hiram*. Now, what other men do in the privacy of their bedchambers is their own business, but I was preparing to tell him to exhibit a bit more subtlety or risk getting his neck stretched, duke or not. But to answer your question, *no*, Chatham has never courted any lasses. He danced with your sister to please me and for no other reason."

Sylvester nodded at his friend and turned to Hy. "You see? *You* are the only woman I've ridden half-way across Britain for. And I'd ride ten times that distance for you. In short, you are the only woman I've ever *wanted* to marry, darling." He couldn't help smirking. "And I did so. And now you are mine."

She was blinking rapidly, her eyes swimming with tears although none had fallen, thank God. "What is it, sweetheart?" he asked.

"I thought…"

"Yes?" he asked softly, taking her hands in his, not caring if Fowler's eyes were bulging out of his head.

"I knew you'd danced with Selina. My aunt thought you were going to offer for her."

"Ah." He exchanged glances with Fowler, who's face reddened under his chiding stare. "Was that the reason for the rather alarming letter to Lady Selina?"

She shrugged. "Maybe a little."

"No, that was not my plan, darling. I've already told you that you are the only woman I've wanted."

"I thought you didn't mention courting Selina because it was the gentlemanly thing to do."

He raised her hands to his mouth and kissed them. "I told you I'd never lie to you, Hy. And I meant it."

She suddenly threw her arms around his neck, her embrace squeezing the air from his chest.

Sylvester met Fowler's stunned gaze over Hy's shoulder and narrowed his eyes. *Go away*, he mouthed, his glare threating death or dismemberment if Fowler interrupted this moment.

The Scotsman hastily turned away and wandered over to where his horse was calmly grazing.

Hy clung to Sylvester the way he'd sometimes seen children cling to the people they loved—without embarrassment and with their whole heart.

He stroked her back and kissed every part of her he could reach—neck, cheek, and ear. "What is it, my love? Why are you so upset?"

"I'm not upset," she said in a warbly, emotional voice he wouldn't have believed his stoic lover was even capable producing. "I'm—I'm… oh, Sylvester, I think I'm in love with you."

Sylvester cast his gaze skyward and mouthed, "*Thank you.*"

To his emotional wife he said, "I wanted you even if you only *liked* me, but I must admit hearing you say you *love* me exceeds all my expectations. Indeed, it makes me want to do silly romantic things like write poetry or sing beneath your window."

She pulled away just enough to meet his gaze. "You sing?"

Sylvester laughed. "Have you ever heard a tomcat in heat?"

She gave a watery chuckle. "That bad?"

"That bad," he admitted, and then he kissed her with abandon, not giving a damn who might see them. He kissed her breathless and until tears no longer sheened her eyes, and then, reluctantly, he released her.

"I'm afraid we'll have to delay our bridal journey to Chatham, my love."

She nodded and brushed the back of her hand against her cheeks, as if she feared a few tears had sneaked out.

"You'll take me with you to go fetch her back?"

"Yes, you know I can deny you nothing. Besides, I am weak and selfish and don't want to be without you, so of course you will go with me. We'll send a message to your aunt from the next inn, just to let her know we are going after your sister." He had already sent word to Lady Fitzroy that they'd married in Skipley.

Hy glanced over his shoulder. "What about Fowler? Should we take him along?"

"I doubt we could keep him away. He'd follow us like an abandoned puppy if we rejected his help."

"He may come, but I want you to promise me you won't force Selina to marry either your toad of a cousin or anyone else. I don't care if she needs to live in a stone hut in the Orkneys to avoid the stigma. I just don't want her stuck in a loveless marriage for the rest of her life."

"I promise I won't force her to do anything. I just want to be there and offer her… options."

"Options," Hy repeated and then nodded. "Yes. One of which is to live with us and never marry if she doesn't wish to."

"Yes."

Hyacinth

"She can hide at Chatham or come with us to London next year when you force me to wear a hideous court gown and kowtow to our monarch."

He snorted. "Yes. She can do that, if she wishes."

She gave a firm nod. "Good. Then Fowler can go with us. I suppose there is no time like the present."

She turned to go, but Sylvester caught her arm and pulled her to him. "Say it one more time for me, my duchess."

Hy bit her lip, looked to make sure Fowler was nowhere near, and leaned in close enough that he felt the whisper of hot breath against his cheek. "You are the man who convinced me love exists, Sylvester."

He squeezed his eyes shut for a heartbeat and then kissed her savagely before wrenching himself away.

"Right," Sylvester said, offering his arm to the love of his life. "Let's go and fetch your sister, shall we?"

Epilogue

Seven Weeks Later…

Hy made her way through the lower gallery, hurrying toward her favorite room—and favorite person—in the house, her heart fluttering at the unprecedented message from Chatham in the middle of the day.

Curiosity consumed her. They rarely saw each other between breakfast and dinner, each of them busy with the myriad responsibilities of running a huge country estate.

Usually, Hy was fine with their time apart—which only made their reunion all the more… passionate. But today she was glad he'd sent for her because she had a piece of news for him—something she'd been keeping to herself for more than three weeks, until she could be sure.

Her courses had never been regular, and she was often off a week or two in either direction. But this morning, after she had left Sylvester's bed, she'd spent five minutes throwing up into a basin while her maid—a young girl Hy had hired despite her new mother-in-law trying to force a sophisticated French dresser on her—had wrung her hands and paced nervously, begging Hy to allow her to summon His Grace or a doctor.

But Hy had wanted to savor the news for a while—to accustom herself to the shocking but not unwanted thought that she would be a mother—before sharing it.

She hadn't needed long, just a few hours to marvel at the change in direction her life had taken since that rainy evening in April when she'd walked into Jensen's gambling parlor.

Hy smiled as she laid a hand on her still very flat stomach, eager to share her news now that she'd had it to herself for almost four hours.

She had been at Charles's cottage preparing it for his arrival next week when she'd received her husband's message.

Hyacinth

It had taken some persuasion, but she'd convinced her friend to cut short his stay in Skipley and move to Devon, with its far gentler and warmer climate and she was very excited to have him nearby.

It was a long walk to the library from the entrance in the east wing of Chatham, but she enjoyed every single step through the magnificent house.

While she'd lived her first fifteen years in a house that was every bit as old, if not as large, Wych House had always been dusty and dowdy because there had been too few servants, and it had been decrepit and neglected because there'd been too little money.

Chatham Park was impeccably maintained, both the immense house—there were seventy-eight guest rooms and Hy had only seen thirty of them—and the rolling park and manicured gardens.

Her new husband was not a man to rest on his laurels and woke up every morning early to ride and then visit a different part of his estate.

If he'd been surprised that first morning when Hy had shown up in the stables garbed in riding gear—she'd worn a proper habit rather than breeches and top boots, not wishing to shock the neighborhood (at least not yet)—it had been a happy surprise.

They rode together most mornings and—since her second week—Hy was now mounted on the most superlative gray mare, a creature who was so perfect for Hy she might have been made for her—thus earning the name Perfect. Thunder now lived the life of a gentleman of leisure, growing fat and lazing his days away.

Once their morning ride was over the duke kept busy with tenant meetings and other estate business.

Hy's new mother-in-law—who had invited Hy to address her as *Your Grace*—was determined to turn her into a duchess even if it killed both of them in the process.

"You don't have to do anything she says," Sylvester had assured her even before Hy had met the dowager. "The house has run smoothly for over a decade with Parker at the helm, so don't let her browbeat you into believing you must embrace dinner menus or linen purchases or anything else of that nature. Other than planning house parties and occasional redecoration, my mother has never managed this household—not even when my father was alive. It is Parker who does it all and he will be happy to continue."

Justin Parker, Sylvester's secretary, was a quiet, dignified man a few years older than his employer who seemed to manage not only the duke's schedule but the rest of the household without any visible effort.

Hy liked the coolly controlled man a great deal and appreciated how much he did not only to make her life easier—like managing domestic matters which would, in most households, be handled by the lady of the house—but also how he'd quickly learned about the sorts of things that she *enjoyed* doing and made sure there were more of them.

Things like improving the course offerings at the local school to include upper mathematics and science classes, along with the hiring of a new teacher to fulfill those duties.

Hy had also volunteered to serve as a judge for two events at the annual equestrian pageant that took place every fall before hunting season.

Parker could not get her out of some tasks, of course—like receiving visitors and paying morning calls—but for some reason those duties seemed far less arduous without her mother present. Indeed, she'd made a new friend of the local squire's wife, an older woman who was engaged in some fascinating plant grafting with grape vines and several species of trees.

Hy had always enjoyed gardening in the small home farm at Wych House—although her mother had forbidden any of her children to work in food cultivation—considering it the purview of servants—limiting them to helping with the flower gardens.

But at Chatham, Hy could engage in any sort of agricultural pursuit she wanted. The duke didn't just tolerate her interests, he seemed proud and pleased when she'd inspected both the extensive home farm and the dairy, which made cheese not just for the household, but also for sale at the local village market.

Life at Chatham was so different from what she was accustomed to. There was no shame to feel over neglected tenant farms—as she'd constantly experienced growing up—and the servants, villagers, and tenant farmers were all far healthier and happier. The town was vibrant with bustling shops, unlike Little Sissingdon, which had always felt as if it were one step away from closing its doors.

She had never been happier. And if she experienced the occasional twinge of anxiety when she thought about next Season—when she'd be forced to assume her position in *ton* society—she knew she'd have not only Chatham, but also his clever secretary by her side. She'd not be alone. And this Season would be different from the last in that she didn't need to seek a husband; she'd already married the most sought-after bachelor of the decade.

Hyacinth

Hy was still smirking to herself over that thought when she reached the library and nodded to the footmen who were always stationed outside any door the duke—or Hy—happened to occupy.

As ever, she reveled in the smell of old paper and well-oiled leather when she entered the ancient library.

Her gaze went immediately to the magnificent desk, behind which sat her magnificent husband.

Hy raised the note in her hand. "You wanted to see me, Your Grace."

His lips pulled into that snarl of a smile she loved so much. "Lock the door and come here, Hyacinth."

***

Sylvester waited impatiently as his wife obeyed his order.

He had pushed his big leather chair back from his desk and rested his hands lightly on the arms, keeping his feet spread wide enough to ease the pressure on his aching balls.

He'd been at least half-hard all bloody day long thinking about this moment and his cock was currently jammed against the placket of his oldest, most comfortable pair of buckskin breeches, his shaft throbbing and slippery with arousal.

The sight of his wife—whose delicious body was garbed in a rather severe dark blue gown whose tight, square-necked bodice set off her long, elegant neck to perfection—only made him harder.

When she came toward him, he saw that her lids had lowered over her brilliant eyes and her lips were pulled into that faint smirk that drove him mad with desire.

He pointed to a spot on the floor between his spread feet. "Stand there."

She complied immediately, but without haste.

"You have been naughty," he said, allowing one hand to rest over his throbbing erection, amused when her breathing quickened and her gaze fixed on his hand. "Hyacinth?"

"Hmm?"

"Look at me."

Her eyes snapped to meet his.

"You have been naughty," he repeated.

"Have I?"

He smirked. "What is today?"

Her brow furrowed. "Tuesday?"

Sylvester heaved an exasperated sigh. "Not what day of the week—what *date*?"

He saw the moment comprehension dawned. "Ah, it is my birthday."

"You forgot your own birthday?" he accused, not really surprised. A few weeks of marriage had taught him that his wife's mind was rarely on the mundane.

"Yes." She shrugged. "How did you know? Oh," she said, before he could respond. "Parker."

"Exactly. You cannot hide anything from Parker."

"I didn't mean to hide it. It just doesn't matter."

"It does to your husband," he said sternly.

"Oh."

He couldn't help chuckling at her response. Sylvester suspected that even when they'd been married for fifty years, he'd still not be able to predict his wife's reaction. He adored that about her.

"Open the box on my desk," he said.

Her eyebrows lifted, but she did as he bade her.

Sylvester saw her grimace before she could hide it.

She lifted the necklace out of the box and turned to him, her smile laughably unconvincing as she looked from him to the truly hideous piece of jewelry in her hands. "For me? You shouldn't have."

Sylvester laughed. "Are you lifting your nose at the famed Chatham Diamonds, Your Grace?"

"No, no, they are very… unusual."

He grinned. "They are hideous. And that is what you deserve for not giving me time to buy something you might like."

"I don't need jewelry," she protested, just as he'd guessed she would.

"Then perhaps you might like my second gift better." He jerked his chin at the priceless diamond necklace. "Put that back in its box."

She obeyed with amusing alacrity.

"Look what is beneath the box."

She moved the box and he heard the soft gasp she made when she saw the familiar green leather book. "I have placed a book marker inside. Open it."

When she did, Sylvester stood and went to look at the erotic illustration with her.

Hyacinth

"As you don't want your birthday gift, I have decided you can give one to *me*."

She wrenched her gaze from the exquisite image. "But it is *my* birthday."

"I thought you said they didn't matter?"

She narrowed her eyes at him, but he could see by her flushed cheeks how excited the illustration made her.

"Have you done this one before?" he asked, tracing her sinful lower lip with a finger.

She swallowed and shook her head. "No, Your Grace."

Sylvester smiled. "Good." He carefully closed the old book and set it aside. "Get up on the desk."

"But in the illustration, she is on a chaise longue."

He gave a dismissive cluck of his tongue. "Think of this as artistic license. Up."

Sylvester watched in admiration as a flush spread from the swells of her snugly corseted breasts to her throat and finally her cheeks.

Once she was perched on the desk he said, "Lift your skirts."

Her breathing quickened as she slowly pulled up her dress and petticoat.

"All the way, until I can see your pretty red bush."

Sylvester grunted when she bared her flaming curls. "Good. Now I want you to spread your thighs and show me what is mine."

Her pupils swelled so fast that Sylvester could actually see them swallowing the irises.

She swallowed convulsively and lowered both hands to her sex, her fingers shaking slightly as she slid them into her curls and then parted her sweet little lips.

"Fucking beautiful," he murmured, smirking when she jolted at the taboo word. "Wider," he ordered. "Yes, just like that," he praised when she complied.

Sylvester's chest felt like it was about to explode. By God she was gorgeous, her expression cool and proud, her pussy all pink slickness and visibly engorged. He wanted to plunge inside her so badly that he shook with need. But first he wanted something else. Something suitably naughty for his very wicked lover on her birthday.

"Flex your inner muscles for me—show me how tight you're going to squeeze me when I fill you."

Her breathing was much faster now, and raspy as she clenched for him, the sight making him dizzy.

"Yes," he whispered, mesmerized. "Now, I want you to show me how you pleasure yourself."

***

How had Chatham known what Hy's secret, taboo desire was? The source of her shame all those years ago was also her most private fantasy. Even with Charles she'd never done this.

"Don't be shy," the duke urged, his hand resting over his obscene bulge. "I've been imagining you performing for me—just for me—for weeks now. Show me, Hy."

She *was* shy, which wasn't her normal reaction to sexual matters, at all, but she also wanted him to see her this way, to watch as she gave into irresistible physical sensation.

With her eyes on his face, she slid a finger inside her body.

"*Bloody hell*!" he hissed, his lips parted and his gaze riveted to her.

She was so wet it didn't take much to slick her finger, but she teased him anyway, plunging to the knuckle before withdrawing her wet digit and using it to caress her throbbing bud.

A shudder racked his body and his gaze flickered to hers, the look in his eyes hungry and raw.

Hy had never become so aroused so quickly from her own touch and knew it would be his gaze that incited her. "This is what I did at my aunt's house the night I first met you," she said. "I imagined you in that green robe you wore—and I pulled the sash and bared you."

His eyebrows shot up. "Indeed?"

She nodded, her finger moving faster, her inner muscles squeezed tight against an orgasm that was already building to something beyond her control. "I thought of how you looked earlier—at the Pigeonhole—when you were stroking that woman, your hand on her breast. Her thigh."

"You liked that, did you?"

"I wanted it to be me."

An explosive growl burst from his lips and he yanked his chair toward the desk, until he was right in front of her. He pushed her thighs wider and leaned so close she felt hot breath on her sex. "Do it. Make yourself come."

Hyacinth

Hy distantly heard him say her name as the dam broke and she shook with the force of her orgasm.

He was on her and in her as the first wave of her climax rolled through her body.

"Yes," she whispered in his ear as his hips pumped and his hot mouth sucked the skin of her neck so hard she knew there would be a mark. "Fill me, Sylvester."

He gave a primitive roar as he obeyed her command, thrusting himself deep and pulsing inside her, flooding her with warmth.

***

It was the sound of Hy's heart, strong and fast, that woke Sylvester from his semi-doze.

"Sorry," Sylvester murmured as he realized that he was crushing her with his full weight, her back pressed against unforgiving wood. But when he began to lift off, her arms wound around him as tightly as jungle vines.

"No, stay."

He pushed up onto his elbows and stared down into her flushed, beautiful face. "But I am crushing you."

She gave him a sultry-eyed smirk. "I like it. And thank you for my birthday present. I will remind you about my birthday next year, now that I know the sorts of gifts you give."

He laughed. "I am rather brilliant, aren't I?"

"You are." She caressed his face, the side that was scarred, her eyes no longer opaque, but so loving it made him ache.

"I have a birthday gift for you, Sylvester."

"But it isn't my birthday—not for another nine months."

"I'm afraid this gift won't wait that long. If my math is correct—"

"—and it always is," he teased.

"This gift will wait no longer than seven months before I will have to give it to you."

Sylvester cocked his head. "Seven months? What—" His jaw dropped as he stared at her smug grin, realization slowly dawning. "*Really?*"

She nodded. "Really."

"*Seven* months? That means—"

"That means you made me pregnant outside of wedlock, Your Grace."

He grinned.

"I can't help but notice that you don't look especially guilty about that. What happened to male honor?"

Sylvester laughed. "Oh, stuff that." He claimed her mouth and kissed her savagely as he rolled them over, until she was on top of him. "Are you happy?" he asked.

Her lips curved slightly as she brushed a lock of hair from his forehead. "I'm very happy. What about you?"

"There hasn't been a word invented yet to express how I feel, darling." He slid a hand between them and stroked her flat belly. "I can't wait until I can see something."

She snorted. "I will look like a snake that has swallowed a goose egg."

"You will look beautiful, just as you always do."

Her eyes softened and she kissed him, her gaze thoughtful. "Will you care terribly if it is a girl, Sylvester?"

"I only want him or her to be healthy, my love. And *you* to be healthy."

"You don't want an heir?"

"That used to be important, Hyacinth, but not anymore. Now all that is important is that I have you."

"Are you trying to make me cry again, Sylvester?"

He laughed.

Suddenly, she groaned.

"What is it?"

"I'm just thinking about how insufferable Charles will be—how much he will tease me."

"Because you have fallen in love?" He still got a chill when he realized this intelligent, fearless, wonderful woman loved *him*. Not his title or his wealth, but *him*, scarred face, perverted fetishes, and all the rest of his foibles.

"Yes. He will be relentless," she said with a sigh. She smiled down at him—one of the rare, open blinding smiles she gave out less rarely now. "But you are worth all the teasing and more, Sylvester."

He slid his arms around his love and held her tightly. "It was the luckiest day of my life when I stopped to pick you up that wet, rainy night all those weeks ago." Sylvester waited for his pragmatic wife to say what she always said: *there is no such thing as luck.*

Yet again, she surprised him.

Hyacinth

"It was lucky," she agreed, kissing him lingeringly. "And it was also proof that even the worst storms can blow something truly wonderful into one's life."

The End

Dearest Reader:

I hope you loved Hy and Sylvester as much as I enjoyed writing them!

Every time I sit down to write one of these letters, I realize I whine about the same thing—how hard it was to get the characters to *behave* and do what I want them to do.

Hy was a harder than usual character to get to know and she refused to allow me to boss her around. It took me a great deal of time to get to *know* her as she was as secretive and inexpressive to me as she often was to poor Sylvester.

I always visualize my characters, but they usually don't look like anyone "famous". I must confess that I had the image of Tilda Swinton in my mind's eye as I wrote this book. I personally think she is beautiful, but she is undeniably unconventional looking and, at six feet, a very tall woman.

Hy is probably more of a "horn dawg" heroine than I normally have in my books and I trace part of her development to a contemporary romance book I was reading where the hero said at one point that he had a strong sex drive—that all the men in his family did. I can't recall the book right now, but I remember thinking, "Why is it always guys who get to have the strong sex drives in romances and never women?"

I think that question must have worked its way into my brain and came out in Hy. For her, sex is a perfect way to express her feelings. Non-verbal and yet potent.

While there is a little of me in every book I write, I must admit there is more of me in this one. I am intensely private and don't normally talk about personal issues, but this book was very personal. Like Hyacinth, I am touch averse and it has been a lifelong struggle to manage the issue.

Socializing with people I don't know or among large groups is... difficult, mainly because it always forces my touch aversion into the open. For example, when I go to a conference, the non-stop hugging is like a physical assault and I feel battered by the end of the end of the function. If you ask people not to hug you—even politely—they get offended and view you as standoffish and unfriendly. It makes you *odd* in a culture where physical touch is a sign of acceptance.

In any case, I suspect there must have been people throughout history who've had the same condition and I'm guessing there was almost *no* sympathy or understanding in the early 19th century.

I wanted Hy to get some sort of help—something that would at least keep her from despair, but I didn't want to create a situation that was too anachronistic. I also didn't want to get too heavy—this is a romance novel, not a psychological study. Obviously, I couldn't give her a modern therapist and touch aversion therapy, so that was a tough balancing act. I was ultimately very pleased with the result—Charles, who was a fellow sufferer who had a happier childhood, one that prepared him better for life, despite his "issues". I had written a great deal more about Charles and their relationship in an earlier version of the story but space constraints required me to make some painful cuts (this story is already long and could have easily been 600 pages without cutting).

As for Sylvester? Well, he is my favorite sort of hero: sensual and deep and ready to love and be loved. He's been bruised, but not broken. Life hasn't been a bed of roses for him, but he is still open to love, no matter how jaded he believes he is.

With a heroine as reserved and quiet as Hy there were bound to be some misunderstandings because communication is not her forte, but I wanted the misunderstandings to be *understandable* ones. With her clunky sense of what is "logical" I enjoyed writing the scene where she tries to give her lover away to her beloved sister, just because it "makes sense". That was classic Hy in my view.

I conceived of a big part of this story when I read an article about Princess Eugenie's wedding. I almost *never* remember where I get my ideas, so this is unusual, but as I looked at all the photos in the article, I couldn't help thinking that such a spectacular social event would be *hell* to me.

I love the gorgeous dresses and hats and jewels and men in tuxedos, but… it would just be terribly stressful to be part of such a rigid, formal culture like that of the British royals.

For the first time, I accepted that I probably would not have married a duke even if one had proposed.

Luckily that is not a problem I have to worry about, LOL.

Some of the fun research I did on this story…

Squeak beef means to tattle, but you probably figured that one out.

You'll be glad to know the word *fart* has been around for a long, long, long time. When I used it in the story I thought, "Wait, would this word be around in the early 1800s?"

It turns out that it was used in Chaucer's *Miller's Tale*, so that is 14th century! Wow! People have enjoyed fart jokes for a long time.

Yes, sheep do use a salt lick (I'm embarrassed by how much time I wasted to create that single line of text...).

The card playing research was a lot of fun. I found numerous young men's "sporting guides" to London that gave explicit information about all the sorts of things young guys liked doing—from hookers to cock fights to gambling parlors—the guides even mentioned specific women's names, how long they'd been plying their trade, and whether they had any diseases (yeah, stuff we don't mention in romance novels). I also read about the various games played in popular hells. I've made some changes to the style of 21 that people played, but I haven't tampered too much with the game.

All the terms I use for masturbation come from Jonathan Green's Timelines of Slang, which I adore. There really are about 10 zillion terms for male masturbation and 2 for female masturbation. Go figure.

So, what am I working on next?

I've got book one in a brand-new series, BALTHAZAR: THE SPARE coming up on May 18th, so that is what I've got next. After that is SELINA in August.

I'll be putting up preorders for my sci fi series: THE TIME CONTROL TRILOGY sometime this next month.

As usual, I'm working on about three or four books at a time, most of which aren't anywhere on my schedule. I just write when an idea hits me, so I have lots of partials that sit around until I have time to come back to them.

I'm also going to include a brief description of the books I've written. I put this into an answer to a reader on Goodreads and then thought, "Hey, this might be helpful to more readers."

So, here it is, I'm going to leave it in a different font so you can easily see where it starts and stops:

I write 3 different levels of *steam* so that is usually how I break up my books.

While I have open door scenes in all my romance stories, I'd have to say that THE OUTCASTS & REBELS OF THE TON are probably the mildest (although that is relative, LOL)

Those two series are also interconnected. I would read 1-3 in THE OUTCASTS and then 1-3 in REBELS OF THE TON. That will give you the best experience, IMO.

THE ACADEMY OF LOVE is a tiny bit spicier and it is a self-contained series. These books stand alone really well. There are currently 5 of the 7 planned out, so a nice little binge waiting to happen.

THE MASQUERADERS trilogy is complete and it is also spicy with more intense themes. These stories are best read in order as the characters are interconnected pretty tightly. Especially the heroes from books 1 and 3.

THE BELLAMY SISTERS this is a 5 (maybe 6) book series that has 1 book out, PHOEBE, and one out in a few days, HYACINTH. It is my first family series and I really, really like it. It was inspired by Balogh's BEDWYN series and now I'm crazy about writing siblings. It has a similar steam level to the series above

THE SEDUCERS is a hot trilogy that focuses on sex trade workers (i.e. prostitutes) from the Regency Era. This has serious themes and lots of steam. This series is probably my most polarizing. If you like pretty, frilly, sunny Regencies in ballrooms with dukes, you won't like these.

VICTORIAN DECADENCE
This is my erotic Victorian romance series. These books are hot and break just about every taboo there is. They are intense and not for everyone. Yes, they are very very EROTIC! (I'm just saying that twice, so if you don't like sex scenes, avoid them)

They aren't porn and they have received 2 reviews from Publishers Weekly, which is--frankly--very flattering because they don't usually review erotic books. That said, proceed with caution. If you are easily triggered, just avoid them entirely.

I also write historical mystery under S.M. Goodwin, if you read that genre. Those book have mature themes but have only mild romantic elements. There are 2 books in THE LIGHTNER & LAW series right now and I have at least 5 more planned.

The only connected series are the first 2 I mention.

> As usual, if you read my book and enjoyed it—hell, even if you hated it—I'd love it if you gave me a review.

I REALLY love to hear from readers about what stories they'd like to hear next or what they really liked about something they've already read.

I read each and every email and always respond, so keep 'em coming. If you have sent me anything on INSTAGRAM or FACEBOOK and I haven't responded then chances are I haven't seen it—because I'm bad on those platforms.

My email address is: minervaspencerauthor@gmail.com

Have a great 2023 and stay safe!

Minerva

About S.M. & Minerva

Minerva is S.M.'s pen name (that's short for Shantal Marie) S.M. has been a criminal prosecutor, college history teacher, B&B operator, dock worker, ice cream manufacturer, reader for the blind, motel maid, and bounty hunter. Okay, so the part about being a bounty hunter is a lie. S.M. does, however, know how to hypnotize a Dungeness crab, sew her own Regency Era clothing, knit a frog hat, juggle, rebuild a 1959 American Rambler, and gain control of Asia (and hold on to it) in the game of RISK.

Read more about S.M. at: www.MinervaSpencer.com

Printed in the USA
CPSIA information can be obtained
at www.ICGtesting.com
LVHW030339230424
778121LV00011B/315

Meet the Bellamy sisters, five youn[...] **anything to save their siblings and k**[...] **door.**

Lady Hyacinth Bellamy's plans were flawless. Until fate dealt her a hand she never saw coming…

Romance isn't for the plain, shy, and awkward—a painful truth that Hyacinth knows better than anyone. But Hy refuses to let anything or anyone stop her from living life on her own terms. Independence—and the opportunity to secure her family's future—is finally within her grasp. But then Hy crosses paths with a meddling duke and everything changes…

Sylvester Derrick, Duke of Chatham, is bored. Even gaming and debauchery have lost their appeal. And he's fed up with women who can't see that he's more than a title, a collection of scars, and unusual…appetites. Then he spots a young card sharp who is anything but boring. Clearly, Hy is the person who can make Sylvester feel something again…

It's not long before Hy and Sylvester realize they have more in common—in and out of the bedroom—than they ever thought possible. But is happily ever after in the cards for a man who has been broken by love and a woman who doubts its very existence?